BLOOD AND ROSES

BY

JORDAN PETRARCA

EXODUS

So, what did happen all those years ago? And we're not talk'n just a few years back. We're talk'n like over a thousand years ago. Back when this gigantic nation supposedly didn't exist. Yea, you heard right. Hundreds of years ago our world of *Exodus* didn't exist. It was nothing. Just a slab of unused land. There were no skyscrapers built thousands of feet high strewn across the major cities looking like a field of concrete crops. There were no means of transportation, like our cars, buses, limos, and ships; some of which can fly around the bustling metropolis's full of busy citizens. Could you imagine that? Only using your feet to get around? Sure, there were probably animals that you could get on the back of and ride, but damn if that wouldn't hurt your ass after a while. That's what it must've been like back in the day. Just a big pain in the ass.

Let me digress even further. Hundreds of years ago there were no *Families*. The *Seven Blessed Families* to be exact. But what they *should* be called are the seven crime families of Exodus. They run this nation. There wouldn't be an Exodus if it wasn't for the Seven Families. They built this place from the bottom up, using any means necessary to cultivate this land into a blood-soaked playground. That's right. They use the cities to play in…But that's because they can. The Seven Families possess the instruments of control. The tools for corruption, violence, and unstoppable power. That's why the authorities won't put an end to their dishonest and downright wicked ways of doing business. Because they can't. Even the *President* pretends to be blind to what really goes on deep inside the dark underworld. Their godless ways will continue to go on, and the authorities in Exodus will continue to turn their heads if the Seven Blessed Families stay in control of their precious magical items. And what are these items that they have? *Relics*, of course.

Relics are what the Families use to amass their wealth. The Seven Blessed Families are not hurting for money. No, they are the richest humans in Exodus. Wealthier than all of the most successful business owners, merchants, athletes, and authoritative figures

3

combined. And that's because they own *everything*. They are in complete control of every aspect of human life, and possession of the Relics makes this possible. But let's not get into what Relics really are right now, because quite honestly, a regular citizen of Exodus doesn't know too much about magical items and the like. All we do know is that there are seven Relics, and each of the Seven Blessed Families possess one. Of course, there's something rather mysterious about them, but only the highest members of the Families know the entire truth about what they are and how they work...Not us. Nope, not the average village idiot.

So, the basic question on every citizen's mind in Exodus is-*How did the Seven Blessed Families receive these tokens of dominance?* Well, if we're still being honest about our oblivious nature to this world, then the answer is rather simple. We don't know.

We don't know what caused the sudden immigration into this piece of unused land, and we don't know how and why the Families were given these Relics. Maybe they were the first humans to stumble upon magical objects, or maybe something happened that's unexplainable and out of our realm of comprehension. Sure, it's possible to dig down deep into the *Archives*, but who has the time and money to take a long trip into the heart of the city of *Juna*, and visit the *National Archive Building*? It could just be a waste of precious time. You could spend many days and nights researching the history of Exodus, and come up with absolutely nothing. That makes you wonder. Do the highest members of the Seven Blessed Families want the average citizen to know the entire truth? Probably not...Actually, most definitely not! They are very secretive about their powers. And why shouldn't they be? It's not anyone else's business but their own. They don't care about the average Joe. The higher-ups only worry about themselves, which is why they are so successful. Keep it in the family, and don't dwell on what's outside the box. Inside the box is what matters. Words of fucking wisdom.

We still got some other ground to cover before we move on to the drama and bullshit of these ritzy ditzy fuck-heads. So, let's get more familiar with who the Seven Blessed Families are. The first family we're gonna talk about is well known around the nation as quite possibly the most powerful of all the Seven Families. *The Rose Family*. Led by their great patriarch, a man who they call *The Father of Gangster-Don Maretto*

4

Rose. Maretto calls all the shots in not just his own Family, but he's also considered the most powerful man in all of Exodus...The man is a legend. Just say his nickname one more time, and listen to how bad-ass it really is. The Father of Gangster. Holy shit...It's a nickname passed down from one patriarch of the Rose Family to the next. It's sort of a Family tradition started way back in the day when the term *gangster* started floating around Exodus from one local yokel to another.

Maretto Rose had risen to his throne at the tender age of twenty-five, soon after the death of his father. Kind of young to lead the most powerful clan of gangsters in Exodus. But his age never got in his way. He grew up fast under the tutelage of his famous father, *Victorio Rose.* And he married a prize piece too. A spectacular piece of work, *Malayla Rose* was. It's too bad she met her maker at such a young age. She was the perfect partner for the Father of Gangster. She was Maretto's heart and soul, and although she could be one feisty broad, she was also a charmer and a sweetheart.

Don Maretto has six children. Four sons: *Jonero ("Jon-Jon"), Altonio ("Alto"), Georgiano ("Georgie"),* and *Ricalstro ("Ric"),* and twin daughters: *Ritta* and *Nattia.* Most of his sons follow their dad's way of life, except for the youngest, Ric. Rumor has it that he's a runaway, who drinks his life away at the downtown clubs in Juna, and does an obnoxious amount of smack on the street. Supposedly, he's a bum...But who are we to judge. We don't know what kind of life he must have being the youngest son of the most powerful man in Exodus. So, let's just keep our comments to ourselves for now.

And then there's the *Cicello Family.* The next most powerful Family, who like the Roses, reside in the great city of Juna. Now these assholes are something else. Not the kindest souls of the Seven Families, the Cicello's are led by their patriarch, *Don Xanose Cicello,* and he has five children of his own, including his eldest, *Zasso.* Both father and eldest son are pieces of work (and you'll learn exactly why later), but so far, they have kept a lasting peace with the Rose Family. They even have some sort of alliance against the lower Families...But peace never lasts forever. At any time, there could be a break in the trust. Especially between two Families with egos out the wazoo, and who both thirst for power.

5

Well folks, it's not necessary at this moment to discuss the rest of the Seven Blessed Families. Eventually you'll find out who they are, and what role they're gonna play in the future of Exodus...And what is Exodus's future? Is there gonna be a fallout of the Seven Blessed Families? Is it only a matter of time until these crime families seal their doom because of their unholy acts and bloody business practices? We shall see now, won't we...Yea, we shall see. Because very soon there's gonna be an event that's gonna change everything between the Seven Blessed Families of Exodus. Yes, blood will be shed...It's a crazy journey ahead, so just sit back, relax, and enjoy the ride. Watch what happens when this nation of ours changes...Because in Exodus, gangsters make the world go round...

Sincerely,

Your fuck'n Narrator

Don Maretto Rose

And the Tragedy at the Grand Theater

His office smelled a little funky. The odor of his brother-in-law's smoking tobacco pipe made his nose cringe. But Don Maretto Rose wasn't the kind of man to tell one of his family members to stuff away his habit while talking business. He wanted everyone in his private office to feel comfortable. Don Maretto could put fear in the hearts of men. Even family members. *Especially*, family members. He was the grand master in charge of it all, so it could be a little intimidating to be sitting across the Don, while he looked upon you in his dark oak chair that was shaped like a throne. He didn't have a desk in front of his chair. He wanted every confrontation to be the utmost personal.

Maretto sat back with his legs crossed and left hand under his chin, fingers rubbing the stubbles of facial hair. His gold wedding band glistened in the undertone of light coming from the large fireplace behind him. *Oh Malayla, how I miss you,* he always thought to himself when the ring caught the attention of his dark, puppy dog eyes. He could see the flames dancing in the reflection of the gold. Their anniversary was next month. He had to make sure he bought her something nice and made reservations to their favorite restaurant. He still enjoyed celebrating their wedding day, even though she has long been deceased. *Oh, how beautiful that woman was. What I would give for one more night with my sweetheart.*

Maretto stopped rubbing his chin, and slid a couple fingers through his wavy black hair that was streaked with lines of gray so straight, that one could assume he had it colored that way on purpose. It felt greasy. Almost wet. Maybe he put a little too much mousse in it this evening. Nah, there was never enough grease. He didn't even like washing his hair with shampoo, because he liked his hair to be extra greasy. It complimented his olive oil skin. Even his mustache would get the extra oily treatment. That was his look, and the look of most of his family members. *Grease balls*, is what citizens of Exodus would call them. Dirty, greasy, no-good gangsters. That would always make Don Maretto chuckle. His family wasn't dirty. They were the richest people in the world.

Well, fuck all that shit. Maretto shouldn't be thinking about his appearance right now. He had an important matter to discuss with his brother-in-law, who was sitting in the minute chair in front of him, puffing on that pipe of pungent smoke. It stung the nostrils a bit. Smelled like tobacco and ass.

"I don't know what to tell you, Don Maretto," his brother-in-law said after blowing out a puff of smoke, pipe still hanging in his mouth. "He's a talented athlete, but gets into too much trouble. Maybe if he worried more about his pitching than banging broads and having all-night drinking binges, then I wouldn't have to come to you and complain. But I just can't deal with this son of a bitch. He gives me too much shit."

Palco Valone married Don Maretto's sister, *Peppi*, right around the same time he wed his wife, Malayla. He was good to his sister, or so he has been told. And Palco is not only his brother-in-law, but also one of his Underbosses. A pretty talented moneymaker, Palco was. Only one of his brothers was still alive, so he gave him the honor of being his Underboss, because he could trust him just as much as if he were blood related. That didn't mean that he wouldn't still piss him off a little here and there. *He's still a Valone and not a Rose. His baldness is a dead giveaway of that. But he still tries to comb the few strands of hair that lie on top of his head, the dipshit. And I wouldn't wear those goggles he calls glasses, if I were paid to.*

"You know I don't follow these *batball* players as much as you do, Palco. What do you want me to say to this guy? Stop having fun, and start concentrating on your game? That's a job for the coach...or his agent," Maretto said, eyebrows raised and eyes locked on Palco's.

The one thing Palco could make money on more than anything was professional sports. He was an agent for a number of batball players in the EBL, or *Exodus Batball League*. And his agent business brought in a lot of dough for the Rose Family...*a lot* of dough. We're talk'n millions here. So, it didn't bother Maretto when Palco would come around and bitch a little about his clients.

"He obviously doesn't want to hear it from me *or* his coach, but if he heard it straight from *your* mouth, then maybe he would wise up."

Maretto frowned at the notion, and looked over at his eldest son, Jonero, who was sitting behind a desk in the corner of the room. Jon-Jon just shrugged his shoulders. Don Maretto looked back at Palco. "So, you want *me* to take time out of my day and call some jock about his party habits?"

"It wouldn't hurt," Palco brashly replied.

Don Maretto frowned again.

Palco cowered at the look on Maretto's face before saying, "Well, maybe a written letter would work just as well. Anything coming from you would do the job."

"Writing a letter would take even more time out of his day, you dipshit," the Don's second eldest son, Altonio, expressed as he stood behind the bar in the other corner of the office, making himself a drink. "Haven't you told this asshole who you work for?"

"I try not to disclose that information upfront. Sometimes it scares the clients away," Palco replied to Alto.

True, true, Maretto thought to himself as he made a gesture with his hand. "I'm sure he'll hear it from other players who know you, if he hasn't already. What's his name?"

"Bryant Strattburn."

The Don smiled and said, "That's a good name."

Palco wasn't as impressed. "Yea, a good name for a talented ball player who makes millions of dollars, but can't seem to stop fucking whores and snorting powder. He's going to sabotage his career, and make me look like a fool." His face was getting redder by the second. "And besides that, we'll be out of a hefty chunk of change. This bastard could ruin my name!" he yelled out, then put his head down and rubbed his forehead.

It only took a second for Maretto to reply, "Then let him go."

Palco popped his head back up and said, "What?"

"You heard me…Let him go."

Stunned by his boss's advice, Palco replied, "But we're talk'n millions here, Maretto. Scouts have been up his ass ever since he was thirteen years old. And not only is he gifted in batball, but he's got a face that's a marketers dream. It was sheer dumb luck that he even picked me as his agent. I just can't give him up that easy!"

"You let him go, and then let another agent pick him up and deal with his foolishness. He ruins that agent's name, and then another, then another after that, until he loses all his sponsorships and deals. Then, when he finally sobers up and realizes what a shit he has become, he'll remember the agent who didn't put up with his nonsense from the beginning…And he'll respect that. He'll be begging you for your services. But this time around, you let him know that if he ever screws up again, then the Rose Family will personally make sure that he never plays for another team in the EBL for the rest of his life. We'll make sure that his career is ruined no matter how good he can still play the game."

Palco thought for a moment. "You really think that will work?"

Don Maretto Rose stood up, wiped a speck of dust from the shoulder of his black tuxedo and said, "Frankly, Palco, I don't give a damn about this Bryant Strattburn. He can die of an overdose, or his dick can fall off for all I care. A couple million dollars isn't going to make or break this family. We have quite enough money to go around." Palco lowered his head once again, and Maretto could sense his disappointment. "But if this client means that much to you, then listen to my advice and let him go. He'll be back. I guarantee it."

Lifting his head back up, Palco grinned as he rose to his feet. He stepped forward, and embraced Don Maretto. "You're probably right, my brother. Thank you for listening to my complaining once again." He grabbed his boss's hand and kissed it as a gesture of respect.

"Good," Maretto casually replied. "Now get the hell out of here so I can go celebrate my birthday with my sons." He chuckled then lightly slapped Palco's cheek.

Georgiano-Maretto's second youngest son-came from behind Palco, and escorted him to the door. "Maybe you can get me Strattburn's autograph before you let him go," Georgie said with a smile. "I'm kind of a fan."

Palco laughed and smacked Georgie on the back. "I'll see what I can do." He turned around to say one more thing before he exited. "A very happy birthday to you, Don Maretto!" He waved goodbye and left.

After shutting the door, Georgie casually walked across his father's office. His footsteps echoed off the wooden floor, bouncing around the ominous room. Maretto preferred his office to be quite under lit to set a serious mood. He usually had the window drapes shut during the day, but at night he would let the moonlight in and a view of practically the entire city of Juna displayed for guests. The Rose Family lived in a high-rise mansion in the upper-class region of the big city, and it cost a pretty penny.

The Don sat back in his chair/throne, and crossed his legs as usual. His black shoes were shined to look like fucking mirrors. As his three sons gathered around him, he adjusted the tie under his vest, relaxed himself and said, "You boys look good." His sons were all dressed in black tuxes with black dress shirts underneath. Their vests and ties were blood-red like his. "It's a wonder why none of you are married yet."

"Married?" Alto quarried. "Hell, I'm still trying to play the field, pap. It's gonna be a while until a Mrs. Altonio Rose comes around. Your best bet is Jon-Jon. He's been dragging his girl around long enough now."

"I think you've got them mixed up, Alto. She drags his big ass around," Georgie ribbed his eldest brother.

"At least I've got a girl. You guys make me wonder sometimes," Jon-Jon retorted.

"I know you're not talk'n about me," Alto said. "You see the dimes I bring home almost every night, Jon-Jon."

Jon-Jon laughed out loud and said, "Dimes? More like a couple nickels and some pennies. Don't flatter yourself, Alto."

"Yea, Alto. It's about quality, not quantity," Georgie chimed in.

"Oh, you really wanna say something, Georgie? When's the last time I even seen you talk to a girl? Hmm, let me think. Maybe it was when Aunt Babs came to town last." Alto pulled a silver case filled with cigarettes from out of his coat pocket, taking one out.

"It still counts," Georgie said with a grin.

"You sick fuck," Alto said, before lighting up his cig. He sucked it back and let out the smoke. "That's a really sick fucking thing to say."

Georgie responded by just shrugging his shoulders and smiling. He did have a sick sense of humor sometimes.

"You're doing the right thing by waiting for the right girl to come along, Georgie," Jon-Jon advised his younger brother. "You don't want to follow this guy's example when it comes to women. You'll be at the clinic getting antibiotics in no time."

"I got some in the medicine cabinet right now if you need it sometime, Georgie," Alto said, not missing a beat.

Don Maretto sat back and chuckled. *God I love my boys,* he said to himself while listening to them go back and forth at one another. He was proud of these three boys. Here they were, deep in the family business with him. Each of them with different talents and different personalities. Jon-Jon, the eldest, was tall and handsome with honest dark eyes and wavy hair like his own. He was the quiet one, but smart and responsible. Alto was the shortest of the three, but was very handsome as well with his black curly hair and blue eyes. He had a fiery heart and could lose his temper easily, but he had balls of steel and would rip your lungs out if you crossed him. Georgie had a medium build, straight hair and brown eyes. He was the most innocent looking of the three and had a heart of gold, but that didn't take away from the fact that he was a talented fighter. As a matter of fact, all three of them were powerful. *Someday these boys will be as Blessed as I have been.*

His youngest boy, on the other hand, was a different story. *God, I hope that boy will find his way again soon,* Maretto thought for a moment. *I shouldn't have let him get rid of us so easily. I should've made him stay. I don't let the other boys see it, but I worry about him night and day.*

In the midst of thinking about his youngest son, Maretto heard Jon-Jon say, "Well, tonight's not about us anyway, so let's pay a little more attention to the birthday boy." He gave a slight grin to his father.

"Today is just another day, boys," Maretto humbly said.

"Yea right, pap," Alto disagreed. "You don't turn fifty years old every day. And we don't go to the *Grand Theater* everyday either, so get you old ass up and let's get moving." He extended his hand to help his old man up from the chair. His father gratefully accepted the courtesy, and stiffly rose to his feet.

"Alright, then," Maretto said as he patted Alto on the back. "Call down for Vego, and tell him to get the limo ready." He slowly walked over to the window, and gazed upon the ever so enigmatic nightlife of Juna. "This great city belongs to the Rose boys tonight," he stated with a proud look.

The black stretched limo cruised around the outer edge of the city, crossing the *Avrahem Lonell Bridge* that stretched across the *Vile River*. It was a perfect night. The outskirts of the city seemed peaceful, but downtown Juna would be filled with excitement. Don Maretto sat in the very back of the limo, stretched out on the leather seat. He stared out the window and thought, *this city is home. Home to my family. Home to the Rose Family. It's been our city to play with for generations now, and no other Family has tried to take it from us. We control most of everything in Juna, and throughout the entire nation of Exodus. We are so very blessed to dominate this world, and we are so very blessed to be in possession of the most extraordinary Relic of all.*

As the limo neared the inner city, Maretto observed groups of homeless people huddled on the street corners. He immediately thought about his youngest son again. *Where are you son?* He asked himself. *And what have you done with my precious little boy? Your mother would be worried to death right now if she knew you were running around on the streets. She would've never let you go. She would've done everything in her power to keep you safe at home...So, why did I let you go?* He started fiddling with his wedding band.

13

Noticing that his father was in a deep trance, Jon-Jon said, "Hey, dad." Maretto instantly snapped out of it and gave his attention to his eldest. "Are you okay?"

He rapidly blinked his eyes and replied, "I'm fine, son. I just got lost in the view of the city."

"This part of town?" Jon-Jon knew he was lying. His girlfriend, Jeena was sitting next to him. He draped his arm around her as he kept regarding his father. "What's on your mind, pap?"

Maretto adjusted himself on the seat and answered, "Oh, I was just wondering if we should ask Martell if he wants to go out and have a few drinks with us after his performance tonight. It would be nice to spend some time with him. But I don't know if we should bother him. He's a very busy man." Martell Vienis was the lead actor in the play they're about to see. He's one of the most famous people in Juna, and the Rose Family had substantially helped him with his career.

Jon-Jon knew he was lying again. He could sense why his father was daydreaming. It was Ric he was thinking about.

"I'm sure Martell will have no problem going out with us after the play. He is all about the nightlife. I've heard many rumors about his party habits," Jeena chimed in. She was wearing an expensive red dress, and was done up real nice tonight. A blonde-haired, blue-eyed knockout.

Alto and Georgie were talking amongst themselves for most of the ride, but when Alto heard about Martell's party habits, he blurted out, "She aint kidding, you know. Martell is a professional boozer along with his professional acting. These celebrity types all get down like that. A line up the nose for every drink down the gullet."

"And how many times were you with him, shoving stuff up your nose?" Georgie asked his brother.

"Too many times. Now shut your mouth," Alto replied with a grin.

Maretto smiled and looked back out the window. The limo entered the tunnel that led into downtown Juna. Lights from the inner walls flashed across the car windows at a high speed. It was as if the press were riding alongside, flashing their cameras right into the car.

As the limo neared the exit of the tunnel, Alto said to everyone, "It's Showtime."

The dense and murky tunnel opened up into the glitz and glamor of the downtown Juna nightlife. Four multi-lane streets intersected in the center of the city where a large skyscraper displayed a massive video billboard, highlighting all the major events of the evening-including the play they were about to see at the Grand Theater called *The Prince of Ancient Exodus*; a fictional tale about the beginning times in Exodus when a royal family supposedly ruled the world.

This epicenter of the city was called *Juna's Heart*, and on every corner, there was a massive building with a video billboard, radiating advertisements in bright lights. The streets were bustling with cars (flying or not), regular Juna residents, and out-of-town tourists. The crowds were fussy and moving fast. The smell of the night was filled with petroleum, fried foods, and body odor. Vendors were yelling at anyone they could to try their particular brand of foods. Horns were being honked to keep the traffic moving.

The limo took a right turn out of the chaotic scene of Juna's Heart and into another one. The outside of the Grand Theater was a spectacle in of itself. The building was amazingly big. It was wide as it was tall, and constructed of white marble. Large columns lined the main entrance at the top of a steep incline of stairs. Two oversized spotlights produced a magnificent effect of white light. They rotated in all directions like they were signaling the authorities for an emergency. The main entrance also displayed the name of the play that was now showing on a large and square matinee sign.

When the limo pulled into the front of the theater, a swarm of press and media flooded the area as if they were waiting for the arrival of the most predominant members of the Rose Family...And they were. The Rose Family were like royalty. They were celebrities in Exodus. Whenever the media had a chance to film Don Maretto Rose in public, they were all over it. He was the patriarch to the most powerful family in the world. He was like a fucking king. And the press loved him. He was a media darling, and they

15

all sucked on the nipple he nourished them with, whether it was television, papers, radio, or any other form of communication.

Don Maretto's head of security and main bodyguard, *Vego Rainze*, stepped out of the passenger side of the limo, walked to the back, and opened the door for his boss. Maretto was the first to step out of the car, which started a hallucination of paparazzi. The light bulbs flashed as the crowd erupted into a frenzy of one person trying to yell over another. The security guards of the theater had to intervene before all hell broke loose.

An SUV full of Rose Family guards parked directly behind the limo. They and Vego Rainze escorted the Don along the red-carpeted walkway leading to the theater, through a tunnel of media held behind a velvet rope on either side.

The rest of Maretto's entourage followed behind him, but were not paid as much attention as the Don. As Maretto waved and smiled to the eccentric crowd of people, hounding him like a pack of street beggars, he was asked a barrage of personal questions.

One reporter shouted, "Don Maretto, do you think that it is morally right for the local churches to accept substantial donations in the name of your family?"

Maretto responded, "The churches accept my donations because my family are dedicated members of the *First Church of God*."

The same reporter shot back with, "Even though your family practices in business are considered morally wrong?"

"My family keeps the peace in this great nation of Exodus," he answered back.

Another reporter yelled out, "Don Maretto, do you believe that there would be even *more* peace in Exodus if the Seven Blessed Families were not so affiliated with crime?"

"There is crime in this city and in every other city in Exodus every day that is *not* affiliated with the Families, and like I just said, *my* family tries to keep the peace. We are involved in legitimate business all over this great nation, and our businesses make the world go round."

The reporter replied, "So, are you saying that *gangsters* make the world go round?"

He did not respond to that question but kept moving forward with his security. Vego looked annoyed by the media's questions.

Before Maretto and company made it to the front main entrance to the theater, yet another reported shouted out, "Don Maretto, do you believe it necessary that the Seven Families control the only Relics in Exodus? Why are average citizens deprived of such powerful objects?"

For that specific question, Maretto turned towards the reporter who asked it, and replied, "The Relics were given to the Seven Families in ancient times as a gift. If you want to know how and why they were given specifically to us, then I suggest you go to the National Archives and do some research…I am at this theater to celebrate my birthday with my sons, so I bid all of you a goodnight and make God bless all of you."

The ferocious gathering of press shouted his name and more questions, but Maretto did not acknowledge any of them and continued his way into the Grand Theater. His company followed suit, and soon they were inside and safe from further interrogation.

The main lobby of the theater was luxuriously decorated in an archaic style. It had a marble floor and columns of gold. Twisting staircases led to higher levels of the theater, covered by red velvet carpeting. Don Maretto and his sons were taken up one of the staircases that led to the main luxury box that sits high above the normal seating, with a straight-on view of the stage. Many of the guards set up different perimeters around the theater for extra protection of their great leader.

The luxury suite had black velvet chairs and a balcony of gold sculpted with fancy décor. Maretto took his seat in the middle with Alto and Georgie at his sides, and Jon-Jon and Jeena sitting behind. It was a magnificent view to the stage from their spot. The large red curtain with gold trimmings was down and blocking the stage. Maretto took in the breathtaking sight of the theater as crowds of attendees filed in. It was three levels high, the balconies were all made of sculpted gold, the ceiling was a dome with exquisite artwork and bright golden chandeliers, and tapestries made from the highest quality fabric hung down the walls. An orchestra pit was built in front of the stage, and they looked ready to start playing their instruments at any moment.

Georgie noticed the glow in his father's eyes, and the happiness his face portrayed, so he leaned over to him and simply said, "Happy birthday dad. I love you."

Maretto's eyes looked as though they were welling up. His mouth formed a heartwarming smile. "I love you too son. Thank you for this wonderful night." He embraced Georgie, and then got more comfortable in his chair.

In a matter of minutes, the band struck and began playing the overture. Soon after, the curtain separated, and the stage was revealed. *The Prince of Ancient Exodus* was about to begin.

Long ago, in a time when kings ruled the world of Exodus, there was born a baby boy. A bastard baby boy. Left behind in the royal lineage, because his mother was a whore. A whore that laid down with the king. A king who had a reputation of ruthless aggression. But when it came to his bastard boy, he had a heart of gold. He made sure this boy and his mother were taken care of, until the day the queen found out about his adultery with the whore. The queen vowed to kill the whore, and to sacrifice the bastard boy to the gods, in order to rid the mortal sin of the king. The mother was slaughtered immediately, but the bastard prince would get away, and escape to a faraway land where he would be raised by an old warrior who was now a master in the art of magic...Soon enough, the bastard would return to the kingdom, and attempt to take his vengeance on the queen...

The play went on. Martell was magnificent in his portrayal of the bastard prince of Exodus. The audience was moved by the dramatic story of his revenge, and they were eating up every scene. They were hypnotized. Frozen like sculptures of ice from the words coming out the characters mouths and articulation of their bodies. Especially Don Maretto Rose. The story had always been captivating to him. His father used to take him to this play when he was a little boy. *My father was a great man*, he thought during the first act. *If only he could have been around for just a little bit longer...I sure do miss him.*

When the first act ended, there was a brief intermission. Don Maretto and his sons talked about what had happened in the story thus far for a few minutes, until it was time for the second act to begin.

So far, it had been the perfect birthday for Don Maretto Rose. Well, maybe not perfect. His youngest son was not present for the celebration, and it hurt the powerful man very much on the inside. But it was still as close as it was going to get to being perfect.

But sometimes, when you least expect it, the unexpected happens...And everything goes to shit.

Outside the Grand Theater, two black extended SUVs came flying from around a nearby skyscraper, and hovered towards the ground. They landed on the street directly in front of the red-carpeted entranceway. As soon as they were grounded, the doors on each SUV flew open, and gangsters came pouring out like water from a spout. One of the Rose Family guards and two theater security went into immediate action to stop the probable unwanted guests from entering the theater. An array of other guards and security lined the stares and main entrance.

Now, a lot of the gangsters spilling out of the cars looked pretty much the same, dressed in regular black suits and fedoras, but there were two in particular that were dressed a little nicer and a little weirder. They both took their good ole time striding towards the main guard as the other gangsters filed behind them. The one in front was tall and lanky, wearing a royal blue suit with a matching necktie and white dress shirt. He bore a blue fedora over his silvery black hair that hung down to his cheeks. His eyes matched his hair, and his face was thin like his body. He was draped in gold jewelry around his neck and had gemmed rings on almost every finger. The pride in his walk signified that he was a man of importance. And he was. The man was none other than Zasso Cicello, son of Don Xanose Cicello.

Walking closely behind, was a shorter man dressed in a shiny silver suit and black dress shirt. His face was round but came to a point at his chin, and he bore a pair of sunglasses that could be mistaken for a couple of round mirrors. His long and thin hair was shoulder length and was black with a bluish tint. He, also, had a certain pride to his walk. And that's because he was Zasso's personal protector and assassin, *Razo Malvagio.*

As Zasso and Razo approached the main guard, he put up a hand to signal them to stop and said, "I'm sorry gentlemen, but this is a private viewing and you need to show credentials to enter the theater."

In the blink of an eye, Razo came whirling around Zasso, holding a pistol-gripped sawed-off shotgun. It was pointed directly at the guard, and Razo didn't hesitate to pull the trigger. There was a loud burst, and then the guard's hand exploded clean off his arm, along with half of his face. His limp body collapsed on the red carpet. A puddle of blood formed underneath the other half of his face.

"*There* are my credentials," Zasso said to the corpse.

The two theater security guards reached for their firearms, but Zasso was too quick for them. Like a gunslinger, he drew a small pistol from his waist and fired multiple shots. Blood burst out of their chests, and they perished before they even touched their guns. Zasso and Razo continued on, with their entourage following behind.

The Rose Family guards and theater security wasted no time opening fire at the oncoming murderers. They fired numerous times whether it was with a handgun or semiautomatic rifle. But it was to no success. Upon the masquerade of bullet-fire, Zasso raised a hand and magically constructed a transparent yellow force field that deflected the bullets. Then, all hell broke loose.

Zasso's gangsters came storming around him and returned fire upon the guards and security. Zasso and Razo went on the offensive as well with their short-arm weapons. Blood started spilling, and bodies were falling everywhere. When Zasso reached the bottom of the stairs, he extended his left hand and bolts of electricity spewed from his fingertips in the direction of his targets. And at the same time, he kept on firing shots out of his pistol with his right hand. His targets were electrocuted and blown away by bullets at the same time. Zasso was *Blessed* with magical powers by his Family's Relic, which made him a very dangerous killer.

While a few of his men were taken down, Zasso and Razo came away from the chaotic scene unscathed. The Rose Family guards and theater security were all dead. It was now time for them to enter the premises of the theater, and accomplish what they came here to do.

Vego Rainze was casually walking down a hallway near the entrance into Don Maretto's balcony suite. He was the Don's head bodyguard, and took his job very serious. He had the entire perimeter of the theater secured with men. His first and foremost job was to protect the patriarch of the Rose Family, in which he did with a sense of pride and dignity. He was the perfect man for the job.

Vego had a hard face with an afternoon shadow, short grayish black hair, and brown eyes. He was always dressed in an all-black suit and dress shirt, and sported sunglasses everywhere he went, even inside. That's because his sunglasses were special, and you'll soon find out why.

While the play went on, Vego had the inclination to contact the main guard outside the theater. Call it a hunch, but something just didn't feel right in the air tonight.

Using a small device attached to his shoulder, he paged the main outside guard and said, "Perimeter One, what's your status?"

There was no immediate response.

"Perimeter One, are you there?"

Again, no response.

Vego changed the channel on his voice transmitter and said, "Perimeter Two, come in."

Right away, the man on the other end replied, "Yea, Shades, Perimeter Two is here."

Stopping his pace around the hallway, Vego said, "I received no response from Perimeter One, so I need you to immediately go out and check the first perimeter, and then relay me his status. Do you copy?"

Almost sounding annoyed he replied, "Yea, yea I copy. I'm going right now to check on Perimeter One. I'm sure that big son of a bitch is just dicking around out there." He laughed a bit.

"Yea, everything is always so fucking funny," Vego mumbled to himself. He began pacing around the hallway again, waiting for a response. Hopefully a quick one.

After a few moments, Vego's transmitter buzzed, and with a shaky voice, Perimeter Two said, "Shades? I think you should…"

The voice cut out, and Vego started freaking out. "Perimeter Two! Perimeter Two, are you there?" When there was no response, Vego yelled, "Fuck!" And then he bolted down the hallway towards the exit.

Electrifying bolts flashed out of Zasso's hand. The intensity of the electrocution lifted the guard and sent him flying backwards through a glass cabinet. With his other hand, he pulled the trigger of his firearm and blew another man's heart clear out of his chest. Razo was right next to him, blowing guards away with his shotgun. The main lobby of the Grand Theater was a bloodbath.

When the chaos in the room stopped, Zasso saw a survivor on his hands and knees, trying to crawl to safety; wherever that may be. Zasso hurriedly walked over to the man and kicked him in the gut. The man doubled over in pain, and lied on his back. With his right foot, Zasso stepped on his neck and aggressively said, "Vego Rainze is in this building and stationed in a delegated hallway. I can smell him. Tell me, which staircase will lead me to him?" His voice was ominous but sort of high-pitched. Its tone was dark and sadistic.

The man coughed up a little blood and replied, "The eastern staircase," he barely got out.

Zasso half smiled and said, "Good." With one pull of the trigger, the carpet was decorated with brains. The young Cicello walked back over to where Razo was standing and said to him, "We take the western staircase. I'll enter through the first floor, which

22

will take me directly to the stage. *You* know where you are to go. The rest of our men go to Vego and deal with him. Let's move."

Zasso and Razo made their way to the left side of the lobby and climbed the staircase, while the gangsters who accompanied them to the theater trekked up the other staircase. Before Razo went his own way, Zasso grabbed ahold of his shoulder, yanked him close and said, "Don't fail me now, friend. I'm counting on you."

Razo replied in a dark, twisted tone of voice of his own, "Of course, prince of the city. You cement your legacy tonight." Zasso smiled at his right-hand man and let go of his grasp so Razo could move ahead.

Vego Rainze was in for a surprise once the gangsters reached him, but Zasso would be damned if he himself was going to run into the old-time mobster. Vego was a threat. A very dangerous threat, and Zasso didn't have time to deal with anything like that. He had other plans. He had a surprise of his own for Don Maretto Rose, and the rest of the patrons inside the theater. It was his time for a grand performance.

The door burst open. Gangsters started firing immediately. Their main target was Vego Rainze, but he hadn't made it into this stretch of hallway just yet. Rose Family men were caught by surprise, and the walls were now painted with blood. It happened so fast, that this perimeter of guards had no idea what had hit them…But Vego was on his way. His hunch unfortunately was correct. Something was wrong, and there was going to be little time to react to the chaos at hand.

The next hallway over, Vego Rainze had heard the shots. He knew what was awaiting him on the other side. A fight for life or death. He could run back to Don Maretto's balcony suite and warn his boss of the impending danger that was about to transpire, or he could stop it himself right now, before the threat even has a chance of reaching him…He chose the latter, and geared himself up for combat.

Vego reached into his coat pocket, yanked out a comb, and slicked back his greasy ass hair. After returning the comb to its proper location, he placed his hands behind his back, under his suit coat, and retrieved a pair of semi-automatic handguns. The barrels were black and the grips were decorated in flashy gold. They were big, badass, and lethal. And Vego was an ace marksman.

A group of guards formed behind Vego, and before he stepped towards the golden double doors that separated them from the oncoming enemies, he said to his men, "Beyond those doors, any man we encounter that is not one of us, we shoot to kill. Capeesh?" His men all nodded their heads and repeated, "Capeesh."

"Get ready for some serious shit," Vego uttered before he pressed a tiny button on the side of the right frame of his sunglasses. A pattern of fluorescent blue light appeared around the dark lenses. And then with a violent kick, he broke open the double doors.

Extending both arms and aiming at his targets, Vego wasted no time opening fire and taking out gangsters. And he didn't cower behind his men whatsoever. No, Vego was in the front lines, going to war for Don Maretto Rose and his Family. He didn't flinch when the gangsters fired back at him. He believed that the bullets wouldn't touch him. And they didn't. They flew every which direction but into his body. He had the mindset of a vicious predator, and these unwanted guests causing havoc in this theater, were his prey.

From Vego's point of view behind the sunglasses, the advanced technology of the lenses produced bright-red digital targets that locked onto the vital spots of approaching enemies. He shot with the clear-cut precision, and gangsters were dropping left and right. Blood splattered against the walls, ceiling, and floors. Any objects in the hall were subject to destruction. Bullets were busting through anything they came in contact with. It was complete mayhem, and Vego had to finish them all off in a hurry, so he could get back to his boss. There had to be something else going on. This was just too easy.

It was the most dramatic scene in the play. The backdrop was a night sky at the very top of a castle tower. The queen had a knife to the throat of the bastard prince's simpleton lover, and Martell was engaged in a song, professing his love, and begging the queen to leave his lady alone. It was the end of the road for the queen, for she knew she would not make it off of the tower alive, so why not take the life of her enemy's love as one last sadistic maneuver in a web of unholy acts in her life.

Don Maretto was entranced. He had witnessed this scene played out many times before, but Martell had perfected this most dramaturgical moment. When Martell's voice hit its highest octave, Maretto leaned forward in his seat ever so harder, allowing his ears to be filled with the nourishment of beautiful music. The gratifying sound wrapped around his inner soul. He closed his eyes, and for a moment, thought about his beautiful wife…When he reopened his eyelids, that wonderful moment of peace in his soul was replaced by a scene of horror.

Coming from the crowd on the western side of the stage, an erratic lightning bolt zigzagged its way up into the ceiling and struck the base of a golden chandelier. Sparks flew, and the chandelier plummeted towards the stage. The queen and the simpleton lady screamed bloody murder just before they were crushed by the large ceiling decoration.

The crowd erupted in hysteria as more lightning bolts made their way up to the ceiling, causing a few more chandeliers to fall into the seats around the stage; including the orchestra pit. Innocent lives were being lost by the second. Mobs of people were knocking each other out of the way while trying to escape the dreadful events the night had turned to.

Along with his sons, Maretto Rose abruptly rose to his feet. His face turned to dismay as he watched the violent murder of innocent theater patrons, and the chaos that was ensuing below. He also watched Martell, who seemed frozen in time on the stage. The actor was looking in the direction where the lightning came from, and out from the crowd, a tall man in a royal blue suit slowly strode into full view. The man then jumped high into the air, performed an uncharacteristic acrobatic maneuver, and landed on the stage. Using his magical lightning skills, he began electrocuting the hell out of Martell so bad, that it lifted him off his feet. When Martell was in midair, the man used a semiautomatic pistol to finish the actor off. His burned and bloody lifeless body coasted backward and crashed through the painted backdrop, leaving a gaping hole in the canvas.

It didn't take long for Maretto to recognize who this murderer was. It was the son of his supposed ally. For a second, he wondered why Xanose would want to have actors of the Grand Theater killed, but then it hit him like a slap in the face with an iron glove. Zasso Cicello wasn't here to murder the actors in the play and innocent patrons. This wasn't an act of terrorism. He was sending a brief message before unleashing his ultimate plan. And the message was to him. Zasso was here for Maretto Rose!

After strolling to center stage, Zasso looked towards the Rose's prominent balcony suite, and extended his left arm. A vibrant ball of electric energy formed in the palm of his hand. Then, he just simply yelled, "Whether you want to or not, Don Maretto Rose, you are coming with me!"

The audacity this young man has! Maretto instantly thought to himself. His son Georgie leaned forward, and shouted, "The fuck he is!"

Maretto grabbed Georgie's shoulder as a gesture to tell his son to calm down.

Without further delay, Zasso blasted an intense bolt of lightning towards the gold covered balcony. The Rose Family members dove out of the way as the bolt buzzed past and hit the back wall, causing an explosion of marble shrapnel. Jon-Jon crawled over to his lady-who was screaming very loud-and protected her with his own body, while Maretto and Georgie got back on their feet to face the foe.

Zasso wasted no time sending another destructive bolt of magic towards the balcony. This time Maretto was ready to defend the attack. With a simple wave of his hand, a sparkling red force field-shaped like a rose-engulfed the entire balcony, and deflected the lightning into the ceiling.

Zasso looked frustrated, and attempted to injure Maretto and his family again. But it was to no avail. The protective shield was just too strong. Don Maretto Rose was powerfully Blessed by his own Family Relic. And that Relic was no joke. It was considered the most powerful in the whole fucking world.

The crowd was having a hard time conforming to the rules of a panic situation, so people were still struggling to exit the theater. Zasso noticed this and yelled, "You're coming with me, Maretto, or you will watch me destroy more innocent lives! I will kill everyone in here, and not give two fucks! Get your ass down here, and I'll stop the death!" He pointed his hand in another direction and sent another blast of magic. Four patrons were electrocuted to death upon impact.

"I'm going down there, dad," Georgie urgently said to his father.

"The hell you are. You stay right here, son!" His reddened face was draped with worry, because he knew that no matter what he said, Georgie was going to try to be a hero for him tonight.

Georgie looked over at Maretto with a sorrowful face and said, "I'm sorry, dad. But he's not going to leave until he has you, or kills as many people as possible...I love you dad."

Before he could stop his son or even shout *NO*, Georgie took a giant leap off the balcony, crashing directly through the crimson shield. The shield broke into magical pieces that looked like glass shards until they disappeared. It seemed as though he hovered through the air and defied the laws of gravity, until he landed with a thud on the stage. He was in a crouching position, then stood up, and faced the enemy.

Zasso slowly shook his head back and forth and said, "You've made a fatal mistake joining me on stage, my old friend. You're interrupting my business with your father. What do you think you're going to prove, Georgie?"

"I should be asking *you* that question, Zasso. But I know you won't tell me, so I'm going to stop this madness, you son of a bitch!"

"Wrong answer!" Zasso extended his left arm, formed his hand like a claw, and delivered a magic bolt towards Georgie.

Georgie raised his hand in front of his body, forming a rose-shaped red force field. The lightning bolt dissipated into the magical shield. Zasso gave a scowl as he tried another attack, which was unsuccessful again.

Meanwhile, Don Maretto was about to stand on the balcony ledge and take a leap of his own, when his son Alto grabbed the back of his tux, stopping him. "You can't go down there, pap," Alto said.

Turning to face his son, Maretto had fireballs in his eyes when he said, "He's going to get himself killed! That's your brother down there!"

"He's doing it to protect *you*!" Alto had some fire in his irises as well. "We gotta get the fuck out of here. You don't know what else he's got planned. Be smart, pap!"

Looking back down at the stage, Maretto thought, *He's right. We have to go before we all get killed...But I can't just let my son die! I need Vego.* He aggressively turned his body, brushed past Alto, and shouted, "Where's Vego? Somebody tell me where the fuck Vego is!"

Coincidently, Vego entered the balcony. His suit was draped in blood. Enemy's blood. He had successfully rid of the gangsters Zasso sent after him.

Maretto grabbed Vego by the arm and ordered, "Get your ass down to that stage and help my son! I'm escaping with the rest of my family. Get down there quick!"

Vego nodded, and without a word he did as he was commanded. Maretto and Alto helped Jon-Jon and Jeena to their feet, and together they left the balcony suite to make their escape out of the theater.

Zasso Cicello had had enough of the magic bullshit. It wasn't going to work on someone just as Blessed as he was, so he removed his royal blue suit coat, tossed it aside, and said, "You've successfully ruined my mission tonight, you boy scout piece of shit! So, I have no other choice but to take it out on your ass!" With his right arm, he reached behind his back, and unsheathed yet another weapon from his arsenal. It was a short sword with a golden hilt and cross-guard. The blade was made of a shiny black metal, and bordered by a yellow transparent glow. Zasso waved the sword around gingerly and took his position for a fight.

Georgie removed his coat as well. He reached behind his back and revealed his own magical blade, except that his hilt and cross-guard were made of silver, inlaid with diamonds, and the border around the blade was a transparent crimson. He too readied himself for battle.

And then in the middle of the stage, like a grand theatrical performance, the fight was on. They connected swords, red and yellow sparks exploded from the blades. Zasso spun around and tried to connect with a swirling offensive attack, but Georgie fended it off with ease. Zasso came at him with an array of more swings, causing Georgie to backtrack towards the edge of the stage. In response, he jump-flipped over his opponent, and gave him a stiff kick under his chin. Zasso flailed back, grabbed his jaw with his non-fighting hand, and began to laugh.

"Not too bad, old friend. I guess Don Maretto *has* taught his boys how to fight like men."

Georgie wasn't the least bit amused. "Yea you keep talking, wiseass. You and your family are going to pay for the peace that was broken here tonight!"

Eyes widened, Zasso replied, "Peace? You talk of peace? When was there ever peace? We have been fighting you for years, right under your noses. The Rose Family is just too arrogant and stupid to notice!"

Zasso charged with an aggressive attack. Georgie held up his magical blade and deflected the vigorous chop. Then it was his time to go on the offensive. He went after Zasso with a multitude of spin attacks, cutting the air with every swift motion. His blade was buzzing with fury, and Zasso was having a difficult time fending off the hostile swings. Zasso ducked under one swipe, and tried taking out Georgie's legs, but Georgie was quick to jump over the blade, and then tried to end the fight with a chop across the neck. Zasso's instincts were quick, and he leaned back, barely escaping with his head.

"Enough!" Zasso shouted. "I tire of this!" His body was suddenly engulfed in a fury of golden lightning bolts. He levitated in the air and burst forward while his body spun horizontally.

The magical charge was furious, but Georgie engulfed himself in a crimson shield, and shoulder-rammed the spinning lightning vortex. Georgie's attack was the mightier, and Zasso was violently pushed across the stage, landing on his back while lingering bolts still surged through his body.

Nonchalantly walking towards his opponent, Georgie said, "You underestimate my family, Zasso. You especially underestimate me. I know what you want. I know what your *family* wants. The Cicello's were always the jealous type."

"Fuck you!" Zasso yelled, still lying on his back. Slowly, he rolled over and started rising to his feet. "Fuck you *and* your fucking family."

Georgie stopped in his tracks, raised his blade and said, "On the contrary, Zasso. Fuck *your* family…Right to hell!"

As Georgie was about to charge at Zasso with another attack, the entire theater began to rumble and shake. With a bewildered look, Georgie gazed up into the ceiling…and that's when it happened. The marble ceiling imploded as a flying extended SUV crashed through. Georgie had to jump forward, diving out of the way of oncoming debris.

When he quickly stood up, he was amazed to be standing face to face with his enemy. But what was more shocking, was that Zasso's sword was sticking through his chest and protruding out his back. He was defeated and he knew it.

A slowly dying Georgie stared into the eyes of Zasso, and with heavy breathes uttered out, "You'll never get your hands on *it*…My family is too damn strong."

Gazing back into the eyes of the dying man, Zasso tilted his head, gave a leering grin, and replied, "Hardly going to listen to the noise of a soon-to-be dead guy."

Zasso lifted his sword upwards, and split Georgie's upper torso into two. A massive spray of blood coated Zasso's face and clothes. He closed his eyes, seemingly enjoying the bath of gore. Georgie's limp body fell lifelessly onto the stage.

When he opened his eyes, he could see Vego Rainze running for the stage and opening fire upon him. He surrounded his body with a yellow shield, deflecting the bullets.

As Vego came closer, Zasso looked up at the flying SUV that saved his ass, and noticed Razo in the driver's seat. With a nod, a rope was extended down to Zasso. He wrapped it around his body, and was airlifted off the stage and out of the theater.

Vego hopped onto the stage and continued firing up at the departing hovercraft. But it was no use. Zasso had escaped, and lying in a pool of blood in the middle of the stage, was the dead body of Georgiano Rose. Vego removed his special sunglasses, and with a look of dismay, stared upon Don Maretto Rose's dead son.

Ricalstro Rose

And the Utter Depths of His Darkness

Ric Rose was going to pound-town, and he was taking the two-bit skank that he happened to fuck from time to time with him. The busty brunette was always good for a random screw. He had a thing for big tits. He loved them. Sure, a nice round ass was good for the soul too, but if he had to choose which he liked better, Ric would usually go with the big boppers. *Tits don't take a shit,* he always surmised in his head.

So anyway, Ric was pounding out this stupid bitch and was ready to make a deposit into the splooge-lagoon at any moment. He was having it rough with her. She didn't deserve to be banged in any decent way. If she was willing to come over, do some smack, and then the nasty without any hesitation, then she was gonna get railed like the Metro City Express Train. This trick wasn't a prostitute, but she might as well have been. But whatever. To Ric she was just a local cum-dumpster that he had quick access to.

Ric let out an almost angry grunt when he was finished. He tossed her ass to the side and got out of bed immediately. There was no cuddling or any of that nonsense when it came to fucking this bitch. And that was more than cool with him.

As Ric stood in the tiny bedroom of his meager apartment, he sniffed the air. The room smelled of alcohol, sex, and bad perfume. He even smelled his own ass. He farted a couple times at the end. *Maybe I gotta take a shit...Nah, it's probably just the drugs fucking with my stomach*, he happened to think while standing completely in the nude. His unit went soft quick. Looking down at his junk he thought, *Yep, that's the drugs too.*

Ric was almost six-foot-tall and had a slim, but toned build. He had olive oil skin like his father, brown eyes, and dark brown-almost black-hair that was wavy and a little messy. Ric had always been a very handsome young man, but lately some of his facial features have become distorted because of all the alcohol and drugs he ingested from day to day and night to night. The darkness under his eyes made it look as though his eyeballs were casting shadows. Right now, his face didn't look too healthy either, but there was a time when Ricalstro Rose's face could make any woman powerless to his charms. Being the youngest son of Maretto Rose didn't hurt either. He got bitches.

As he started getting dressed, the brunette got a bitchy look on her face and asked, "Where do you think you're going?"

"I'm going out," he replied while pulling a tight black t-shirt over his head. His voice was usually smooth, but a slight rasp had developed since last year.

"So, we're done here already?" She seemed pissed.

"Yea we're fucking done. What the fuck do you think?" He noticed her bra on the floor so he picked it up. Size D. Big tats.

"But I still want to fuck!" She yelled so loud that the neighbors probably heard her stupid ass.

"Then go fuck yourself!" Ric said back, then threw the bra at her face. She looked disgusted, *but fuck that bitch*, he thought. "Get dressed and get the fuck out."

Angrily, the skank gathered her scattered clothes, got dressed, took a hit of some leftover powder on a small mirror with a crack in it, and then stormed out of the apartment. Ric was glad to see her go so early. He satisfied his urges, and there was still plenty of nightlife left. A drink sounded damn good right now, so a trip to his favorite club was next on his agenda. Plus, he needed to score some more shit, and he wasn't going to find any drugs between the couch cushions.

Before he opened the door to leave his apartment, Rick took a glance at his rundown shithole. He had his own nickname for his place. *The room of depression.* Once upon a time the small apartment didn't look so drab, but after a couple years of drug abuse, alcoholism, sex with bitches, and all-night parties that always ended with a few things being broken, it turned slum-like. The dishes were stacking up even though he doesn't eat hardly much anymore. His appetite is for smack. Whether it's shooting something in his veins or sniffing the shit up his nose, that's what Ric Rose lives for. Fuck all the wholesomeness in life, Ric wanted the bad and the ugly; to be the fool in the darkness. *I* am *the fool in the darkness. Killing myself slowly and I'm only twenty-two...Look at this fucking life I live.*

He opened the door, took one more glance at the place and said to himself, "Fuck it." Rick slammed the door, and was now on his merry way to the wonderful world of debauchery. *Fuck this life I live.*

La Bella Scoundrel. The Beautiful Scoundrel it means in the language of today. *La Bella* is but a couple of words left over from the language the ancestors used before their flight to Exodus-whenever the fuck that supposedly happened. He was taught that in middle school. It was a special school that consisted of students who had any relations to the crime syndicate-that the rest of the world calls *Families*-in or around the city of Juna.

But school was the last thing Ric wanted to think about as he walked under the bright lights of the club's logo. He needed a drink. Well, more than *a* drink. He wanted about five to ten. If there was a chance that he didn't score some good smack, then he might as well get drunk as all hell. Maybe more than ten drinks would suffice.

The big bald security guard that was dressed in all black gave him the nod to go inside. Ric was a regular at the Scoundrel, so his face was recognizable by all the doormen. He nodded back and entered, getting off the crummy streets of the lower eastside. It wasn't always sparkly and glamorous in downtown Juna. The lower eastside was like a pit of hell. No respectable native would venture through this part of the city. It was rough and hard. *Just like the way I gave it to that skank. Hah ha.*

The tunnel that led to the main bar had a row of black lights that lit his outfit up like a starry night sky. Every single piece of dust and fuzz was visible on the black t-shirt and pants. The gold chain around his neck and gold belt buckle turned into God knows what kind of color. The dandruff in his hair was probably showing too. *I bet it looks like someone grated cheese over my hair.*

The music was blaring, but Ric could give two shits. He wasn't there to make any small talk with people he didn't know. He wanted to be left alone. The only conversation he wanted to be involved in was a drug deal. He had to keep his eyes peeled for that, but anything else was beneath him tonight. But usually, he didn't get left alone. Someone always wanted to chat with the son of the most powerful man in Exodus.

The bar and stools were made of transparent glass that displayed cheery colors, lit by neon. Ric had to admit that he hated the bright colors of the bar, but that was the place to get his drink on, so fuck it. The burly bearded bastard bartending stood in front of Ric in an instant. He was always quick to wait on him.

"What can I get you tonight, my friend?" the bartender asked with his abnormally deep and gutted voice. He had his large and hairy arms stretched out on the bar as he waited for an answer. Rows upon rows of liquor were in the background. They too were alit by bright cheery fucking lights.

"The same thing I always start out with, Nester," Ric answered back. *Nester. What a bitch ass name for such a big ass fucking man.* But Ric kind of liked him. He was actually a cool guy.

"Coming right up." Nester slapped the bar counter and went to work. Watching him make a drink was like watching a performance. He must have gone to Mixology school with a minor in theater.

Nester slid the drink down, and Ric scooped it up. It was a grand mix of several liquors that turned the liquid a light blue when all blended together. And it tasted good as hell. Ric went to town on it immediately, and Nester didn't hesitate to mix up another one for him. That one went down even easier. In fact, they all went down easy. All the time. He was good at drinking booze. It gave him a smooth buzz…And when you mix the drugs in later, then it's a whole new ballgame.

It was getting late. But you couldn't tell Ric that. He would drink until the sun came up. So far, nobody had ventured over to the seat next to him to try to strike up a stupid conversation with him. Maybe it was his lucky night…That was until a short and stalky dark-skinned fellow made it his business to stand next to his stool and stare at him with big white eyes.

Groggy and drunk, Ric looked up at the muscular dark man, dressed in a white sport coat and pants with a halfway buttoned teal undershirt. "Can I help you, big guy?" Ric slurred.

"My boss wants to have a word wit' you," the dark man replied. His accent was very street.

Ric looked behind him but didn't notice anyone. Was he too drunk to see? "Where the fuck is he?"

The dark man just nodded his head a little to the left while crossing his big forearms. "Right over there, motherfucker. Sitting in the VIP booth. Can't you fucking see that far?"

He finally was able to and noticed some silly man waving him over to the booth. *Why the fuck do I have to deal with this right now?* He had to ask himself. "Do I really have to?" his drunk ass asked with a fart-face.

The man leaned in and said, "Listen, motherfucker. I don't like wasting my time getting up and walking over to ask some asshole to come to my boss's table. I don't wanna look like no motherfuck'n errand boy. But I do what I gotta do cause he pays me to do it, so get the fuck up, follow me to his booth, and don't ask me any more stupid ass questions."

Ric nodded his drunken head and said, "Sounds fair." A sloppy mess, he got off his stool and followed the dark man over to the VIP booth. Nester watched Ric's every move, his face very serious.

The silly man appeared to be excited to have Ric visit his area. He hastily put out his cig in the ashtray and stood up to greet his guest. Using both hands, he grabbed Ric's hand and shook it, almost nervously. But it probably wasn't nerves. This guy most likely has been snorting powder all night.

"Ric Rose, Ric Rose, damn glad to see you." The silly man let go of the handshake and motioned to the booth. "Have a seat, have a seat." His smile was big and his teeth bright. A fro of curly black hair covered his round head. He had bushy eyebrows and a thick mustache. The white suit with black pinstripes looked expensive, but that could be a front. *This guy looks like someone from one of those pornography videos,* was Ric's initial thought. *And why the hell is he wearing sunglasses in a place that's already dark as hell?*

Ric sat down and spread his arms across the back cushions of the booth. He didn't say a word. It wasn't his idea to come over here, so he waited for this weirdo to initiate the conversation.

Continuing to smile big, the porn guy asked, "You smoke? You wanna smoke?" He snagged the pack of cigarettes off the table and flung one out.

"Nah, I'm good."

"Okay, okay." The man lit up the cig and puffed on it a couple of times. *Does he do everything in twos?* "Do you recognize me? Do you know who I am?"

A waitress arrived at the booth and dropped off a couple drinks for them. Ric picked his up right away and threw it back before replying, "I have no fucking clue."

"Are you serious? Are you serious right now?" He still smiled. "It's okay if you don't. It's no big deal. I guess it's easy to forget a face when you're higher up in the food chain of the Families."

"I guess," Ric agreed, taking another sip of his drink.

"*Augusta Rocca.* I'm the son of *Don Maximo Rocca* of the Rocca Family. Remember me now?"

"I don't remember you, but I sure the fuck have heard of you." Ric looked behind Augusta, and stared at the large bald man with a bushy beard standing behind him with his mammoth forearms crossed. The dark-skinned guy was standing not too far off to the right. "Who the fuck is that guy?" he asked, nodding to the bald white guy.

Pointing his thumb back, Augusta dropped his smile and replied, "Who? That fucking monster behind me? That's Karn. You don't want to fuck with that guy." He then pointed a finger at the dark-skinned man. "And that's Jamele. You don't want to fuck with him either. These are my guys. They're big and they're assholes. Get it? You catching me?"

37

"I hear you." Ric slammed the rest of his drink and set the glass on the table. The remaining ice jingled. "So, what the fuck do you want from me? I was enjoying my time alone at the bar. I don't like being bothered when I'm trying to drown myself in booze."

"I get what you're saying." Snapping his fingers at Jamele, Augusta said, "Hey, go get sweet-tits and have her bring me and my friend here another drink." He brought his attention back to Ric as his guy went on his mission, all pissylike. "I'll tell you why I wanted to hang with you for a minute or two. I saw you sitting there and recognized that you were Ric Rose. I was hoping that I would run into you tonight. I heard this is the spot you usually hang. I thought you could help me if I helped you. You *are* a Rose and everything."

Man, he talks fast. Has to be the powder.

Ric laughed and said, "I think you got the wrong Rose Family member. I'm not much help to anyone these days."

"Oh, I don't think so, Ric Rose. I don't think so at all. You *are* the one Rose that can help me. Not any of your other brothers can, and definitely not any of the other fucking Families around. I have to pull teeth to get any help in this city. The Rocca Family aren't the biggest stars in town. We grovel at the feet of most to make our ends."

Which is true. The Rocca Family is one of the smaller of the Seven Blessed Families. They dwell in a small city to the south called *Vena,* and own one of the finer casinos on the strip.

"It's pretty fucked up what I have to do to pull some tricks, but the good thing is that someone always wants my shit. And I tell you right now, that I got the best shit in Exodus." He pointed his finger down, tapping the table as he said, "Pure premium grade-A fucking shit that will knock your fucking block off."

Very intrigued now, Ric asked, "What are we talking about here?"

Jamele was back, and not a moment after 'sweet-tits' set down two more drinks. Ric picked his up while Augusta waited for the waitress to leave before he answered, "Only the finest fucking smack this nation has to offer."

Yes! Ric shouted in his head. This is what he *really* came to the club for tonight. It was time to score some good drugs. He didn't have much money on him, but he could probably get enough smack to last him the night.

"You got my undivided attention now," Ric said, taking another healthy swig of his fresh drink.

Augusta's smile was even bigger now, if that was at all possible. "Hey now, Ricky, that's my boy, that's my boy. Now, I'm not a stupid village idiot, Ric. I know the kind of shit that you're into, and that you're a user and not a dealer. I'm not here to judge. I get it, I get it. Unlike the other yuppie fucks in this city that carry your name or the name of those other motherfuckers, you like to get down and dirty. And I respect that, and I like it. And I like you. That's why I came to *you*. *You*, Ric Rose, are on the other side of my glory hole." He made a circle with his left hand, and motioned his pointer finger with his other hand in and out of the circle. "And all I'm trying to do, is get my dick through to your side."

What? Was Ric's initial thought. He looked perplexed.

"And smack, my friend, is how I'm going to get that dick on your side. Because it's what you want. You want this dick on your side. You need my help. I can help you. All I need, is just a little tug from you to get it all the way through. Just a little help from you. Are you feeling me, Ric? Are you feeling the poke? Can you tug on it a little, so I can get through? If you can't, then I understand. I'll understand." Augusta must have snorted himself silly tonight, because he was just a rambling fool at the moment.

Ric was more than confused, but at the same time, he kind of understood the weirdo. "So, are you trying to get me to suck your dick, or are you offering me some smack? Because I'll tell you right now, I'm not interested in any dick."

Augusta leaned his head back and howled to the moon. "Oh, you little devilish bastard. You know what the deal is," he said, nodding his head up and down. "You know what the deal is."

"Actually, I don't know what the deal is, because you haven't told me yet."

Pointing his finger at Ric, Augusta said, "I'll tell you what the deal is, Ric Rose. It's a genuine clear-cut offer from me. Something to get you through the next, I don't know how many fucking days." He paused while Ric listened intently. "How about a whole pound of my finest shit for you, for free?"

Ric's droopy eyes opened up wide, but then he thought why this guy would randomly give him free smack. "Of course you're not gonna just give me free drugs."

"You're not a village idiot either, Ric. This is where I need your help sliding my dick through."

"Well, slide it on through and tell me what you need from me."

Augusta's laugh was almost giddy, but then he calmed himself and put on a more serious face. "Vena is a shithole, Ric. Besides the strip, it's old, it's rundown, and it's almost empty. Juna is where all the action is. This," he said, tapping his finger down on the table once again, "is the hotspot in Exodus. And *this*, is where I have to come to make my money.

"I have enough smack and powder to get the whole nation high, but not everybody in Exodus has the money. Especially not in Vena. It's a dried-up piss hole, I tell ya. Too many assholes are throwing their money away in the casinos." He paused to let his words soak in, but Ric didn't really give a fuck. He just wanted him to get to the point. "But I've been having some problems as of late. The Juna Police don't take too kindly to out of town gangsters. The Rose Family, The Cicello Family, those people can get away with this type of shit, because the authorities know better not to fuck with them. But the Rocca Family is out of their jurisdiction, and they must feel like they have to maintain some authority over the Seven Blessed Families, so they like to pick on the smaller ones. And Families like *yours*, don't give a shit if the police pick on us, because of course, they believe that nobody else should be in their territory. But to me, this place is free game. All of it."

Now Ric was getting impatient. He wanted his drugs. "Get to the point, Augusta. What do you need from me?"

Putting his hands up, Augusta replied, "Alright, alright, alright." He put his hands back down. "It's real simple, Ric. You know someone important that can get some of the police off my ass. The last couple of months have been rough. My men have been busted three or four times in the last two months, and that means that my product has been confiscated as well. That's a lot of business right down the toilet. Just flushed down into the sewer system. I lose a lot of money when that happens, my friend, so this is where I need you." Ric leaned in a little as he continued in a softer voice, "I know about your relationship with a certain officer of the law. *Detective Melroy Statz.* That name rings a bell now, doesn't it?"

Ric looked down at the table and slowly nodded his head. *Does he really want me to get Melroy involved? Fuck.*

"You guys are what, childhood friends?" Ric doesn't answer, but Augusta still goes on. "Anyway, all I need is for you to have a little talk with Detective Statz, and have him tell his other detective buddies who specialize in illegal drugs, to back off a little. That's all I need. Just a little backing off. I just want to be able to cruise into town, deliver my goods, and get the fuck out without any problems. Whatever happens after I make my delivery, is of no concern to me. I just need to make my money, and that's that. Do you feel me? Do you feel my dick poking through the glory hole?"

Eyebrows raise, Ric replies, "Oh, I feel you. I feel it poking." *I just want the fucking drugs you lowlife asshole, so I'll feel anything you poke at me right now. Sure, I'll talk to Melroy. Maybe when I've used up the whole pound of smack I will.*

"Good," Augusta smiles, his big teeth glowing in the neon lighting. He lights up another cig. Who knows how many he's smoked since Ric sat down? "It's a real simple deal, Ric. Your guy tells his guys to back off, and me and my guys are as happy as a rainbow taking a shit. Next week, when I bring my new shipment in, I should have no problems with the authorities. Right Ric? No law-abiding scumbags dressed in ugly trench coats tampering in my business. Am I right, Ric? Can I count on having no interruptions in my deal next week?"

Crossing his arms, Ric shrugged his shoulders and said, "Sure. No problem." He wasn't sure, though. Even if he did have a sit down with Melroy, there was no way he would consent to this. Melroy Statz was by the book. Clean as a whistle. Cleaner than cleanser. Not a speck of dirt on him. You get the fucking picture.

This time, Augusta wasn't smiling. Instead, he reached under the table, pulled out a small black satchel with a strap, and placed it on the table. "My payment for you is up front." He slid the satchel across the table. It stopped in front of Ric. "So, you better hold up your end of the deal. If my shipments come through without any disruptions from now on, then there's plenty more where that brick came from…But if I do have some problems, then Karn and Jamele won't be standing around just for show. They'll rip your fucking head off. Is that cool with you?"

Ric casually grabbed the satchel and hid it under the table, setting it on his lap. "Yea, that's cool," he replied. *Oh, he's gonna be pissed if his men get busted next week, but what's the chance of that happening? He said himself that he's only had a few problems in the past couple months, so fuck it.*

Standing up, Augusta brushed the front of his suit with both hands, then said, "Alright then. I'll be seeing you around, Ric Rose. Don't let me and my boys down, now." He left the VIP booth, walking quickly to the exit. Karn and Jamele mean-mugged Ric as they slowly followed behind their boss. They *did* look like a couple of big mean assholes.

Ric sat back in the booth, and finished the contents of his drink. He looked down at the satchel on his lap, running a few fingers through his messy hair. *Damn my hair is greasy,* he thought. *But that's the way it should be.* He tapped his fingers on the satchel. There it was. The score of the night. And it was a big score. A *really* big score. Supposedly some of the finest smack in Exodus. *Well, there's only one way to find out if Augusta's telling it true.* It was time for Ric to get high. Really, *really* high. He slid out of the booth, and he and the satchel left the club together.

Lying back and relaxing on his couch, Ric wrapped a rubber tube around his arm to pop out a good vein. Then the needle filled with some Vena Gold was stuck in his arm. The plunger was pulled back, Ric's blood mixed with the now liquid smack. The plunger was pushed forward, and Ric's vein was filled with chemical nirvana. In a matter of moments, his eyes felt like they were going to roll into the back of his head, and his entire body turned to jelly. It was a euphoria he hadn't felt in a while. *This is some good shit,* he thought, high as high can be. He grabbed a glass filled with ice and brown liquor and took sip after glorious sip.

He didn't realize that he was standing up until he was actually on his feet. His head was swirling with thoughts. Not good thoughts. Very bad thoughts. The mind plays around with you when you're as high as a mountain peak. *My family,* was his first thought as he mindlessly walked towards the kitchen. *My family abandoned my trust when I needed it the most. My brothers are traitors in my heart, though they never really caused any harm to me.* He was now standing barefoot in the kitchen. *Oh, but they did harm me. They took my revenge away from me, those bastards.* Ric removed his shirt and was now bare-chested. *They should've known how much that revenge meant to me. It was the only treatment I had left for my soul.* A tear fell from his right eye. *Those bastards! She was relying on me…That was my revenge!*

A vision appeared before him. A vision of the past. It was so real that he felt as though he could reach out and touch it. So he tried to. He closed his eyes, extended out his arm, and reached for the vision…There she was with the cute blonde hair and with eyes of jade. They were walking together through an alleyway. They were laughing. Enjoying life with one another.

Oh, how beautiful she was. My God did I love her…I never wanted any harm to come to her. She was my everything.

Ric was only eighteen. He and his girlfriend, Galia, just had dinner together at their favorite restaurant. It was a romantic evening. It was about to get even more romantic.

We talked about our future together that night. About getting married. Having kids. Maybe having four of them. I kept losing myself in those hypnotizing green eyes. Oh, how beautiful she was…My God did I love her…

It was a dark and decrepit ally. Probably not a good idea to walk down this way. But it was a shortcut. A shortcut to get home faster, so they could envelope each other under the covers…But it was never meant to be. At gunpoint, a street thug demanded their money and jewelry. There were others too. A whole group of thugs ready to rob them.

We gave them everything we had. But it didn't matter. They were after more than just our riches. They were after our dignity, our self-respect, and our lives…

Back in the kitchen, Ric grabs a butcher's knife off the counter without even thinking about it. Then, he held the knife to his chest, with the sharp edge against the bare skin.

I can feel the pain right now. The first couple of blows brought me down to my knees. There are a couple of my teeth on the ground. I was spitting globs of blood. It was painful. But not as painful as watching what he was doing to her…I never meant any harm to come to her…

The thug that initially held a gun to their heads punched Galia directly in the face. She went down in an instant. Her jaw was realigned. Ric could only watch the horror. The other thugs were holding him down now. One was kicking his sides, cracking his ribs. He yelled for them to stop. He yelled for them to leave her alone.

They laughed…Those sons of bitches just laughed at me!

Ric ran the blade of the knife diagonally down his chest and to his abdomen. Not deep enough to kill himself, but enough to shed blood. He wanted to feel the pain. But no matter how much pain the blade caused, it would never be as much as that thug caused *her* that night.

The thug threatened to rape her. I begged and pleaded him not to do it. I even told him my name. I yelled to him that I was Ricalstro Rose! But it didn't work. They didn't believe me…

She was raped. Terribly. She yelled, cried, and screamed…But the thug laughed. Laughed and went to town on her. Ric shouted louder and harder for him to stop. But the other thugs just beat him repeatedly, until he was about to lose consciousness.

The thug stood over her ravaged body. She had passed out from the pain and fear. He aimed his gun at her forehead. I couldn't bear to watch, and I had no strength left in me to beg for her life. But with little strength I had, I shifted my eyes and saw something a ways down the alley. It was someone in the shadows. Hiding there. Almost as if the person was watching the action...

The thug shot her between the eyes just as Ric went unconscious. Galia was dead, and now it was Ric's turn. While he wasn't awake for what happened next, Ric would later find out that one of the thugs holding him down checked his wallet and let the rest of his crew know that his ID said he was in fact Ricalstro Rose. Immediately, they all got spooked. This was a grave mistake. The Rose Family would come after them with full force. But what would also spook them, was the sound of police sirens. The shot had been heard and the authorities had been called. So, not taking good aim with his shot, the thug who killed Galia, fired a round at Ric's head. It seemed as though it was a direct hit, but the bullet only grazed him.

The thugs ran away...But they wouldn't run for long. My family would catch up with them quick...But I didn't want them to yet. It was me who would find each and every one of them, bring them to their knees, and listen to them beg for mercy right before I blow their brains all over the pavement...They took my precious Galia. She was going to be my wife someday. Oh, how beautiful she was...My God did I love her...

Somehow, Ric was now lying on his couch, staring up at the ceiling of his apartment. But what he saw wasn't actually his ceiling. It was the hospital ceiling. Ric had been in a coma for a week as a result of the trauma to his head. But now he was awake. And Jon-Jon was the first person he saw, sitting by his bed, gracing him with a smile. He went on and on about how thankful everyone was, since he was going to survive, and how excited everyone was to see him now that he was awake...But he didn't mention Galia. She was dead and he wasn't. It was time for revenge, so that's all he wanted to do as soon as he was out of this place.

Ric was now alert, and sitting up. His brothers were all surrounding his hospital bed. They joked around for a little while, but Ric was having a hard time being amused. There was a revenge to plot.

"I need to get out of here, and then it's time to go find the guys who did this to me and Galia," I said, eyeing down Alto, who I interrupted in mid-talk.

They all looked at me with blank stares. Then they looked at one another. Their heads went down. Jon-Jon spoke first. "Ric, there's no need to go find the guys responsible. We already found them."

The news got me excited. My brothers found them for me already. I was now in the driver's seat, on my way to getting my revenge. "Good! So, let's get me the hell out of here and go get them." I fumbled around with some of my tubes, until Georgie grabbed my arm to settle me down. I gave him a confused look. "What?" They all were looking at each other strange, but nobody would give me eye contact. "What is it?"

Alto finally looked me in the eyes and confessed, "We already took care of it for you, Ric. We couldn't wait until you woke up and risk them running and getting away for good. They were captured three days ago. They're all dead and gone now. All five of them."

I couldn't believe what I was hearing. I drew heavy breaths. A panic attack was on the horizon. Those bastards did what? "What are you talking about?" Georgie tried to comfort me by putting a hand on my shoulder. I aggressively shoved it away. "What the fuck are you talking about? You went out and got those assholes without me?"

"Calm down, Ric," Georgie told me. But I didn't.

"Are you serious? Are you guys fucking serious right now?" They remained silent. I guessed that they were serious, but I wanted to hear it one more time. I pointed at Alto and said, "Is it true, Alto? You guys already found them and killed them!"

Alto hesitated for a moment and then answered, "Yes. It's already taken care of, Ric."

I sat there, still for a moment, and then I ripped the IV right out of my arm, feeling no pain. I threw the tube at Georgie and yelled, "You sons of bitches! How could you do this to me? She was my life! I was going to marry her! I had to watch them rape her and blow her head off, and now I can't do a damn thing about it!" They all tried to calm me

46

which made me even more irate. "No! No! No! You had no right to avenge her death for me! That was for me to do! That was my revenge!"

The flashbacks were gone, but Ric could still see Galia's smiling face.

My heart still aches for her, and my wounds were never able to heal…Oh how beautiful she was…My God did I love her…

That was my revenge!

The next morning, Ric was awoken by the vibration of his cell phone. For some reason, he was lying face-down on the floor, and the phone was buzzing right next to his head. The name on the caller ID said ALTO. He grabbed ahold of the phone and slid the answer button.

"Hello?" Ric groggily said, phone held to his ear.

"Hey Ric, its Alto." There was a short pause. "You better come home. Georgie is dead."

Detective Melroy Statz

And the President's Special Agent

It was quite possibly the most infamous crime in the history of Exodus. Georgiano Rose had been slain at center stage in the middle of a theatrical performance at the Grand Theater. But he wasn't the only fatality last night. Considered the best actor of recent memory, Martell Vienis was brutally murdered as well. Along with two other actors, about a dozen theater patrons, and a multitude of gangsters from the Rose and Cicello Families…It was a fucking massacre. And word has quickly spread across Juna that the main figure responsible for the heinous act was none other than Zasso Cicello.

What was that asshole thinking? Melroy asked himself, still lingering around the theater at the crack of dawn. He had already talked to members of the Rose Family-who he was very familiar with-and they told him that Zasso's plan was to actually kidnap the leader of the Rose Family, Don Maretto Rose. Instead, he ended up murdering one of his sons and a bunch of other people at the performance. But why? *What was he trying to accomplish by kidnapping the most powerful man in Exodus? And who could've talked him into such a bold idea? His father?* Detective Melroy Statz asked these questions to himself over and over again, but he wouldn't be able to come up with a clear-cut answer. Not until he did some real investigating.

The sight of Georgiano Rose's butchered corpse was a haunting picture for Melroy Statz. He had grown up alongside the four Rose brothers. Especially Ric and Georgie. He and Georgie were the same age, but he was closest with Ric. Georgie was always up his father's ass, getting groomed to be a Blessed family member, so he found himself hanging out with Ric, acting as an extra big brother as they went on fun adventures together when they were kids. Melroy never really did have a father. His biological dad was already dead before he was born. Some drug deal gone wrong or something. His mother sort of raised him, but she was always working or whatever else she did with her time. And she didn't exactly make enough for him and his two older half-brothers. Those two assholes never gave him the time of day either. They were a couple of dickheads for sure.

One day, when Melroy was about eleven, Ric and Georgie left school early, and took a back alleyway as a shortcut to get home. As a matter of fact, it was the same alley that Ric's girlfriend was murdered in. *This happened right before I graduated from the academy. The criminals were never caught alive. They were all found dead in the basement of some shithole club,* Melroy reminisced. Anyway, the two brothers found Melroy scrummaging through one of the trash bins. He was scavenging for food and looked as though he hadn't bathed in a week. Ric and Georgie brought him home, and Don Maretto Rose fed him, gave him a bath, gave him new clothes, and some extra money. From that day on, Melroy looked up to Maretto Rose like a father, and he was always welcomed into their home. He almost became a permanent fixture in their family...*Almost.*

To Melroy, those days were very special. When he was a kid, he believed Maretto Rose to be a genuinely kind-hearted soul, and that the Rose Family members were all saints sent down from God...Oh, how time can change everything. As he grew up on the outer edge of the Rose Family, he would eventually see the corruption with his own eyes. They weren't saints at all. Far from it. Saints don't have other people killed to satisfy their business needs.

But he would stay loyal to the Rose Family. Although corrupt, they still helped a poor kid from the street, whose mother was absent most of the time. And Melroy was very grateful. Even though Don Maretto wasn't too delighted with his choice of occupation, Melroy would do whatever he could to help the Rose Family if they were in need...*And that time is now,* Melroy thought, staring at the blood-soaked stage. *If there was ever a time I could pay them back for all the hospitality they gave me, it was now. I'll get to the bottom of this. I'll not only find out who gave him this crazy order, but I'll also find out where that bastard ran off to.*

Melroy was young for a detective, but he was one of the best at his job, and didn't join the police force to be a uniform guy. His ambition always had been to be a detective. He worked his ass off to get where he was today. But today, his job has put him in a rut. Sure, he knew exactly who the culprit was in the newly titled 'Grand Theater Massacre' case, but *why* Zasso committed this heinous crime was nagging his brain. *Someone higher up gave him this order,* Melroy thought, while finally leaving the grounds of the theater early in the morning. *But who? Would Xanose Cicello actually give such an order? He was never this ambitious. And why kidnap Maretto Rose? What did they want from him?*

On and on the questions kept bouncing around his mind. He had to sit down in a quiet environment and think this over, so he walked to a local diner that he often visited. The coffee at *Crist's Eatery* was good and strong, and the breakfast food was the best kept secret in town. He sat in a booth and only drank coffee for the time being. He wasn't hungry yet. The questions from last night's assassinations had suppressed his hunger. Maybe after a while of thinking things through will get him in the mood to have a bite.

He was alone in the diner, except for the two waitresses and the cook in the back kitchen. It was a small hole in the wall, and you could see the cook doing his work from where you were sitting. Right now, he wasn't doing a damn thing, but when it gets packed, he'll be seen sweating over a hot grill. The inside looked aged and a little dirty, but that's what made it unique. Fuck the five-star restaurants that the Rose Family goes to all the time, this is where Melroy Statz was more comfortable. This shitty diner fit him properly.

The entrance has a little bell that chimes when a new patron enters the diner. When it jingled, it alerted the waitress. It didn't alert Melroy. He just stared at the blackness of his coffee, pondering his next move. Little did he know, he was about to have a visitor in the next few seconds. The waitress asked the new patron if he wanted a cup of coffee and the patron said, 'yes please'. Thinking it was probably just some fool off the street, Melroy kept his eyes in the cup, until a clean-cut dark-haired man sat himself across from him. The man was dressed in a jet-black tailored suit with a plain white dress shirt and an ordinary black tie. He was wearing sunglasses, and must have forgotten to take them off.

The man's freshly tailored suit was a contrast to Melroy's drab outfit of a casual brown suit coat and pants, cheap dress shirt and tie. A brown fedora was also usually donned on his head. This man's face was taken a lot better care of too. Melroy was beginning to grow a beard and mustache. Shaving had become bothersome to him lately.

He knew this guy though. Yea, he recognized his face, even though there were thousands of guys that looked just like him. His outfit was the dead giveaway. He was in law enforcement too. One of different proportions. He wasn't just a protector of the city

50

of Juna, he was part of a special unit that monitored the entire nation. The *ESFU*, which stands for, *Exodus Special Forces Unit*, is the elite unit that works directly for the President of Exodus. When talked about, it is usually just shortened to SFU...They were a strong group of men who did the President's bidding without any questions asked, and they were also a big group of fucking assholes. Especially this one, *Special Agent Kelvin Strain*.

Strain acted like he was the greatest thing around since the invention of electricity, and he played the part well. Always dressed real tidy, clean shaven and handsome. Probably banged a lot of broads in his life, or maybe he was into guys. Who knew with these dickbags? They all kept true to their oaths to the President, and were fairly hush-hush when it came to their personal lives. The members of the ESFU were anomalies. They no longer had true identities. They were whatever the President wanted them to be. Strain was no exception. Nothing about this guy's past life was ever brought out onto the table.

While the waitress prepared Strain's coffee, the special agent broke the silence in the diner. "It's useless to dwell on a case like this, Statz. I know that's what you've probably been doing since you got word of the crime. You detectives are all the same." Strain had a deep, intimidating voice for a douchebag. Those were probably two credentials needed for the job. An intimidating voice and douchebag persona. "It's a cut and dry case, my friend."

Melroy finally stopped staring into the coffee, and looked directly into the douchebag's sunglasses. "Oh yea, well humor me, Kelvin." Melroy's voice was not as deep, and he definitely had a street accent.

"Agent Strain," he corrected.

Douche.

"I'm sorry, Special Agent Kelvin Strain," he muttered with some sarcasm. "Please tell me your point of view on why this is such a cut and dry case."

A little annoyed, Strain said, "In a second. I want to have my beverage in front of me. Where the fuck is this bitch?" As if the waitress heard him, and she probably did, his coffee was promptly set down in front of him. He smiled at her and said, "Why thank you, ma'am. I'm sure this will be delightful." As soon as she walked away, his smile disappeared. He took a sip and looked rather surprised. "Hmm. Not too bad." He looked back at Strain. "Now, where was I?"

"The massacre at the Grand Theater."

"Like I really forgot...Now, Melroy..."

"Detective Statz."

"Whatever." He looked very annoyed now. Melroy was loving it. "*Melroy*, you can sit here all day long, drink coffee until you piss your pants, and think of all the different conspiracies your feeble mind can coax up, *or* you can just take it for what it is. Zasso Cicello committed this crime, plain and simple. He may have been advised by someone else, but that someone else didn't destroy a number of lives last night."

Melroy shook his head. "That someone else devised a plan to kidnap Maretto Rose. *The* Maretto Rose. Maybe you've heard of him before?"

Strain turned his head. "Don't talk to me like I'm some village idiot. I know what you have been told, but your sources are from the Rose Family itself. Can you really trust the word of a criminal empire?"

"I can trust you?" Melroy quickly asked.

He turned his head again and replied, "Come on, Melroy. We're both on the same side of the fence. We play for the same team."

"Oh, do we now? You work for the President of Exodus and I work for the city of Juna. We're not even on the same playing field anymore." He was correct with this statement. The President has kept his affairs quiet, quiet, quiet, as of late.

"Think whatever you want, Detective. Our departments both hold up the same standards of law in this God-forsaken nation. And the law was broken last night, *in public*. Over a dozen innocent people were slaughtered at a high-profiled gathering, highlighted by the appearance of the man of the hour, Don Maretto Rose. His arrival was broadcasted live throughout the nation, and the people of Exodus grovel at his feet like he's the fucking king." He sounded slightly agitated when mentioning the patriarch of the Rose Family. "Well, grovel all they want, but he's the *real* problem in Exodus. And since his appearance brought on national coverage, the tragedy that ensued is now under the investigation of the SFU, and we strongly believe that we will find Zasso Cicello sooner rather than later. The President will strike his justice hard on the Cicello prince, and he will undoubtedly pay the price for his immoral act. You can bet on that, *Detective Statz*."

Strong words for a strong believer in his President. But Melroy wasn't buying any of it. The President and the ESFU are the ones who usually grovel at the feet of the Rose and Cicello Families. They were just going to cover this up and try to keep a war from happening between the Families. War meant more death. The last thing the President of Exodus needs on his plate is nationwide coverage of inner-Family murders. The crime syndicates must keep the peace, or the nation will spin out of control. It has happened before. Long, long time ago. And it wasn't pretty.

"So, you want me to just step away from the case and watch," Melroy assumed.

"Not completely step away. Maybe just take a step back. Let us dig deep into the dirty secrets of the underworld. But you can ask questions around town if you want, I have no problem with that. You can even help us out and fill us in with whatever tidbits of information you find."

This made Melroy chuckle a tad. Such a dickhead douchebag. "Are you sure I won't be a disruption to your work if I just ask a few simple questions around the city?"

"Laugh all you want, Detective, but that's what you're supposed to do anyway, isn't it? Asking questions is your job. I'm sure every low-life scumbag in this city will have an opinion on the whereabouts of Zasso Cicello. And if you do happen to hear some interesting information, the SFU will be more than happy to have that information shared. Maybe we'll even give you a reward…Opening day is coming up for the EBL. I'm sure we can easily get you some boxed seats for any game you'd like."

Staring back into his cup of coffee, Melroy picked it up, took a sip and said, "That sounds really enticing, Agent Strain. Opening day tickets just for me. Wow, you guys are generous."

Strain's mood was deterred. "Let's cut through the shit, Melroy. I'm going to let you in on a little secret."

"Ooh, can't wait to hear this," Melroy said, faking his excitement.

The Special Agent finally removed his glasses and revealed his cold, dark eyes. "I know the nation thinks that the President just sits on his ass and watches the criminal empires in Exodus play around like this land is some fucking playground, but for a number of years, he has been planning something big pertaining to the Seven Blessed Families."

Suddenly, Melroy's attention had been ceased. "Like what?"

"Well, my friend, let's just say that the President is fed up with all the senseless violence in Exodus, and it's about time to punish those mainly responsible for it all. Sure, all the violence doesn't stem from the Families, but more often than not, they *are* the guilty party. And the President is sick of it. *He* is the true leader of this nation, and he's tired of bowing down to groups of murderous gangsters who spill blood on the streets that our kids walk on every day. The Seven Blessed Families believe that they can just do whatever they please, because they possess those sources of power called Relics.

"But let's be honest here. Relics are a curse to this nation. If the Seven Families didn't have these sorcerous powers, then their leaders would be nothing more than two-bit criminals running around the streets. I think the Relics should all be destroyed, but our President believes that they should be contained and used for good causes. To him, they are being wasted on crime syndicates. Why should law-breaking murderers have the good fortune of possessing such items? The government would use them in a clean and inspiring way."

"Like how?" Melroy asked.

Strain shrugged his shoulders and answered, "I don't fucking know. However, the President wants them to be used for. I don't really give a good damn what he has in store for the Relics, but I sincerely believe that the President has a valid point. The Seven Blessed Families are ruining Exodus, and it's about time that they pay for all their crimes. And recent events are proof that the President's future plans will be validated by the average citizen of Exodus. The death of innocent civilians will not be tolerated by our government from here on out. You'll see."

Taking another sip, Melroy turned his head and gazed out the window. *This is big. This is really big. No one person has ever stood up to the Seven Blessed Families. Especially not the President himself. How will he succeed? He just doesn't have enough power.*

"I know you'll probably run to the Rose Family and leak this information out to them. Everybody in the SFU knows your close-knit relationship with Maretto and his sons. Just be careful with your actions, Detective," Strain informed.

Immediately, Melroy said, "I'm not gonna say a word to them. They can fend for themselves. This is not my fight."

"Good," Strain responded.

"But I'm still gonna do my job, and find Zasso before he completely disappears, or tries to capture Maretto Rose again. *And* I'm gonna figure out who gave him the order. He didn't act alone on this, you have to at least agree with me on that." Melroy had a spark in his eyes and Agent Strain noticed it. He smiled at the Detective, put his sunglasses back on, and stood up from the booth.

"Okay, fine. I'll agree with you on that. Zasso Cicello took an order from someone higher up. But that only leaves two suspects. Xanose Cicello and your friend, Maretto Rose. But would the great Father of Gangster fake his abduction to have his own kid killed? I'm sure *you* would strongly disagree with that notion, but I wouldn't put it past him. So, that leaves only one."

Melroy slightly nodded his head in agreement.

Before he left, Strain knocked on the table a couple of times with his knuckles and said, "Just ask questions. We'll take care of the rest...See you around, Detective."

With a jingle of the bell above the entrance, the diner was now empty again, except for Melroy, the two waitresses, the sweaty cook, and his empty coffee cup. The waitress came over and filled it up. Just like his head was now filled with new and vital information about the future of the entire nation.

Exodus is in for a long road of turmoil. The Seven Blessed Families will not succumb to the President so easily, Melroy thought to himself, sipping his last cup of coffee for the day.

Zasso Cicello

And the Mystery Guest

His mission ended up being a complete failure. More than a failure. It was a disaster. The result of last night couldn't have been any worse, except for if he himself was the one to get viciously mutilated. *Well that wouldn't have been any good,* Zasso thought in his head. *This world needs me. I have so much more to do.* It would be a shallow thought for some inbred loser who didn't contribute shit to this world, but Zasso Cicello was going to make a significant impact in history. It was his time to shine. He would soon be engulfed in the spotlight…But right now he had to hide. The now infamous event at the Grand Theater was his doing. The people of Exodus will be angry for the time being, but soon enough they will come to terms with his actions. Just as soon as the master plan has been fulfilled, the people will praise him, rather than shun him. But he's still going to have to take some heat from the individual who gave him the mission. *Things just got out of hand really fast last night,* would be one of his excuses. Still, the higher ups are probably very unhappy.

The SUV that saved him had to be dumped part way to their hideout spot. It was their plan B. If something went wrong at the theater, and they had to hide from the authorities, then the plan was to abandon the SUV and pick up the alternate transportation, which was a regular car that blended in with traffic. If the initial plan was being carried out successfully, then it was a straight shot to their destination. There was no time to fuck around with Maretto Rose in their grasps…Obviously, it didn't go the way they planned, and Zasso and Razo had to go through the hassle of changing vehicles and traveling a lot slower to Plan B's destination; an abandoned shack on the northern outskirts of the city, just a small distance beyond *Dumond's Pond*, which was surrounded by a small forest.

It was a shitty little shack, but it was dark and hidden from Juna. The only way they would be found, is if someone happened to come upon the shack by accident. The odds of them ever being captured were definitely in their favor.

The fire was crackling in the hearth. There was no electricity in the remote forest, so Zasso and Razo were huddled around the fire, as it was their only light source. They acted like fools. A botched mission didn't seem to bother the two elite gangsters. A botched mission of grand proportions *should* bother them. And when they started drinking and doing a good amount of powder, they started to care even less. *Big deal if we fucked up this time around. At least I got rid of one of those Rose assholes,* Zasso's fucked up mind thought. *It was Georgiano's fault that the mission was a failure. Screw the higher powers that be. One day everyone will suffocate under my feet. Fuck...everyone...else.*

They were both wearing street clothes now. Those damn suits were too uncomfortable. It was bad enough that they were stuck in this dirt-ridden shanty, cobwebs attached to every dark corner, piles of dust accumulated from lack of habitation. Just sniff the air and the smell of rotted wood and decomposed vermin filled the nostrils. This was not their usual form of residence. They were used to the luxury of penthouses with butlers, maids, and nonstop women coming in and out. At least they had wine and a shitload of drugs. They could at least put on a nice buzz while waiting for their contact to arrive.

Razo threw back a splash of wine and said, "To me, the look of that Vego bastard's face when he saw his boss's son dead at center stage was worth the failure. I wish I could have seen the way the rest of the Rose Family looked when you started electrifying the theater. They were probably shitting bricks."

Laughing ignorantly, Zasso said back, "Oh, they were shitting themselves alright. Except for that wannabe hero who thought he was going to save the day. Good riddance to that fool." *He did put up a good fight, but I'll be damned if I give him that credit out loud.* "See you in hell someday, Georgiano Rose."

Both of them gave a menacing laugh, and at the same time lifted their glasses, clinking them together. It was a gesture of agreement that they were both happy the Rose Family member was dead.

Before Zasso took a sip, he swirled the contents in his glass, and glared hard into the ruby liquid. "Wine," he hoarsely said. "It always reminded me of blood. A little less dense, but it has the color. When I see a man bleeding profusely from an open wound, it always makes me thirsty. Thirsty for wine. Thirsty for more blood." Half of his face was glowing orange from the fire, and the other half was dark in shadow.

Razo took a generous sip from his own glass, never taking his eyes off the menacing human across from him. He wiped his mouth, removing the remnants of wine, and listened intently to the man he worked for.

"Tonight, we spilled a lot of blood. And my good God did it make me thirsty. My mouth was drooling, the hairs on the back of my neck stood like needles. I think I might have even been aroused a little." He cracked a half-grin. "Call me sick, or twisted, or psychotic. But after I carved into that Rose faggot, I couldn't wait to get to this shack and crack open a bottle of wine." He finally drank the contents in his glass. As he swallowed, he kept his eyes closed, and let out a satisfying moan. "Now that's what dreams are made out of."

Razo didn't look disturbed, but he didn't seem very comfortable either. He just kept drinking, staring, and listening.

"I never tasted actual blood before, and I'm sure the two don't taste nearly the same. But what about satisfaction? Maybe it quenches the thirst just as well as wine. Maybe the taste of blood is more gratifying." He was a monster by his actions and also by his words. "When I see blood pouring out the wound of some unlucky fool, I sometimes have the urge to bend down and take a sip." He motioned his lips, almost as if he was actually thirsty right now for the taste of blood. "I wonder if it would entice me to take a bite of the flesh."

There was a sudden flash of lightning that brightly lit the darkened shack for a split second, followed by a loud crack of thunder. And then, the rain came hammering down outside. It couldn't have happened at a more appropriate moment.

Now looking into the fire, Zasso went on with the sadistic soliloquy. "When I stare into fire anymore, I don't just see the flames. I see an object. A silhouette of a rose. A burning rose. Shriveling into a black misshaped mass, until it disintegrates into a pile of ash." His eyes grew, the reflection of the flames were dancing in his irises. "And then I begin to see something else. I can see a figure. It could be a man, but I'm not quite sure. The figure's eyes are red. But not just any red. A fiery red. Like the end of a metal poker that's been lying in the coals of a brazier." He squints. "It looks at me. Stares deep inside my soul. It's like the monster that my father would tell me stories about as a kid, who haunted me in my nightmares…We meet gazes. It grows a pair of horns, and then gives me a ghastly grin. Black saliva drips from its teeth…It laughs. A horribly deceitful laugh. Like it knows something about me that has yet to become…But what? What does this *thing* see?" His complexion goes pale. He almost seems spooked by his own tale. "What do you see, my old friend?" he asks the fire. Then he abruptly stands up and shouts, "What the fuck do you want from me you son of a bitch? You demon! You fucking fiery demon of hell! What the fuck are you looking at?"

Suddenly, Zasso whipped out his pistol and started shooting aimlessly into the fire. The bangs were extra loud, reverberating through the confined shelter. The shock of the abrupt gunfire caused Razo to fall off of his seat and cover his head.

Click, click, click. Drawing heavy breathes, Zasso's eyes were filled with demented fury as he kept firing his pistol, even after the clip was emptied. When he stopped pulling the trigger, he let his arm drop, but his eyes were still focused on the fire. His black and silver hair was drenched with sweat.

Rising to his feet, Razo said, "What the hell was that?"

Slowing down his breathing, but not losing his gaze on the hearth, Zasso replied, "I don't know. I think I snorted too much powder."

A small mirror, covered with lines of powder, lied on the floor between their two chairs. Razo picked it up and said, "Speaking of which." Using a thin silver tube, he snorted a line the length of the mirror. After the big sniff, he tilted his head back and let the powder do its job. "Maybe I'll see some demon fuck in the fire now."

Zasso shook his head and said, "You don't want to." Rapidly blinking his eyes, he snapped out of his drug-induced hysteria. "Now let me get another line of that shit."

Just as Razo offered the mirror to his boss, a set of bright headlights shone through the windows and cracks of the wood-built shack. Their attention was immediately turned towards the light. The sound of a rumbling engine was heard outside. The next sound was a vehicle door opening and quickly slamming shut. The contact had arrived. Zasso wondered if he was alone. Most likely he was not, but they only heard one door open and close, which meant that the contact was going to at least enter the shack with no protection. If things turned ugly, Zasso was sure they could handle just one guy.

The door to the shack slowly creaked open. The contact didn't bother knocking. He just barged right in. With the headlights of the vehicle still shining into the shack, at first it looked as though a shadow with a fedora and long coat was standing in the doorway. Then, the man stepped further into the untidy room, and the contact's identity was revealed.

Both Zasso and Razo had never actually met the contact in person, so this was the first time they were face to face with the man. He was tall, broad-shouldered, and had a sinister appearance. Rain droplets dripped from his black fedora, which was shadowing his eyes. The long black knee-length coat had its collar up, covering the bottom half of his face. A flash of lightning lit the parts of his face that could be seen, but he was still unrecognizable at the moment. Then, he untied the front of his coat, slipped it off, shook off some of the water, folded it in half, and draped it over his arm. His suit was just as dark as his hat and coat. He bore a white bowtie instead of a regular necktie, tightly knotted around the collar of his pink dress shirt. The mystery man used his other hand to slightly lift his fedora to completely reveal his face. A strong jawline complemented his physique, and his eyes were a shade of gray. There were visible scars that crisscrossed his face.

This guy must have gotten sliced up by a pair of hedge clippers or something, Zasso unrealistically thought. *Or he was in one hell of a sword or knife fight...Obviously he came out the victor.*

"So," the mystery contact spoke, "who's going to be the first one to tell me what the hell happened last night?" By the tone of his deep and strong voice, he wasn't pleased at all.

"As soon as you tell us who the hell you are," Zasso disrespectfully answered back.

"Oh, I'm sorry. I must have forgotten my courtesies." The man stepped closer towards Zasso. "I'm the one who's been relaying your orders over the phone. My name is *Solace Volhine*." He extended his right arm for a friendly handshake.

61

Looking down at the stranger's open hand, Zasso sighed and then offered his own hand to accept the shake. But instead of a handshake, Solace slapped the shit out of him. So hard, that Zasso stumbled back a few feet as he shouted an obscenity. With no hesitation, Razo whipped out his handheld shotgun and aimed it at the man with balls of steel.

Solace turned towards Razo and said, "And what are you going to do with that useless thing?" With his free hand, he scrunched his fingers into the shape of a claw, and concentrated hard on the shotgun.

To the astonishment of Razo, his special weapon was crystalized by ice. The grip became so cold that it started freezing his hand. He let go of the shotgun and it dropped to the floor, shattering into a thousand pieces of ice crystals. Razo looked dumbfounded. And he showed a hint of sadness by the loss of his favorite weapon.

Rubbing the side of his face, Zasso asked, "How the hell are you Blessed?"

"Don't you worry about that right now, tough guy. I want to know some answers." Solace made his way over to the hearth to warm himself. He noticed the bottle of wine and an empty glass, so he took it upon himself to make a drink. He tossed it back, and then poured another right away. "You were given a direct order to abduct Don Maretto Rose at the Grand Theater last night. Instead, you killed one of his sons, and Maretto remains free of our capture." His eyebrows raised when he saw the mirror with lines of powder. He picked it up and snorted a healthy bump. The hit caused him to quiver, but he was noticeable satisfied by the feeling. "So tell me. What the hell happened last night?" With his finger, he rubbed the remnants of powder on his teeth.

"It wasn't our fault. Everything was going to plan until Maretto's wannabe hero son intervened. He fucked it all up," Zasso tried to explain. "We did exactly what we were supposed to do, but sometimes things just don't pan out." He kept rubbing his cheek, still irritated by the slap.

"Really?" Solace queried. "Is that really going to be your excuse? Sometimes things just don't pan out?"

"What the hell else do you want me to say?" *He's cocky and I hate him already,* Zasso already decided. *I'm the cocky one. I'm the heir to the Cicello Family. Who the hell is this guy?* "I'm the one who just risked my life doing what I was told, and now I have to hide because my name is being broadcasted throughout Exodus. Plus, the entire Juna Police Department is probably out on a manhunt looking for me, so what the fuck do you want me to tell you? I did what I had to do in the moment I was thrust into!"

Biting his lip and then grinning, Solace yanked a pack of smokes out of his breast pocket. As he took a cig out of the pack, he began walking towards Zasso. "I guess you're right, young Cicello." Whipping out a novelty silver lighter with a depiction of a skull, he lit the cig and blew out some smoke. Shoving the lighter back into his pants pocket, he said, "You *were* put in quite a predicament ordered to capture the one and only Don Maretto Rose. And you did rid one of his talented sons, who could have been a nuisance in the process of our grand mission." Only a step now separated the two. It was now a face to face discussion. "But your job wasn't to kill the young Rose. It was to bring the main target back with you, so we could take the next step in finding what we most desperately need if we are to fulfill the ultimate dream. And the patriarch of the Rose Family is the one who contains that crucial information, as you well know."

"And I failed," Zasso cut in. "I failed and now we have taken a step back." He spit on the ground to his right. "I accept that responsibility, scar-face."

Solace smiled. A sinister smile. "I'm glad you accept it like a man." With a little more oomph, he reached back and slapped the shit out of Zasso again. This time, Zasso didn't act nearly as stunned and actually took the slap rather manly. Solace noticed and said, "You *are* a tough guy, aren't you? I'm rather surprised. You rich mafia goons have had a golden spoon shoved up your ass since birth, and usually have the toughness of a little girl playing tea party. But not you, Zasso Cicello. No, you have a lot of inner strength built inside that greasy body of yours."

Zasso was about to agree with him, when Solace grabbed him by the shirt collar, roughly pulled him closer, and said, "But don't you dare think for one moment that you have the brass down between those skinny legs of yours like I do. I came from the streets, Zasso. I once sliced a man from neck to nuts, scalped him and then sent it to his mother.

63

There's nobody on this slab of land we live on that I wouldn't kill! Do you understand, young Cicello?"

Impressed by his demeanor, Zasso replied, "I think I'm starting to get the picture, Mr. Volhine. But if you're going to kill me for my failure last night, then just do it and get it over with. I don't like being toyed with."

A satisfying grin formed on the mouth of Solace, and then he let go of his grasp. He straightened Zasso's shirt out a little and said, "Maybe I will kill you someday. Or maybe you'll kill me. Who knows? But those aren't my orders."

"Then what *are* your orders? Do we even take orders from the same source?"

"What do you think?" Solace said, making his way back to the hearth to warm himself. The rain was giving the air a cool bite.

"I don't know what to think," Zasso responded, not moving at all. "I just do what I'm told, because obviously I don't have any other option in my life. I was groomed to perform last night's mission, but all the preparation in the world couldn't have prevented Georgiano Rose from protecting his father. The Rose Family gets underestimated and underappreciated all the time. They aren't the most powerful of the Seven Families for no reason, Mr. Volhine. They have a uniquely defensive Blessing that makes Don Maretto and his sons extra strong and dangerous. I know the theater was a good opportunity to catch him in the open, but we shouldn't have attempted to abduct him with his sons around."

Solace flicked his cig to the ground and stomped it out before he said, "Very good point, young Cicello. You and your friend over there *were* put up against bad odds, and that is why you both are exempt from persecution."

"And I thank you for that, Mr. Volhine."

"But that doesn't mean that you are exempt from making up for last night's failure."

"I didn't think we would be. We will be honored to be given a second chance."

Nodding his head, Solace said, "And a second chance you *will* be given." Clasping his hands behind his back, he started walking towards the door. "There will be little preparation this time around, though. Time is precious from here on out. We must strike while most of us remain anonymous, and that means that we have a short window to complete this mission before questions start to be asked and answered about what transpired last night; besides the fact that you and girly-hair over there made headlines across Exodus." Razo looked bothered by the insult to his appearance, but of course Solace wouldn't give a shit. He just stood in front of the door and continued to talk like nothing negative was said. "What the rest of the world doesn't know, is that you are well protected beyond their realm of notion, and it will continue to be that way if you successfully retrieve Maretto Rose without getting caught in the act. Furthermore, young Cicello, you will be rewarded with what you have desired in return for the Rose patriarch. Juna *will* be your playground…But if you do not succeed this time around, I assure you, the consequences will be brutal."

Even though Zasso and Razo didn't care for the man, they still had to conform and do their duty, and the reward was worth dealing with the asshole, so they both nodded in agreement. Zasso did have one more question for the mysterious guest, though. "I have been to every city and countryside in Exodus, Mr. Volhine. I have been around just about every member of the Seven Blessed Families, but I have never met or seen anyone outside the Families use powers of a Blessing, except for *one* man. So, I want to ask you again, how the hell are you Blessed?"

Solace opened the door to the outside, and once again the headlights to his vehicle beamed in, passing through patches of fog produced by the cool night air. He stood in the doorway and answered, "Let's just say that I'm the other guy who has had a Blessing, and maybe that it's now safe to say that the Seven Families aren't the only beings in Exodus to have that privilege." He extended his arm, and a blast of snowy wind was expelled from his fingertips. The target was the hearth, and the fire was put out in an instant, casting the shack into darkness. "Sleep tight, gentlemen. You will be hearing again from me shortly." He exited the shack, slamming the door shut behind him. After he entered his vehicle, it slowly rumbled off into the night.

Standing still in the darkness, Zasso and Razo kept a silence between them. The Cicello heir had just one thought after the departure of Solace. *If we succeed in capturing Don Maretto Rose, it will not be easy to get the information needed out of him...I wonder how much suffering he will endure to keep them from getting what they want.*

Don Maretto Rose

And the Revelation after the Loss

It's been three days since the death of his son, and the funeral was about to take place. Since the tragic night at the theater, Don Maretto Rose had been mourning in the darkness of his office, trying to forgive himself for letting his son jump onto that stage with Zasso. *It was his own decision to try and protect our family, but I should've tried harder to stop him. This is all my fault,* he thought over and over again. *If I would've let Zasso take me, then my son would still be alive.*

The Rose patriarch was inconsolable. Jon-Jon and Alto did their best to try and comfort him, but they too were broken down with an insurmountable amount of grief. It was a terrible time for the Rose Family. The atmosphere in their high-rise mansion hasn't been this somber since the death of the wife and mother, Malayla Rose.

The night before the funeral, the Don was sitting in the master chair of his office with his legs crossed and head held up by his hand. He was dressed in a casual red dress shirt and black slacks. It was completely dark, albeit the fire blazing behind him, and all Maretto could smell was the burning embers. He wanted to be left alone, unless his youngest son happened to make an appearance. Maretto was praying that Ric would walk through the doors of his office, and that night, his prayers were answered.

The double doors opened wide and stepping through, wearing a black and white zip-up jacket as if it were cold, was Ricalstro Rose. Tentatively taking steps into the room, his footsteps racked off the walls. Maretto lifted his head, but did not display a trace of emotion. His eyes just followed Ric as he made his way closer to his father.

There he is. It's been so long. He looks awful, Maretto noticed. And then his mind repeated the same thought that has come into his head for the past couple years. *I should've never let him leave. His mother would've never let him go.*

"You look terrible," Maretto directly commented.

Ric looked down at his outfit. "These are new clothes."

"I'm not talking about how you're dressed. I'm referring to your physical appearance. You're killing yourself with junk on the streets," he speculated. "Are you junked up right now?"

Shaking his head, Ric replied, "Of course this is the first thing you ask me after all this time."

"You're my son," Maretto strongly pronounced. "It's my job to be concerned for your wellbeing. And when you step into my office looking like a walking stick, it's only natural for me to say what's on my mind. You need to eat something, son. I'll have Grunzo cook you up a nice meal."

"Don't trouble yourself," Ric quickly said.

With a deep sigh, Maretto leaned back in his personalized chair. Slightly shaking his head, he said, "I don't want to get into an argument, Ricalstro. That's the last thing I want after not seeing you for so long."

Ric nodded in agreement, and that was the end of that.

"Your brother is dead." Rolling off his tongue, the words brought a shot of pain through his chest. "He died with honor trying to save his family." Tears swelled up his eyes. "He would've done the same thing for you, Ricalstro."

Taking a deep breath, Ric simply said, "I know."

"Did you get to talk to him recently?"

Walking towards the draped windows, Ric replied, "Yea, actually I did." Between the two large office windows was a panel with a couple of buttons on the wall. He pressed the one on top, and the drapes automatically spread open, revealing the Juna night skyline. Gazing out into the city, he said, "We spent some time together not too long ago, but I told him not to tell you."

"Oh, did you?" *Not surprising.*

"Yep," he walked away from the window and started to make his way across the room to the bar area. "Just a few months ago, Georgie called me up and wanted to hang out for a night, so he came down to my apartment and we went out." Grabbing a bottle of wine and a glass from the cabinet, he poured himself a drink. Ric knew his dad would have some of the good stuff. A bottle of purple *Pin'e* from the best vineyard in southern Exodus. "We had a good time, me and Georgie. Stayed out pretty late, had a bunch of drinks and a lot of laughs." He took a refreshing swig of wine. "At least I can say that the last time I saw Georgie, we had a great time together."

"I'm glad to hear that." He really was. Maretto and his other sons were having a great time with him too, *until that Cicello kid had to ruin everything. Damn him.*

Taking another healthy sip of wine, Ric went on, "When we left the club, we walked back to my place taking a shortcut through an alleyway. Almost like the one Galia and I took when she was killed."

Here we go, Maretto painfully thought.

"We saw *him* again, you know. Just like I saw him that night before I went unconscious."

"Oh, Ricalstro." *He must be on the junk. God help my poor little boy. I'm sorry he turned out this way, Malayla.*

"He's been following me ever since. Watching me," Ric said, before slamming the rest of his drink. "Which means that we're all getting followed. Georgie's death compromises that notion. I didn't think the Cicello Family had that kind of brass to kill a high figure of one of the Seven Families."

"It was *me* they were after."

Squinting his eyes, Ric replied, "What was that?"

Rising out of his chair, Maretto joined his son at the bar. Ric quickly snagged a glass from the cabinet and filled it up for his father.

"I wanted you to come home right away, so that I could explain in full detail what happened the other night, before you heard a silly story from some nut-job on the street or at the club." He took a generous sip of the expensive wine. *Damn that's good.* "Zasso Cicello's initial plan was to abduct me. He barged into the theater using his lightning powers to kill innocent people, and then yelled to me that I was going with him whether I wanted to or not. He threatened to kill more people unless I complied, and that's when your brother took it upon himself to save all of us. We all escaped before we saw what happened to him, but I was told that Georgie fought bravely against our Cicello friend. It's still hard to accept that Zasso bested him. Your brother was skillfully Blessed with powers."

"And I'm skillfully not."

"Is this really all about you?"

Ric stayed silent for a moment, then shook his head and said, "No." He put his head down, almost ashamed that he was being selfish at a time of mourning for his brother.

After taking another sip of the good shit, Maretto said, "You're right about the Cicello Family, Ric. I never would have thought they would make such a bold move, either. Xanose Cicello has never made such a drastic decision in his tenure as the patriarch, and I'm finding it hard to believe that he even concocted such a mission. Capturing me would destroy every relationship the Cicello Family has with all the other Families. Especially, if none of the others were asked to join him in this endeavor. They would believe this to be a selfish move, taking over the Rose Family without the rest of their consent."

"But who else could it be?" Ric intriguingly asked. "Do you really think that Zasso acted alone?"

Without hesitation, Maretto shook his head and said, "No." He pounded his fist on the bar counter. It startled his young son. "And that's the problem, Ricalstro. I have no idea what is going on."

Ric was used to his father knowing everything that was going on in the world of Exodus, so he looked a bit surprised to hear him sound so perplexed. "What are you going to do?" was the only question Ric could ask.

"Find out the truth, of course," he answered with a cunning grin. Then the grin quickly went away. "And find the asshole who killed your brother."

Just as Don Maretto threw back some more wine, his two eldest sons came striding into his office. Without words or emotions, they stood next to both their younger brother and father. Alto lit up a cig, and Jon-Jon kept his hands in his pockets. They were both dressed in casual shirts and pants of the red and black variety.

"Welcome home, Ric," Alto broke the silence. All he got in return was a bit of a nod. "You look like shit."

"Thanks," Ric satirically replied.

Jon-Jon always had the kinder soul. He patted Ric on the back and said, "It really is good to see you, Ric. I hope you're able to stick around for a while."

"I'm here for Georgie's funeral. And then I'm going back home."

"This is your home," Alto said. "That shit-kicker place you got on the lower eastside is not where you should be living, brother. You belong here."

"He's right, Ric," Jon-Jon agreed. "You always have your room in this house and you know that. You don't need to hide yourself on the streets anymore. The Family needs you more than ever right now."

"Does it really?" Ric asked, studying his glass of wine. "I don't know, Jon-Jon, the streets seem a lot safer than this house right now. The Family is under attack."

"I dare someone to come here and try to penetrate these walls," Alto chimed in, then taking a puff of his cig. "No member of the Rose Family is going to be taken prisoner by some Cicello fuck, who thinks his balls suddenly grew a bit bigger overnight! We are gonna do what we always do, and stay strong!"

"Settle down, Altonio," Maretto tried to calm his son.

71

"No, pap! Ric needs to understand what being a member of the Rose Family really is. And it's not sticking needles in your arm and chasing the pink dragon, while the enemy is trying to invade the sanctity of your Family!" Alto's eyes were beaming so hard, that it looked as though he was staring straight through his younger brother. "It's about becoming Blessed, and learning how to be a *real* Rose Family member. Which means putting your Family's well-being first, in front of your own. It's about being selfless!"

Words would not come out of Ric's open mouth. His brain was too mushed to give a response, so his father spoke for him and said, "This is not the time to be discussing such things. We will have another chance to talk about Ric's future."

Now Ric had a response. "My future?" he asked, perturbed.

Maretto paid no attention to Ric's question, but said, "Soon enough, we will determine whether or not Ric is ready."

"He should've been ready a long time ago," Alto said. "He needs to learn now, and we as a Family need to strike the enemy before they strike us again! We need to plan our revenge!"

Both Ric and Jon-Jon were about to say something in response to Alto's rant, when Maretto slammed his fist on the counter and yelled, "Can we please bury your brother first!" Tears instantly cascaded down his face. "I want to mourn the death of my son. I don't want to talk about revenge, or about Blessings, or about sticking needles in your arm…None of you have the slightest idea of what it's like to lose a child. He should be the one who has to bury me, not the other way around. That's how the world is supposed to work. Not like this. This is the unnatural process of life, and I just want to sit in silence and try to contemplate why this is happening. But all you three want to do is bicker about your fucking selves!" His face got beet-red during the lecture, but then the olive tone came back and Maretto sunk into helplessness. "I just want to weep for my little boy!" He then covered his face and broke down.

Maretto's sons had never seen their father so vulnerable before. At least not since their mother had passed away. Jon-Jon and Alto both hugged him as he wept, comforting the man who brought them into this world. Ric, on the other hand, just stared at his father.

72

Stared into the deep, depressing abyss that his father has fallen into, but did not try to comfort him. He was the outcast. He was alone.

The next morning, Georgiano "Georgie" Rose was laid to rest. The funeral took place at the First Church of God, followed by the burial at *Heaven's Rest Cemetery*. The ceremonies were private, but the procession from the church to the cemetery was highly publicized. Residents of Juna lined the streets, hoping to catch a glimpse of predominant members of the Rose Family as limo after limo drove by, while also paying their respects to one of the princes of the city. Members of the media were present during the procession as well, turning the funeral into a worldwide social event. News station's ratings were going through the roof as the coverage was broadcasted live on television. It was a day that citizens of Juna-whether rich or poor-would not soon forget.

To Maretto Rose, the entire day was a blur. It was not his intention to forget the consoling words that were spoken, or the prayers that were said to the Heavenly Lord up above in regard to his son. It just happened. He was in such a distressed state of grief, that his mind went completely blank. It was emptiness. A dark hollow tunnel that led into a deep and desolate pit of despair.

Though, there was one moment during the burial that he would always remember, when he looked upon the faces of his children. His daughters, Ritta and Nattia, were teary-eyed and flustered under veils of black. Jon-Jon was gazing up at the gray sky as if he was trying to find an answer to the loss of his brother in the clouds. Ric just stared at the coffin, unable to process his brother's death in his mind that was riddled with grief and most likely drugs...And then there was Alto. Alto looked straight ahead, almost emotionless. Not really paying attention as the minister prayed over the grave. *Is he thinking about getting revenge, or is he not thinking anything at all?* Maretto pondered. *Does he really care? What lies deep in your inner soul, Alto?*

When the funeral was finally over, Maretto and his sons went back to the high-rise mansion to relax and have a few drinks. The grieving process will never end, but their lives must go on. That night, Maretto held a meeting with the most significant male members of the Rose Family. Seated in two leather chairs in the middle of Maretto's office were Palco Valone and Arlo Telasassio-Maretto's childhood friend and his other

73

Underboss. Maretto sat in his throne/chair, Jon-Jon was behind the desk in the right corner, and Alto and Ric were having drinks at the bar. The Don's only surviving brother, Victorio "Vetti" Rose, stood alone leaning against a bookshelf, stocked with books, on the wall opposite the windows, and the bodyguard, Vego Rainze, was guarding the door.

From the start of the meeting, Alto was heated. But that's because he's a fucking hothead. "I don't even know why we're discussing whether or not Xanose had anything to do with this," Alto busted out, "the man's son was responsible, so that makes him responsible. And there is no way in hell that he had no knowledge of Zasso's plan. They've never worked apart before, and I'll be damned if I believe they didn't work together to try and abduct pap." He lit up a cig, blew out some smoke, and snagged his drink off the bar counter. "These fucking Cicello's have been jealous of our success for decades. They still regret not getting their hands around the oil and auto industries."

"I doubt that the attack had anything to do with money, Altonio," Arlo Telasassio said. He was a very tall and burly man with a full head of gray hair, a mustache and beard. His voice was very deep and he puffed on a big brown cigar. "What would they accomplish by abducting your father? Bribe companies into siding with them, or they'll kill him? I really don't think so."

"Then what the fuck do you think they want, Arlo?" Alto responded.

Arlo shrugged his shoulders and answered, "What does every leader of the Seven Families want?"

"Power," Maretto strongly blurted out.

"And what ultimately gives the Rose Family its power?" Arlo asked the group of men.

"You're not talking about the Relic, are you?" Palco Valone questionably answered first.

"Well, what else could it be?" Arlo said, raising his eyebrows as he puffed on his cigar.

"Well, maybe Alto is right," Palco said. "Maybe it does have to do with the industries we control. The Cicello Family has been bitching about how they were dicked over for about a hundred years now. They can't possibly believe that getting their hands on our Relic would be a good idea for their Family. We don't even know if we can be Blessed by other Family's Relics." He puffed on his pipe that gave out the pungent tobacco odor.

"No," Jon-Jon almost shouted, finally joining the conversation. "You're wrong, Palco, and so are you, Alto."

"Oh yea," Alto said. "And how the fuck do *you* know, Jon-Jon?"

"Because money can only get you so far, Alto," Jon-Jon answered right away. Alto shook his head and looked away, but everyone else in the room was paying attention to the heir to the Rose Family throne, including Ric, who has been silent ever since the funeral. "I think that all of the Seven Families have been naïve when it comes to the powers of the Relics we control. I mean, does a Relic really have the notion to choose which Family will have control over it?" He almost began to laugh, but stopped himself. "A stationary object isn't going to jump to the Family it wants to own it, the Family is going to choose for itself. And since those choices were made so many years ago, the Families went on to believe that they are solely attached to those Relics."

"What are you trying to say, Jon-Jon? I think you have us all lost in here with your bullshit," Alto said after taking a puff of his cig.

"I'm saying that if another Family has the idea that controlling our Relic will help them control the rest of Exodus, then that Family is going to try and capture the man who is in the highest control of it." Jon-Jon's response to Alto now had everyone thinking large.

Don Maretto folded his arms, and without looking over at his son, said, "Jonero, are you trying to tell us that the Cicello Family wants control over the *Rose Quartet*?" The Rose Quartet. The diamond in the rough. The Relic of all Relics. A further explanation of the powerful Relic was soon to come.

Nodding his head, Jon-Jon replied, "Think about it, dad. Even if my theory on Relics is far from the truth, merely having control of the Relic can become a power boost. Without the Rose Quartet, the younger Rose Family generation could never be Blessed, which means our Family would never grow. But the Cicello Family would…unless we wiped them all out, of course."

"And that's exactly what we should fucking do, no matter if Jon-Jon is right or not. Those assholes killed one of our own!" Alto shouted out.

Maretto held up a hand and said, "Relax, Alto. We need to keep our minds straight right now, and not lose our grip on things with anger. We must listen to what Xanose has to say for himself and his Family first, before we go on a killing spree."

Alto made a gesture that said, 'the hell with that'. Jon-Jon gave him a dirty look and said, "Listen to dad, Alto. We're not going to stoop to their level and just start killing everyone because we have the muscle to do it. The rest of Exodus already has negative idealistic thoughts on the Rose Family, and a complete massacre of another Family will just prove their thought processes are right."

Squinting his eyes, Alto said, "I don't know what language you even speak anymore, Jon-Jon. Are you trying to make me feel like a stupid piece of dog shit on purpose, or what?" He didn't respond to the question, so Alto went on and said, "And oh by the way, you're confusing the absolute shit out of all of us. It sounds as though you think the Cicello Family *is* responsible and that they have this master plan to get their hands on the Rose Quartet, but you're also trying to tell me to back down and find out the entire truth before we make any moves. But I'm gonna tell you right now, that if there's even one member of their Family involved with this horrendous attack on *our* Family, then we should take the fuckers down and punish them for what that Zasso fuck has done!"

"Well, Alto, it's not ultimately my decision on what we should do about the Cicello's. It's the leader of this Family's order," Jon-Jon said, then looked in his father's direction. "What do you think, dad? Is Xanose Cicello after the control of our Relic, or is Zasso responsible on his own account?"

Maretto thought it over for a moment, while everyone else in the room waited for words to spill out of his mouth. *This could be bigger than I first expected, but it could also be smaller. What the hell is going on here? How is Zasso Cicello causing such problems?*

Before Maretto gave an answer, Arlo spoke up, "This is all just not right. If someone wants our Relic this desperately, then this Family is in a lot of trouble."

"This Family, Arlo, will persevere no matter what anyone outside of it tries to accomplish," Maretto finally spoke up. "Even if they did succeed in abducting me, do you really believe that I would give up the information needed in obtaining the Rose Quartet?"

Arlo leaned forward in his chair, staring hard into the eyes of his best friend and leader. "You would be tortured beyond your threshold of pain, Maretto. They might even end up killing you, and then the Family would really be in trouble, and that can't happen. You are our great leader, father, and friend. The Father of Gangster, Don Maretto Rose."

Maretto gave Arlo a grin for their friendship.

Then Palco came out and asked, "So, why would they go after Don Maretto in the first place? Wouldn't it be easier to abduct one of us, when we least expect it? It's a much safer route to go after one of his Underbosses that are not blood, but still have knowledge of its whereabouts."

"Then I guess you better start shaking in your shoes, Palco, and go into hiding," Alto said with a grin. "You can go hideout at Ric's place. Nobody wants to have to go down to the lower eastside in those shithole neighborhoods." He laughed and smacked Ric on the back. Still, Ric just kept to himself.

"The men in charge of this whole operation want Maretto so they can get rid of him after they've received the information they need about the Rose Quartet," Vetti spoke up out of nowhere. "It will be a massive blow on the Rose Family, and I'm sure they expect us to be catastrophically weakened."

By his appearance, Vetti Rose was a strong presence. And so was his voice. The third son born to the late Don Victorio Rose, Victorio Jr., was taller and physically bigger than his older brother, Maretto. His head was completely bald and the surface was so smooth that it glistened in the light. His baldness was a personal choice, though. If he didn't straight-razor his scalp, then his head would have a prolific mop of gray hair. After the grayness was taking over the black in his later years, Vetti thought that going for the completely shaved look would make him appear more intimidating. It sure worked. The man looked like a complete badass. And the circular spectacles with darkened lenses he adorned over his black eyes, added to his tough guy image.

Not only is Vetti Rose one of the highest figures in the Rose Family being the younger brother of the patriarch, but Maretto also named him the *High Consultant*. This title makes him the Don's right-hand and most significant advice giver for important matters. Also, the High Consultant works closely with the Family's Relic by studying its powers, discovering new ones, and training other Family members in the maturation process and privilege of being Blessed.

"You really think that the Cicello Family, or whoever the fuck else is involved with this crazy plan, is willing to execute the most powerful man in the world?" Palco asked in a concerned manner.

"Obviously, they are willing to go to any extreme measure possible," Vetti replied. "That was proven with an attack on our Family publically at the Grand Theater, which I think was a fatal mistake on their part. But that doesn't mean that they won't try it again. Whoever is responsible for Maretto's attempted abduction is not going to sit back and just give up on their mission. He will be attacked again, but when and where will be another surprise. Most likely, it will be at a more discrete location, and not involving the Juna public."

Maretto clasped his hands on his lap and said, "Which is why I will be taking extreme caution everywhere I go from now on. Vego will be at my side at all times, and we will take an entourage of his best men with us if there is a need to leave my home." The Don was looking straight at Vego after saying this, and his bodyguard gave him the nod of agreement.

"That's all fine and dandy, pap," Alto cut in, "but you're still avoiding your decision on what we do with the Cicello Family. Are we going to make a hit on them or what?"

Not hesitating to answer, Maretto said, "I thought I made it perfectly clear that we would listen to what Xanose had to say for himself and his Family first, my son. I'm not going to allow my Family to act like a bunch of savages. I always stress to the media and to the President that the Rose Family tries to maintain the peace between the Seven Families and the rest of Exodus. Just because we are lavished in riches and control the ultimate Relic, doesn't mean that we are to use our powers to make our own judgment before listening to any reason. This Family will not be regarded as the tyrants of Exodus."

Shaking the ice in the glass he's been drinking out of, Alto said, "So that's really going to be your stance on this situation? Sit back, relax and wait for that kingpin to give us his account of what his son did."

"Yes, Alto," Jon-Jon answered for his father. "That's what our father, the patriarch of our Family, is ordering."

Lowering his head, he gave a multitude of slight nods, and continued to shake the ice in his glass. Then, with a burst of anger, he launched the glass into the cabinet behind the bar. It shattered into sharp pieces, causing Ric to cover his face, just in case a rogue shard happened to try and pierce one of his eyeballs.

"This is fucking bullshit, pap!" Alto shouted.

"Alto! That's enough! You need to relax," Maretto responded to the lash-out.

"No, pap! I'm not going to relax! Not when my family was threatened with an attack and my little brother was killed because of it!" He was pointing in his father's direction with eyes that were on fire. Sweat was starting to drip from his dark curly hair. Alto was a drunken furious mess. "Zasso Cicello and his thugs went too far, and his Family has to pay the price for it! You're being soft! And the rest of the Seven Families are gonna start thinking that we're weak if we don't retaliate before the Cicello Family attacks us again!" He reached in his pocket and pulled out another cig, popping it in his mouth. "I mean, come on pap!" He lit up his cig, blowing out a substantial amount of smoke. "The longer we sit in here on our fat asses, the longer Zasso and his Family will have to devise another plan to hit us where it really hurts! And this time, they might as well fucking succeed! So let's stop this, 'we're gonna be the good guys' bullshit, and hit *their* asses where it really hurts! Right up there fucking asses is where we'll go! Let's go and take out Xanose Cicello himself!" His last words echoed throughout the room. For a moment, there was nothing but silence.

Then, Jon-Jon broke the quiet. "Are you out of your fucking mind, Alto. Take out Xanose Cicello?"

"No, Jon-Jon, I'm not out of my mind. All of you are out of your minds if you think we should stand down."

"We're not going to stand down," Jon-Jon said, "we're just going to wait until we have more information on the truth!"

"We just can't wait to see what Xanose has to say, but we can't attempt to assassinate him either," Ric said, coming out of left field with an opinion. The rest of the men in the room were shocked that Ric finally gave his piece of mind. But would they really give a shit about what the street junky has to say?

"Well, well, well, the druggy speaks his mind," Alto ribbed his younger brother.

"Shut the fuck up, Alto," Jon-Jon ordered. Taking Ric serious, he asked, "What do you think our move should be then, Ric?"

Everyone tuned in to what Ric was about to say, especially Maretto. It wasn't often that his youngest son had an opinion on Family matters. *Is there hope for this boy yet?* Maretto questioned himself. *God, I can only pray that there is. I want my little boy to become the man he was meant to be.*

Ric took a deep breath and said, "As much as all of us would like to see Xanose Cicello get thrown off the face of this earth, killing him now would only make things worse in the peace between the Seven Families. The problem we have to deal with right away, is finding his son. Zasso is still at large out there hiding somewhere probably outside the city, and we need to track him down as soon as possible," He took a gulp of air before continuing, "We all know Zasso rather well, and even though he's fairly powerful in his Blessing, his mind can be manipulated into revealing to us crucial information. So, if we were to find the whereabouts of Zasso, abduct him before he has a chance to try and get dad again, then I think we can ultimately find out who he received his order from…I mean, if he's stupid enough to be coaxed into attacking our Family at a highly publicized event, then I think he'll be foolish enough to reveal the man who gave him the mission, if we work him hard enough." He took a long gulp of his cocktail. "And after he does give us what we need and we fake the fact that we're gonna let him go," he paused for a brief moment, "then we'll give him a horrific Rose Family death."

At first, nobody in the room said a word. There wasn't even a movement. They were all taking Ric's advice in for the moment, and probably still surprised that he had anything to say at all.

Through eye contact, Maretto and Vetti seemed to be thinking the same thing. They were both proud of Ric for coming up with the appropriate resolution to their problem and it showed in the content looks they were giving each other.

After a few more moments, Alto began to chuckle and shake his head before he said, "Listen to this fucking guy. Who would've thought that the junky off the streets would be the one who would come out with the most reasonable plan? I think I've had too much to drink…Phew!" he exclaimed, then took a slow walk to where Vego Rainze was standing by the door.

"Where are you going, Alto?" Maretto asked his son.

Alto turned and answered, "I don't know. Maybe I'll go for a walk through the streets of Juna, and start asking questions to the bums under the bridges. If one of them reveals to me the whereabouts of Zasso Cicello, then I'll come back and let you all know." He turned back towards the door, brushed past Vego, and left the office without another word.

"Well, he obviously doesn't agree with Ric," Palco said to the group.

"He wants blood and he wants it now," Maretto morbidly said. "His brother just died, so you can't really blame him. I'd be lying if I said I didn't want the same, but like Ric and Jon-Jon agree, it would be a mistake to take out Xanose."

"I'm sorry," Ric softly spoke. "I shouldn't have said anything."

81

Slowly turning his head in Ric's direction, Maretto gave him a stone-faced look and said, "Never say you're sorry for speaking your mind in front of family, Ricalstro."

Nodding his head once, Ric accepted the advice from this father and went back to sipping on his drink.

"So how are we gonna find the Cicello kid?" Palco asked the boss. "Get every two-bit gangster working for us to go out and scan the city and look for him?"

"Absolutely not," Maretto answered. "We do this internally and with the utmost secrecy. You and Arlo go on with business as usual, acting as if nothing happened. If anyone asks the two of you what the Rose Family is going to do for vengeance, you brush it aside and pretend that you could care less. Only money affects the Underbosses of the Don. That's what I want people linked to us to think." Arlo and Palco motioned in agreement. "Within the week, I *will* meet with Xanose Cicello, and I don't want him to hear through an anonymous source that our Family is tracking down his son. I want him to believe that we are considerate enough to hear him out first...Is that understood?"

The two underbosses gestured in compliance again and both said, "Yes, Don Maretto."

"Good. You two are dismissed. I thank you for joining me tonight and mourning the death of my son."

As Palco and Arlo stood up out of their chairs, Maretto did the same. Arlo was the first to approach the Don. He took Maretto's hand, kissed it, and said, "Anything for the Father of Gangster and my dearest friend." Smiling at the gesture of respect, Maretto embraced Arlo in a hug, patting him on the back.

Palco was next. He kissed the Don's hand and said, "For the sake of the son you have lost, Don Maretto, may the Rose Family live on forever." He was given a friendly hug as well from the boss.

It was usually Georgie who would escort his father's guests from his private office, but with him now gone, the two Underbosses let themselves out, saying their farewells to the rest of the men in the room. When they were gone, Don Maretto sank back into his chair/throne. He loosened his tie, unfastened the top button of his dress shirt, and slid a hand through his gray-streaked hair. His brother, Vetti, left his spot against the wall and stepped closer to Maretto, while Jon-Jon and Ric stayed in their spots, until their father said to them, "Boys, come to me."

Doing as they were told, Jon-Jon and Ric attentively stood on either side of their father. "Finding Zasso Cicello in a short amount of time is going to be near impossible. Though reckless, Zasso is not a total fool, so I'm quite sure that he has taken every precaution in securing a tight hiding spot. And if anyone from the high end of his Family is involved, I assure you that their lips are sealed. The only chance we have finding him is from some random talk on the streets. There were a lot of low-level gangsters that abetted him at the Grand Theater. Most were killed by Vego, but some most likely survived and ran back to the streets...Ricalstro, do you know of any Cicello thug hangouts?"

After he thought about it for only a moment, Ric replied, "On the lower eastside not even ten blocks from my place, is a club called *The Danger Zone*. That's where most of the Cicello grunts go out for drinks on a nightly basis."

"Have you ever been inside and drank with any of them?" Jon-Jon then asked.

"Only a couple of times with some friends on late night tips. None of them even knew who the hell I really was."

Maretto made eye contact with Vetti, and without saying a word, a decision was made. It was as if the two brothers communicated through some sort of telepathy or some shit like that. It must be just brotherly intuition.

"Then that's where your nightly hangout is going to be for the next week, Ricalstro," Maretto ordered his son. "Make it a habit to frequent the club, cozy up to these Cicello grunts, make them trust you, and then sooner or later one of them is going to spill their guts about the Grand Theater. And if we're lucky, maybe one of them will have information as to where Zasso ran off to...Can you do this for us, my son?"

Ric lowered his head. He looked reluctant to follow his father's orders. *Come on, Ricalstro. This is your time to prove yourself more than just a drug addict,* Maretto thought as his son contemplated the mission.

Knowing that his brother wasn't fully comfortable with the job, Jon-Jon stepped in front of him and put a comforting hand on his shoulder. "Listen, Ric. I know you haven't been happy with your family in recent years, and I don't blame you for your anger. So, don't do this for us. Do it for Georgie. Do it so your brother can rest in peace."

Lifting his head back up, Ric gazed into his eldest brother's eyes. Jon-Jon bore down on him with a bloodline trust. He then took a glance at his uncle, who also appeared as though he had faith in his ability to get the job done. Finally, he met eyes with his father. *Make me proud, Ricalstro,* was what Maretto was trying to infuse into his son by his look.

"Okay," Ric finally agreed. "I'll find out what I can."

A smile of pride grew on Maretto's face. "Very good." *There is hope for you yet, my son. Thank the good God, there is still hope for you yet.*

Ricalstro Rose

And a Long Night Out with the Enemy

As soon as Ric agreed to help his father, he immediately regretted his decision. He could've simply said *no* and went on his own way, but Jon-Jon persuaded him when he said to do it for Georgie. Besides, he *was* the perfect man for the job. Nobody else in the upper echelon of the Family could infiltrate that club.

It wouldn't take much time. *Not even a few days,* Ric thought to himself about the small mission. He knew exactly how to cozy up with any lowlife gangster on the streets. Drugs. That was the way to get someone to talk. Do some good smack with them. And the best part was that Ric had plenty of that shit to go around. A few drinks, a few laughs, an offering of the best smack in town, and then stories will come flying out of mouths like bullets out of a loaded semiautomatic.

The shitty part about it though, was that he had to spend his nights at The Danger Zone. A Cicello thug hangout where you had to make sure you went strapped. One wrong move, and you were looking down the barrel of a loaded gun. Sure, Ric had been to the club before, but it wasn't like he ever felt safe while he partied there. And if anyone happened to figure out who he was, then there would be a major problem. Ric was certain that the Cicello mob was on high alert.

If any of the gangsters from the Grand Theater were smart, then they wouldn't be seen in public for a long time, Ric thought. *Who knows if I'll even run into any of them?* But he doubted those assholes had a shred of intelligence. They were wannabe Family members. Wannabes were stupid and sloppy.

After he said his goodbyes to his father and Jon-Jon, Ric decided to take a stroll through his childhood home before he went back to his grimy apartment. Taking his time down the master staircase, Ric slid his hand down the smooth and glossy oak railing. When they were kids, he and his brothers used to see how long they could last sliding down the steep railing before falling off. He hurt himself a bunch of times, but more often than not, he would usually win the contests. Ric had steady balance and unwavering patience. Thinking back now, maybe Alto was right. Maybe he *should* be Blessed by now. Drug addiction aside, Ric had the talents necessary for a Blessing…But he just didn't give a fuck.

Speaking of Alto, when Ric was finished reminiscing about sliding down railings, he spotted his brother waiting for him in the lounge at the bottom of the stairs. It was decorated with a few black leather sofas, a couple of antique chairs, an elegant coffee table, a couple of dim gold-based lamps, and a brick fireplace in the corner. The hardwood floor was partly covered by a red ovular rug with gold tassels. Alto was spread across the large sofa next to the coffee table, smoking a cig and sipping on dark liquor. His eyes were glossy and hair a mess. The only sound at the moment was the fire hissing and cracking. Hung above the fireplace mantle was a painted portrait of his late great-grandfather *Eltassio*, whose eyes seemed to follow him everywhere in the room.

Holding up his glass of liquor like a salute, Alto said to him, "Here's to a long road to recovery for our Family, Ric. Things will never be the same around here." He tipped the glass back, and the brown fluid flowed down his gullet. He took a quick drag of his cig afterwards.

Deciding not to ignore his brother and just leave, Ric braved encountering the drunk hothead. As he stepped closer to the sofa Alto was stretched out on, he glanced at his great-grandfather. *Yep, he's definitely looking at me, the creepy fuck,* he thought, in reference to the haunting eyes. He sniffed the air a couple times. *Damn, it smells like hell in here.*

"Sometimes it's hard to embrace change, Ric," Alto spoke out again. "Everything was in its right place until the other night. Georgie was still alive, and we had no reason to kill anyone significant." He let out a little chuckle. "Well fuck if that hasn't all changed now." Lifting his glass in another salute, he said, "Here's to the end of an era of peace between the Rose's and Cicello's." He tipped back another big gulp. "Awe fuck me."

Ric didn't have anything to say to him. He already spoke his mind enough tonight, and it caused him to receive a job that he didn't want to participate in…And he didn't want to further piss off his brother. Alto could snap at him at any moment.

But instead of snapping, Alto looked Ric up and down and just gave him a drunken smirk. "You still hate me and Jon-Jon, don't you?"

"I never hated you guys," he quickly replied in a soft tone, almost mumbling his words.

"But you blame us for the way you turned out. You blame us for your addiction."

Shrugging, he said back, "I blame a lot of people for a lot of things."

Laughing out loud, Alto said, "I hear that. Welcome to the life of a Rose." He went to take another sip, but the glass was empty. He shrugged and tossed the glass into the fire. It broke upon the burning logs.

Ric was about to sit next to Alto, but before he could make a move, his brother wobbled to his feet. As he brushed the front of his shirt, Alto said, "Thinking back on it now, I understand why you were angry with us. I mean, I would be fucking pissed if you guys went under my nose and carried out a vengeance that I wanted." He took a deep hit of his cig, tossed it to the floor, and rubbed it out on the nice carpet with his foot.

Looking down at the now ruined carpet, Ric thought, *Ah man that is not going to make our dad happy. He loves this old rug. It belonged to old creepy eyes over there.*

Stepping closer to Ric, almost face to face with him, Alto said, "I'll tell you something right now, Ric. It wasn't me who made the decision to go find those assholes before you woke up. I wanted to wait for you."

Turning his head away, Ric said, "Come on, Alto. Let's not talk about this right now."

Alto grabbed his shoulders with both hands, forcing him to look at him eye to eye. "No, Ric. This is the perfect time to talk things out. Georgie would want us to forgive and forget. Especially on the night he was laid to rest." His eyes were so red. So, so fucking red. "The others, they didn't take your feelings into consideration, Ric. They just wanted to get revenge for what those dirt-bags did to you as soon as possible. It all happened so fucking fast, it was like a whirlwind of emotions and everyone got so caught up in the fury...But I was on your side, Ric," he solemnly said while shaking him a tad. "And I'm still on your side. I've never given up on you, and you shouldn't give up on yourself."

Ric put his head down and thought to himself, *But I have.*

Cupping Ric's cheek with his right hand, Alto continued, "I care about you, ya know. You still got a future ahead of you and I envy you for that." He gave him a light love slap to his cheek. "You're my little brother and I love you."

Ric nodded his head while Alto swiped a speck of dust off his shoulder, grabbed his face, and gave him another love slap. "I'm sorry for putting you down upstairs and trying to tell you what to do with your life. You do what you want to do, ya hear me? Don't let anyone else tell you otherwise. Not even pap...And definitely not me." He gave a crooked smile as Ric kept nodding and agreeing. "Be careful out there, Ric. Don't get yourself too deeply involved in all of this."

With a curious look, Ric asked, "Why's that?"

Alto draped his arm around his brother and escorted him out of the lounge and towards the front entrance of the high-rise mansion. "Because even if you were to get Blessed in the near future, the best thing to do is to stay out of this new war. You're better off sitting on the sidelines, while the rest of us take care of the future of the Rose Family."

He still thinks I don't have what it takes to be a Rose like him. No matter what he says, he'll never have complete faith in me, Ric pondered as they walked side by side to the door. *I'm always gonna be that street junky to him.*

Right before Ric exited the Rose mansion, Alto gave him a big brotherly hug, patted him on the back a few times, and said, "You take care of yourself, ya hear? I'm only a phone call away if you need me. Don't do anything stupid from here on out. You hear me?"

Nodding, Ric replied with a simple, "Yea."

"Huh?" Alto replied as if he didn't hear Ric's response.

"I hear you."

Letting go of the embrace, Alto lightly punched Ric's shoulder and said, "Alright. Now get the fuck out of here." He gave his younger brother a smile and that was that.

Moments later, Ric was taken back to his apartment by a private limo, and when he arrived, he immediately injected a healthy dose of smack into his veins. He'd been salivating all day for the Vena Gold, and now he was back into a comatose state, trying to heal from the long day of grief. He was also trying to block out the job he had to do in the next week, but that was easier said than done. Even on smack, Ric was getting nervous about his trip to The Danger Zone.

After a couple drug-induced days of planning, Ric was ready to fulfill his father's request of him. While he sat on the couch in his apartment that night, two of his street friends, Jonas and Lex, accompanied him. Jonas was tall and slim with shaggy blonde hair and blue eyes. Lex had brown wavy hair, brown eyes, and was stalky and a lot shorter. Both were wearing appropriate dress clothes for a nightclub.

Dressed in a flashy black coat over a tight black t-shirt with a gold chain draped upon his chest, black dress pants, and shiny shoes, Ric stretched his arm out, and injected a needle in the most protruded vein. Euphoria. That's what the needle brought into his soul. Mindless euphoria. Nothing was going to go wrong tonight. He had it all worked out…Or did he? *What am I getting myself into tonight? If I pry into someone's business too hard, am I gonna die?* Ric suddenly asked himself…Paranoia.

Jonas and Lex were fucked up as well. That was the only way Ric could convince these guys to go with him to The Danger Zone. 'Hey, why don't you guys come along with me while I take care of some business at that place we all hate? I'll feed you smack all night if you do'. Then, his two idiot friends answer, 'Sure thing man'. The dumbasses. Ric was taking them into a bomb that was on the verge of exploding. But he didn't have a choice. He sure the hell couldn't go there alone.

So, after they were all tuned up on their fix, Ric and his two friends left the apartment and set out for a long walk across the lower eastside. To Ric, the streets were extra dark tonight, but every car that flew by had extra bright headlights, beaming through the misty night air. He sniffed fumes from the sewers and bitter smoke from burning barrels. His sense of smell was greatly enhanced now. There was the possibility that he got a whiff of shit. Someone must have taken a dump right around the corner of an alleyway. A common toilet for a homeless man.

Shadows were creeping along the streets. They were everywhere, lurking in the dark before jumping out into the moonlight. Those fuckers were trying to dissuade him from completing his job. *Turn around,* they kept whispering in his ears. *Turn around before you get you and your friends killed...*But Ric wouldn't listen to the shady shadows. Nothing was going to scare him into going back home. Sure, hanging out at his apartment would be safe and not so tedious, but he wanted to prove to his dad and brothers that he wasn't just some junky fuck. No matter how much smack he did, Ric was still a Rose. The kings of Exodus. Fuck them haters.

Then, without even knowing it, they made it to their destination...The Danger Zone.

The name of the club was in huge letters, flashing on a sign in neon red lights. While Ric and his friends were waiting in line, the color red glowed on their faces as the ultimate warning not to enter the building. But the way they're minds were lost in a cloud of drugs, you could smack them on the face with a DO NOT ENTER sign, and they would still venture into the hostile environment.

A couple of muscular security guys dressed in tight black T's surrounded the trio when they got to the front of the line. One of them was dark skinned and bald, and had a set of gold teeth. Flashing his metal shiners, he said, "I don't recognize any one of you motherfuckers. What business do you have here?"

Ric has been through this spiel before, so he answered, "It's my friend's birthday, so we decided to go bar hopping tonight and this looked like a pretty hot fucking joint. Are we not allowed in?"

"That depends," the bald black guy replied. "Are you motherfuckers packing any heat?"

"Wouldn't you if you were skipping around these neighborhoods?" Ric sharply retorted.

The big black guy grew an awful grin, baring those gold smackers that were replacements for real teeth. "I catch your drift, my man. Just behave in there, and there won't be any problems."

They were let through. One of the other security guys said, "Have a good time, gentlemen."

And then they were in.

A dark hallway, lined with blinking white lights on the floor, led the way into the nightclub. It felt as if Ric was in slow motion as he confidently strode through and entered the main lounge. The music playing wasn't the loud thumping bullshit he was used to. It was a lot classier. In fact, The Danger Zone was a lot classier than La Bella Scoundrel. Where the Scoundrel had bright neon lighting up clear glass counters, stools, shelves, bottles of liquors, railings, and even the dance floor; this place had hard-wood flooring, leather seats, railings made of brass, oak bar counters and tables, and a candlelight atmosphere. Cig, pipe, and cigar smoke reigned supreme in the air, but the club also had the pleasant odors of perfume, cologne, and incense.

The band playing on stage were striking a classy rhythmic tune. Their main instruments were a guitar and bass, drums, and a couple of brass horns. The patrons in front of the stage danced slow and with elegance. The males had their shirts unbuttoned to reduce the heat caused by their movements, and the females were dressed scantily, grinding all over their male dancing partners.

After purchasing some inexpensive cocktails at the main bar, Ric decided it would be best to venture up a stairwell to the upper floor, and snag a balcony table, so he could scan upon the entire club from a high point of view. When they sat down, their drinks emptied rather fast as the drugs were making the alcohol go down like fresh lemonade on a hot summer day. But as soon as their drinks were empty, a cute dark-haired waitress with perky tats was on the scene. After they ordered more cocktails, she gave them a flirting smile and shook her ass as she strutted away.

Wasting no time, Ric scanned the lower floor. There was nothing unusual to see. Just a bunch of thugs off the streets having a good time drinking and trying to get laid. He knew these thugs were mostly Cicello dogs, but were any of them participants in the massacre at the Grand Theater? There was a promising group in a booth near the bar, but he didn't recognize a single soul.

Noticing that Ric was entranced by what was happening below, Jonas asked, "So what you got to do here, Ric? Some assholes fucking with your Family?"

"You could say that," he shortly replied.

"Pussy is what we should be looking for. I'm in the mood to get my dick wet...Bigtime," Lex said loudly, so Ric could clearly hear him.

"You can worry about getting laid later, Lex. I told you I have business to take care of while we're here. If you don't like it, then you can get the fuck out of here and go home."

"Fine with me." Lex stood up, acting as though he was actually going to take off.

Without looking at his friend, Ric pointed a finger down and commanded, "Sit the fuck down. I need you and Jonas to keep me company so I don't stick out like a dick in a row of vaginas."

Lex did as he was told without an argument. *Why would he want to leave me tonight anyway?* Ric questioned his own mind. *I'm the one with the load of killer smack. And he's the broke-ass fiend who always follows me around.*

The cute waitress came back with their round of drinks. Ric handed her some cash, including a nice tip, and she went about her business to other tables. Sipping on his cocktail, Ric once again peered over the balcony and spotted a private booth right next to the stage. It was hard to see the faces of the men sitting there through the clouds of smoke, but he did perceive that they were dressed rather formal. And when some of the smoke dissipated, there was a new revelation to behold...He recognized the man sitting directly in the middle of the booth between two goons in gray fedoras...But it wasn't a good thing.

Oh shit, he instantly thought as a sharp feeling of anxiety coursed through his inner sanctum.

"Oh shit," he then expressed out loud.

"What is it, Ric?" Jonas curiously asked.

Turning his head towards his friends to hide his face, he answered, "There's a guy down there who I know. And he sure the hell knows who I am too."

"Are you serious?" Jonas started to turn his head to take a peek.

"Don't fucking look!"

Now a bit panicked, Jonas said, "I thought you said nobody would recognize you here. You said there was nothing but a bunch of lowlife thugs that have no idea what you look like here."

"Well then, I guess I was wrong now, wasn't I."

"Figures," Lex snidely remarked.

"Shut up, Lex," Ric said with a hint of annoyance.

"Well, who the hell is it?" Jonas asked, very worrisome.

Carefully peeking over the balcony, trying to keep his face covered by his hand, Ric squinted his eyes and studied the man over again. *Yep, it's definitely him,* Ric concluded. *Fuck...me.*

"It's *Miro Cicello.* AKA, Miro 'The Magician'."

"Is he one of Don Xanose's sons?" Janos asked.

"Yea, his second eldest. A bigtime prick."

Janos nodded, crinkled his forehead, and then asked, "Why is he called 'The Magician'?"

Ric slowly turned his head towards Jonas and morbidly answered, "Because supposedly, he has a very special talent with his Blessing, and he can make your body disappear." He raised his eyebrows after saying the last part.

Taking a big gulp of air, Jonas seemed completely spooked. Lex, on the other hand, just laughed it off.

"But that's just hearsay," Ric offered as comfort to his druggy friend. "Probably just some stupid nickname he came up with himself to make him seem tougher than he really is." At least that was what Ric was hoping. He wasn't too familiar with Miro. Zasso and the youngest brother, Michiela, he knew rather well from his younger days and past *Gatherings* of the Seven Blessed Families. Miro, though, sort of shied away from all the Family hoopla bullshit. He still did some work for his father, but he was mostly into his own lines of business; which was mostly prostitution, drugs, and pornography...Yep, he was heavily into smut films.

As a matter of fact, Ric was sure that the scantily dressed women sitting at his table were some of his actors. *They're pretty hot,* Ric inferred, as he checked the women out. *In a slutty kind of way...* But Ric had no problem with that. He was into skanks these days.

While staring at the slutty women, Ric noticed another person. He wasn't sitting in the booth like everyone else. This guy was standing in attention next to the booth as if he was some kind of bodyguard. He looked a little familiar to Ric, but he couldn't deduce exactly who he was. The man did seem a bit older than he and Miro, being bald and all, but that didn't mean he couldn't kick the shit out of anyone who acted a fool in front of the boss he was protecting. The guy was a beast...And to make matters worse for Ric and his friends, the big bald bodyguard was staring directly up at their table.

Quickly turning his head away-which was probably not a smart move on his part-Ric urgently said, "Alright, I think it's about time we should go."

Perplexed, Lex said, "Already? Come on, man. Let's at least get another drink before we walk all the way back to your place. There's some hot ass in the building."

"No," Ric sternly said back. "We have to go now."

"What's going on?" Jonas asked with noticeable concern.

"Just follow me," Ric said, instead of giving an answer. He abruptly got out of his seat, and hastily made his way to the stairwell leading back down to the ground floor. Brushing past their waitress, she said something along the lines of 'have a good night', but the three paid her no mind. When Ric made it down the stairs, he had to push and shove his way through a crowd of people in order to make it to the front entrance. Some of the patrons were irked by his inconsideration, but he didn't care. His goal was to make it out of the club without interruption, and he was almost there.

Ric and his friends were only a few lengths away from the dark hallway with blinking lights when the worst-case scenario happened. He felt a massive hand tightly grip his shoulder to the point of it almost being painful, and when he turned around to observe who it was, not surprisingly, it was the big bald bodyguard.

Once again, Ric said to himself, *Fuck...me.*

"Ric Rose?" the bodyguard said as if he wasn't certain. Maybe he should lie and tell him he's got the wrong guy. "Oh yes, you are definitely Ric Rose." Then again, maybe not.

"Can I help you?" Ric asked the man as if he hadn't noticed him a short time ago. Jonas and Lex stood behind Ric, cowardly hiding their faces from the big man.

"I'm Bruto Valvoni. It's a pleasure to meet you, young Rose." He extended his hand, and with polite courtesy, Ric shook it. Although it was a hard grip, the handshake was rather friendly.

"Nice to meet you too, Bruto. I don't mean any disrespect to a man of your size, but me and my friends were on our way out, so I'll catch you again some other time." Ric tried to let go of the shake and hurry on his way, but Bruto didn't let go and tugged him closer.

"Come on, Mr. Rose. How about you make some time for my boss tonight? He would really appreciate your company. It's not every night that a Rose comes strolling through here." Bruto's crooked smile on his jar-shaped head was fake, but the invite wasn't. His eyes dug deep into Ric's. They were very dark. Pretty much black.

Ric peered around the big body that filled a silver suit. Miro had already made room at his booth for Ric and his friends. "You have a boss, big guy? A man of your size should answer to no one."

Letting out a chuckle, Bruto replied, "The Cicello Family pays well for my services. It's a hard job to turn down...But I thank you for the compliment."

He finally let go of Ric's hand. "No problem." Ric took a glance over his shoulder. He was surprised to see that Jonas and Lex were still around. He was sure they would've booked out of there...*If they were smart they would've. But once again, I'm the one with all the smack.*

"So, how about it, Mr. Rose? Miro Cicello is waiting for your presence." Another fake smile. It looked unnatural on him.

"You can call me Ric."

Now Bruto looked a little annoyed with him. "So, how about it...Ric? Your friends are more than welcome to join too. It's all on the house tonight."

"Hey, if drinks are on the house tonight, then I'm in," Lex butted in.

Ric wanted to backhand the shit out of Lex, but right now wasn't the time or place. Later he would...If they survived the night. *This is no good. What a rut I've gotten myself into now. I guess I didn't really follow Alto's advice on staying out of trouble.*

With no further contemplation, Ric nodded and said, "Well, show us the way, kind sir."

Bruto gave a smirk, followed by, "Right this way." He extended his arm toward the private booth by the stage. He led the way, obviously not worried that Ric and his buddies would take off. If they did, he would have no problem tracking them down in the crowded nightclub.

Before arriving at Miro's booth, Ric thought of three scenario's that could result after tonight. *Scenario one*: Ric and his friends have a few drinks and a few laughs, and leave the nightclub with no problems. *Scenario two*: Ric and his friends have a few drinks and a few laughs, do a ton of smack with this Cicello guy, and he ends up spilling his guts about the whereabouts of his brother. He completes his father's request, and lives to see another day. *Scenario three*: They all end up dead…Of all three scenarios, the third seemed more probable to Ric. If they don't play it cool, Ric, Jonas, and Lex were going to be taken out with the trash at the end of the night…But Ric still kept his hopes up. *Maybe I'll end up completing my job after all, and then my family will finally have a lot more respect for me.*

Miro Cicello was already standing up when Ric and company made it to the private booth. Immediately, he extended his hand for a friendly shake. Ric extended his hand as well, and Miro clasped it with both hands and shook vigorously. Like someone who snorted a good amount of powder this evening.

Speaking over the rhythmic music, Miro said, "It's an honor to be in your presence, Ric Rose." He let go of the handshake and slicked back his silvery black hair. It wasn't too long, hanging just below his eyes, but it was definitely thick and greasy. Miro also dressed rather odd. The glasses he was sporting were just a ruse. They were white frames with no lenses. His shiny multi-colored dress shirt was halfway unbuttoned, exposing a patch of chest hair, and his white slacks had small thunderbolts imprinted on his ass…Kind of strange, but hey, he's a fucking Cicello.

Ric was facing Miro at eye level, so the guy wasn't nearly as tall as his older brother. He had more pounds to his figure though, compared to Zasso's thin frame. "I don't know if I would call it an honor to be around a guy like me, but I thank you, Miro. How's life treating you these days?"

"Take a look around you," Miro answered, and Ric complied. "This is how I'm living these days. Drinking, dancing, snorting, and fucking," he said with a cheesy smile. He then motioned to the booth. "Please. Have a seat."

Just a short time ago, there were fellow thugs occupying the booth, but now it was empty, so Ric, Jonas, and Lex filed in and tried to make themselves comfortable given the circumstances. Miro followed and slid down the leather, taking a seat right next to Ric. In a matter of seconds, a hot blonde waitress was serving them all cocktails.

Snatching his drink off the table, Miro held it up and said, "A salute to you and your friends, Ric Rose." They all nodded and clinked glasses. "Let's have ourselves one hell of a night." At once, they all took large sips of their beverages. Everyone except Bruto, who stood next to the booth as a bodyguard should.

Placing his drink down, Miro reached into his pants pocket and pulled out a pack of cigs. He offered one to Ric, but he declined. After lighting it up, he said, "So tell me, Ric. What the hell brings you here?"

"I was just gonna ask you the same question," Ric retorted.

Miro let out a slight chuckle. "Well, I venture down here quite often, my friend. I own the place, so it's my responsibility to be here."

"Really," Ric said with a bit of surprise. "I had no idea."

"A Cicello hangout should be owned by a Cicello, don't you think?"

Ric responded with an agreeing, but debatable shrug.

"Actually, I used to let this two-bit fucker that worked for us run the joint, so I could concentrate on my real passion, which is the porn business if you didn't know." Ric did know. "But the stupid fuck kept stealing a good amount of the profit every night, so I eventually had to let him go, if you know what I mean."

"I think I do know what you mean." *I'm sure the guy probably magically disappeared.* "How *is* the porn business going these days?"

Tapping the ash off his cig, he smiled and replied, "As long as people want to fuck for money, then I'm gonna be in business. And boy do these Exodus smuts love to fuck for money." He laughed his ass off at his own comment, and Ric laughed along with him. "I tell ya, Ric. There's nothing like making porn. I watch women get the bejesus fucked out of them on camera, and then get a piece of them myself when the cameras stop rolling…It's a fucking dream job!" he exclaimed, laughing harder.

Ric tried to keep laughing along with him, but it was hard feeling comfortable enough to do so. Even though Miro was being rather courteous and friendly, he was still caught in the middle of hostile territory. He slammed the rest of his drink, hoping that the alcohol would help the anxiety, but what he really needed was something stronger.

Miro must have picked up on the tension from his guest, so in a more somber tone, he said, "Hey, Ric. I know you're going through some shit right now, losing your brother and all. And believe it or not, I can relate." He took a long drag of his cig and blew out a cloud of smoke. "I watch the news. I know it was my own brother who committed that heinous act at the Grand Theater. And I'm not stupid. I figure you probably think I know where he's hiding."

Shit. He's on to me. I knew it.

"But trust me when I tell you this." Miro leaned in closer toward Ric for a more private chat, even though there was no way anyone else could hear them talk with the loud music in the background. "I have no fucking clue what the hell is going on with my family. I usually never do. Sometimes my father and brother go over the top when conducting their own private businesses, and I try to stay out of the loop so I don't get caught up in any of their stupid bullshit." He took a quick puff of his cig and continued, "Zasso is a menace to our society. He's a loose fucking cannon, and sometimes, I want to stay as far away from him as possible. He's always trying to fuck everything between the Seven Families up, and this time, he definitely went too fucking far."

Ric was listening, but surely taking everything with a grain of salt.

"As for my father," Miro went on, "he's got the intelligence of a retard trying to become a chemical engineer."

Ric gestured as if he was about to agree, but thought better of it. Instead, he placed a hand on Miro's shoulder, and explained, "If what you say is true, and we're both gonna try to trust each other, then I'm gonna tell you that I didn't come here to find out anything that has to do with your brother's hidden location. I'm the outsider of my Family, just like you. They don't trust me with shit. To them, I'm just a drug abusing fuckup with no future of my own, and my father didn't even want me to come home for my brother's funeral. He rather me stay at my shit-hole apartment, and stick needles in my arm until I overdose and die." A total fabrication, but by the look on Miro's face, it appeared as though he believed him, and was actually sympathizing with his situation.

Putting his arm around Ric like they've been friends for life, Miro said, "That's why guys like you and I should put all of our Family bullshit behind us, and work together on our own shit."

Agreeing with Miro by putting his own arm around him, Ric said, "I think that's one hell of an idea."

They both smiled at each other and started to have a laugh.

Letting go of the embrace with his new friend, Miro lifted his drink high into the air and shouted, "It's a celebration, Ric Rose! To our new friendship! May it last a long time, and fuck the rest of our Families!" He burst out laughing, clinked glasses with Ric, chugged his drink, and slammed the empty glass on the table.

Amazing, Ric thought during all the joyful madness. *We might actually make it out of this place alive after all. And all because this crazy asshole has more spite against his family than I do…I wonder how my friends are doing.*

He looked over his shoulder and saw that Jonas and Lex were busy chatting it up with a couple of beautiful women in tight revealing dresses…Good for them.

While observing his friends, Ric felt a sudden smack on his back. It was Miro grabbing his attention.

"So how about another drink, my friend? The booze is going to flow all night long," he said with a big drunken smile. "And that's not all that will be flowing tonight. I gotta nice surprise for you in the back of this joint. Something that's right up your alley."

Drugs. And lots of it, I'm sure. He might not accomplish what he came here to do, but the night might not be a total loss. Ric was going to party like there was no tomorrow…And for a few moments tonight, he definitely thought there wasn't going to be a tomorrow. Good thing this Cicello was just like him. He liked to get down and dirty with mind expanding substances.

At the waning hours of the night, Miro Cicello and his bodyguard, Bruto, escorted Ric and his friends through an arcane hallway, leading to an even more obscure dwelling in the back of the club. When Bruto opened the metallic door and Ric walked in, he couldn't decide whether to be impressed or perturbed by the back room.

"Welcome to the *real* VIP room of the club, my friends," Miro expressed with open arms. But it wasn't your average VIP room. It was kind of desolate and gloomy. The walls were brick, some pieces cracked and chipped. The floor was cement, gray and dusty. There was a fireplace near the far corner, a fire blazing and supplying most of the heat and light. A large sofa was placed in front of the fire, and a few wooden chairs were scattered around two wooden tables.

The room was what had Ric perturbed, but the tables were what had him impressed. Inserted in the middle of both tables, were large mirrors, strewn with piles of sparkling white powder. There was even a large glass jug sitting on the edge of one of the tables that was filled with a clear liquid; which Ric knew for sure wasn't just plain water.

This guy doesn't fuck around when it comes to late night partying, Ric thought to himself as he and his two buddies entered the room and took a look around.

"Make yourselves comfortable, gentlemen," Miro said, before he walked around the tables and began cutting up some lines of powder. Bruto leisurely leaned against the fireplace, showing that fraudulent smile.

"So," Ric said, scanning his surroundings, "this is what you call a VIP room?" He sat down on the sofa and tried to make himself comfortable. Jonas and Lex sat down as well.

Chuckling a bit while still chopping up lines, Miro replied, "I know it's not your usual VIP hangout, but I just started refurbishing the place. You should've seen it a couple weeks ago. It looked as though it hadn't been occupied in over a century." Picking up a thin silver tube next to the mirror, he snorted a major line of powder, tilted his head back and shouted, "Yes fucking sir! That's what the fuck I'm talking about!"

Ric smiled at his enthusiasm. *This fucker is a good time.*

Grabbing a couple more silver tubes, Miro pointed them at his three guests and with wide open eyes said, "You guys are up. It's time to make something of your lives…Dream big, boys. Dream fucking big!"

Ric and his friends didn't know what the hell he was talking about, but they had no hesitation getting out of their seats and following orders. Free powder is free powder. It was time to get funky.

While they helped themselves to some of the best powder in the city, Miro strutted very awkwardly to the opposite side of the room and flicked a switch located on a lonesome panel on the wall. Two balls of multicolored lights dropped from the ceiling, and the wall slowly opened and spun around, revealing a high-tech music system. He pressed the power button and within moments, a loud upbeat song with distinct guitar riffs and drum beats started booming on the loudspeakers.

High adrenaline drugs pumping through his blood, Miro Cicello started moving his hips back and forth to the beat of the music, while still facing the wall. Ric watched as the thunderbolts on his ass swayed from side to side, and his arms went up into the air like he was trying to stretch before a workout. Ric then looked over at Bruto, who was pounding the side of the fireplace with his fist along with the beat. He had an intense look on his face as he watched his boss groove.

What the fuck? Ric thought in his mind that was now running wild from the extremely potent powder. Things were beginning to get weird.

When the vocals of the song broke in, Miro swiftly spun around, pointed a wavy hand at his guests, and lip-synced every word that he knew by heart:

Once you were lost…but now it's time to get found,

You got caught up in the fire…and then pushed to the ground.

You thought the worst was over...but it had only begun,

Cause the flames melted your heart...and now you're out on the run.

Miro spread his arms out, tilted his head back, and busted out into the chorus while still diligently swaying back and forth:

Ooooooh, ooh, ooh,

This is the last of your Games!

In a bizarre dance with strange articulate motions, he grooved across the room during a short instrumental break, and then the second part of the chorus came in:

Ooooooh, Ooh, Ooh,

So just get trapped in my Flames!

A longer period of voiceless music played and Miro's movements became even odder while he danced his way around the two tables. Putting a firm grasp around the neck of the large jug of clear liquid, he said, "No joke, this forest brewed back-road shit will literally put hair on your ball-sac the instant you take it down. It will look like a brown lagoon down there...It's pretty damn close to being straight alcohol and strong enough to catch on fire. It feels like flames going down your throat." He laughed a naughty laugh, hoisted it up to his lips, and took a nice-sized swig. After he set it back down, a look of pain engulfed his face before he coughed multiple times. He then smiled and looked satisfied...Plus instantly more intoxicated.

"Holy fucking shit!" Miro yelled out. "This shit might disintegrate your stomach!"

Ric and his buddies laughed pretty hard as they were now back chilling on the sofa. Miro brought the jug of killer booze with him as he stood in front of his guests. He held out the jug for Ric to take it away from him. And when Ric gladly adhered to his host's offer, Miro broke into the next verse of the song with his crazy flamboyant movements:

The time is ticking on down...cause here I come,

I've already made my mistake...thinking you were the one.

I had the world in my hands...but let go of it for you,

Now I'm gonna grab my world back...and start to see a better view.

During the next instrumental, the movements became weirder and weirder, with hand gestures across his face, gyration of his hips and crotch, and leg kicks and spins.

Ric followed his every movement with his eyes and became more freaked out, but entertained at the same time. *Who would've thought that Miro Cicello was this fucking weird? My God what is he doing? This guy gets crazy when he's high...I guess he's not the only one though,* thinking of himself when he's all doped up on smack; the downer drug.

The wild Cicello sang silently with the repeating chorus:

Ooooooh, ooh, ooh,

This is the last of your Games!

And then Miro got behind Ric, Jonas, and Lex, and gyrated his crotch back and forth near the back of their heads when the second vocal part of the chorus came in:

Ooooooh, ooh, ooh,

So just get trapped in my Flames!

It was now time for the big guitar solo in the song, which Miro fanatically imitated with his arms and hands. His dance moves became ever more expressive and outlandish. The gyrations, spins, leg kicks, ass shakings, and struts were so eccentric and freakish that Ric started to question Miro's sexual orientation in his mind...But hey, who doesn't get a little carried away when the drugs are flowing and everyone's having a good time? Jonas and Lex didn't seem to mind. They were both high as fuck with cheesy smiles stuck on their faces...The powder was good.

When the guitar interlude calmed down a bit, Miro pointed a finger directly at Lex, and signaled for him to get to his feet and follow him to the tables of ecstasy. Gladly, Lex got up from the sofa and made his way behind the tables. Miro then chopped up a line of powder that stretched across the entire mirror, which would be a fitting task to take it all down in one snort. With uncharacteristic hand movements, Miro gestured for Lex to rip the whole line. Lex had no problem complying.

Ric and Jonas sat on the edge of the sofa and curiously watched their friend in action. Chances were, Lex wouldn't be able to complete the entire line, but it was still going to be entertaining to watch.

Taking a deep breath, Lex bent over the table, stuck his thin silver tube up his nose, and began snorting from one end. And as soon as he was halfway through, the night of bliss dramatically changed...

During Lex's big snort, Miro suddenly stopped his foolish dance and reached under the table. As if it had magically appeared out of nowhere, he pulled out a silver handgun, cocked it, and then aimed it at the back of Lex's head. Ric and Jonas barely had any time to stand up before Miro pulled the trigger. The front of Lex's face exploded into a cloud of pink and white. Chunks of skull, tissue, and brain matter scattered across the table and onto the floor. Lex's limp body then bounced off the table and fell lifelessly to the ground.

Ric's initial thought process was that he was about to get shot dead, but Miro's next move wasn't even aiming the gun at him. Instead, he lifted his other arm, spread out his fingers, and blasted a surge of electrical power directly at him. Ric was pushed backward by the blast of magical energy, and then fell on his back. His body was paralyzed by the electrical surge and all he could feel was an intense tingling and burning sensation before he blacked out from the pain.

The next thing Ric felt was a stinging slap across the face. Slowly opening his eyes, his blurred vision saw the outline of a large mass in front of him. When his vision eventually cleared, big ole Bruto was standing in front of him with an uncanny smile drawn across his face. Bruto reached back and slapped him again, and that's when reality began to sink back in.

In the open space between the fireplace and sofa, Ric was tied to a wooden chair with his hands behind his back. He had been stripped of his weapon, and most likely the stash of smack he had on him. About ten lengths across the way, Jonas was also tied to a chair, but had a strap of black tape covering his mouth. He was breathing heavy through his nose and sweating profusely with a look of fear and panic. Ric realized in an instant that they were now Miro Cicello's captives…*Oh shit, what have I gotten myself into?* Ric asked himself. A feeling of terror was settling in. He could see Lex's dead body on the other side of the tables, immersed in a pool of blood.

Bruto was holding the jug of fiery booze when he said to Ric, "You want a sip of this shit, Ric Rose? I think you might need it." He took a long gulp of it himself and then spit the contents all over Ric's face. Ric closed his eyes and cringed his face. The strong alcohol burned the skin a bit.

Letting out a sinister laugh, Bruto then said, "There you go, shithead. Let me know if you want some more."

Remaining silent, Ric just watched as Bruto laughed some more, stepped to the side, and placed the jug on the ground next to the fireplace. Then, his eyes made contact with Jonas again, whose eyes were bulging with horror.

From the side, Miro came into view, slowly striding with a more serious approach to the now drastically turned night. He walked directly behind Jonas and slid a hand through the poor guy's hair. Jonas started freaking out and shaking in his chair. It wouldn't do him any good though. They were both trapped and now prisoners of this weirdo.

"It's funny how things work out for me sometimes," Miro sadistically spat out. "I was told to keep a close watch on the club after what my brother did at the Grand Theater, and low and behold one of the Rose brothers happens to venture in…Coincidence? I think not!" He reached back and smacked the shit out of the back of Jonas's head. Jonas's yells were muffled behind the tape, as his body squirmed in the chair some more.

Ric couldn't just sit there in silence and watch his friend get beat up, so he yelled out, "Let him go, Miro! He's got nothing to do with us."

Eyes now seemingly curious, Miro said, "So there *is* a reason why you came here tonight, huh? Are you admitting that you were sent here to find out information about my brother's whereabouts?"

I'm fucked, Ric thought before he replied, "Let my friend go and then we can hash it out. He's an innocent civilian who just wanted to come out and party."

Smiling oh so pompously, Miro said, "Well then he came to the right place, my friend." Once again, he smacked the hell out of Jonas. This time, with a closed fist to the side of the face. Jonas grimaced in pain as his cheek swelled up. "Ooh, now that's gonna leave a mark," he remarked, shaking his hand.

Ric lowered and shook his head in disgust. "What do you want from me, Miro? What do you want me to tell you, that I came here tonight to spy on your family?"

"You don't have to tell me that, Ric Rose. I already figured that out the second Bruto spotted you." Once more, he wound up and cracked Jonas across the jaw. This time Jonas didn't let out a peep. He was almost unconscious from the blow, and his body slumped forward, held up only by the leather straps tied around him and the chair.

With a subtle grin, Miro left Jonas alone for the moment and approached Ric, crouching directly in front of him. His eyes pierced through his lens-lacking glasses and seemed to be radiating a bright yellow charge in them. As if his Blessing was heating up inside him.

"What really intrigues me, Ric," Miro said in a calm fashion, "is why the hell your Family would send a piece of shit, junky trash bag like you, to seek out crucial, if not historic, information about what *my* Family seeks to gain in attempting to abduct your father...It just blows my fucking mind." He let out a chuckle that was laced with mockery.

My Family believed that I would blend in with the crowd, Ric answered Miro's riddle to himself, but dared not to reply aloud. *And they sure weren't expecting your weirdo ass to show up.*

Not expecting Ric to respond back to his quarry, Miro continued on, "Oh well. It's all going to be ancient history soon, so I might as well let you in on a little secret about this fucked up world of ours, because I'll admit, it's killing me to keep holding it inside."

Ric figured this was coming. He was as good as dead, so why not tell him important information that's been bundled up in his mind, just aching to get out.

Placing a hand on Ric's leg, intruding in on his comfort zone, Miro explained, "This world we live in, this *Exodus*, is in for a historical transformation, Ric Rose. A major power shift is imminent, and the Rose Family is merely just blocking the way. The Rose Quartet is a necessity for this change, because without the Relic, your Family will be reduced to nothing...But if *we're* in control of the most powerful Relic in Exodus, then the transformation can be completed, and my Family will continue to prosper in the years to come." He leaned in closer towards Ric's face, and with a more intense look, continued, "The Rose Quartet is what we're after, Ric Rose. And your father is the one man in your Family who knows exactly where it is...Sure, we could've gone after your Uncle Vetti, but he would never disclose that type of information. He has too much pride. He probably rather die...But your father, on the other hand, cares too much about the rest of his Family. He loves his children and would rather give up the Relic than watch his kids get destroyed. Because that is what will happen if he doesn't give us what we want...You, your brothers, and your sisters, will all be killed off one by one." He pointed his finger between Ric's eyes, twiddled it around, and then poked him on the nose. "And it so happens, that it started last week with your brother, and will continue tonight, with you."

Not wanting to keep looking into Miro's eyes after what he just disclosed, Ric peered to his right and watched as Bruto lifted the jug of extreme booze to his lips and take a big swig. He wiped his mouth before placing the jug back on the ground...A jug of flammable alcohol, right next to a live fireplace.

Miro saw that Ric wasn't paying attention to him, so he aggressively grabbed Ric's jaw, steadying his face and making him look into his eyes. "Pay attention to me, you junky fuck! You think I'm playing around here, you think this night is some kind of fucking game! You are going to die tonight, asshole, and I'm going to send severed pieces of your body in the mail to your Family!" He shoved his face, before letting go of his grasp. After standing up, he walked back over to Jonas, who could barely keep his eyes open.

Inside, Ric was furious. The Cicello Family had a master plan to rid of the Rose Family...The nerve of those fuckers. Always wanting to be more significant than they actually were. The dreaded thought of the Cicello's being in control of his Family quickly popped in his head, and it caused his body to squirm in the chair he was tied to...*Wait a second,* he thought after his movements made the chair creak. *This wooden chair is fairly brittle.*

Meanwhile, Miro stood behind Jonas and decided it was a good time to rip off the piece of tape fastened over his captive's mouth. Instead of yelling out or screaming, Jonas simply mumbled incoherent words. Miro caressed his cheek and under his chin, and then moved his hand up to the top of his head where he gently coursed his fingers through Jonas's hair. His actions were unnerving to Ric. Miro was making him sick.

"Stop fucking with him!" Ric hollered. But all he got in return for caring for his friend, was a quick slap across the face from Bruto. The bodyguard then stepped away from him, and now stood directly in front of the fireplace.

"You know, you're right, Ric. I should stop fucking with your little friend here, and get down to business." Miro patted the top of Jonas's head, and then made a claw-like grip with his fingers upon his skull. This action caused Jonas to stir a little more. He fully opened his eyes and looked at Ric for help...But that was asking a lot at the moment.

"I'm sure you've heard of my nickname before," Miro said, with his claw grip still fastened on Jonas's head. "There's a good reason why I'm referred to as Miro 'The Magician'. I do this little trick with my Blessing, where I can make someone disappear." His eyes and fingers began to light up like neon lights, while electrified currents surrounded his hand. An evil sneering grin grew upon his face. "It's a little messy...but it's a hell of a lot of fun to witness." He laughed uncontrollably, and then suddenly, a massive current of energy flowed from his shoulder and down his arm, before bursting through his fingertips.

Instantly, Jonas's eyes grew the size of saucers, and he let out an ear-splitting shriek that would cause a ghost to cringe. Smoke began to rise from the top of his head, and his body started to convulse. His face broke out into mini seizures. He was being electrocuted...severely.

Ric didn't want to watch, but couldn't take his eyes off the performance. Jonas's face was turning all sorts of colors; from yellow to orange to red. Considerable amounts of smoke puffed out of his ears, nose, and eye sockets...Ric couldn't let this go on much longer. "Stop! Stop this fucking shit, Miro!"

Once again, Miro let out a despicable laugh. "There's no turning back now, Ric Rose! I've only just begun!" His eyes appeared ever more devilish as another surge of energy flowed from his arm and out his fingers. The effect was devastating.

The hair on Jonas's head was burned off, and the skin on his face began to melt, revealing blood and tissue, which fizzled away into ash in a matter of moments. His eyeballs popped out of the sockets and rolled onto the floor, which amused Miro and Bruto. They were completely engulfed in the horrendous Magic act, and weren't paying too much attention to Ric.

This is my only chance.

Amidst the chaos, Ric began to sway his upper body back and forth. The wooden chair was about to give. Hopefully, it would break apart upon impact on the hard ground.

Laughing hysterically, Miro continued to electrify the hell out of Jonas. He was already dead, but the disappearing act was still not complete. It would take a little longer to burn his entire body into a pile of ash, and that delay is what Ric desperately needed for a possible escape.

It's now or never.

The left legs of the chair were completely off the ground, and the right legs collapsed under Ric's weight. He toppled over and hit the floor with a great thump. And like a divine miracle, the chair broke into pieces, freeing him from the straps. It was in that short moment that Bruto noticed what had just happened. He drew his gun, but it was too late for him.

Ric landed with his legs right next to the jug of flammable booze, and with a powerful kick, it flew into the fireplace.

BOOM!

An orange fireball and shards of glass burst out of the fireplace, and flames completely engulfed the large body of Bruto. He dropped his piece and started frantically running around in circles, yelling and screaming while he started to burn to death.

Miro was so shocked by the turn of events that he stood motionless behind Jonas's corpse and watched as his bodyguard flailed around the room in a ball of flames. Ric seized the opportunity by rolling on the ground a few lengths and grabbing Bruto's gun. He instantly sat up, aimed towards Miro, and opened fire. Miro dove out of the way as bullets flew over his head. A couple shots struck the burned body of Jonas and also hit the back wall. Ric didn't empty out the clip, though, as he wanted to preserve the bullets left in the handheld cannon.

While Bruto's burnt to a crisp, lifeless body crumbled to the floor, Ric and Miro both stood up from their respective spots. Ric shot off a couple more rounds, while Miro tried to electrify him with a protruding lightning bolt. The bolt missed Ric completely, instead blasting the music system on the back wall, but Miro was hit in the shoulder by one of the bullets. He fell to his knees, grasped his shoulder, and yelled to high heaven from the pain.

I injured him, Ric quickly thought. *Now it's time to go.*

Ric hastily made his way to the exiting door without looking back. An electrified bolt of energy hit the side of the doorframe, just as Ric escaped the unholy room of death. The dreadfully dark hallway felt like it was a mile long as Ric ran down it at as fast as his legs would take him. He heard himself breathing heavy and then yells coming from Miro.

"You won't escape me, you junky son of a bitch!"

But he was wrong. Ric was going to escape. Maybe not forever, but he was definitely going to get away this night. He turned down another long and dark hallway, and spotted a door that was most likely an exit that led to a back alleyway. When he burst through the door, a man dressed in a suit and fedora just so happened to be leaning against the outside wall. Before he could even ask Ric what he was doing, Ric put a bullet in his brain, splattering the wall with blood. He wasn't fucking around anymore. If anyone else got in his way, they were going to die.

The back alleyway was littered with garbage and rats, but all Ric concentrated on was the full sprint he was in. He didn't want to look back, but he had to take a peek over his shoulder and see if he was being followed. And low and behold, he caught a glimpse of Miro trying to catch up to him. Miro tried hitting him with scattered lightning bolts, but they kept missing him by mere inches.

This guy just won't quit, Ric thought as he turned the corner and entered another alleyway that opened up into a true street. There was an abandoned car in the middle of the alley, so Ric jumped up onto the trunk and dove over the roof, landing on the front windshield, before sliding off the hood. He hid behind the car and waited for Miro to turn the corner next. When he finally came flying around, Ric relentlessly opened fire upon his enemy. Miro didn't even have a chance to return fire. A couple of shots hit their target, and he fell hard to the ground.

But just as Ric fired off his last round, a car with flashing red lights zoomed into the alley before coming to a halt. The driver's door flew open and the occupant stepped out with his own firearm pointed it in Ric's direction.

"Lower your weapon and put your fucking hands in the air!"

Detective Melroy Statz

And the Interrogation of Ric Rose

He had trouble going to sleep tonight, so he set out on a late-night patrol, and just so happened to be in the area. Call it luck, or what you will, but just as he was about to devour his roast beef sandwich with peppers and onions, Detective Melroy Statz heard shots being fired down the alley right around the corner from where he was parked. Immediately, he tossed the sandwich to the passenger seat, switched on the flashing red lights above the dashboard, and sped around the corner and into the alleyway. The headlights beamed through the darkness and shone directly at the culprit. The man was dressed in all black with his weapon drawn, and fired one last shot. He could barely see the silhouette of the other man being fired upon, but he was positive that the man took off running.

Like regulatory police procedure, Melroy exited his vehicle, drew his firearm, aimed it at the suspect and yelled out his demands. "Lower your weapon and put your fucking hands in the air!" It was close enough to normal protocol.

The suspect didn't resist whatsoever. Actually, the man did as he was told without any hesitation. He threw the firearm to the ground and slowly raised his hands up, surrendering himself. He must have known right away that it was a cop in command. A street thug or gangster would've just blown him away without a word.

"Now turn around and face me, keeping your hands up where I can see them!" he commanded with more authority, gun still pointed at the suspect.

Still doing as he's told, the man casually turned around. And that's when the real shock came. Melroy recognized the suspect at once. *You got to be shitting me,* was his initial reaction. The gunman was none other than his best childhood friend, Ric Rose.

The beaming headlights must have made it impossible for Ric to be able to see who his arresting officer was, because he made no reaction and was squinting rather hard. It was only when Melroy stepped away from the vehicle, approached Ric, and was about a few lengths away, he finally recognized who the officer really was.

It was in that moment of recognition that Ric's mouth grew into a smile of relief. He dropped his arms back to his side and curiously asked, "Melroy? Is that really you?"

There was not going to be a happy reunion at this time. No friendly embrace with open arms. Melroy was pissed that it was Ric who was breaking the law and shooting at someone, so instead of acting like a friend, he grabbed Ric by the arm, aggressively turned him around and shoved him face-first onto the hood of the abandoned car, and assertively said, "You're under arrest for disturbing the peace, discharging a firearm in public…and attempted murder."

Face down and with his hands being handcuffed behind his back, Ric yelled out, "Attempted murder? What the fuck are you doing, Melroy? It's fucking Ric Rose! Your best friend!"

"I know who the fuck you are, Ric. Do you think I'm stupid?" he replied back, putting the finishing touches on the handcuffs. "But you're still under arrest. I saw you firing your gun at another person, and now I have to take you in."

"You gotta be shitting me, Melroy! That guy I was shooting at was trying to kill me. I was only trying to defend myself, and it's not even my gun!"

"Then whose gun is it? Your father's? Maybe one of your brothers gave it to you."

"Ha, ha. Real fucking funny. If you really need to know, I was just caught up in a fucked-up situation, and barely got out of it alive. I'm actually lucky to be getting arrested by you right now," Ric explained as a plea to let him go…But Melroy wasn't going to budge. He was angry with Ric…and very disappointed.

"Well then your luck is going to get even better, because I'm taking you downtown to the station and throwing your ass behind bars," Melroy conveyed with heat. He knew Ric was really going to flip his lid now. He grabbed him by his shackled arms, and escorted him over to his undercover vehicle.

"Come on, Melroy, you don't have to do this. We can just talk this out and I'll explain to you everything that just happened to me," Ric pleaded some more, trying to reason with his friend.

"You can explain yourself down at the station," is all that Melroy had to say as a response to the plea.

Now Ric was really heated. Melroy could sense his blood boiling on the inside. And when he opened the back door to shove Ric inside the car, his friend expressed a derogatory thought towards him. "Fuck you, Melroy!"

Melroy stuffed Ric inside the car, slammed the door shut, and pretty much to himself said, "It's good to see you too, Ric."

During the ride to the station, Ric pretty much kept quiet in the back seat. *He must be pretty pissed at me if he's not even gonna try to plead his case some more before we get downtown...Maybe he wants to be in lockup for the night, so he can be safe from whatever did happen to him tonight,* Melroy pondered as he drove. *But I will give him the benefit of the doubt and let him explain to me what happened soon. I just want to teach him a little lesson first.*

Before they arrived, Ric did have one more thing to say to his officer friend. "I didn't see you at Georgie's funeral. I hope it's because you were too grieved to attend. But knowing you, you probably didn't want to be seen mourning the death of a Rose Family member."

Melroy didn't want to respond to an accusation like that. Mostly because it was sort of true. Attending the funeral would have made it seem as though Melroy was biased to the Rose Family, and considering that he was working on the case of the Grand Theater massacre, it wouldn't have been a good idea to be seen there...But the biggest reason for his absence was that he didn't want to witness Don Maretto Rose bury one of his sons. Especially, the one with the kindest heart.

"My dad would've been happy to see you there, Melroy," Ric continued saying. "He was like a father to you too, you know...And Georgie was like a brother."

Waiting a few seconds before a reply, Melroy said, "I know what your Family was to me, Ric." It was a simple, straightforward response in a solemn tone.

Ric just simply replied, "Do you?"

The conversation in the car ended there. Melroy parked his car next to the sidewalk in front of his precinct. The *Juna City Police Department*, or JCPD, was located about ten blocks west of Juna's Heart, the epicenter of the city. It was a rather large building, about three stories high, resting atop a steep incline of cement stairs. The walls were built of dark-gray brick, and the windows were all tinted, besides the clear glass doors at the entrance. Melroy escorted his prisoner up the steps, walking past a group of uniformed officers taking a smoke break during their late night shifts.

Entering through the glass doors, Melroy took Ric to the front desk, booked him, and then a couple uniformed guys showed him to his jail cell. Ric remained quiet, did not resist, and went without a fight. Melroy then went to sit at his desk and began filling out the paperwork for the arrest. After only one page, he threw his pen across the room, lounged back in his chair, and picked up the mug of coffee resting on the desk. He sipped the coffee over and over while he thought of what to do with Ric. He couldn't keep his best friend locked up, he just couldn't do it. So, he decided that he wouldn't waste any more time and go see him. It was now time for a nice long chat with his longtime friend. It was time to get to the bottom of exactly what happened tonight.

Standing in front of the Interrogation Room One-A window, Melroy watched Ric as he sat in the lonely room with his arms crossed, deep in thought. *I wonder what he's thinking about,* Melroy thought. *He looks kind of spooked. What the fuck did he just witness?*

As he continued to watch his friend, a tall and slender older man dressed in a navy blue suit and tie joined him by the window. The older gentleman had snowy white hair, slicked back to cover up the bald spots, and a gray mustache that extended to his chin.

"Good morning, Captain Riccard," Melroy respectfully greeted his superior.

"Good morning, Detective. What do you have cooking inside there?" the Captain asked, peering through the deceptive window. Inside the room, the window was tinted so you couldn't see who was studying you on the outside.

"Just some idiot who was disrupting the peace."

Taking a closer look at the suspect, the Captain's eyebrows raised as he said, "Holy shit, Melroy. I hope you have a damn good reason why Don Maretto Rose's youngest son is sitting alone and twiddling his thumbs in that shit box." His voice was deep and vibrant. Perfect for someone in charge of law enforcement.

"I'm just doing my job," Melroy calmly answered, as if it was no big deal.

"Maretto Rose is a good friend of mine and a dedicated supporter of this department, and he wouldn't be too happy to know that his son was being interrogated for some petty bullshit." Riccard didn't sound too pleased.

"Don't worry, Captain. You know that the Rose Family and I go way back too. Especially me and Ric. I just want to teach my old friend that he can't be running wild on the streets and shooting guns as he pleases. Don Maretto would understand." *Actually, he probably would be pissed at me.*

"Shooting guns? At who?" Riccard asked with concern.

"That's what I'm about to find out," he replied. "With what happened at the Grand Theater, we can't have one of the Rose sons causing trouble and making the family look bad while the investigation is in progress. I won't keep him here for much longer, Captain. I just want to ask him a few questions."

After contemplating Melroy's actions for a few moments, Riccard said, "Fine. But you get his ass out of here as soon as you can. I don't want him kept in that box for more than an hour. Do you understand?"

"Of course I do, sir."

"I mean it!" he exclaimed, pointing a bony finger at Melroy. "If I get an angry phone call from Maretto Rose himself, then I'm gonna take it out on your ass, and you'll

117

be dressed in a uniform, pulling traffic duty for a month. It's very important that I keep a good standing relationship with the Rose Family, and I don't need it fucked with!"

"I absolutely understand, Captain."

"Alright then," Riccard said, lowering his tone and his finger. "Go get your interrogation over with, Detective. And I don't want to see another Rose in this building again, unless *I* bring him in." As he stormed away, the clomping of Captain Lan Riccard's shoes echoed down the hallway until he exited into another corridor.

Melroy stared through the window for a few more moments before he opened the door and entered the interrogation room. As soon as he stepped through the doorway and slammed the door shut behind him, Ric looked up from the table in front of him, directly at Detective Melroy Statz. Ric was slouching in his seat and his hands were placed upon the table, fingers fidgeting. As far as Melroy could tell, he was coming down from an intense high.

Before he sat down, Melroy said, "Can I get you anything, Ric? A bottle of water, a cup of coffee. Maybe a smoke?"

The last offer made him chuckle a bit. "It's funny how many times I've been offered a cig since I quit smoking. When I did smoke, nobody offered me shit."

As Melroy pulled the opposing chair out from the table, it screeched across the hard floor. As he sat down and made himself as comfortable in the rickety wooden chair as he possibly could, Melroy said, "What's really funny is that you quit smoking cigs opposed to quitting dangerous drugs. At least cigs will take many years to kill you."

"Well, since you put it that way, I'll take you up on your offer."

Patting down his brown coat, Melroy said, "Oops. Seems as though I left them on my desk."

Ric smirked and shook his head.

Leaning back in his chair and crossing his arms, Melroy stared directly into Ric's eyes and said, "So, Ric. Were you having a little fun tonight?"

Cunningly, he answered, "I don't know. Maybe I should bring in a lawyer before I give you any information, *Detective.*"

"Fuck a lawyer," Melroy snapped back. "This is all off the record, so just answer the fucking question. Why the hell were you shooting at someone, Ric? Was it over drugs? Did somebody rip you off, maybe give you some low-quality shit for the price of the high-quality stuff?"

"No. It had nothing to do with drugs."

"Oh, okay." Melroy paused and thought about the next possibility. "Did you not pay the full price of a prostitute, and her pimp chased you down?"

Ric shook his head, not even bothering to answer that scenario.

"Maybe you owed money to some drug kingpin and he let out the dogs on you. Were you being chased down for not paying what you owed for some smack?"

"Cut the shit, Melroy," Ric said with slight aggravation. "It had nothing to do with any of that bullshit." He removed his hands from the table and crossed his arms as well. The two friends looked like mirror images, sitting across from each other in the same position.

"Then enlighten me," Melroy simply put.

Ric took a deep breath and sighed before he explained, "After Georgie's funeral there was a long discussion within my family about the events that occurred at the Grand Theater. Besides Alto, everyone agreed that our next action should be locating the whereabouts of Zasso Cicello, since he was the main perpetrator involved. If we could find Zasso, then we could get the answers we need out of him."

"What answers?" Melroy promptly asked.

"Important ones, like what he was trying to accomplish by abducting my father, and what the hell he wants from my family. Also, why the fuck would he do it at a public gathering. You know, shit like that...But the most important information we need from him is, who the fuck gave him such a bold order. He risked his entire Family name that night. The other Families are going to shun the Cicello's for what they did." He paused for a quick moment and then said, "Unless they all had prior knowledge of the attack."

That theory was something that Melroy had not thought of yet, but it was also highly unlikely. The Cicello's were scum-bucket assholes. It wasn't in the best interest of the other Families to side against the Rose Family. Maretto could give the other Families so much more...Unless if it wasn't the Cicello's who gave the order in the first place...But that was a farfetched theory as well.

Nodding his head, Melroy ordered Ric to go on.

"So, when the meeting was over, my father, Jon-Jon, and my Uncle Vetti talked to me in private, and asked me if I could infiltrate some popular Cicello thug hangout and possibly find out some crucial answers into Zasso's whereabouts. I really didn't want to do it at first, but Jon-Jon convinced me when he said that I should do it for our slain brother...And besides that, I wanted to prove to my father and brothers that I wasn't just some worthless street junky. That I could give more to the family." He slightly lowered his head in disappointment with himself and continued, "But I should've known better and rejected their request, because I failed them like I always have...The biggest disappointment of all my father's sons."

Listening intently to his best friend's story, Melroy asked, "How did you fail? And what's the name of this Cicello hangout?"

Staring off into oblivion, Ric answered, "It's called 'The Danger Zone'. I've been there before with no problems. Usually, there's nothing more than your average lowlife thugs packing in the joint, and I figured last night would be no different. My plan was to cozy up to some random Cicello thugs and hopefully get them to spill some rumors about where Zasso ran off to...But little did I know that I was in for a big surprise. One of Xanose Cicello's other sons is the owner of The Danger Zone, and he so happened to be in attendance last night."

"Which son is that?" Melroy quarried, ever more interested.

"Miro Cicello. Xanose's second eldest. A weird motherfucker this guy is." Ric slowly shook his head, obviously remembering the night that had unfolded.

"So, then what happened?"

"Miro's bodyguard, Bruto Valvoni spotted me in a matter of minutes, and pretty much forced me to go have a drink with his boss. So, I did." Ric stopped slouching and sat in his chair with better posture. "At first, everything seemed fine. We were having a bunch of drinks, a lot of laughs, and as fucked as this Miro guy was, he actually seemed like a friendly dude." He lowered his head and rubbed the skin above his eyebrows. "Anyway, I had a couple of friends with me, so he invited us back into a private room to do some late-night partying, if you know what I mean. And that's when the night just got all fucked up.

"Now, this Miro guy, I've heard his nickname before. He's known as Miro 'The Magician'. And after we did a bunch of powder, he showed us why he's called that...To make a long story short, he blew one of my friend's brains out, tied me and my other friend up in a couple wooden chairs, and performed his Magic act."

Melroy's eyebrows crinkled. *What fucking Magic act is he talking about?* He asked himself.

"Basically, Melroy, he used his electrifying powers of his Blessing to electrocute my friend's head until his face melted off."

"What the fuck?" Melroy exclaimed, shocked by what he just heard.

"That's what my initial reaction was," Ric replied. "But luckily, I was able to break free, take out his bodyguard, and escape that hell hole with my life."

Taking the story all in, Melroy then said, "So I take it he chased you out of the building and into the alleyway."

"That's exactly what happened...I was able to retrieve the bodyguard's firearm and hit Miro with a shot before I escaped the room. Then, he proceeded to chase me out the back of the building, and down a couple alleys, trying to hit me with that lightning Magic he possesses. And when I was hiding behind that abandoned car, I opened fire on him when he came running around the corner. I know for a fact that I got him a couple more times and he fell on his back, but when you ordered me to put my hands in the air and lower my weapon, I noticed that he was gone."

Thinking back on what he witnessed as well, Melroy nodded and said, "Yea, I saw a guy running away from the scene."

"That was Miro," Ric agreed. "Oh, and there's one more thing."

"What's that?"

"I killed a guy right outside the back of the club," Rick blurted out. "Blew his brains clean out of his head."

As soon as Ric made the confession, Melroy almost fell out of his chair. "Don't tell me that shit, Ric! What the hell are you thinking? I'm a fucking officer of the law!"

Acting nonchalant about the revelation, Ric said, "What? I already confessed about taking out Miro's bodyguard."

"But that's different," Melroy replied, leaning forward. "You were trying to escape a volatile situation. It was in self-defense."

"Well, this was kind of the same thing. The guy was obviously a Cicello thug who would kill me if he had the chance. I'm sure his résumé in life isn't exactly clean."

Fucking Ric, he thought to himself as he leaned back in the uncomfortable wooden chair, shaking his head in disapproval.

Avoiding eye contact with his friend, Ric continued, "Anyway, don't worry about that fuck. The Cicello's will just chop him up and toss him in the river. I'm sure you're familiar with that technique of getting rid of bodies."

He definitely was. All too familiar with it. The thought of a man being chopped into pieces brought a childhood memory back from the grave. But Melroy quickly dismissed it and returned to the matter at hand…Ric's stupid ass.

Instead of delving further into the unfortunate situation Ric was thrust into last night, Melroy wanted more info on the Grand Theater massacre, so he asked, "So, does your Family believe that Xanose Cicello was the sole mastermind in the attempted abduction of your father?"

Ric sighed and slouched back in his seat. "Maybe. Maybe not. Alto thinks it was definitely him, but the rest of my family doesn't believe Xanose has the brass to pull off such a major move against us...But I really don't know, Melroy. I think I'm just gonna stay out of the way of family business from now on."

Nodding, Melroy said, "I see." *He's holding back on me. Even though we're old friends, I still have to keep in mind that I'm a law-abider and he's a Rose. He'll never tell me the full truth. Especially now that he's out of trouble at the moment.*

Clasping his hands behind his head, Ric seemed to notice Melroy's disappointment in the lack of information he provided. "If you really want to know my opinion, Melroy...I think that this city, and all of Exodus, is in for a major overhaul."

Interesting, Melroy thought before he asked, "And why's that?"

"Just call it a hunch," Ric replied, diverging from what he really knows. "But if you really want to know what Xanose's role in all this is, then maybe you should go talk to the man himself."

I will, Melroy immediately thought...And that was that. Melroy ended the interrogation of his friend, and then proceeded to drop all the charges against him. Ric had been through enough, and it was time for him to go home.

Melroy sniffed the early morning air as he led Ric down the department steps. It was crisp and uncontaminated, unlike the city of Juna and the vermin known as the Cicello's that have infested it with their tainted filth. *A Magic trick that melted a man's face off? My God, help us all. Maybe Agent Strain was right. The main source of problems in Exodus start with the Seven Blessed Families.*

Melroy's burgundy classic four-door was parked in front of the department building, so he left Ric's side to tend to his baby. He roughed it up a little last night, screeching around the street corner before encountering Ric, but there was no damage done. It was still in pristine shape for an older model.

Ric stood on the sidewalk and watched him admiring his pride and joy. "Sorry you had to put that thing to some use last night. I hope she didn't get a scratch."

Brushing a speck of dirt off the white top, he said, "Nope. Not one scratch on her pretty ass since I bought it two years ago. Luck of the lady, I guess."

Ric smiled. "It is a nice ride. Maybe you could take me for a cruise in it one of these days."

"Maybe," Melroy quickly answered.

Nodding a couple of times, Ric hesitated a moment before he asked, "Hey, do you want to go sit down and have a cup of coffee, or some breakfast or something?"

He inserted the key into the driver-side door, unlocked it, and pulled it open while he thought about the offer. "Nah, maybe some other time."

Nodding again, Ric turned his body and began walking the opposite way of the car.

Watching his old friend slowly walk away, Melroy thought about the old Ric for a moment and instantly began to miss him. He also wondered if he would ever see him again after today, so he said, "Hey Ric," before he could get any further. When Ric stopped his stride and turned around, Melroy asked, "Do you want to know the real reason why I took you in last night?"

Flashing a bright smile, Ric responded, "Okay, tell me."

He hesitated to answer at first, almost as if he was embarrassed to say it, but then he finally blurted it out. "Because I wanted to spend some time with you. I miss my old friend...I miss the Ric I used to know."

Ric's smile faded. He didn't respond back, but instead stared up into the sky, lost in thought.

Realizing in that awkward moment that the old Ric was probably gone for good, Melroy went back to business and said, "I'll keep my eyes peeled for this Miro guy while I work your brother's case. I doubt he went running for daddy, but I have a feeling he might run for his older brother."

Ric shook his head and said, "Don't bother. He's my problem." And then he was gone. Back onto the streets, blending in with the downtown scumbags of Juna. Not a fitting place for the son of the most highly regarded man in Exodus.

A short time later, Melroy found himself driving aimlessly through the city, reminiscing about the old days with Ric. At one point in his youth, they were inseparable. Always getting into trouble, and at the same time, trying to stay out of it. Whether it was going down to the local arcade to pump some coins into action-packed video machines, or stealing adult magazines and cigs from a hole-in-the-wall shopping mart, it was all fun and games in their preteen years...*We didn't care about nothing back then. We did whatever we wanted, and didn't worry about consequences. It felt as though Ric's family was my family. And I loved his father like he was my own.*

But on one particular day in his youth, that feeling of love for the Rose Family would change...

Melroy was twelve. Ric was pushing eleven. They were in the back seat of a limo, riding around town with Don Maretto. He had said to them earlier in the day that he needed to run some important errands, so of course Ric and Melroy begged and pleaded their hearts out to go with him. He finally caved in and brought them along. Riding around the city with Maretto was the best thing in the world to the two young boys.

Partway through the day, Maretto had the limo driver stop in front of an old apartment complex that appeared as though it hadn't been renovated in decades. It was an odd place for a highly respected man such as Maretto to be visiting, but the boys thought nothing of it at first. They followed him out of the limo and into the main lobby, which was in need of a major paint job, new furnishings, and all new carpeting. It was drab and unappealing to the eyes. Someone needed to dust the fucking place too.

Maretto ordered the boys to stay put in the lobby as he disappeared down a corridor with an older gentleman dressed way too nice to be staying at this shithole. And there was no one sitting behind the front desk to keep an eye on them, so after time started dragging on, and they began to get restless, Ric had the spontaneous idea to go venturing through the complex. "There's gotta be something cool about this place for my dad to be here," was Ric's rationality. So, they went exploring.

They climbed a reclusive stairwell, because the elevator looked ancient and probably hadn't been operated since the beginning of time. Each floor they reached seemed to be abandoned. There were no signs of life and the hallways were in total darkness. But then they spotted a door that had a sign posted on it. 'Do Not Enter' it said, written in red letters as a cautionary warning. So instead of heeding the sign, Ric said, "Let's check it out."

Melroy doesn't remember how, but at some point during their exploration of the 'Do Not Enter' hallway, he lost sight of Ric, who must have found something to his delight and disappeared into one of the rooms. And that's when Melroy saw something that sparked intrigue. At the end of the hall was a room with the door cracked open, spilling out a shred of light. It was a little unnerving, but Melroy was young and brash, so he slinked his way through the partially opened door and tiptoed into the room. Immediately, he spotted a trio of men around the corner, sitting at a dining table, eating a meal consisting of spaghetti and meatballs. They were slobs, all three of them. Slurping down noodles like it was going to be their last meal. The irritating scrapes of their forks along the plates made his ears cringe. But not as bad as the classical music coming from the old-school record player. It sounded like a jumble of stringed instruments trying to play on top of each other.

Then he heard it. A loud *thud* that came from a room down the apartment hallway. He heard it again. Then again. And again. He crept down the hall as silently as possible. The three spaghetti slobs had no idea he was there. He was damn quiet. Like a cat creeping on a mouse.

There was a room with a light on. *Thud...thud...thud...* The closer he got to the room, the louder the *thud*. It was distinct now. It sounded as if someone was chopping at a piece of beef. And when young Melroy finally peeked around the doorway, his twelve-year-old eyes experienced a scene of horror in which no young boy should ever witness.

126

Tears instantly filled his eyes and the breath in his lungs was swept away as he looked upon a nude body hanging upside down above a bathtub. The dead body was riddled with bullet holes from the toes down to the head, and blood streamed down the naked skin, filling the porcelain tub with a coat of red gore. The victim's mouth was hanging open and the eyes seemed to stare straight at him. The look of terror on the corpse was the same look Melroy was broadcasting now.

On a wooden table set up by the sink, lied another body. And standing there, hacking down on the other corpse with a meat cleaver, was a grotesque blob of man with a hairy back. He was wearing a white t-shirt and a cooking apron to block the blood splatter. The man took one more hack and slowly lifted up the piece he amputated. It was a person's arm, cut off at the elbow. Flesh and bone hung out of the severed end.

Melroy gasped and fell backwards into the hall. The blob of a man turned around to see what the commotion was all about, and when he saw a little kid, he shouted, "Hey, you little fuck! What the hell do you think you're doing in here?" Meat cleaver in hand, the fat fuck started charging towards him. His eyes were dark and sunken in, lusting for more blood and death.

He pissed his pants as the fat guy drew closer. He wanted to yell and scream for help, but who would listen? Those guys slurping spaghetti into their gullets weren't going to do a damn thing, so he just stood up, closed his eyes, and accepted the fate that was approaching.

But fate was on his side that day.

Maretto Rose pushed Melroy to the side, drew out a golden pistol from his waist, and fired multiple shots at the disgusting fat man. The shots were deafening in the closed capacity of space, so he covered his ears and watched as the fat man's chest and face exploded in a cloud of red. His enormous body then collapsed face-first to the ground. A river of blood quickly gushed towards Melroy, but Don Maretto grabbed him by the arm and took him away from the violent scene before the blood could reach him.

Melroy didn't remember much after that, except that he worried what the other three men in the apartment were going to do. To his surprise, they didn't do anything, and once Ric was in Maretto's possession as well, he escorted them down and out of the building.   Once in the limo, Maretto tried to calm him down, but he couldn't catch his breath. The scene was so terrifying and so horrific that Melroy made a life-altering decision after that day...

He wasn't ever going to be a member of the Rose Family.   Instead, he was going to dedicate his life to the law.

Don Xanose Cicello

And the Necessary Apology

The finish was rather sloppy. In fact, his whole technique was dwindling down to only a couple of moves lately. He wasn't the sex machine he used to be in his younger days. No, Don Xanose Cicello was getting older, and the whores he paid top dollar for were getting younger and freakier. Especially the one he just fucked. That cum-guzzler was into some fucked up shit. *Was it necessary for her to want to do all those positions?* Xanose contemplated while he got dressed. *I would've complained, but I need to keep an open mind in my older age.*

It didn't matter anyway. She was dead now. When they were done, he went to the bathroom and came back with a piano string that was hidden in his coat pocket. Xanose strangled her to death, and then sat next to her lifeless body, serenading her with a ballad in the old language. It was one of his addictions after screwing the same whore multiple times. He didn't want anyone else to experience them after he'd had his way over and over again. It was an evil vice. It was his thing.

After pulling up his white slacks, he buttoned up his baby blue dress shirt, and then slipped on a snazzy suit coat that was whiter than a rainless cloud. No matter how older, hairier, and fatter he got, Xanose still maintained a high standard of style. Yea, maybe he dressed the same way as his kids, but he'd be damned to be caught wearing morbid black and red suits like the Rose Family. A flashy and ritzy presentation was the Cicello way. Expensive gold chains, watches, sunglasses, and fancy clothes were a necessity.

Xanose casually walked into the bathroom of the hotel he was banging the whore in, and checked himself out in the mirror. Slicking the greasy black hair he had left on the top of his head, he noticed a few grays showing in his perfectly trimmed mustache. Oh well, the same was happening to the hair on the sides and back of his head. He squinted his already squinty eyes and thought, *there's nothing I can do about that. It's all part of getting old. I'm fifty-two fucking years old. More than half my life is already fucking over.*

In another twenty years, I'll be partway over the waterfall...if I don't fall over it sooner than that.

Leaving the roadside hotel, Xanose jumped in an extended white limo with navy blue leather seats, and ordered his driver to take him to *The Classic*; one of the many high-class casinos located on the downtown strip in the epicenter of the city of Vena. The hotel and the whore was only a small pitstop during his trip to Vena. He had to leave Juna for at least a couple of days, so he could get away from the bullshit that was piling up as a result from his eldest son's sloppy actions at the Grand Theater. The Rose Family was not happy and most likely blame him for the death of Don Maretto's son, so a visit to his close friend in Vena was a good option for now.

Cruising down the strip, Xanose admired the view of large modern buildings with flashing neon lights that turned the night sky so alit that it was a rarity to spot any stars. The warm climate of the south also produced exotic trees that bore rare fruits, which were lined in the grassy dividers between the roads leading in and out of the strip. The *Vena Strip* was the hotspot for high-roller casinos, five-star hotels, and fancy restaurants...It was his kind of place. Xanose thought about moving his Family to this city many times, but Juna was just too important to let go of. Besides, the strip was the only area of Vena with any prosperity. The rest of the city was a rotting pile of garbage.

Pulling up to The Classic, Xanose noticed a few renovations to the casino. A marble fountain with a life-like statue of an old king was placed in the middle of the parkway, spitting streams of water into a pool with multi-colored lights. Also, pillars of gold stood in front of the main entrance, and the valets were now dressed in sparkling suits of silver. His old friend was definitely trying to out-class the rest of the competition in town, and was succeeding.

Xanose's bodyguard stepped out of the passenger's side, walked to the back of the limo, and opened the door for his boss. *Rondo* formerly served for the ESFU, so he was a well-built physical machine, standing well over six lengths. He was originally from the deep south of Exodus, so his skin was naturally tanned and his short head of hair was a deep auburn. The man never smiled, but that's because he didn't have much to smile about. His wife and kids were slaughtered by a fellow agent of the ESFU, which coaxed him into leaving the President's personal unit and join Don Cicello in a life of murder and mayhem. Rondo never revealed the entire story of the reasons behind the slaughter of his family to his boss, but Xanose didn't give two shits anyway. Just so Rondo did his job in protecting him, he didn't care what happened in his past.

An SUV filled with Cicello thugs parked directly behind the limo. The pack of men exited the vehicle and followed closely behind Xanose and Rondo as they entered the casino.

Bells rang, coins jingled, and lights flashed over and over the moment Xanose stepped into the casino. The aroma of stale smoke, booze, and perfume smacked him in the face. Laughter and conversation meshed to produce the noise of a dull crowd. The place was packed with gamblers from all over Exodus, dishing out their hard-earned money for a chance to make themselves wealthier. Levers were pulled, cards were dealt, and roulette wheels were spun, adding fortune to some, but for most, the disappointment of a loss.

In a matter of moments, the head overseer of the casino greeted Xanose and his men in the front lobby. He was dressed in a black suit with a silver dress shirt, tie, and cuffs, and his long blonde hair was slicked back and tied in a ponytail. When Rondo whispered something into his ear, the overseer immediately broadcasted a flashy smile and motioned for the group to follow him.

The main floor was littered with slot machines, and the bells, chimes, beeps, and other pestering high-pitched sounds were already annoying the patriarch of the Cicello Family. Don Xanose preferred his gambling to be in a private room on a card table with soothing classical music playing in the background, while he smoked an expensive cigar and drank aged wine. Card games such as Poker and Twenty-One were a decadence compared to the lever-pulling machines that the spit of society liked to play.

The stink of the main floor was getting to him as well. A cloud of cig smoke hovered above the slot machines like a dense fog on a mid-summer night, and cheap perfumes and colognes invaded the nostrils with the putrid stench of lower class. *Fucking bottom dwellers,* Xanose thought of the casino patrons inhabiting the slots. They were all trying to get a quick piece of the action by hardly lifting a damn finger.

Elevator doors with a gold shine retracted into the walls, and the overseer led Xanose and Rondo inside. Xanose motioned for his men to stay on the main floor before the doors closed shut. The elevator carried them up only one floor and then the doors slid open again. The second floor was an open circle full of card tables, and was bordered with panes of glass, overlooking the main floor. The ceiling was a collection of mirrors with an eye in the sky camera, accompanied by a handful of silver chandeliers. Straight ahead, in the center of the circle, was a giant room closed to the public by a pair of white doors with gold handles, blocked by beams of transparent blue light.

The overseer opened a hidden panel next to the doors and punched in a code. The beams of light disappeared, and with a welcoming smile, the overseer opened the double doors, motioning Don Xanose to enter the room. Before he stepped inside, Xanose noticed a bit of commotion going on at a table on the far side of the open circle. A young man with curly black hair, wearing retro glasses and a cream white suit, violently threw down his hand of cards, smacked his stack of chips unto the floor, and reached across the table, grabbing the dealer by his shirt collar. The young man looked infuriated. It must not be his lucky day.

Noticing the curiosity in the Don's eyes, the overseer said, "Don't worry about him. It's just Don Maximo's youngest son, Lucius. He gets that way when he's on a losing streak."

"I can see that," Xanose replied, before stepping into the private room. Rondo did his duty and waited outside as the overseer shut the doors and initiated the barricades of light.

Don Maximo Rocca sat behind a large marble desk with a glass top, and just finished snorting a long line of powder as Don Xanose entered his private office. Rising out of his brown leather chair with a beaming smile across his face, Maximo opened his arms and welcomed his guest. "Don Xanose, my good friend. Welcome to the new and improved Classic casino." His smile was plastered on his face in the shape of an upside-down triangle. "How do you like what I've done to the place? Pretty impressive, huh."

Xanose took a long look around his surroundings. The walls and ceiling were made of white marble while the floor was a hard glass with neon lights projecting underneath. The wall on the right side of the room had an array of glass shelves, littered with expensive bottles of liquor behind a mini oak bar counter, while the left wall contained a giant aquarium built into the wall with an oceanic-like ecosystem and rare colorful fish. In front of Maximo's desk was a set of leather chairs, small tables with round tops, and a white rug with gold tassels and a fancy blue 'R' in the center. Behind his desk, a clear window overlooked the main floor, and a giant flat-screen video monitor was anchored just above it.

His eyebrows raised when he answered, "Very nice, Don Maximo. I see that the casino is treating you well these days." He sniffed the air and his nose was filled with the sweet aroma of herb smoke.

Maximo waved a hand and said, "The expenses threw me back a bit, but as you saw downstairs, my casino is bringing in some coin." He walked around his desk directly towards Xanose. With open arms, he embraced the Cicello patriarch and then kissed him on both cheeks. "Your mind wonders, my friend." He motioned his hand to one of the leather chairs. "Have a seat."

"I rather stand for now," Xanose replied, looking the Rocca patriarch up and down. Maximo aged rather well with only streaks of gray in his curly fro of black hair. The skin on his face was a golden tan with only slight wrinkles, and there were no dark circles under his big round eyes that hid behind black-rimmed glasses. He stood almost a length taller than Xanose and had a thin frame in his snazzy white suit with black pinstripes. Maximo never bothered to wear a tie. He let the top of his shirt unbuttoned, spilling out straggling chest hairs.

"Hey, if you wanna stand, then that's no sweat off my sac. How about a couple lines of the finest powder in the city?" Maximo offered, pointing a finger at his desk.

Shaking his head, Xanose replied, "I can't do that shit anymore at my age. That's just asking for a heart attack."

Maximo walked around his desk, snatched up a small metal tube, put it to his big nose and said, "Suit yourself. This is the only shit that keeps me going sometimes." He snorted a long line of powder, causing his bushy eyebrows to crinkle his forehead. Rubbing some of the remnants on his yellow teeth, he then asked, "So is there something you want to tell me, Don Xanose?"

Folding his arms, Xanose answered, "Like what?"

After doing a smaller line and rubbing more bits of powder on his teeth, Maximo sat down in his brown leather chair, put his arms behind his head in a relaxing position, and said, "Your son, Zasso, pulled a nice little stunt at the Grand Theater. The attempted abduction of Don Maretto Rose, and the murder of one of his golden boys. Now, I have to tell you, Xanose, it seems as though the Cicello Family is up to some pretty heavy business, and I'm just sitting down here in Vena shoving powder up my nose and playing with my dick. I figured you would inform an old friend if you were going to move in on the Rose Family. I thought we had an agreement." He placed his hands in front of him and started tapping his fingers on the desk, antsy from the high-octane powder.

Lowering his head and giving a half-grin, Xanose replied, "You know I wouldn't make any moves without talking to you first, Max."

"Then why is your son attacking Don Maretto Rose?"

"I have no idea."

"Bullshit!" Maximo shouted as he pounded his fist on the desk, nearly shattering the glass surface.

There were a few moments of silence between the two Family leaders. Maximo leaned back in his chair with a scowl on his face, while Xanose casually walked over to the bar area.

When Xanose grabbed a glass and one of the brown liquors off the shelf, Maximo said, "Sure. Have a fucking drink."

Ignoring his friend's bitter attitude, he poured a healthy sized portion of booze in the glass, swished it around, and took a sip. Xanose nodded his head, gave an impressed look over at Maximo, and said, "Not bad. A little spicy, but not bad."

"Are you gonna play with my emotions all night, or are you gonna tell me what the fuck is going on?" Maximo asked, trying to keep himself calm.

Carefully placing the glass of liquor on the bar counter, Xanose replied, "There has been no change in what we've talked about, Max. My friendship with you continues to be loyal as always."

"And why should I believe you? I'm always left in the dark down here in this shithole, rubbing elbows with the other grease monkey-fuck Families. They've been getting on my case about your son, asking me what the fuck your Family is up to. And what am I supposed to say? That I don't know?"

"Well, that is the truth."

Jumping out of his chair and flailing his arms about, Maximo said, "This is just unbelievable, Xanose. Unbelievable!" He pointed a finger directly at Xanose and shouted, "How can you lie right to my face after all that we've talked about and planned out? We go back a long way, me and you, and you never once lied like a fucking fiend to me before."

Xanose threw back the rest of the liquor, slammed down the glass and said, "And I'm not lying to you now, Max!" He paused and let the burning sensation of the spicy liquor in his throat secede, before he continued, "My son acted on his own accord. I had no prior knowledge that he was going to attack the Grand Theater and try to take Maretto Rose. If I would've had any knowledge of this plan, then I would have put a stop to it immediately, because it was stupid…Attacking the most renowned man in Exodus in public is just plain idiotic. The last thing I wanted was the public spotlight to be on *my* Family. Underworld business is not something the media and the public needs to witness firsthand, and now the President, the Legislation, and the rest of Exodus is going to be pointing a red-hot poker in my face until my son is found…Do you think I want to be the center of attention, Max? Do you think I like to be under the microscope of the media?" Xanose didn't give Maximo any time to answer his question. "The answer is no! No!

Maretto Rose might like to flaunt himself and his kids in front of the cameras, but I'm a man who takes pride in the secrecy of what the Seven Blessed Families do when the rest of the world isn't looking."

Folding his arms across his chest, Maximo's mouth formed a sly grin before he said, "Okay Xanose. I'll put my trust in our friendship and believe what you tell me."

"Thank you," Xanose said back, then poured himself another drink.

"My eldest does the same shit sometimes. Always making trips to other cities, pushing his product and getting himself into precarious situations. He never listens to a fucking word I say."

Xanose cracked a smile and sipped on his drink.

"My youngest, Lucius, on the other hand; I can't seem to get him the fuck away from me."

The remark made Xanose chuckle a bit. "I can't seem to get my youngest the fuck away from other men."

The comment caused Maximo to roar in laughter.

"It's like one dick after another with that kid. If he puts any more jiz in his stomach, he could open his own sperm bank."

Maximo laughed so hard that he was on the verge of tears. "I'm amazed that you're able to joke about it. I would've killed my sons if they brought home another man."

"Well, I *did* have some of the men Michiela brought home killed, but he keeps bringing more back. It's like he's growing faggots in our back yard."

Laughing hard again, Maximo bent over his desk and shoved some more powder up his nose. When he straightened back up, he tilted his head back and took a couple hard sniffs to get the powder to the back of his sinuses and down his throat. After a fit of coughs, he said, "I'm glad that you took time out of your busy life to come see an old friend, Xanose. There's a lot of business that I've wanted to discuss with you in person."

Reaching inside his coat pocket, Xanose brought out a silver case engraved with an 'X'. He opened up the case and snagged one of the brown cigars being stored inside. "Well, I'm here, so what business do you want to discuss?"

Maximo snatched a fancy lighter off his desk, made his way over to Xanose, drew a flame, and helped him ignite his cigar. Xanose puffed on it a few times and then blew a couple of smoke rings in the air. Maximo then put out the flame and softly said, "You know what I want to talk about…The agreement we made. Our alliance against the Rose Family."

After another round of puffs, Xanose cordially responded, "And that alliance still stands. More than ever now that the Rose Family believes that I'm responsible for the Grand Theater massacre."

"Yea, well I'm sure you can't really blame them. Your son is under *your* command."

The comment drove Xanose to frown. "My son is rebelling against me. He's taking matters into his own hands."

"And what matters would that be?"

Seemingly not pleased, Xanose stared directly into Maximo's eyes and said, "You still don't believe me, do you Max? Why is it you lack so much faith and trust in your closest friend? Is it so hard to believe that my oldest and most powerfully Blessed son would take it upon himself to make a move against the almighty Don Maretto without consulting me first?"

Maximo simply shrugged his shoulders.

"Zasso is an ignorant young man, who doesn't follow the old rules of order between the Seven Families. He doesn't care about an allegiance between Families. He thirsts for power."

Shrugging again, Maximo said, "Well, I suppose that's plausible."

Grinning and shaking his head, Xanose ran a hand through his thinning greasy hair and puffed on his cigar. "Of all the patriarchs of the Seven Blessed Families, I never thought I would have to convince *you* of my innocence."

"If it were my son who committed the attack on the Grand Theater, wouldn't you be skeptical of my participation? I know your son is strong and gifted, but he is also very young and easily influenced by others of higher power...Especially his father." Xanose gave another frown, but Maximo continued regardless. "But I know you Xanose. And the Grand Theater massacre isn't your style. So, do I believe you? Yes, I suppose I do. Like I said before, my own son has taken the initiative of conducting business deals that I highly disagree with. He even tries to partner up with our own enemies. But that doesn't mean I don't have the right to be a little skeptical of the whole situation. If I wasn't, then I wouldn't be a very good leader of my Family."

Nodding his head once, Xanose said, "This is true."

Maximo put his right hand over the area of his heart and said, "But I swore to you on my life and the lives of my children that I would never defy you and forever be a loyal ally in our endeavor to reign over the other Families together. And that is how it will remain." His words brought a slight grin on the face of his partner. "I can see the future now, my friend. The Cicello Family and the Rocca Family, ruling the nation of Exodus as one."

Impressed with his friend's words, Xanose grabbed a second glass from under the bar and filled it with brown liquor. He offered the glass to Maximo, who graciously accepted the act of kindness. Xanose then raised his glass in a salute and proclaimed, "To the future of our Families, and to the end of the Rose Family. May Don Maretto Rose someday *not* rest in peace."

Nodding in agreement with a drawn-out smile and clinking glasses with Xanose, the Rocca patriarch pronounced, "A salute." He tossed back the entire contents of liquor, cringing from the spiciness, but also letting out a refreshed gasp of air.

Xanose let out a refreshing gasp as well. *I have Maximo exactly where I want him still,* he deviously thought to himself. "Now, back to our business with the other Families. How are our informants coming along?"

"Very nicely. They are all fully infiltrated deep into the other four Families. I have received valuable information from all of them."

"Good. Now fill me in," Xanose commanded.

Without hesitation, Maximo exposed the secret information. "Don *Alfonto Triglione* is sick. Bedridden and deathly ill. I'm not sure how much time he has left, but the informant has assured me that his eldest son, *Petoro*, has a key that he wears as a necklace at all times. That key could be the access to the *Triglione Family* Relic, but to be sure, he is going to follow Petoro more closely when he is not sitting bedside with his father.

"Don *Elmonzo Flagella* has quite the weakness for young and beautiful girls. And we're not talking about young women in their twenties. He likes them in their teens. Delicate flowers that have just begun to bloom into their bodies. His weakness is so bad that my informant has heard rumors that he will give a young lady a private viewing of the *Flagella Family* Relic, just to get her pants off. A bony old tree is not so appealing to an attractive young flower, until the tree shows the flower an intriguing and powerful root he has hidden underground."

"So, I take it you and the informant will be planting your own delicate flower for Elmonzo," Xanose deciphered with a cunning grin.

Maximo's mouth formed the triangular smile. "Yes indeed, my friend…As for the lovely Miss *Lamora Luccetta.* She has still not given up her husband's power to her son, insisting that he is far too young for the responsibility of patriarch to the *Luccetta Family.* But that works to our advantage, because a woman can be easily persuaded to reveal a secret if she is enticed by a handsome and charming man to replace her dead husband. Our informant fits the bill. Soon enough he will be seducing our lady friend into showing him where the Luccetta Family Relic is. He specializes in fucking old cunt. He has a knack for it."

After a slight chuckle, Xanose asked, "And what about our friend in *Sonia*. I hope he's not soaking in too much sun to get his duty done."

Maximo slightly hesitated before he answered, "I haven't heard from that friend for a couple weeks now."

Eyebrows scrunching, Xanose looked deterred when he said, "You just said that all four informants were deeply infiltrated into the other four Families. So what about the *Javoni Family?*"

Pouring himself another drink, Maximo explained, "Well, the last time I heard from him, he told me that he and Don *Calio Javoni* were becoming quite close. The young patriarch took a liking to him immediately since they both have a love for the game of batball. And since Calio owns the Sonia Sultans, they were planning to attend a lot of games together this season and placing heavy bets. From what he told me, everything was going according to plan, and he would find the location of the Javoni Family Relic in a matter of weeks...The problem is, is that I haven't heard from him since. Not a phone call or anything...Nothing."

"He's dead," Xanose blurted out without a thought.

"You don't know that."

"Trust me, he's dead. Either that, or he turned against us; which would make him a dead man anyway." Xanose puffed on his cigar with a distasteful look on his face.

Staring off into nothing, Maximo sipped on his beverage, most likely thinking about the possibility of his informant turning on him. "Well, if that's the case, then I'll just have to send someone new down to the Deep South. It's not hard to convince one of my men to hang out in a city built on a beach."

Xanose didn't say a word. He just shrugged and smoked his cigar.

"We and the other Families have always placed the Javoni Family at the bottom of the food chain. It was for a good reason in the past. I mean, Gasto Jovani was a drunken fool and a terrible patriarch, but there's something different about his son. Calio could become a menace," Maximo said, still staring off into space and thinking hard.

140

This Calio guy has him spooked, Xanose thought as he watched Maximo walk away from the bar toward the windows overlooking the casino's main floor. *He could end up being a threat to my plans...Or an even younger and stronger ally...*

Staring down at the casino patrons pumping coins into the slot machines, Maximo put a hand on the window and asked, "So, how are you going to convince Maretto Rose that you had nothing to do with the death of his son? This is not a good time to have friction between your Families. Your son has certainly stirred things up."

Scratching the stubble on his chin, Xanose replied, "The Rose Family wants to have a private meeting with me. And even though I deny having anything to do with Zasso's actions, they still want an apology for what he did. Don Maretto believes that it is my responsibility as a parent, the smug son of a bitch."

Looking over his shoulder, Maximo said, "Then that's exactly what you need to do. Apologize for Zasso's behavior."

With a heckling laugh, Xanose said, "I rather die than apologize to a Rose."

"Then die you will. If you don't apologize and right the relationship that has taken a turn for the worse, then they will strongly believe that you *did* give the order to Zasso, and will hit you with everything they got."

"I'd like to see them try," Xanose arrogantly proposed.

"Oh, they'll try," Maximo hoarsely said, staring back out the window. "And it could be detrimental to our allegiance. You must apologize and ask for their forgiveness, so they could be convinced that your Families will remain on decent terms. It is necessary for the future of our Families, Don Xanose." He turned around to face his friend, who was muttering obscenities to himself while puffing on his cigar. "If the Rose Family catches wind of anything that we are planning, then I fear for both of us," he morbidly uttered. "I have no doubt that we can fight them and beat them when they are not looking, but when you awaken the beast that is Maretto Rose...you might get your head bitten off."

After a few more drinks and conversation that didn't have to do with business, Don Xanose decided it was time to leave Maximo's casino and depart the city of Vena. He was in no mood to stay up all night gambling, and give away his hard-earned money to the Rocca Family. He wanted to go back to the comforts of his own home, no matter how strenuous matters were back in the city of Juna. Problems were eventually going to have to be dealt with. Hiding out in another city wasn't going to solve anything.

His bodyguard, Rondo, walked alongside him out of the casino, followed by the entourage of thugs behind them. His private white stretch limo was waiting for him, and Rondo dutifully opened the back door for his boss. "Tell the driver to take this thing to the skies whenever we hit the highway. I'm ready to go home," he ordered.

Rondo adhered to the command with a nod and closed the door when his boss was securely inside the vehicle. When inside, Xanose closed his eyes and took a long and deep breath, trying to keep his head from spinning after consuming more liquor than he wanted to while spending time with Maximo. When he opened his eyes back up, he was shocked to notice that he wasn't alone in the limo. Sitting in front of the tinted window that separated the driver from the rest of the vehicle, helping himself to a glass of wine, was his eldest son Zasso.

"Why hello there, papa," Zasso greeted his father with a cheesy smile. "Hope you don't mind that I dipped into your wine. I got kind of thirsty while waiting for you." He was dressed in his commonly worn royal blue suit and fedora. A small mirror with remnants of powder was propped on the seat next to him.

Xanose's face reddened at the sight of his boy. "What the hell are you doing here? And how did you sneak into my limo?"

"It's good to see you too, papa," Zasso replied, raising his glass.

"Cut the fucking shit, Zasso. You better hope no one saw you."

Zasso leaned back and said, "Relax, nobody saw me. Papa didn't raise no fool."

142

"Are you sure about that?" The color in his face went back to its normal pigment as he unbuttoned the top of his shirt and lounged back in the leather seat. "Fools do foolish things."

"Uh oh, I feel a fatherly lecture coming along," Zasso mockingly said. "You're not angry with me about what happened at the Grand Theater, are you? It's not like I wanted the situation to get out of control like it did. It was rather misfortunate."

"Misfortunate? I don't ever recall running into a building like you own the place, and killing everyone you see, a misfortunate situation."

A sly grin grew across Zasso's face as he replied, "Well, to be quite honest papa, I pretty much *did* own the place that night."

Xanose leaned forward, and with red-hot eyes yelled, "You murdered one of Maretto Rose's sons!"

"A bonus in my eyes," Zasso snidely remarked.

The Cicello patriarch's eyes seemed as though they were going to explode out of his head. "You did it at a public event! The murder of the most renowned man in Exodus's son in front of everyone! And innocent people! You even killed the most famous actor in modern times!"

Zasso waved a hand at his father as if he didn't care what he did. "Oh well. Even if I didn't kill Georgiano and the rest of those fools, the whole nation of Exodus would be on my nuts about me attacking Maretto Rose; the one and only Father of Gangster. Exodus's favorite son." A scowl draped over his face. "If the people only knew how despicable he really is." After taking a hard swallow of wine, he threw his glass at the window, shattering it into pieces.

Paying no mind to the lack of respect for his limo, Xanose said, "If I knew you were going to try to capture Maretto Rose at a public event with hundreds of bystanders watching, I would never had agreed to let you carry out the mission. It was a sloppy move, and the Cicello Family is better than that. Now I have to convince everyone that I had nothing to do with the attack; especially the Rose Family. Deny, deny, deny! That's what

I have to do on a daily basis from here on out." Xanose calmed himself back down, fixed his ruffled suit coat, and tried relaxing back in his seat. "I've been doing the same damn shit ever since you were a kid. Denying that it was *you* who stole donation money from the church. Denying that it was *you* who convinced that kid to poison your teacher. Denying all those murders that *you* committed since you were a teenager. And denying to myself that *you* enjoy watching other men rape and kill helpless women…That denial is the hardest one of all. My own son with a sick and twisted fetish."

His father's condemning words didn't seem to bother Zasso. Instead, he smiled and said, "We all have our sick fetishes, papa. I don't believe strangling prostitutes after you've had your way with them, translates into a healthy pastime."

This time Xanose waved a shoving hand at his son, and watched out the window as the limo picked up speed on the highway. The roads were clear of other vehicles, so the driver pressed the ignition switch for manual flight. High octane boosters replaced the back taillights, and with a booming infusion of power, the booster released blue fire, lifting the limo into the air.

While gazing at the shrinking ground, Xanose said to his son, "I'll have my driver land on the outskirts of Juna and drop you off. It is a must that we take every precaution. You cannot be seen with me."

With dead-staring eyes, Zasso replied back to his father, "I'll be exiting the limo long before that."

Curiously, Xanose asked, "How?"

"You'll see," Zasso simply answered.

Xanose looked back out the window and pondered a thought, which he didn't keep to himself. "We've gotten ourselves into a deep mess."

"A mess that will be easily cleaned up," Zasso responded.

"I wish I could believe your words, my son," Xanose said, shaking his head. "But we've made a critical decision that's going to alter everything within the walls of the Seven

Blessed Families. Soon enough, life in Exodus will never be the same." His tone was morbid, almost regretful.

"As if we had a choice, papa," Zasso said with a smirk.

Xanose slowly turned his head, looked upon his son with hopeless eyes, and nodded.

Zasso rose from his seat, having to slightly duck in the oversized limo. "Oh, by the way, your other son came looking for me the other day. I thought you told no one of my new residence for the time being."

"Who? Miro?" His son nodded. "I didn't tell him anything."

Zasso drew a coy smile. "You're right, papa. I told him…Just testing you."

The Cicello patriarch wasn't in the mood for tests. "What the hell did he want from you?"

Pressing a button on the panel next to the sunroof, the limo was now exposed to open air. Zasso took off his fedora and let the wind blow through his long, black hair. "He was running away from an interesting encounter with one of the Rose boys. Seems as though Don Maretto was trying to infiltrate one of our clubs in order to find out where I was hiding."

With a curious tone of voice and eyebrows raised, Xanose responded with a drawn out, "Really?" He then asked, "Which Rose boy was it? Jon-Jon? No, Jon-Jon is the heir," he answered himself. "Maretto wouldn't send the shiniest of his golden boys to do some dirty work…Then it must have been that hothead, Alto."

Zasso simply shook his head as a no and said, "He sent the youngest…Ric Rose."

Don Xanose was flabbergasted by the revelation. "The junky?"

As an answer to that question, Zasso nodded and grinned from ear to ear. "It was a smart move. Maretto Rose is an asshole, but he's the smartest of the assholes…It's just too bad for him that Ric Rose cares more about his next fix than he does about his own Family." Zasso reached in his pocket and pulled out a shiny silver disk. He tossed it to the floor in front of his feet, and the small disk protracted and grew itself into a large saucer. He stepped forward and stood on top of the disk that now looked like a big shiny shield. Shackles automatically strapped over his feet as a glowing blue light appeared underneath.

The silver saucer began to hover off the floor as Zasso gave his father a salute with his hand. "Arrivederci, papa," he said goodbye in the old language.

Xanose gave a slight nod and watched with intrigue as his son boosted through the sunroof and flew off into the night sky on the hovering saucer. His only thought was, *Ric Rose, huh? Hmmm.*

Salic Stone

And the Don of the Deep South

Delightful bright rays of sunshine penetrating on white-sand beaches along the coast of a deep blue ocean that expands to an infinite horizon. Extravagant beach houses with ocean-view balconies surrounded by tropical palm trees, overlooking the masquerades of tourists soaking up the deep southern sun. Piers that stretch hundreds of lengths out into the water and docks with luxury ships and boats that turn the ocean into an aquatic playground. Hotels, bars, clubs, casinos, and boardwalks that extend from the sand into the mainland where an entire city is encouraged to never sleep a wink…Sonia. The Deep South of Exodus…A tropical paradise. A city that inhales the daytime sun, and exhales the festive nightlife under starry night skies.

That is the view of many who live in the southernmost major city in Exodus. And that is how *Salic Stone* viewed the city when he arrived a handful of months ago. His breath was taken away by its beauty. *How could any of the other Families live so far up north where it gets cold and dreary half the year,* is what Salic would think to himself every day, as he woke up to such peace, tranquility, and warmth. The salty smell of the ocean and the sounds of waves crashing into the shoreline is what he would fall asleep to every night. He never had such good sleep. Not in the big cities up north. The sounds were irritant, and the smells were god-awful. How can you compare the sounds and smells of a beach to that of a sewer system? The answer, is that you can't.

It didn't take Salic long after he arrived to realize that Sonia is where his home really ought to be. Not Juna. And especially not Vena. Sure Vena's weather was a bit comparable to Sonia, but most of the city was a trash bag…But not Sonia. Every inch of the oceanic city was enchanting to him. The white beaches, the palm trees, the blue sea, the docks, piers, boardwalks, batball fields, daytime cookouts, nighttime festivals of lights, drinking cocktails in the sun, riding high-powered boats through the tides, beautiful tanned women, the robbing of helpless victims, and the ease of getting away with murder…Everything.

It was a new life for Salic, and a life that he fell in love with. He also fell in love with a man, but not in the gay kind of way. He loved his new boss. The man he was sent to spy on. The Family that he was ordered to infiltrate by his boss up north; Don Calio Jovani, the leader and patriarch of the Jovani Family.

Salic Stone was a Rocca Family thug. He grew up on the hard streets of Southside Vena. A rat's nest. When he was a boy, his abusive alcoholic mother would turn tricks at night and would complain all during the day that his father was a no-good deadbeat who gave them no money. And the reason his father was a deadbeat, was because his father was *dead*. Killed in the line of duty for the Rocca Family when Salic was just three years old. It always gave him a bitter taste in his mouth when his mother would bitch about his poor father. Who the fuck gives a man shit because he died trying to provide for his family? The whore. The motherfucking whore of a woman.

Anyway, Salic Stone was a hard earner and a trustworthy, loyal follower of Maximo Rocca and his sons. He would've done anything for the Rocca Family. Robbery, extortion, drug dealing, murder…anything. So, when the day came that Don Maximo personally asked for his services and ordered him to do cozy up to the Don of the Deep South, infiltrate deep into the Family, and discover where the Jovani Family kept their sacred Relic, Salic said 'yes' before the words even came out of his mouth. 'I would be honored, Don Maximo,' was the exact verbatim. A trip down south to get away from the streets of Vena and do his loyal duty for his leader was the perfect opportunity for Salic…*Loyalty*. Oh, how things can change at the drop of a hat.

One month around Don Calio Jovani and the rest of the Jovani Family. That's all the time it took to change his mind and his lifetime allegiance. One fucking month.

Salic's facade was that he was a drifter from one of the small villages on the southeastern shores, looking to make some real money in the big city. His expertise was robbery and explosions; which in fact was true about him. Salic loved stealing. It was his passion. But he also loved using explosive devices for certain business transactions.

Usually murder, but he enjoyed intertwining his two passions as well. Using a bomb to cause a chaotic scene amid a robbery was a sure way to get to the money or valuable items he was after.

The first night he arrived in Sonia, Salic stole a small speedboat and drove it out into the black waters about a couple hundred lengths away from Don Calio's yacht; which was anchored off the shore and in the middle of a late-night boat party. He set the timer on an explosive, jumped overboard, and with a bag full of cash tied around his waist, he started swimming towards the beautiful white yacht in the distance. When the bomb detonated, there was an awesome display of fire and debris that blasted off the water and high into the night sky. When Calio and his men witnessed the awe-inspiring blast, their focus of attention was no longer the music, drinks, and women happening on the yacht. It was the huge explosion and the man slowly drifting in the water towards their location.

Without any questioning, Calio's men threw a rope over the side of the yacht and pulled Salic up to safety. Everyone aboard was rather intoxicated from the night's festivities and impressed with the grand explosion on the water, so instead of interrogating the mystery swimmer right away, they let him dry off, change into new clothes, have a drink and a snort of some powder, and then allowed him to join the party. He was an instant hit. Salic told an entertaining story of a robbery gone awry, and the escape by the skin of his teeth, he had to make into open waters on a stolen boat. The explosion was for safe measures to trick his pursuers into thinking he had been blown to bits.

After the impressive tale, Don Calio had him brought to his private room, and then the interrogation started. Salic simply told the Jovani patriarch that he'd been drifting from one village to another along the southeastern shoreline, until he finally ended up in Sonia, where he hoped to make the big bucks performing daunting heists, instead of the petty thievery he'd been doing his whole life.

Don Calio bought every word of it. And he also enjoyed Salic's company. Very much so after Salic handed him the bag full of cash and assured him that there was a lot more where that came from if he was allowed to do some work for his Family. Calio agreed, and soon enough, they became close friends. They had many things in common, including a love for the sport of batball, the taste of women and fine herbs and powders, and the thrill of crime and murder.

So, in no time at all, Salic was working high-end jobs for the Jovani Family, and running personal errands for Don Calio himself. His impressive talent for robberies and explosions came in great use for the Don, and after a good month and a half, Salic Stone was initiated into the Jovani Family. He accomplished his initial job, and would soon be told of the location of their Relic, known as the *Triad*...But there was a problem. Salic Stone didn't want to help Don Maximo Rocca steal their Relic anymore. He was in love with Jovani Family, and wanted to stay permanently. Don Calio Jovani gave Salic a lot more than just money and other gratitude in return for his hard work and dedication. He gave him respect. Respect that he would never receive from Maximo. Maximo was a prick. In all honesty, Don Maximo and his sons would most likely repay him for his duties with an early grave. An informant didn't last long in this business. To the Rocca Family, the solution for keeping one silenced forever was to kill and get rid of the evidence.

When a few more months went by, and his relationship with Don Calio grew closer and closer, Salic couldn't deal with his conscience anymore, so he decided it was time to come clean. He'd been reporting to Don Maximo every two weeks, coming up with bullshit stories about his infiltration, but he let an extra week go by without checking in, so that Maximo would start to believe that something had gone wrong and the Jovani Family had taken care of the spy that had been fooling them. Well, the Jovani Family *was* about to find out that there was a spy in their midst, but Salic was going to reveal it to them on his own accord.

It was a rather cool and breezy morning when Salic paid an impromptu visit to Calio's ocean-view mansion, and without reservation, he told his new boss the truth. He was a spy for the Rocca Family. The disgust and heartbreak on the face of Calio almost brought the usually rugged and fearsome Salic to tears, but he remained calm when he explained why he was coming clean. He didn't want to be a Rocca thug. He wanted to be at Calio's side from here on out. He would die many deaths for the Don of the Deep South, and would pay any penance necessary for his deception. Even if it meant his death.

Calio was furious. He wanted to hear nothing more from the man who deceived him, so shortly after Salic unveiled the truth, he was immediately bound and shackled, and thrown into a hidden cell underneath his mansion, rarely used in recent times. It reminded Salic of an old dungeon cell that he visited on a school field trip. Cold, dark, and gloomy. The walls were cracked and dripping water from the crevices as if it were sweating out the southern heat. The ceiling was caked with mildew and the floor was nothing but dirt and small rocks. The bars to his cell were black with spots of rust. The rotten smell of decomposed vermin took over the room. In the area outside his cell there was only an old wooden chair and small table, but during the three long days he was shackled to the wall with iron chains, not one Family member sat down to keep him company. He was given one piece of bread and meager rations of water. The man who was given the job to bring him that water, *Petro Palini*-Calio's Underboss and right-hand man-was just as disgusted with him, since they too became close friends since his arrival. Now, Petro treated him like a disgraceful human being. Not even worthy of small chat during his trips down to his cell.

During the three brutal days of captivity, Salic still held onto a slight ray of hope. One of the initiations into the Family is the diamond-studded piercings in both earlobes and the middle of the forehead, symbolizing a triangular effect that represents the Triad Relic. When a member is deemed a traitor to the Family or killed for insubordination, the piercings are immediately ripped off them to signify the end of their membership…Salic was not stripped of the diamond studs, which led him to believe that his punishment could only go as far as being held captive for some time. But during the third night, his hopes were diminishing. He was stripped of his shirt and bare from the waist up, and the underground chill was causing him to shake uncontrollably and produced a fever. Maybe their plan was to starve him and let the fever kill him during one of the nights, before they ultimately removed the piercings. The fever was causing delusions. He saw visions of himself lying on the floor, gasping for air as his skin rotted off his tissue and bones, while slimy white maggots crawled all over his body. His demise would be of suffering.

The next morning, or so he surmised it was morning time, the latch to the wood-planked door of the underground prison clicked, and the door creaked open. Standing like a shadow in the darkness, with a lit candle in his right hand and a set of keys in his left, was Petro Palini. Petro was tall with a toned muscular build. His blonde spiky hair had streaks of black in it, and his golden tanned face brought out the radiance of his bright blue eyes. He had little facial hair besides the small blonde patch under his bottom lip. He was wearing a neon orange short-sleeved shirt made of fine silk and white pants. One thick gold-chained necklace was draped around his neck.

Stepping inside the murky room and towards the cell, Petro showed the keys in his left hand to Salic, jingled them around and said, "Your time is up, spy. Don Calio would like to speak with you now." The tone of his voice was flat with no emotion. Not the usually high-spirited tone he was used to.

The iron chains of his shackles clinked and clanked as Salic weakly rose to his feet. With a tight grip with his hands, he pulled the chains closer to his muscular chest. His arm muscles bulged out when he flexed. With his brown eyes barely open, he let out a grunt and said, "That's too bad. It was just starting to get cozy down here." Salic's curly black hair was in disarray. Some of the fine curls covered his ears and dangled at the neck. Cold sweat dripped off the tips and down his tanned face.

A half a smile slipped from the corner of Petro's mouth. He knew all too well of Salic's sarcastic humor. *We shared a lot of laughs together, Petro and I. I'm sure he hasn't forgotten how much fun we had. We drank, gambled, chased women, robbed, and murdered together…Shit, we even shared the same broad one night.*

Letting out a simpering sigh, Salic said, "Hopefully you will forgive me someday, as I hope Don Calio will." His voice was deeper and raspier than normal.

Petro took one step closer to the cell. "I've already forgiven you, my friend." His words caused Salic's eyes to light up. "The work you did for our Family never went unnoticed. A normal spy would not infiltrate as deep as you did, and I believe that you had a change in heart when you realized how much this Family cared for you. No other member was ever given the special treatment that you were, and no other member climbed the ranks as fast as you did. You are a good friend of mine, and that is hard to come by in the business we are in."

With almost a sigh of relief, Salic said, "I'm glad that you see it that way, Petro."

"But I'm not the one who has the final say. Don Calio is. And he hasn't spoken about your confession since the first day you were sent down here. All he said was to keep you locked up until he was ready to speak to you." With two fingers, he held a single key from the rest of the key ring. "And now he is ready. So, let's go and meet your fate." He shoved the key inside the keyhole of the iron lock that was connected to a thick chain wrapped around the cell door. There was a loud click when the lock popped, and then Petro unwrapped the chain and pulled open the door. It gave a shrieking creak that pinched the eardrums.

Petro escorted Salic through the ocean-view mansion, which was three stories high with the walls all painted white. Don Calio spared no expense when it came to accoutrements in his home. Most of the walls were decorated with expensive oil paintings with mostly uplifting depictions of different types of beautiful scenery. He also owned all the latest technology in home entertainment, appliances, and lighting, and had a state-of-the-art gym built on to the side of the first floor, so his men could come and work out their bodies to become more physically fit. Don Calio took great pride in the appearance of his Family members, so his men spent an avid amount of time getting into shape in his personal gym.

When the two men finished their hike to the third floor, they entered the master bedroom, furnished with a king-sized bed, a couple nightstands and dressers made of marble with gold knobs, and a video monitor that was the size of the entire wall. The closet doors were a collection of standing mirrors, and the darkened bathroom appeared to be almost the same size as the bedroom. A glass sliding door separated the bedroom from the outside balcony, so Petro slid it open and motioned Salic to step through.

The balcony was the same white color as the rest of the mansion, and extended out over the first-floor patio that reached to the edge of the sandy dunes leading to the beach. An extensive glass table sat near the railing with a large umbrella posted in the middle to shield occupants from the blazing hot sun. And sitting near the end of the table, with his legs crossed and enjoying an early morning cocktail and cig, was the Don of the Deep South himself, Don Calio Jovani.

The Don was wearing a pair of dark sunglasses with golden frames under his thin eyebrows. His hair was dark brown, his face an orange-hued tan, and he had a hard jawline. A thin strip of facial hair extended from his sideburns down to his chin and connected with a thin mustache. The diamond studs in his ears and on his forehead sparkled even in the shade as he puffed away on his cig. His upper body was adorned with a gold chain inlaid with diamonds and a white buttoned-down shirt that exposed his hairless chest, tight enough to show off his muscular toned body. Instead of pants, he sported a pair of white shorts with brown sandals.

When Salic entered through the sliding glass door, Don Calio shifted in his chair to make himself comfortable. Salic slowly walked towards the glass table with Petro following closely behind. The shackles that bound his hands in front of his body clanked with each step. When Salic reached the table, Don Calio had a disgusted look on his face. *He looks pissed at me,* Salic thought as he approached the patriarch. *And I don't blame him one fucking bit.*

With a wave of his hand, Calio said, "Are the shackles really necessary, Petro? Take them off."

Both Petro and Salic looked confused. *So, he looks disgusted because my hands are bound?*

"You were the one who told me to use the shackles, Calio," Petro said back, eyebrows raised.

Now Don Calio was the one who looked confused. "Oh, did I?" With another wave of his hand he said, "Well, I must have been shitfaced drunk and in one hell of a bad mood when I made that decision. Take them off."

Salic tried not to show a smile. The sound of Don Calio's voice did that to him. His voice was soft and flowing, but had an easy rasp and a distinct flavor to it. It was the coolest sound he ever heard.

Stepping in front of Salic, Petro used a different key from the keychain to unfasten the shackles binding his hands. When they were off, Salic rubbed his hands and felt a sense

154

of relief. But he wasn't out of trouble yet. Don Calio could be very conniving. One second he's smiling in your face, and the next he's slashing your throat.

Calio looked Salic up and down and said, "You look terrible. Your pants are so dirty. What were you doing down there? Rolling around in the dirt?" Salic didn't say a word. He didn't know if he should. "What's wrong with you? Did Petro cut out your tongue as well?"

Slightly shaking his head, Salic softly replied, "No, Don Calio."

Leaning back in his chair and shrugging, Calio said, "What? We're gonna be formal all a sudden? 'No, Don Calio'," he mimicked and laughed, then took a long drag off of his cig. He motioned a hand towards the chair next to him and ordered, "Have a seat."

Almost timidly, Salic took a seat. He wasn't sure how to act in front of the Don. Especially when he didn't know what was going to happen to him after telling him the truth. *All I can do is tell him the complete story, and hope to whatever god there is that he'll believe me and let me stay as a member of his Family...But I'm pretty sure I'm a dead man.*

After a yawn and a light scratch of his cheek, Don Calio asked Salic, "What am I gonna do with you, Salic?"

Salic was perturbed. He had no idea how to answer him, so he looked behind him at Petro for some support.

"Don't look at Petro," Calio sternly told him. "He can't help you right now. Only you can help yourself at this point, Salic."

He instantly returned his eyes back to Calio. *Don't screw this up you asshole, or you're dead,* Salic told himself. "I don't know what to say right now, Calio," Salic answered with a slight stutter.

With a more serious look on his face, Calio tilted his head to the side and said, "You don't know what to say, huh?" He tilted his head to the other side. "Four days ago, you confessed to me that you were an informant for the Rocca Family. Like a gentleman, I

155

didn't rip your throat out with my bare hands, but instead, let you suffer in a cell that was probably constructed over a thousand years ago…And when I bring you in front of me to let you explain yourself, all that comes out of that traitorous mouth of yours is that you don't know what to say?" He leaned forward in his chair and with quick hands, whipped out a dagger made from a distinct black metal with a sandy white grip and a transparent orange glow surrounding the edge of the blade. Salic has only seen Don Calio bring out the odd dagger a few times, and it never went to good use to the man facing it…He also remembered him having another identical one.

With the blade pointed at Salic's face, the Don whispered, "The time to genuinely explain yourself is now, Salic Stone. I should've killed you the second you confessed to me, but I seem to have a soft spot for you. And I also want more information on the Rocca Family." He spat on the ground and yelled out, "Those fucking pieces of shit bastard motherfucking prick assholes!"

Most men in his position would cry like a baby and beg Don Calio for his life…But Salic Stone wasn't most men. He was tougher than the average thug, and wasn't going to show weakness in this critical fight for his life. He'd been through too much shit in his life to lie down like a bitch now.

Looking down at the magical glow of the blade, Salic took a deep breath and said, "You know what I think you should do?"

"I'm all ears, my informant friend," Calio replied.

Leaning a bit forward, Salic said, "I think you should stop pointing that fucking thing in my face, and listen to my story in its entirety. I've made a lot of money for you in the short time I've been here, and I've killed a lot of men. So how about you treat me like a man instead of threatening me with a silly knife."

There was a moment of silence before Calio's mouth grew a small grin. "This knife is far from silly, Stone. I could stick it through your skull without the slightest shove if I wanted to."

Leaning in even closer, with the blade right between his eyes and the fiery orange glow reflecting off his irises, Salic said, "Then do it." His voice had some authority to it and his face was as hard as his last name.

There was a short pause, and then Calio suddenly grabbed ahold of Salic's neck with his free hand. He added pressure to his grip, squeezing enough for Salic to begin losing air. With the dagger in his other hand, he slowly moved it closer and closer to his forehead, shoved the tip under the diamond stud, and plucked it out. Salic let out a painful yell as the diamond clanked off the table and hit the ground, bouncing a few times before coming to a rest.

Calio let go of the grip around Salic's neck and sat back down in his chair, shoving the magic dagger behind his back. Salic put his hands to his forehead as he let out grunts of pain. *He took away one of my studs. The triangle isn't complete... This is not good.*

Leaning back in a more comfortable position, Calio grabbed his cocktail, took a deep swig, and said, "I'm taking away one of your diamonds. That is your punishment for now. You can thank the evening stars that I didn't kill you just now. But I need you alive, so today is your lucky day. But luck never lasts forever, so from now on, you better do as you're told."

Still holding his forehead and breathing heavy from the painful pluck of the diamond, Salic replied, "I will do whatever you ask of me, Calio."

Nodding without even the slightest emotion, Calio said, "That's good. That's really good for you, and even better for me." He looked in Petro's direction. "Petro, can you please go put together a clean outfit for our friend? I'm sure he wants to take a bath soon, and frankly, he smells like a pile of shit."

"Of course," Petro complied. Before walking away to do his task, he placed a comforting hand on Salic's shoulder and gave it a squeeze. Salic gave his hand a pat as a response to his gesture of friendship. They were both grateful that he was kept alive.

When Petro exited the balcony, Don Calio got down to brass tacks. "Now, your first obligation to me in your new journey to get your diamond stud back and validate yourself to this Family, is to fill me in with everything you know. But first I have to ask you a question." His face was an iron plate when he asked, "Do you truly love this Family and truly want to be the sworn enemy of the Family who gave you the assignment of spying on me?"

Sucking in the pain and removing his hand from his forehead, Salic put on the straightest face that he possibly could, looked Don Calio directly in the eyes and answered, "Don Calio, I swear on my father's grave and the life of every single member of this Family that I am solely dedicated to you and the rest of the Jovani Family. For the rest of my life, whether it be short or long, I will spend it trying to make up for the deceit that I have committed by destroying whatever enemy you may have…Especially the Family who sent me to you. I will make them suffer."

A smile finally came across the face of Don Calio. "All in good time, Stone. All in good time." He grabbed the pack of cigs lying on the table, took one out, and threw it to Salic. Taking a cig out for himself as well, he used a lighter to ignite the tobacco stick and then tossed it over to Salic. "First things first. I want you to tell me the exact reason why Don Maximo Rocca sent you down here. What does he want?"

After lighting up the cig and taking a drag, Salic let out the smoke and revealed the answer with no hesitation. "It's not just what *he* wants. It's what they want. And what they want is the Relic. They want all the Relics."

For a moment, Don Calio didn't say a word or move a muscle. *He has to be shocked. Who in their right minds would go after another Family's Relic? Don Maximo Rocca would, the son of a bitch.*

"So, it's not just Don Maximo?" Calio asked. Salic nodded. "There's another person outside of his Family working with him?"

"Yes," Salic simply replied.

"Who is this asshole?"

Taking a deep breath, Salic answered, "Don Xanose Cicello."

There was an awkward moment of silence, until Don Calio started laughing his ass off. He didn't stop for nearly a minute. He just kept laughing and laughing. But Salic didn't understand why. *What could be so funny about Maximo Rocca and Xanose Cicello joining forces to capture the other Family's Relics?* To Salic, this notion was downright unnerving and a threat to every other Family and their business dealings...*That's if they can pull it off, though.*

As soon as his laughter stopped, Don Calio asked him another, more complex question, "So, if Maximo and Xanose somehow get ahold of all the Relics, what do they plan on doing with them?"

Clearing his throat, Salic replied, "I honestly don't have an answer for that question, Calio. Maximo would only let me in on so much information. I was just a grunt to him. A thug who would do anything he asked. I don't think he even tells his kids the entire truths of certain operations, especially this one. His sons probably have no idea who I am. In order to find out what their objective with the Relics is, you might have to torture it out of him."

With a wave of his hand, Don Calio said, "And if I did that, do you think he would ever reveal it to me?"

"Never."

Calio nodded his head and said, "That's what I thought. He's an asshole, but also a stubborn asshole. He has too much pride for a man who runs dirty casinos and lets his kids deal smack on the streets...Not a very good father I suppose. Never really had a decent conversation with the man. He thinks he's too good for small talk with a young patriarch, the cock-licker."

Salic scrunched his eyebrows at the rambling of his boss. The hysterical laughing after the revelation of Xanose Cicello was still confusing him too, so he asked, "Why did you find it so funny when I told you he was working with Xanose Cicello?"

"Because it works out in my favor."

Even more confused, he asked, "How is that? That's two of the more powerful Families working together. This is some serious shit."

Before answering Salic's question, Don Calio rose out of his chair and took a few strides over to the railing. He stared upon the majestic scenery. The white sand beaches were bright and serene. The morning breeze drifted calmly through his dark, spiky hair. Waves crashed into the shoreline sounding like subtle rumbles of thunder. The deep blue hue of the *Never-Ending Sea* was a sight that some northerners may never have the privilege to document in their memories.

Salic was just about to ask his boss the same question again, but before he could, Don Calio spoke. "The Rocca and Cicello Families might be two of the more powerful Families, but they aren't the *most* powerful. That distinction belongs to the Rose Family, led by the great Father of Gangster, Don Maretto Rose."

The Rose Family, Salic quickly thought about for a second. *The most distinguished of the Seven Blessed Families.*

Calio continued on, "I've always admired Don Maretto Rose and his Family. Not only because of their power and wealth, but because Maretto never treated me like I was an incompetent leader being as young as I am. When he first became the patriarch of his Family, he was around the same age as I am now, so he understands me. We are a lot alike him and I...It's just too bad that we are separated by miles and miles of earth. The Rose Family would make a great ally for our Family."

An allegiance with the Rose Family? Is he crazy? The Jovani Family is considered to be the smallest of the Seven. The Rose Family would never join forces with us. Unless they had good reason... "What are you trying to say?" Salic curiously asked.

"The Rose Family recently had a misfortunate incident on Don Maretto's birthday. Everyone in Exodus is aware that his son was killed by Zasso Cicello, the heir to the Cicello Family."

"Well, of course. It's the biggest news to hit the airwaves since the death of his wife."

"Exactly," Don Calio assertively said. "And Maretto Rose can't be too pleased with the Cicello Family right now. Word is, that the murder of his son was a botched attempt to abduct him." He put his finger to his lips and pretended to think very hard when he said, "Hmm. I wonder what the Cicello son was going to capture him for."

A light bulb flashed in Salic's head. It definitely made sense. "The Rose Family Relic."

Crossing his arms, Don Calio gave a quick nod in agreement. "If Maximo and Xanose are working together to obtain the Relics of the Seven Blessed Families, then they had to be the masterminds in the plot to abduct Maretto Rose at the Grand Theater. So, now is the best chance for us to become allies with the Rose Family. If we do Maretto Rose the great service of eliminating his enemy, then he will accept us as an ally, and the Jovani Family will grow to heights that my ancestors never thought possible. They're skeletal remains will shiver with a chill up their spines in their dark, cold graves." A bigger smile was now casted on his face.

This is nuts, Salic thought to himself as he shook his head. "And how the hell do you suppose we pull that off? Maximo and Xanose are always heavily guarded."

Displaying a conniving grin, Don Calio replied, "We have the perfect weapon for the job."

"And what's that?" he quickly asked.

Don Calio turned around to face Salic and with a pointed finger, replied, "You."

Salic nearly laughed at his boss. "Me? How the fuck am I the perfect weapon?"

"Maximo Rocca sent you to do a job, and you're gonna go back home with that job completed. In two days, you will go back to the city of Vena and bring Maximo the good news that you have successfully found the whereabouts of the Triad Relic. I'm sure he will be delighted by the news and accept you back into the Family with open arms."

"You're joking, right?" Salic said with a hint of cynicism. "He's going to have me executed and thrown into the garbage no matter what kind of news I bring. I'm just a puppet in him and Xanose's masterful play."

Shrugging his shoulder, Calio said, "Maybe so, but there's a chance that he might give you a promotion in the Family. He may have a greater trust in you and put you close by his side. You will become an asset that is not so expendable. *You* will be the only man around the Family who knows how to get to our coveted Relic.

"And if you are unfortunately killed because you know too much about Maximo's plans, well then, I guess that is the hand of cards you are dealt for being a deceiver of two Blessed Families." Calio pointed to his right eye. "The Relics can see you. They can sense deception. I firmly believe that the Relics at one time were joined together, sharing their powers and teaching lessons to each other, evolving so that they could survive this world and live amongst people."

Salic scoffed at Calio's thoughts on Relics. "You act like they are alive or something."

"Well, they are," the Don replied at once. Salic gave him a frown. "You would look at me like that because you have no idea what Relics really are. Not being blood-related to a Family, you never once came in contact with a Relic. To you, a magical item is just that. An item. Not something that lives and breathes the same air as people." Salic scoffed at the idea once again.

"You are blind to the power of Relics, Salic Stone. The Triad could see right through your soul."

Now the Relics just sound plain creepy, Salic thought, but was trying to keep an open mind.

"Maybe if you ask the Triad for forgiveness, it will keep you safe when you travel back to Vena and encounter Maximo Rocca."

Shaking his head in the disbelief of such nonsense, Salic said, "That means that I would have to actually come in contact with the Triad. And like you said before, I'm not a blood-related Family member, so how the fuck am I supposed to ask for forgiveness?"

Casually taking a few strides toward Salic, Don Calio looked down upon him as if he were his child. With a stone-cold face and in a darkened tone, he said, "The Relics are very mysterious anomalies, my friend, and for some reason, I have a feeling that they don't discriminate against individuals outside the Families. I just think they discriminate against the weak."

Salic was now looking up at his boss in a state of wonderment.

"And even though it is not usual for someone outside the blood of the Family to encounter a Relic...rules are meant to be broken." Don Calio tilted his head and continued, "So, Salic Stone. Do you want to see the Triad, and ask for forgiveness of your deceit?"

Eyes staring directly into Calio's, he searched for the right answer to the yes or no question. Suddenly, he was afraid. Scared to encounter a real Relic. The magical powers that those things produce is something unimaginable in his mind. It's inconceivable to someone outside the Family...But Salic didn't want to show any weakness to the man who spared his life and gave him one more chance to prove his love and loyalty to him and the entire Jovani Family. *So, there is no other option in the matter. I have to do what I have to do.*

The boat ride out into the depths of the Never-Ending Sea went on for hours and hours. When they finally came upon a small piece of land in the middle of the ocean, the entire day had run its course. The nighttime sky was overtaking the brightness of day. The stars were beginning to appear out of nowhere as the sun settled below the horizon. A collage of reds, pinks, and purples were casted over their heads.

The small piece of land had a dock built for the speedboat they used to get to their destination, and a tunnel of palm trees made a pathway into the heart of the island. When Salic, Calio, and Petro reached a stone cavern on the other side of a clear pond, Salic was directed into the dark entrance, barely alit by torches attached to the walls.

Taking trepid steps, he slowly made his way down the tunnel of torches, until he reached a doorway that was blocked with a shield of orange flames. Out of nowhere, Calio and Petro appeared behind him, and the fiery blockade disappeared in an instant.

Then, Don Calio moved his face close to Salic's and whispered, "Enter the dwelling of the Triad, and ask for its forgiveness."

Shaking on the inside and scared beyond belief, Salic stepped through the doorway. But the moment his eyes gazed upon the magical Relic, all of his fears dissipated. As his eyes widened at the captivating mystique in front of him, a bright aura of fiery orange engulfed his entire body. It was the most beautiful site he had ever seen.

Alana Rae

And an Interview with Don Maretto Rose

After the widely popular and controversial news special, *Exodus: A World Created by Crime*, hit the airwaves, it was only fitting that the most dramatic incident in recent history happened shortly thereafter. 'The Grand Theater Massacre' is what the media had dubbed the horrific event, and the tragedy that took place exemplified the very nature of her report. *JBC News* reporter, Alana Rae, opened a great deal of minds with her subjective view on the history of the Seven Blessed Families and their impact on the world of Exodus. Though the way of life for the people who inhabit this land of solitude have been made easier with advancements in technology and wealth brought in by the Seven Blessed Families, violence and corruption have been at the forefront of the dramatic movement into the future. The time was now for the average citizen of Exodus to see more clearly into the truth of who and what is in charge of everything. And who better to deliver the truth than a woman who has firsthand experience of how despicable the Families really are.

Waking up from a few off and on hours of sleep, Alana quietly slid out from under the sheets of the strange bed she stayed the night in, and grabbed her personal phone off the nightstand. The naked man still fast asleep under the covers would wake up alone this morning and wouldn't get the pleasure of a repeat from last night. He was just a one-night stand in a need to fill her sexual desires, although the need was still vacant after a piss-poor performance by the young hopeless romantic she met at a club. Usually she wouldn't be out the night before she had an important assignment to do the next morning, but it was a Saturday night and her apartment was feeling like a desolate cave of depression.

When Alana arrived at her apartment, located about a quarter mile north of Juna's Heart, she took a quick shower to wash the sex off her body and hastily did her makeup before getting dressed. After zipping up the back of her black skirt and buttoning up her white blouse, she brushed her long wavy dark hair repeatedly until it was as straight and as perfect as could be. Before leaving the apartment, she checked her purse to see if she had enough money for a cab, and then grabbed her recorder and mini microphone, along with her personal notepad.

Alana Rae was trying to make history. Her anticipated follow up to the report she gave about the Seven Blessed Families and how their corruption relates to the history of Exodus, was going to be an exclusive sit-down interview with the Father of Gangster himself, Don Maretto Rose…The only problem, was that he has failed to reply to her requests for the interview, and that he has no notion that she was about to show up unannounced outside the First Church of God, following the Sunday service. *He's not going to be very happy with me when I barge in on his personal time, but I have no other option but to be persistent,* Alana thought to herself as she sat in the back of the cab, on her way to the church. *This could be a dangerous move to make, invading on the Father of Gangster…But if you want to be a successful journalist, you have to take risks.*

She knew, without a doubt, that Don Maretto Rose was going to be apprehensive in talking to her. The special news report she conducted was a direct stab in the chest towards the Rose patriarch, and the rest of the Seven Blessed Families. Her intentions were to wake up the public and put the immoral images of the Families right in their faces, and to also get them prepared for a new future in Exodus. A future in which the Seven Blessed Families were not in supreme command of the world. There were many rumors swirling around reliable sources that the President is going to put the hammer down on organized crime in the major cities, and take command of Exodus with the Legislation behind him.

I also wanted to make a name for myself by reporting something that everyone else in this chicken-shit world is afraid to, she thought, smiling proudly to herself.

The yellow cab pulled up to the curb in front of the church. Alana stared out the window for a few moments before paying the fare to the driver. The First Church of God stood tall, the steeple pointing high into the blue sky. The bronze bell near the top rocked back and forth, sending an echo of rings across the city, signaling the end of the service. Worshippers were beginning to file out of the white brick building, built by the strong hands of ancestors over a hundred years ago. She watched as normal God-fearing citizens exited the church as loving families. Fathers, mothers, daughters, and sons dressed in their Sunday best and walking side by side down the concrete stairs. Most families made it a ritual to have a feast after church at home or at their favorite restaurant…The life of the average citizen of Juna.

My life could have been just like theirs. A normal loving family who went to church on Sundays together, ate together, and shared a happy lifestyle together…But it wasn't meant to be for me. When dad died, everything in my life changed. Normal wasn't a possibility anymore.

She stopped her mind from wandering just in time to catch sight of the man she came for. He was one of the last to come filing out of the church, but there he was, standing regal and divine with his entourage of family members and bodyguards. There was one man with greasy black and gray hair wearing dark sunglasses and looking rather sharp in his all black suit, posed directly in front of him. *He might be the one who makes it hard for me to talk to the Rose patriarch,* Alana thought as she exited the cab, closing the door behind her before it sped off in a hurry.

With slight trepidation, Alana climbed the stairs and readied her microphone and recorder. While fiddling with her work tools, she kept her eye on the prize, Don Maretto Rose. He was even more magnificent in person than any news station, magazine, or newspaper could depict him. She was in complete awe of his presence. The perfectly streaked grays in his wavy black hair, the black and red suit adorning him from neck to toe. An olive oil face that barely showed a wrinkle at fifty years old, and a sharp jaw that clenched together like a metal compressor. His godly appearance was starting to make her feel nervous, but she had to stay strong. She could show no fear in front of the man.

Standing directly next to Don Maretto was his eldest son and heir to the Rose Family, Jonero "Jon-Jon" Rose. If there was any male in the Family more handsome and more magnificent than the Father of Gangster, it was Jon-Jon. For a second she locked eyes with him. If she hadn't known any better, she would've thought that he gave her a flirtatious grin…But she knew better, and it was more than likely just a grin out of kindness towards a random female on the church steps.

When she was only a few lengths away from Don Maretto, she found the courage she needed, and with a strong tone she shouted, "Don Maretto Rose!"

As if on cue, the bodyguard with the dark shades, his eldest son, two young women that looked like twin sisters, and Don Maretto turned their heads and watched as the sassy but pretty brunette trudged up the stairs with a waving hand.

"Don Maretto, may I please have a minute of your time?" she asked, just before the bodyguard blocked her from approaching any closer.

"Not a very good time, lady," the bodyguard stiffly said to her.

Ignoring the bodyguard, Alana persisted on getting his attention. "Don Maretto, please. I just want a minute or two to talk."

"I said no, lady. Now back away and leave!" the bodyguard was harsh, but just doing his job.

Don Maretto waved a hand at his bodyguard and said, "It's okay, Vego, let her speak."

The bodyguard moved a step out of the way, but only a step. And he kept his eyes locked on her position. Being as careful with her words as possible, Alana said, "Don Maretto, my name is Alana Rae, specialized journalist from the Juna Broadcasting Company." She added *specialized* to make her seem more important.

"I know who you are, Miss Rae, and I know which station you work for. My Family owns shares in the JBC," he said with a condescending smile down on her level. "Patriarchs of the Seven Blessed Families watch the news just as much as the average citizen."

He put her in her place already, but she wasn't going to stand down. *Even though he has the most intimidating voice I ever heard.* "I know my story pointed a finger in the direction of your Family, but I wouldn't have put together the report if I didn't have good reason to. My call out to the public was also a cry out from my own personal experience as a young girl. I am one of many outside the Seven Blessed Families that have been personally effected by their wrongdoings."

Clasping his hands behind his back, Don Maretto said, "The entire world of Exodus has been effected by the Seven Blessed Families in their own way, Miss Rae, whether

168

positively or negatively. I can't control what every Family does when it comes to their business practices, but I surely can speak for my own Family and say that we have made it possible for the average citizen to live in peace and harmony. Your report was filled with inaccurate information and far-fetched accusations, painting a false portrayal of my Family, and I was surprised, to say the least, that it was cleared to air."

"Even the Rose Family can't control everything the media dishes out, Don Maretto. I always find a way to have my stories heard," she brashly replied. *Whoa, where did that come from?*

Don Maretto looked at his son, Jon-Jon, who simply shrugged his shoulders with an impressed grin. But Maretto didn't look impressed whatsoever. He seemed annoyed with her presence and dissatisfied with the conversation so far. Alana had to maintain a politer attitude toward the powerful man, or their conversation would be ended in the blink of an eye.

"I am sorry that you feel the way you do about the Seven Blessed Families, Miss Rae, and I am also sorry that you had a harmful experience as a young girl, but I am going to have to decline an interview with you today, if that is what you are imposing on me."

The bodyguard snatched Alana's arm to shove her way from his boss, but she resisted him and said, "Please, Don Maretto. Don't you want the world to know your side of the story, so you can clear your Family's name? It will only take a few minutes of your time."

Stepping closer to her position on the steps, Don Maretto gently placed a hand on his bodyguard's shoulder, assuring him that he has no need to use any force on the young woman. "I don't believe I need to clear my Family's name, Miss Rae," he stated as his eyes dug deep into hers, "and minutes of my time are very precious at the present moment. After Sunday worship, I like to enjoy the company of my children. Now, if you'll excuse me."

As the Rose patriarch brushed past her, with the two twins-which she could only assume were his daughters-following close behind, she blurted out, "When I was just a young girl, barely the age of twelve, my father was murdered at the behest of *your* Family,

169

Don Maretto Rose." She tried holding back tears when she made the statement, but her eyes uncontrollably filled up.

Don Maretto abruptly stopped his walk down the stairs, turned around, and faced her with a new look. A look of complete and utter disdain, and deeper intimidation. "Is that so?" he asked in a low, morbid tone. "I would hope that you have solid proof of that statement."

She felt a lump in her throat as she swallowed a big gulp of air. *I went too far. This man is going to have me killed if I dig any further,* she thought to herself as sweat trickled down the side of her face. She could feel the dampness under her armpits. The Rose patriarch was scaring the hell out of her. *But I can't be afraid. I have to do this for myself...and for dad.*

After taking a deep breath and brushing away her fear, Alana responded, "My father's name was Benidine Rae. He and his two business partners owned one of Juna's professional batball teams, the Skylarks. They were a bottom-feeding team when they took over, but in the next decade the Skylarks became a formidable opponent under the ownership of my father and his partners. They brought that team out of the basement and to the top of the EBL."

She took another deep breath before going on. "And that's when the Seven Blessed Families interfered. As the popularity of the EBL grew in recent years, the Families have become more interested in the business ends of the sport. My father and his partners were confronted numerous times by a few of the Families to sell them the team, but my father was not interested in giving it to them. He loved the sport of batball, and loved owning the Skylarks even more. It was one of his passions in life, and he sacrificed all he had when he bought the team. The Skylarks organization was his pride and joy. Almost like a second family to him. It was his dream to retire an old man as one of the owners, and that dream would've come true if a certain Family hadn't stepped in.

"While the other Families laid off after his rejections, one Family did not go away so easily. The Rose Family was persistent. Members of *your* Family, Don Maretto, harassed my father day after day and were not going to give up until the team was theirs.

"Even when his two partners wanted to cave in and adhere to the Rose Family, my father stood his ground and insisted on keeping the team. He was the majority owner and wasn't going to lay down to your Family…A month later, my father and his two partners went missing and were never heard from again." She started choking up with tears again. "While the Rose Family insisted they had nothing to do with their disappearance, my family knew the truth of what happened. My father was killed and his body was thrown away, never to be found, in order for the Rose Family to get what they wanted. Ownership of the Skylarks."

As she wiped the tears off her face, Don Maretto lowered his head and stared at the ground, deep in thought. *I have him right where I want him. He's going to tell me the truth about my father. I just know it. Finally, I'll have closure and hear the truth of what happened to dad.*

When Don Maretto lifted his head back up and looked Alana straight into the eyes, she was astonished to see that he was a bit choked up from her story. Did the man who she thought had a heart of black really have feelings down deep in his darkened soul?

"Miss Rae," he began, "I am so very sorry for the loss of your father. I am too familiar with that type of heartbreaking story." *Of course. His father was taken from him at a young age too…But not as young as she was,* Alana thought, before he went on. "And I want to apologize on behalf of the Seven Blessed Families for their behavior. A team such as the Skylarks must have been a hot commodity back then, and pursuit of the team would've been a high priority for a group trying to make a substantial amount of money." He took a breath through his nose before his next words. "The only problem, is that the Rose Family doesn't own the Southside Skylarks."

What? She thought in her head before asking the quick question for real. "What?" She looked as though she just saw her dad's ghost.

Very calmly, Don Maretto replied, "Some of my men might dabble here and there in the Exodus Batball League. As a matter of fact, my brother-in-law is a high profiled agent for the EBL…But I believe that someone placed a dark cloud over your head many years ago and kept you and your family hidden from the authentic truth. The Rose Family doesn't own *any* of the EBL teams, and quite frankly Miss Rae, we don't need to."

Her mouth was hung out to dry. She couldn't believe the words coming out of the man's mouth, and didn't want to believe them either. "That's impossible, Don Maretto. That's just simply impossible."

"Nothing's impossible in this world, Miss Rae," Don Maretto firmly stated as he brushed past Alana.

Frantically, she turned around to plead her case. "But I've seen documentations, business transactions, bank statements, and whatever the hell else the Rose Family signed upon purchase of the Skylarks."

Without bothering to face her, he said back, "Like I just said, Miss Rae, someone placed a dark cloud over your head and shielded your eyes from the truth."

The bodyguard with the dark shades bumped her to the side as he strutted past her as well, and was followed by the twin sisters. "But wait a second!" she shouted. *I can't lose him! Not now!*

With a backhanded wave of his hand, Don Maretto replied, "I'm sorry, but you've had enough of my time for the day."

No! I have to stop him from leaving! I know I shouldn't reveal this to him, but, "Don Maretto! Were you informed that the President is going to deliver a speech to the entire nation in a couple of weeks, and that he shares similar views of my report about the Seven Blessed Families? My most reliable sources have given me this information on a classified basis, and they have been insistent that he is going to take a stance against the Families in order to lower the rate of organized crime."

Not only did Don Maretto stop and turn around when she blurted out her revelation, but the rest of his entourage gave her their undivided attention. But his reaction was not what she thought she would get back from him. He kept his poise and responded, "I'm sure that if the President was going to give such a speech, he would personally sit down with me and discuss it beforehand. That is how it has always been between us."

With a hardened face, she said, "Well, times are changing, Don Maretto. So, if you would like to have a sit-down interview with me and plead the case of your lifestyle to the public before the President makes his speech, then there is no better time than right now."

Squinting his eyes, the Rose patriarch lifted his head up to the clear blue sky, seemingly looking for an answer from the heavens above. After a few moments of thought, he lowered his head and shook it slowly back and forth. "I think not, Miss Rae. I have faith in my relationship with the President, and I believe that if he has a problem with the Seven Families, then he will discuss it with me first...And as for the public's perception of me; well, they have seen firsthand the anguish I went through losing one of my sons, and now they know that even a patriarch of one of the Seven Blessed Families can suffer a never ending hurt.

"And if I were you, Miss Rae, I wouldn't be releasing classified information in the first place. You can't trust anyone in your line of business. People have been killed for less."

Was that a threat from the Father of Gangster? I should just keep my mouth shut, but...

"You tell me not to trust anyone, but you would trust the President?" she asked, her voice almost cracking when her lips released the words.

"I never said I trusted him. I only said that I have faith in our relationship." Turning his back on her, he ended the conversation by saying, "Good day to you, Miss Rae, and good luck on your follow-up report."

Alana wanted to press him further, but she couldn't. She was speechless. A mute. There was nothing more to say to convince him to do the interview, so she remained silent and watched as he, his bodyguard, and the twin sisters walked toward the extended black limo that was waiting for them. The bodyguard with the dark sunglasses opened the back door, and Don Maretto crouched inside the elongated automobile. The bodyguard then shut the door, and shut out the chance of her getting the story that she needed.

As she lowered her head in a moment of depression and lost hope, she felt a gentle hand grip her shoulder. A bit jumpy, she quickly turned around to see who was touching her.

"I'm sorry, Miss Rae," Jon-Jon Rose said, lifting his hand off her shoulder. "But my father's not too keen on doing interviews. Especially, with someone he just met."

He had an honest pair of eyes to go along with his extremely handsome face. *My goodness is this man good looking,* she thought as she eyed him up and down.

"Well, maybe if we sat down for a drink, or dinner, and talked a little more. He would be impressed with my knowledge of the world, I guarantee it." She was still being persistent even though she lost on this day.

Shaking his head, almost solemnly, Jon-Jon said, "No, I'm sorry, but that's not going to happen."

She lowered her head in another defeat. *I'm not going to get this interview, no matter what I say.*

Then, Jon-Jon did something that sent shivers through her body. Good shivers. A tingling sensation. He softly caressed a sensitive spot under her chin, and lifted her head back up, so he could look directly into her eyes of jade.

"My father might not want to have dinner with you and get to know you better. But I sure would like to," Jon-Jon said with a charming smile.

"Really?" she asked. Her sullen mouth grew into a sparkling smile.

"Of course," he said without a doubt.

Her smile disappeared when she suddenly remembered that the man was engaged to another beautiful woman. Everyone in Exodus saw her standing next to her man during the televised funeral procession of his brother. "But what about your fiancée? I'm sure she wouldn't be too happy with you if you were having dinner with another woman."

A sly smile was now casted on his face when he replied, "It's just two people enjoying a meal together. Besides, I want to help you find out the truth about the ownership of the Skylarks." He looked deeper into her eyes. "And then maybe we can dig up the truth about what happened to your father."

She gave him an almost childish grin and asked, "You would do that for me?"

"Yes, I would. Besides helping you, it would also benefit my Family if you knew for a fact that we had nothing to do with his disappearance. Then maybe, you won't produce any more negative stories about my father," he said in a jocular manner.

With a flirtatious chuckle and a grin, she agreed to the dinner date and insisted that it be in a couple days.

"Okay then," he replied with that oh so handsome smile. "I guess I'll see you soon."

He caressed the side of her face, and then walked his way down to the waiting limo. After giving her a goodbye wave, he entered the vehicle, before it hastily took off down the street.

Alana watched the limo zoom by as she stood alone in the middle of the staircase, wondering if what the Rose patriarch and his son told her was the actual truth. *Criminals are known to be liars,* she thought while making the lonely trek down the stairs and onto the sidewalk. *And that's exactly what the Seven Blessed Families are...Criminals. Criminals leading criminal empires...And that includes the Rose Family most of all.*

After having a few drinks at a small pub near her apartment building, Alana arrived back at her apartment, feeling the need to get a couple hours of sleep before working all through the night conducting more research on the Rose Family and the Skylarks organization. The information that Don Maretto Rose bestowed upon her was still sinking in, and she was still having a hard time believing a word of it. There was so much documentation pointing towards the Rose Family as owners of the Skylarks, but she and her family never did come in contact with the men in charge of the batball organization in person. They were kept hidden from them...But why? Why would the identities of the Skylark management be hidden?

There was so much to contemplate in her head about her situation, but she had no energy to do it right now. What she needed was some rest. And the few drinks she had at the pub were making her nauseated. So, as soon as she walked through the door into her apartment, the need to collapse on the couch was all that she wanted to fulfill. But the second she closed the door behind her, a muscular forearm was wrapped around her neck, cutting her air off in a heartbeat. She tried to scream for help, but her vocal chords were of no use. As her face turned from red to purple, her eyes began to bulge out of their sockets. She was being strangled to death.

Just as she thought she would lose consciousness and eventually die, the muscular forearm eased up a little, so she could take the slightest breath. Then, she felt hot air next to ear and could smell the breath of someone who had more than his fair share of alcoholic beverages.

"My agent let me go, you stupid fucking bitch," the drunkard whispered in her ear.

"W-what?" she tried to say, but was cut off by more strangulation.

"You and your fucking story about the Seven Blessed Families," the drunken man said in a louder, harsher voice. "My agent works for the Rose Family, you cunt. And ever since your story, they've been trying to show a better image of themselves. So they got rid of me!"

She now recognized the voice. It was her ex-boyfriend. A talented pitcher who was under contract with the Skylarks...Bryant Strattburn.

Her ex eased up his grip around her throat so she could speak for herself. "No, Bryant...That's not true," she said in a squeamish voice. "They don't care about their image."

"Bullshit!" he yelled in her ear, causing it to start ringing. "This is my fucking future, bitch! And now the Skylarks want to let me go, because they do whatever the fuck the Rose Family tells them to."

"Wait...What?" she tried to ask, but was cut off by more strangulation.

"Shut the fuck up, bitch!" Bryant shouted, before he ripped the front of her blouse, exposing her firm breasts. Buttons went flying in all directions and bounced on the hardwood floors. He grabbed her breasts, before reaching down her skirt and caressing the

176

well-groomed area down below. Sloppily, he kissed up and down her neck, while shoving his fingers in and out of her. "You owe me big time for what you've done, bitch. Nobody fucks with my money!" He violently pushed her forward, then quickly came up behind her and bent her over the couch.

"Bryant! Stop this!" she yelled as tears streamed down her face, while she was bent over.

But he didn't stop. Nothing was going to stop him from getting what he wanted. If she resisted him, then he would kill her. She knew he would. He was just drunk and angry enough to do it. A man in his state of mind would have no thought of crossing the line and breaking the law.

So tonight, Alana would take the rape that was coming, instead of losing her life.

Ricalstro Rose

And the Fate that Lies Ahead

He stuck the needle in his arm, mixing the drugs with his blood and sent it through his veins. In a matter of moments, Ric was in another world. A tranquil world of forgetting the problems in his life, but at the same time, summoning new ones. His drug habits. Habits that has become all too familiar to him and the rest of the people around him...But that's why he's alone tonight. Alone, so the people around him can't get hurt. Alone, so his father can't give him that look of disappointment in his stern eyes. Alone, so his brothers can't look down on him for turning into a drug infested piece of shit, who never forgave them for carrying out his vengeance. Alone, so no more of his friends could get tortured and murdered right in front of his face.

He wasn't just killing himself anymore. He was killing everything around him as well. Ric was a train wreck, sliding off the track, dragging twisted metal across the terrain, destroying everything in its way and wiping out everyone on board. A heaping, burning pile of rubble is what Ric has laid waste to his surroundings...So why try to fix it? Why not just let his life get worse? It's not like anything is going to get any better.

Fuck it, Ric thought in his muddled head as he lied back on his scruffy couch and stared at the cracks in the ceiling of his apartment. *I can't do anything right. My father gives me one simple assignment, and I fuck it all up. I got two of my friends killed, didn't get the information I needed about where my brother's killer is hiding, and to top things off, I got arrested by my oldest friend...Life is just a used up dirty bitch.*

They're going to try to kill off your Family, Ric. You have to do something about it, is what the other voice in his head was saying. The positive one. The voice that thinks clearly. But he didn't care for listening to that voice, or what was left of it.

What am I gonna do about it? Ric asked his meager positive voice. *Run back to daddy and tell him how his youngest son is worthless, and can't deliver when asked to do something important?* Ric shook his head at nothing. *No way. No fucking way.*

But you did do something. You got Miro to reveal critical information to you. His Family wants the Rose Quartet, and they are going to kill off your Family until they possess it, his positive voice tried to reason with him. *Your brothers and your father are in great danger. You have to go warn them!*

Ric sat completely still with his eyes glued to the ceiling, staring into the realm of absolutely nothing. For a moment, for a slight sliver of time, he thought about going home to his father and brothers. But then…

No! No fucking way am I going back there! That isn't my home. This is my home. This two-bit shitty apartment is my home now. Out of nowhere, Ric took his eyes off the ceiling, stood on his feet, and kicked over the coffee table next to the couch. Dirty plates, glasses, a couple magazines, and drug paraphernalia spilled to the floor.

Those backstabbing bastard brothers of mine stole my vengeance from me! He started taking swings with his arms and fists, hitting nothing but the dry, empty air in front of him. *That was my revenge!*

After the fight with the air, he started breathing heavy, unable to catch his breath. While trying to settle his heartrate down, he caught a glimpse of an object he hadn't seen in a while. It was hidden underneath the table he just knocked over. He put it there months ago because he couldn't stand to look at it anymore. A picture frame. Inside the frame was a picture of him and Galia, taken only weeks before she was raped and murdered in front of his naked eyes.

Slowly, he bent down to retrieve the framed picture. When he grabbed ahold of it, he rose back to his feet and walked a few steps towards the window. Only then, did he notice that it was raining bucketsful outside. The heavy droplets of precipitation tapped on the window as he gazed hard into the beautiful eyes of his lost love. He caressed the edges of the golden frame. A tear fell out of his left eye and dripped onto the glass covering the picture. A moderate flash of lightning brightened the inside of his dreary apartment for a split second, followed by a low rumble of thunder. He sniffed mucus back into his sinuses. All he could smell was the stale sweat running down his forehead.

Oh, how beautiful she was…My God did I love her.

As he continued to gape into the picture frame, his lips began to quiver, and his mouth formed a slight smile…But almost as soon as the harmonious feeling of his love for Galia spread throughout his body, anger swept in and took full control. A deep, hurtful anger that burned the insides of his tainted, drug-infused soul.

Lashing out his anger, Ric put a strong grip around the picture frame, yelled at the top of his lungs, and threw the picture at the window. There was an explosion of shattered glass when the frame busted through, and then it disappeared as it fell hundreds of lengths down to the street below.

Huffing and puffing, eyes glaring out the broken window like they had laser targeting, Ric stood in place and watched as the rain showered into his apartment. And then he broke down and began to sob. He fell to his knees like a beggar who stole from a noble. Like a servant who failed to adhere to his king. Like a Family member who didn't complete his assignment for his Don.

After a few minutes of long, drawn out periods of sobbing, Ric was finally able to control his tears and stood back on his feet. *It's not my fault that she's dead…And I'm not some beggar who stole from a noble, or some servant who failed to do what the king asked of him…But I am a Family member who didn't complete his assignment for his Don…For my father…For my brother.*

Ric had had enough. Shaking the terrible thoughts from his head, he decided it was time to get out of the room of depression. He threw on a black jacket with white stripes running down the sleeves, and hightailed it the hell out the door. He didn't even give his usual look back at the awful dwelling he inhabited and remind himself how fucked his life had become. He just wanted to get the hell out of there.

As he walked down the street, making his way to La Bella Scoundrel, the pouring rain soaked him to the bone. He jumped and dodged around puddles that rain droplets plopped into, creating ripples in the water. The streets were a shiny black, and there wasn't a soul to be seen. It was as if he was the only one in the city to brave the elements of the nighttime storm. He was alone not only inside his apartment, but outside as well. That was until he was inside the walls of the Scoundrel. He then realized that he wasn't the only person in the city who would get drenched just to have a drink. There were more than a few patrons attending the club.

Ric sat in his usual spot, and waited for his favorite bartender to wait on him. Nester, the big scruffy bastard, didn't bother asking Ric what he wanted. He already knew. The light blue concoction was promptly set down in front of Ric. He eagerly threw it back, and in a matter of moments, the empty glass was replaced by another one. It was as if Nester could see the pain in the eyes of his customer, so he was quick to the draw to fulfill Ric's need to drown his sorrows.

For over an hour, Ric sat and drank by himself without anyone else in the club bothering him. No one even sat in either of the stools next to him. Until, a short but stout dark-skinned man took a casual seat to the left of him, while a big and burly white guy sat to the right of him. At first, Ric didn't even realize who the hell they were, until he could feel the eyes of the dark guy to his left staring hard at him. Nonchalantly, Ric glanced to his left, then quickly turned his head to the right. His visitors weren't just some random bar patrons. They were Augusta Rocca's henchmen, Jamele and Karn. Both wore stoic faces, and were obviously not at the club for some amusement.

There wasn't enough time to even panic, before a strong hand clamped down on his shoulder from behind. The voice that emulated behind his ear didn't have to speak for Ric to recognize whose hand it was.

"I sent a major shipment of my Vena Gold into this city the other day, Ric Rose, and the truck was confiscated by the Juna Police Department. Two of my guys are behind bars, and I lost twenty thousand worth of smack. Now, we had an agreement that you were going to talk to your friend and get those assholes off my back, but obviously you didn't follow through, you cocksucking son of a bitch!" Augusta yelled, then gave Ric a slight shove before releasing the grip on his shoulder.

"I thought I had more time," Ric argued, although he knew that he deliberately didn't try to talk to Melroy. What the hell was he thinking?

"More time my ass, Ric Rose. More time my ass. Is that the only excuse you could come up with?" He smacked the back of Ric's head. "I give you a shitload of free smack, and this is how you repay the favor? Business deals don't work like that, Ric Rose. Seems as though you haven't learned one damn thing from your Family." Aggressively, he gripped the back of Ric's neck and said, "You fucked me over bigtime, Ric. And now I'm gonna fuck you...Hard."

"I hope you're not saying that literally," Ric joked. He was so bombed from the dope and alcohol that he didn't give a damn that he was being threatened at the moment...It was amusing to him.

With force, Augusta turned Ric's head to the left, so Jamele could get a good look at him. "Do you believe this guy?" he asked his henchman.

Shaking his head at the sight of Ric's blood-shot eyes, Jamele replied, "He's so fucked up that he don't give a fuck what happens to his ass."

"So, you are being literal," Ric groggily said back.

Augusta began to laugh out loud, and then Jamele and Karn joined in on the amusement. When he finally stopped his outlandish laughter, Augusta said, "I'll give you one thing, Ric Rose. You're a hell of a lot of fun, and I would probably like you if you didn't just cost me twenty thousand...But business is business."

At the exact same time, Jamele and Karn grabbed ahold of Ric's arms from either side and lifted him off his stool, trying to stand him up straight. Ric's knees nearly buckled underneath him from his intoxicated state. They turned him around to face Augusta.

"Are we going somewhere, fellas?" Ric asked, slurring his words.

Patting Ric lightly on the cheek a couple of times, Augusta answered with a smile, "We sure are, Ric Rose. You're gonna join us out in the back alley, so we can teach you a lesson in business."

Ric studied the outfit Augusta was wearing. An all-white suit with black pinstripes. Ric wanted to throw his blue drink all over the suit and permanently stain it, but there was no getting loose from the clutches of his two big henchmen.

"Listen fellas, I wasn't the best student in school, so you're wasting your time trying to teach me a lesson," Ric stated, slurring and wobbling.

Jamele gave a bemused look over to Karn and said, "What the fuck is this guy talking about?" Karn answered with only a growl.

Smiling and showing his big white teeth, Augusta motioned his thumb over his shoulder and ordered, "Take this junky outside."

His henchmen put an even tighter lock around Ric's arms and did as they were ordered without the slightest hesitation. Augusta followed his men from the rear, and away they went to teach Ric the lesson that was coming to him. Behind the bar, Nester watched as the situation was unfolding. As soon as the men were out of sight, he reached into his pocket, pulled out his personal phone, and dialed a number. Patiently, he waited for an answer.

The two henchmen tossed Ric through the back door of the club. He stumbled and fell into the alleyway, scraping his hands and knees. The alley was dark, except for a single lightbulb above the door Ric just crashed through. There was a large dumpster against the opposite wall of the club that reeked of wet garbage from the pouring rain. Everything was completely wet, and now so was Ric's pants and jacket after his fall.

Jamele and Karn lifted Ric back to his feet, and then shoved him into the wall. The thud against the hard brick took the breath out of Ric, and he started to sliver down the wall before they stood him up again. Both Jamele and Karn punched him hard in the gut. He grimaced from the pain and coughed up a lung.

As his men held Ric upright, Augusta stood directly in front of him, shook his head, and said, "It's too bad, Ric Rose. It's just too bad. We could've done a lot of business together, you and I, but you've proven to be as reliable as a hooker without a mouth. I gave you what you wanted, what you thirst for, but in return, all I got back was disrespect, you ungrateful piece of shit." Beads of water dripped from his curly black hair as he leaned in closer to Ric's face. "I hope you enjoyed my free drugs, Ric Rose. But you should very well know that nothing in this world is for free. There's a price to pay for everything. And now it's about time you paid up." Leaning back, he looked at Jamele and ordered, "Light this motherfucker up."

Responding with a slight nod, Jamele wound up and gave Ric a right cross to the side of his face. If Karn hadn't been holding him up, Ric would've fell flat on his back. His face was split open under his eye, and blood ran down his cheek. Somehow, he was still conscious after the violent strike. The slick rain must have softened the blow.

Augusta gave Karn a nod and said, "Feel free to join in, big guy."

Karn smashed his fist into the other side of Ric's face. Blood flew from his mouth as let out a grunt. Then, Jamele took another shot at Ric's gut, followed by a hard smack against his head, and then a sharp knee to his ribs. Karn gave Ric a quick elbow to the temple, a forceful punch to the ribs, and when Ric slumped over, he kneed him in the face.

Blood and bruises covering his face and hardly standing on his own, Ric spit blood from his mouth and said, "Is that all you got you fucking pussies? Why don't you hit me with your tampons next?"

Lowing his head and slowly shaking it back and forth, Augusta said, "A typical Rose. Trying to be a tough guy. Your brother tried to be a tough guy, and now he's dead."

"Fuck you!" Ric blurted out, blood falling from his mouth.

"Throw him up against the wall," Augusta instructed his two men.

The two henchmen gave Ric a mighty shove, slamming him into the brick wall, cracking the back of his head open. It took all his strength to stay on his feet. Ric was a battered and bloody mess. He hadn't taken a beating like this since the incident that took the life of his love, Galia.

Augusta removed his suit coat, folded it up nicely, and then tossed it to Jamele. "Hold this," he instructed the big henchman. He then rolled up the sleeves of his baby blue buttoned down dress shirt, exposing his forearms. Both were covered with detailed tattoos of peculiar objects that looked like gray stones in the shape of faces with teardrops falling from the eyes.

Taking a couple steps closer toward Ric, Augusta flashed him a smile. "Do you know what the Rocca Family Relic is, Ric Rose?" he queried Ric. Not bothering to let Ric respond, he answered his own question, "It's called the *Mourning Stone*. It kind of looks like a face off of a sculpted statue that continuously cries glowing blue tears. Quite an amazing object if you ask me. But what really makes my Family's Relic great, is the power that it gives to those Blessed by it...The continuously flowing tears represent the intense ferocity of water." He extended his arm and shaped his hand into a claw. "Here, let me show you what it can do."

Ric stood motionless, acting as if he was ready for anything to come his way, but he sure wasn't prepared for what happened next. Out of Augusta's claw-shaped hand came spewing forth a gush of intensified water, and it was the brightest blue Ric had ever seen with his own two eyes. The fierce liquid hit him like a punch in the face, even harder than the two henchmen who beat the shit out of him. Ric's head slammed against the wall harder than before as the gushes of water kept coming and coming.

When Augusta finally stopped the magical output of glowing blue water, he and his men laughed at the expense of the victim. Ric spit out the water that ended up down his throat and blew some out of his nose as he tried to catch his breath. He was panting from not only the pain, but the coldness of the magical water.

"Pretty cool, huh, Ric Rose," Augusta said to Ric, who was drenched now from head to toe. "No pun intended." He and his henchmen began to laugh at him again.

Trying to show his vigor and strength, Ric slowly stood up straight and stared at his attacker with a drunken, but intense look. "Is that it, Augusta? What else do you got in your arsenal, bitch?"

All three men laughed at him hysterically, before Augusta replied, "Oh, Ric Rose, you have no idea the power that I possess."

"Then quit being a little vagina and show me."

Crinkling his eyebrows, Augusta said, "It's almost as if you want to die, Ric Rose."

185

Ric spit out some more water and said back, "Maybe I do asshole. So, just fucking get it over with."

A devious grin formed on the mouth of Augusta Rocca, and then he swiped his arm through the air as if he was taking a swing at someone at close range. A bright spark appeared for an instant around his forearm, and then a wave of energetic water was expelled towards Ric. The wave crashed into Ric, slamming him against the wall, before he fell onto his ass. It felt as if he had been hit by a car going at full speed. It took the breath out of him, and soaked him even more than he was before. He tried to get to his feet, but slipped while trying.

"So, how did that one feel?" There was no answer from Ric. He was coughing up water, and still trying to get up. When he finally managed to get to his feet, Augusta extended out his arms and said, "Now, try this one out for size."

In a blur, Augusta started spinning in mind-numbing revolutions. He took the shape of a mini-cyclone, and then burst forward at a rapid rate of speed, charging directly into Ric's body. The impact of the blast sent Ric flying up in the air. He landed hard back to the ground with an impactful thud. There were no words to describe the pain Ric felt from the magical blast. He couldn't move. He felt like he could die right there. The air had been sucked from his body, his muscles all felt ripped, and his bones felt broken to pieces. This was how it was going to end for Ric Rose. In the back alley of the club he loved to attend…Funny, he always thought he would die with a needle sticking out of his arm.

With Jamele and Karn watching the display of Augusta's unique powers, he took a deep breath, seemingly preparing himself for the final blow. "Our friendship was short-lived, Ric Rose, but I did learn a valuable lesson while doing business with you." Ric just lied in a big puddle of water, silent and trying to get a good breath in. "And that lesson is," he raised his hands to the raining skies above, "never trust a Rose."

With one fluid motion of his arms, a funnel of cyclonic water formed above Augusta's outstretched arms. Forcefully extending his arms in Ric's direction, the funnel of water burst forward with a mighty force. Ric was engulfed and tangled in the funnel as it lifted him in the air and repeatedly slammed him to the ground, while drowning him. It was the end for Ric. There was no way getting out of this attempt on his life. The heir to the Rocca Family had finally disposed of the junky son of Don Maretto Rose.

That was until a beaming pair of fluorescent headlights appeared out of nowhere down the alley. The headlights were shining from above the ground, which meant that the vehicle was flying in for a landing. Augusta's magical fury abruptly stopped as soon as he noticed the long black vehicle hovering towards him and his men. Jamele and Karn immediately reached for their handguns, aimed them at the flying car, and began to fire round after round. The bullets hit nothing but hard steel, and the windows of the car had no give. The vehicle was bulletproof.

Augusta's men emptied their clips with no success. "Keep shooting, you fools!" he ordered them.

The two henchmen slid the clips out of their gats, and reached in their pockets to reload them. But it was too late. The car landed on the ground, and doors with tinted windows flew open. Men dressed in black suits and fedoras with red stripes around the base, carrying semiautomatic rifles, stepped out. Immediately, they began to open fire, spraying a hail of bullets toward the three men.

With a quick reaction, Augusta bent to one knee and raised his hands in front of his body as if he was going to block the bullets with just his flesh. Instead, a force shield that appeared as a clear, large bubble encompassed his body and deflected the oncoming bullets…Jamele and Karn, on the other hand, were not so fortunate.

An array of bullets struck Karn in the chest, and it opened up and exploded like fireworks during a festival. The impact to his chest was so intense that the blood splattered all over the outside of Augusta's protective bubble. He freefell on his back and was dead in a matter of moments. Jamele was rather shorter than Karn, so the bullets aimed at him, hit him directly in the face, removing his nose, eyes, mouth, ears, and then finally just exploding his entire head apart. His headless body collapsed to the ground, and even though it was quite obvious he was a goner, the firing squad kept riddling his lifeless corpse with bullets.

When the black-suited men realized that their weapons were no match for the protective shield around Augusta, they lowered their weapons and took a few steps back. For a few moments, the alley was silent, besides the heavy rains tapping the outside of the car and plopping into puddles on the dirty ground. Then, a back door of the black vehicle clicked and slowly opened. A shiny black dress shoe stepped onto the wet ground, followed by the other foot.

Ric found enough strength in himself to lift his head out of the puddle, when he noticed the end of the gunfire and the sound of the opening vehicle door. At first, he saw nothing but a pair of glossy black shoes entering the scene of violence and bloodshed, but when his eyes scanned upwards, he saw the man who had come to join the party. He was tall, neatly dressed in a black suit with red pinstripes and a black tie, his head completely shaved, and sporting dark circular glasses. It was his Uncle Vetti. Arriving at the perfect time to save his ass.

At the sight of the intimidating figure of Victorio "Vetti" Rose, Augusta's bubble shield dissipated, and he rose to his feet. A look of fear struck his face. The older, more distinguished gentleman, stood opposing toward the young heir to the Rocca throne.

Augusta held a hand up in front of his face, turned his head away, and nervously said, "Now, wait, wait, wait just a second. I'm only out here teaching this guy a lesson. There is no need for further confrontation. I was just giving him a slap on the wrist for dicking me over."

Vetti Rose looked over the shoulder of his opponent, and watched as Ric struggled to lift his head out of the water. "A slap on the wrist?" he inquired in a dark and menacing tone. His voice was vibrant and deep. "To me, it looks as if you have been torturing my nephew to the brink of death. Are you sure you want to tell lies to a man such as myself?"

Shaking his hand uncontrollably with his head still turned, Augusta tried to laugh off the situation and brighten the mood. "Now, now, now, come on now. It's all over. My men have been gunned down, and you proved your point. I'll just be returning back to my father in Vena, and we can all forget this night ever happened."

"Oh, I will not forget this night, and neither will Ric. But you certainly will." Vetti took a step closer towards Augusta.

"Wait! Wait! Just wait!" the young Rocca shouted. "Your incompetent nephew did not follow through with an agreement we had, and it cost me thousands. Surely, you can understand why I would be a bit upset with him." His lips were quivering as he spoke. He knew that he was in deep trouble.

Clasping his hands behind his back, Vetti retorted, "The only part of this situation I understand, is that you are doing a great deal of harm to my nephew. My brother's son. The patriarch of the Rose Family. The Father of Gangster." He pronounced the nickname slow and precise for a more dramatic effect.

"I know who his father is, and you must know who *my* father is. And my father will be very pleased if you show mercy on his eldest son and let him return home safely. If not, then you could possibly start a war between the Families, and we both know that that is out of the question." Augusta lowered his hand, put his chin up, and stood toe to toe with Vetti Rose. He tried to act brave and not show any weakness.

"I understand that your father would be quite upset if he were to discover you were killed by a Rose Family member," Vetti calmly said. Augusta let out a sigh of relief as if he was going to be spared. "But your curly-haired fuck father is never going to find out unless I personally deliver your head to his casino."

Augusta's eyes grew big as he uttered, "What?"

In the blink of an eye, Vetti extended out both of his hands and expelled a crimson blast of energy from his palms. The forceful blast struck Augusta head-on, propelling him backwards, until his body smacked against the brick wall. The contact with the red energy caused him to convulse, but he still mustered up enough strength to rise to his feet. Legs shaking underneath him, Augusta tried to plead for mercy, but his vocal chords were failing him.

When Vetti Rose began to step toward Augusta, the young Rocca panicked by raising his hand and expelling a gush of glowing blue water. Instantly, a shield the shape and color of a rose enveloped Vetti's body, and the blue magic was easily repelled off of it. Augusta's effort nearly brought Vetti's face to a smile.

"Nice try, young Rocca," Vetti said, then broke through his own shield by using a shoulder-ram attack, shattering magical pieces into the humid night air. Crimson shadows of himself trailed behind him as the attack struck the target. Augusta was slammed into the wall for a second time, but with more devastating consequences. His skull was cracked and rib bones were shattered. A pitiful young man was convulsing at the feet of Vetti Rose.

Taking no pity on his opponent, Vetti reached down and grabbed ahold of Augusta by his neck. He lifted him to his feet with hardly an effort. Augusta's face was scratched and bruised, and gurgles of blood spilled from his mouth. Vetti shook his head at the sight of the young, battered Rocca heir, and then gripped around his neck even tighter.

Still lying in the puddle, Ric had been watching his powerfully Blessed uncle use his talents against Augusta. But what he saw next was almost unfathomable. His Uncle Vetti twisted Augusta's head completely around, and then with one hand, ripped the young man's head completely off his body, including his spine. Augusta's corpse fell to the damp pavement, and gushes of blood spurt out of the neck, forming a large puddle of dark red. Vetti stood overtop what was left of the body, holding the severed head. The white spine oozed with blood and swayed back and forth, before Vetti tossed the remnants to the ground and shook some blood off of his hand.

At the sight of the carnage, Vetti lowered his head and shook it back and forth. To Ric, it appeared as if he didn't enjoy partaking in the murderous violence…*But he sure is damn good at it,* Ric thought about his uncle.

Ric struggled to rise out of the puddle, so his uncle walked over to him, held out a helpful hand, and dragged him out of the bright blue water that had almost drowned him. Hacking and coughing, Ric lied on his back and looked up at his uncle, who portrayed the look of a caring father over his damaged son.

"I think it's about time you came along with me, Ricalstro," Vetti uttered down to Ric. His uncle held out another helpful hand.

190

He coughed a few more times, then extended his own hand, accepting his uncle's generous assistance. Their hands locked, and as if he only weighed a few pounds, Vetti lifted him off the ground and stood him on his feet. With both hands, he brushed some of the grime off Ric's shoulders, and looked him in the eyes.

"You look terrible, Ric. You need medical attention and a lot of rest."

"I don't need to go to the hospital, if that's what you're trying to say," Ric said, trying not to show how much pain he was really in.

Vetti cracked a grin. "Oh, I'm not taking you to the hospital. I can get you medical attention at the location I'm taking you."

It even hurt to crinkle his eyebrows when he asked, "Where the hell are you taking me?"

Vetti smacked Ric in the back, and his grin doubled in size. "You'll see when we get there." He turned towards the black car and motioned Ric to follow him.

"Do I even have a choice?" Ric asked, his back searing with pain from just a little smack.

"Nope," Vetti replied, without turning around.

Ric sighed, and under his breath, said, "Great."

Limping with every step, Ric grudgingly walked to the car. One of the black suited men was waiting for him and opened the back door. Ric slid into the car, and the man slammed the door shut behind him. The inside of the black car was rather roomy, but it wasn't as big as a standard limo. Vetti sat on the other side of the seat, allowing a comfortable space between him and Ric. The leather seat vibrated when Vetti sank himself comfortably into it.

When the driver ignited the car, Ric twisted his sore neck to his left and said, "Are you gonna tell me where we're going or what, Uncle Vetti?"

Looking straight ahead, Vetti answered, "We're going to where it all started, Ric. But we have to make a quick stop in order to get there."

"What the fuck do you mean where it all started?"

"Watch your language," Vetti sternly told his nephew. "Soon enough, you'll find out what I mean."

The driver didn't bother to use the ground to travel at all. The black car hovered into the air, while the wheels retracted into the wells and were replaced by boosters that fired out bright red flames. The flying vehicle rose above the adjacent buildings, and then accelerated with fury into the rainy night.

It took only a couple minutes for the vehicle to reach its destination. Ric looked out of the window to try and see where they were landing, but the rain was so heavy that the streams of water running down the glass were hindering his vision to the outside world. It wasn't until they were out of the car, did he notice the building they were now parked in front of. Vetti and two of his men helped Ric hurry across the street, so they could get out of the pouring rain as soon as possible. Ric looked up at the enormous construction in front of him. It was the National Archive Building.

"Why are we going into the Archive Building?" Ric asked his uncle, shouting over the heavy rain squalls.

"We're not going to the Archive Building," Vetti replied. He pointed over to a phone booth that was a bit larger than Ric was used to seeing. Plus, phone booths were on the verge of extinction in the city. Everyone was using cellular phones nowadays. "We're going to that booth."

"For what?" he asked, confused as all hell.

Vetti didn't bother answering the question. He and his two men started walking hurriedly to the booth. Ric followed as fast as his beat-up body could. Standing in front of the booth, Ric looked it up and down. It was an enclosed contraption with silver borders, clear glass on four sides, a door that slid open at the touch of the red button located on a shiny metal plate on the side of the booth, and a red sign that read 'TELEPHONE' in white letters that were brightly lit.

The four of them were able to cram into the booth with room to spare. A black phone box with silver push-buttons on the dial pad was built into the corner, and when Vetti picked up the receiver and dialed the numbers five, seven, one, and nine, a loud vibrant sound shook the inside of the booth. Abruptly, there was a loud click, and the floor began to drop at a high speed. Lights flashed consistently as the falling floor took them down a narrow shaft with metal walls.

There was an abrupt jerk and then a loud thud when the descending floor came to a stop. Two heavily plated steel doors split apart, and Vetti and his two men exited the tight confinement. Ric followed slowly behind, entering a brightly lit spacious room with a cement floor and walls of steel. In the background, waiting for arriving passengers, was a modern design three-car express train. The engine and its trailing passenger cars were made of shiny silver steel with tinted windows and automatic sliding doors on the sides. Red flashing lights lined the tops and bottoms, and appeared to blink in a patterned sequence.

Uncle Vetti didn't bother waiting for Ric to enter the train. He and his two men went straight for the front passenger car and stepped inside once the door automatically slid open. After getting a good glimpse of the modern era train, Ric limped into the front car as well, and was amazed to see how clean and high-class the inside was. The floor was draped with a fine red carpet, and there were two booths on each side made of glossy black leather. There were even video screens attached to the top left and right corners of the car, broadcasting a twenty-four-hour news station.

Ric took a seat next to his uncle, easing himself into the opulent leather. Vetti looked upon the face of his young nephew and could see that he was confused, scared, and out of his comfort zone. He had just been through another traumatic life-threatening experience, and now he was being rushed to a mysterious location against his will.

"Relax, Ric, and just enjoy the ride. There is no more harm that will come to you tonight. I guarantee it," Vetti assured his nephew. Ric's only reply was a forward slouch and a glance to the floor. "And you might want to sit back before we get moving."

"Why?" Ric asked, as he sat up straight and leaned back in his seat. But there was no time for a response from his uncle. The hydraulic pressure of the train released with a hiss, and then the boosters on the back car ignited into a fiery crimson. A safety belt automatically strapped itself across Ric's lap just before the express train blasted off through a narrow tunnel.

At first, the train accelerated to a speed that caused Ric's head to stick to the back of the seat like glue, but then the velocity let up a bit, easing the pressure from the force of speed, allowing him to relax his body. He observed his surroundings, first looking to his right at the two men sitting together on the other side of the passenger car. They seemed completely calm, which reduced his own anxiety of the ride. *Hell, if those guys are relaxed, then I might as well stop acting like a pussy. They must've been on this train before.*

He then took a glance to his left and peered out the tinted window next to his uncle. Illuminous fluorescent lights flashed across the windows and reflected off his face. They were traveling through some sort of underground tunnel that had been constructed for the sole purpose of transporting the modern express train he was riding in. Where the tunnel led to, was a question in of itself.

A slight grin grew on the mouth of Ric's uncle as he took his own peak outside the window and then back at his nephew. "Not such a bad ride now, is it?"

Ric shrugged and answered, "It's not too bad." His uncle frowned at his lackadaisical response. Ric just smiled and said, "Okay, okay, it's pretty fucking awesome." And it *was* pretty awesome. With the exception of some windy and jerky turns, and descents that would cause a strange sensation in your balls, the ride was rather fluent and smooth.

Ric looked up at the video monitors. The news anchor was sitting behind a desk, debating with another analyst who was on a live video feed from the deep southern city of Sonia. Apparently, there had been an unusual amount of robberies involving explosions in recent months, and of course they are blaming the one Family that resides there; the Jovani Family.

Taking his focus off the news and back to the windows, Ric's eyes were widened by what he saw next. The outside tunnel wasn't metal and flashing lights anymore. They were now speeding through a clear cylindrical tube, surrounded by green murky water.

"Where are we?" Ric asked with blatant curiosity.

"Near the bottom of *Lake Everence*," Uncle Vetti answered.

Scrunching his eyebrows, Ric said, "But that's pretty far north of the city. Almost a hundred miles."

"Then I guess this train must be moving pretty damn fast," Vetti replied in a dry manner.

Leaning in closer to his uncle, Ric whispered, "Can you please tell me where we're going, Uncle Vetti? I don't feel like getting any more surprises tonight. I've had one hell of a day, a worse week, and an even shittier past couple years. Please, for the love of God, tell me where the fuck you are taking me."

Grinning, Vetti said, "It's not a secret within these walls, Ric, so you don't have to whisper to me." His grin grew wider. "And to answer your question, I'll first ask you a question. Where was the birthplace of the Rose Family?"

Not thinking on it at all, Ric answered, "I have no fucking clue."

"Well, you see, that is the sort of information you should know, Ric. I can't stress enough how important our Family history is to us. Without our history, then we would be lost in our existence of now. The past is what make us who we are in the present, even if the world was so different back then that it would be completely unrecognizable to us now. Many of us forget or don't even bother learning where we came from. What started as a single seed, has branched out into thousands of roots. But it's that one seed that we must remain loyal to. Especially, since that seed gives us the powers we need to convey our strong hold on this world," Vetti rambled on.

Taking in what his uncle just explained to him, Ric paused for a short moment and then said, "Uncle Vetti. I am so lost right now that I don't even know my ass from my face. What the hell are you talking about?"

Letting out a slight chuckle, Vetti replied, "You'll soon find out." He pointed a finger out the window. "We're almost there."

All Ric could see out the window was dirty lake water, but within seconds, the clear cylindrical tube rose out of the depths of the lake and skimmed across the surface. He leaned over his uncle to get a better view of the approaching area. Suddenly, he realized where they were…and why.

The Blessing of Ricalstro Rose

Part One

He didn't care whether he was ever given the opportunity. He didn't need it. Didn't want it. He rather sit his good-for-nothing ass on his couch in his sleaze-bag apartment and get stoned beyond the control of his mind. Maybe back when he was a young adolescent, when he still looked at his father like he was more than just a mortal man and his brothers as if they were the coolest cats in town, he would have followed them to the ends of Exodus and back, doing anything they asked of him.

But a tragic event in his life ended those thoughts of his Family. He was becoming estranged from the Family business in his later teen years, focusing more on his relationship than some silly magical wizardry that he now firmly believes, after two recent experiences, is a taint on society. The rape and murder of Galia right before his very eyes changed his outlook on life completely when he was awoken from a coma and listened to his brothers explain to him that they took vengeance on the men who committed the heinous act, before Ric ever had a chance to carry the revenge out on his own accord. It caused him to think lower of his brothers. It was as if they didn't give a damn about his loss. They carried out the revenge so their Family name wouldn't seem tarnished by some low-life scum on the streets. It has always been about the Family image.

He was angry at his father as well. Every time Ric brought up the tragedy, it seemed as if his father was sick and tired of hearing about it, rolling his eyes each time Ric gave his theory about another man watching from the darkness beyond. The man in the darkness. A conspiracy in which Ric firmly believed to be true. Someone else was watching the rape and murder unfold. Watching in distasteful satisfaction. His father may believe that it was just a bunch of bullshit, but Ric knows what he saw. He knows someone was there.

So now here he was, a passenger in a high-tech speeding contraption of solid metal, converging in on the location where all the mystery unfolds. The mystery of the Rose Family Relic. The Rose Quartet.

I should've know when Uncle Vetti told me we were going to where it all started. And now I realize what he means by the birthplace of the Rose Family, Ric thought as the train sped above the choppy waters of the lake. *He's taking me to a significant part of Exodus. The area where my Family first settled upon arrival to the new land. The place where my ancestors first drew their powers from the Rose Quartet.* Ric took a long and deep sigh at his next thought. *He's taking me to get Blessed.*

Ric and Uncle Vetti were both gazing out the window, reveling in the sight of the archaic building as it came into view. Beyond the shoreline of the great Lake Everence, stood an enormous mansion built out of gray stone from the bare hands of Ric's ancestors. It was more like a castle than an actual house. It was dark, gloomy, cryptic, and dimly lit from the outside. A monstrosity of a building that appeared to be ruggedly uncomfortable to inhabit in modern times. A deep, overgrown forest draped the background of the castle as Ric could see the outline of trees for split seconds when the night sky was brightly alit by flashes of distant lightning.

The speeding train began to slow down as it neared the shoreline. The clear cylindrical tube protecting the track came to an end and was replaced by a wooden overhang next to a stone walkway that led up to the castle doors. When the train came to a complete stop, the pressurized hydraulics were released, and the safety belts around the passengers unclicked and receded back into their rightful positions in between the leather seats. Vetti's two men stood up first and exited the train in a hurry. Their first job was to do a perimeter check outside the castle to ensure the grounds were safe.

Uncle Vetti took the liberty to get out of his seat before Ric. He stepped towards the exit and the automatic door swiftly slid open. Looking over his shoulder at Ric, he asked, "Are you coming, or are you going to sleep in the train like a hobo?"

Ric couldn't move. He was trepid about entering the old castle. He had it set in his mind that he didn't want to get Blessed. "I don't belong here," Ric answered his uncle in a low, sulking tone.

Vetti pointed through the doorway. "That building is your heritage. You have always belonged here. Ever since the day you were born."

Shaking his head, Ric said back, "I haven't been a part of the Family in quite some time, Uncle Vetti, and you know that. I tried to make myself believe that I could help when Georgie was killed, but I failed you and my father."

"I'll be the judge of that," Vetti retorted.

"I failed, Uncle Vetti!" Ric yelled, mostly at himself. "You and dad sent me to find out information on the whereabouts of Zasso Cicello, and instead, I just got two of my friends killed." Ric put his head down and clasped his hands in front of his face. "I fail at everything I do, so what makes you think that I'll succeed in becoming Blessed?" His voice was muffled as he talked into the space between his fingers.

Crossing his arms and giving Ric a hard, stern look, Vetti replied, "You never reported back to the Family what you *did* find out during your assignment, Ric, so how were we to conclude that it was a total failure?"

"Because I didn't find out what you wanted. I didn't get Miro Cicello to tell me where his brother is hiding."

"*Miro* Cicello?" Vetti curiously asked.

"Yea, Miro. I went to that Cicello thug hangout one night and bumped into him. Actually, I didn't just bump into him. We ended up partying all night...Until shit went horribly wrong for us," Ric explained, still talking into his fingers.

"And why didn't you report this information to us?" Vetti asked, not sounding thrilled with Ric's lack of communication.

"Because I was embarrassed. Miro tricked me like a fool."

Vetti frowned at Ric and then said, "Ric, I think you should get your ass off of that seat, and follow me into *Heritage Castle*, because you and I have a lot to discuss, and the night isn't getting any younger. I can see that you are deathly tired and in need of medical assistance, but you aren't going to get any treatment or any sleep, until you explain to me everything Miro Cicello had to say and what he did to you that night." He lowered the dark glasses below his eyes, so he could look at him with his naked irises. "Do you understand me?"

Lifting his head up and realizing his uncle was not fucking around, Ric answered, "Yes, Uncle Vetti."

Nodding his head in approval, Vetti moved his glasses back over his eyes, grinned, and said, "Good. Now let's get moving." He departed the train in a hurry, not waiting for his nephew to follow.

For a moment, Ric sat by his lonesome in the passenger car and thought about how much he wanted a lethal dose of smack right now. His addiction was creeping in. It had been hours since his last fix, and the trauma he went through tonight was not helping his need for drugs. *And there's no chance in hell that this old ass building has any smack. I guess I'll just have to get blind drunk while I'm here. Hell, maybe there's some good pain killers in there to add on to the booze.*

Ric shook his head at his own thoughts. Here he was, sitting outside Heritage Castle, the birthplace of the Rose Family, and all he could think about was his next fix. He brought shame to the name Rose. There was no way in hell that he was going to be Blessed. He would never get through the training involved to step in front of the sacred Family Relic. *And where in the hell is the Relic going to be hidden?* Ric asked his own mind. *This building is not a well-kept secret. I'm sure the higher members of the Cicello Family know the original birthplace of the Rose Family.*

After sinking into his own retched mind, Ric slowly rose out of his seat and limped towards the doorway. He held his side as each step sent a sharp pain through his midsection and into his ribs. Easing out of the passenger car, he stepped awkwardly onto the wooden planked walkway that the express train docked next to. With slow and careful strides, Ric walked to the end of the wooden planks and onto a small road of loose rocks that led straight to the castle.

The rains had let up, but the night sky was still overcast. Bright flashes of lightning enhanced the view of Heritage Castle every few seconds, adding more sinister character to the already fearsome sight. A couple hundred lengths tall and just as wide, Heritage Castle sat in the darkness like a guardian, inviting any trespasser into its halls full of doom. Just ahead of Ric was a drawbridge made of giant logs, sanded and tied together with thick rope. The drawbridge extended over a small river of water that cradled the castle like a mother's arms around a newborn, protecting it from the outside world.

As Ric gimped across the drawbridge, he observed the outside of the castle. The windows were all precise rectangles with wooden shutters that were opened to the sides, and each had a candle burning on the shelf, giving life to the inanimate object. The walls were glossy from the rains as little streamlets of water cascaded down the gray stone like tears down a weeping face. The very top of the castle had protruding spiked stones that were most likely used to barricade behind during an impending attack, but nowadays they served as a strong-arm decoration. In the middle of all the stone spikes was a marble statue of a fully-bloomed rose, with the word *Familia,* carved into the stem. *Familia* means 'family' in the old language.

The entrance to Heritage Castle was a stone archway barricaded by a solid iron gate about fifteen lengths high and ten lengths wide. Vetti Rose stood on the left side of the gate with his arms folded, patiently waiting for Ric to make his way across the drawbridge. Vetti's two men were standing guard on the other side of the gate, evidently awaiting orders from their boss to enter the building.

When Ric finally limped to the end of the drawbridge, his uncle unfolded his arms and spread them out as a sign of welcoming him to the castle. "Ricalstro Rose, this is the birthplace of *our* Family. This is where it all started," he clasped his hands together as if he were about to pray, "and this is where it will all end if one day the world shall come to a climax." Vetti extended his hand toward the solid gate and motioned it as if he was trying to grasp something that wasn't there. His hand was engulfed in an aura of crimson light, and then suddenly, the gate began to rumble and shake, before it started to lift upwards off its hinges. The gate rattled and clanked as it slowly receded into a wide crevice in the stone archway.

There is no key, padlock combination, or crank to set the gate in motion. *It has to be opened with magic,* Ric thought as he watched the gate recede further into the stone. *Magic from a Blessed Rose Family member...No wonder Uncle Vetti's two men are standing there with their thumbs up their asses.*

As soon as the gate's recession into the archway was completed, Vetti motioned for Ric to go inside first. Taking hesitant steps, Ric sauntered through the archway and into the castle. The entrance into the confines of the castle was a shadowy extensive hallway alit by torches attached to the stone walls. Each step he took echoed across the arched ceiling and out through the oncoming doorway, which had no barrier separating the hallway from the next room.

Following closely behind Ric, Vetti urged his nephew to keep moving when he stopped in front of the doorway. Abiding his uncle, Ric limped on and walked through, only to be transfixed by the massive hall that was presented in front of him.

Although the gray stone and dim lighting made the expansive hall seem desolate and tranquil, it was still a vison of unfathomable beauty. The ceiling was raised to at least a hundred lengths high. Four oversized wooden chandeliers, with burning candles branching from the center, hung overhead in a diamond pattern, while a sparkling glass sculpture of a red rose with a green stem and thorns was perfectly inserted in the center. The walls were strewn with burning torches to add light to the under lit hall. Ric was expecting to see tapestries flowing down the walls, as every castle he had ever seen in old pictures, but those must be in storage to keep them from aging, or his ancestors just didn't give a damn about decorating with any. There were doorways, corridors, and passageways throughout the entire hall that all led to their own area of the castle, but Ric had no clue where he would begin to explore if he was left alone to journey on his own. He probably would start by ascending the master staircase on the opposite side of the entrance, furbished with smooth, flossy stone, which spiraled to the second and third floors of the castle. The twisting handrails looked as if they were dunked and soaked in gold. Just one little chunk of the rail would give a poor man a fortune for life.

Besides some tables, chairs, bookshelves loaded with old texts, and four large crimson rugs edged with gold tassels, the grand hall was not furnished with anything else out of the ordinary…Except for one particular object located in the very center of the hall. When Ric took a couple steps forward and gazed up at the stunningly tall and inconceivably breathtaking object, it felt as if the air in his lungs were sucked out through his mouth. It was an anomaly. *There is no fucking way that that thing can be real,* Ric thought, doubting his own eyes.

It was a dynamic and gorgeous fountain with a sculpture of a prestigious man dressed in plated armor and a flowing cape that was tied around his neck and draped close to his ankles. He was holding a uniquely shaped sword in a fighting position over his head, and his other arm was extended outward, his hand in a clenching position, which Ric could only surmise that it represented the badass man casting magic. The statue was sculpted from shiny black marble, which added splendor to its already legendary presentation.

But even more astounding than the greatness of the statue was the implausible liquid that was spewing out from the orifices of his face-such as the nostrils, ears, mouth, and even the eyes-and the fingertips of the man's clenched hand. It was a red liquid. Blood red, but not as thick as actual blood. The bloody water spilled into the base of the fountain that was filled near the top with the abnormally colored liquid. Hundreds of fresh and fully bloomed roses were strewn across the surface of the red water, along with a multitude of single petals floating around them. The base of the fountain was round and made of white marble. Intricate carvings of intertwining roses circumnavigated the circular base and a gold plaque was nailed onto the section facing the hall's entrance.

With wandering eyes, Ric took trepid steps towards the mysterious fountain in order to read what was written on the plaque, and to get an even closer look at the magnificent sculpture that expelled a bloodlike liquid. *Or maybe it was real blood,* Ric conspired in his mind. Knowing the history of his Family and the business practices his father, uncle, and brothers have taken part of during his lifetime, it wouldn't surprise him if they had an ongoing flow of blood in the castle…*But that's a shitload of blood, so what the hell am I thinking? My family isn't a bunch of blood-thirsty creatures of the undead.*

Clutching his injured ribs, Ric kneeled in front of the fountain to read the golden plaque. In bold letters, scribed in a dark red, was the name of the man sculpted of black marble, *Ulozio Manazotti: The First Don.* And written directly underneath the man's name was a hair-raising phrase, scribed in a fancy script that read, *Until the End of Time, When the Lust for Revenge No Longer Imposes, The Family Will Forever Stay Strong and Yearn for the Smell of Blood and Roses.*

As Ric rose back to his feet and regarded the fountain with a gaping mouth, his uncle stepped out from behind him and stood to his left, leering at the majestic object along with him. Vetti placed a gentle hand on his nephew's shoulder as his mouth formed an uncharacteristic soft smile. The mystifying statue and fountain had them both mesmerized.

"Ulozio Manazotti," Vetti dramatically pronounced. "The first Don of the Rose Family. My, what an incredible man he was. Very powerful, but also very wise. He is the model of which every Blessed member of our Family should strive for." It wasn't hard to discern that this man was a hero to Vetti Rose.

"If he's the first leader of our Family, then why doesn't he have the last name of Rose?" Ric curiously asked his uncle.

"It was changed soon after Heritage Castle was built and Don Ulozio became Blessed by the Family Relic, taking his rightful throne as the leader of the Family. He changed his last name to Rose as tribute and undying loyalty to the object which gave him his power. The Rose Quartet." Vetti spoke of the name change with a sense of pride and love for the history of their Family.

"It's a good change," Ric said with a couple of slow nods. "Writing out the name Manazotti over and over again would have been a pain in the ass after a while." He looked at his uncle and smiled after his little joke, but Vetti wasn't amused one bit, so Ric cut off his smile in an instant and turned his attention back to the statue.

"It was in this very castle that Don Ulozio slayed the last king to ever rule Exodus. It was unanimously decided in the first ever Gathering of the Seven Blessed Families that no king should ever be a higher claim to those who possess instruments of unparalleled power such as Relics. Therefore, no other king was ever named and the Rose Family began their ascension into the greatness that it is today."

"By fear and murder," Ric interjected.

Vetti's face remained expressionless, but Ric still felt as if his comment struck a nerve inside his uncle. "There is a lot you do not know about the history of our Family and what it means to be born under the name Rose."

"It means that we lust for revenge and yearn for the smell of blood and roses. It's not hard to learn when it's written right on that plaque."

Shaking his head and displaying an all-knowing grin, Vetti walked away from Ric and the statue, and made his way over to the master staircase. He stopped directly in front of the first step, looked over his shoulder and said, "You have a feeble mind, Ric. But your inadequate thought process will soon be changed once you learn the deep secrets of our Family and the Rose Quartet."

That's what you think, Ric thought to himself.

"Now, follow me and I will show you where you will be sleeping at night and where you can wash up. But before you do any of that, I want you to explain to me what happened with Miro Cicello, so come now so we can get down to business." Vetti began to ascend the steep spiraling staircase that led to two high balconies overlooking the grand hall.

Ric was sure to get lost if he didn't follow his uncle, so he limped his way to the staircase and treaded the stairs, clutching his side as the pain shot through him with each grinding step. He followed him up to the second floor, took a left turn down an open hallway with a balcony to its left, and then a right turn into a closed hallway with golden candle stands lighting the way through. There were a couple of small wooden tables and chairs resting against the walls with a few closed books stacked on top of them. Each table had its own pen and inkwell stationed on the right corner. *When in the hell was the last time someone wrote something down in one of those books?* Ric thought, when he noticed the old-fashioned writing utensils. *I hope Uncle Vetti doesn't think I'm gonna write a fucking book report while I'm here.*

After opening the last door on the left of the hallway, Vetti showed Ric the room he would be staying in. It appeared to be rather comfortable compared to what the rest of the castle looked like. The floors were hard stone, but there were a few small rugs with ornate patterns sewed into the fabric, surrounding a queen-sized four-post bed with crimson sheets, pillows and drapes. A black comforter, decorated with dark green leaves, lied on top of the sheets. There were nightstands on either side of the bed, and both were topped with gold candleholders holding white candles that were lit by a small flame.

A sizeable wooden cabinet was placed in the left corner of the room and a tall standing mirror stood directly next to it. On the right side of the room was a bookshelf with all but five scattered books, accompanied by a wooden table and two chairs. There was nothing but an empty metal goblet and accumulated dust settled on the surface of the table.

To the left of the bookshelf was a doorway that was covered by just a thin tapestry. The tapestry was decorated with fancy 'R's' and stemmed roses that were fully detailed. Vetti walked across the room and pulled back the tapestry to show Ric what was beyond the doorway. It was the bathroom. He would finally be able to take a bath and wash the stink off him. He had been lying in a dirty puddle of magical water and rainwater, plus some of his own blood, so he smelled rather ripe, still dressed in the same clothes hours later.

"I'll have the handmaiden, Alessa, fix a hot bath and lay out clean towels for you when we get back from the den. You stink something so fierce right now that I'm tempted to wait until you've washed up to listen to your explanation of your assignment." He gave the air a couple sniffs, before cringing his nose. "As a matter of fact, that's exactly what I'll do. I can't take the smell much longer. I'll send up a guy named, Jezua, who will take a look at your injuries as well. He's not a real doctor, but he could've been if the Rose Family didn't ask him to drop out of medical school and work for us," he said with a sly grin. "Just make sure you meet me down in the den within the hour."

"And where in the hell is that supposed to be?" Ric asked, already lost in the spot he's at right now.

"I'll have Alessa escort you down. She's a beautiful young girl, but keep your thoughts and hands to yourself. I promised your cousin her hand in marriage."

Ric shrugged and said, "Hey, I'll do my best, but it won't be my fault if she comes on to me. Besides, Veno isn't here to claim her. "

"I doubt she'll want anything to do with you once she takes one breath of your stench. You smell like a garbage truck that just collided with a septic tank. Just one big pile of shit."

"Okay, I get it," Ric said, rolling his eyes.

"Good. Now get to it, so we can have our talk before the sun comes up. I do want to get some sleep tonight." Vetti brushed past Ric and exited the bedroom in a hurry.

Maybe he has to drop a big deuce, Ric derived from how hastily his uncle left the room. *Now where's this hot handmaiden at?*

Uncle Vetti wasn't just blowing smoke out of his ass. The handmaiden, Alessa, was a fine piece of work with her long brown hair, dimples, and razor blue eyes. A little flirting went on between the two, but Ric respected his cousin Veno, so he did as he was instructed and kept his hands to himself. But damn if he didn't want to ravage that young brunette and let out some of his frustration on her sweet spot down below. It would have been a great redemption after the night he had, but there wasn't any time to put any smooth moves on her anyway. The Family doctor, Jezua, came strolling into the bedroom as soon as Ric finished his bath and threw on a red-silk robe.

As young as Jezua was, he still had the appearance of a real doctor, dressed in a white lab coat with a stethoscope hanging around his neck and a thermometer stuffed with a couple of pens inside a pocket protector. Thick black-framed glasses covered his squinty eyes, and he adjusted them just about every five seconds when he was giving Ric a complete and thorough checkup. When he was done feeling around his ribcage, Ric wasn't surprised when Jezua let him know that he had a cracked rib and a couple of deep bruises in his abdomen. The Family doctor advised him to stay in bed for a couple of days-which Ric knew would never happen while he was at Heritage Castle-then wrapped a bag of ice around his abdomen and ribcage and gave him a bottle of painkillers. The painkillers were key for Ric. Not just for the pain, but to give him an extra fix while he drowned himself in a shitload of booze.

Now where the fuck is this den, so I can finally make myself a drink? No smack, no problem. I've got other ways to comatose myself.

Ric had a few laughs with Alessa while she escorted him down a dark stairwell, through several passages and corridors, and then finally toward a set of double doors made of strong oak and bordered with slats of iron. She knocked on the thick wood a couple of times, and almost immediately, the doors slowly creaked and grinded as they spread apart, revealing an area of pure comfort.

Uncle Vetti stood by his lonesome directly in the middle of the spacious room, standing next to a table carved of stone, which was placed on a black bearskin rug with the head of the beast still intact, forever pausing in a state of attack. The rug was surrounded by three black leather sofas, and a regal chair made of the same black leather, but the armrests and legs were edged with shiny beads of gold. A crackling fire burned upon a pile of logs in a stone fireplace attached to the wall on the right side of the room. Above the mantel was an oil painting of a regally dressed man inside an elaborately decorated gold frame. Ric was oblivious to who the man in the painting was, but the guy sure knew how to dress. His ruffled white shirt was covered by a red vest and a black coat with gold plates decorating the top of the shoulders and midway between his biceps. A white cloak was attached to the shoulder plates and hung well past his waist. He wasn't a bad looking guy either. Had to be a distant relative of his.

"That there is your great-great-great-great-who the hell knows how many more greats-grandfather or uncle or something," Ric's uncle explained when he noticed Ric staring at the painting. "There are a lot of gaps in the Family tree, but he's definitely related somehow to the both of us. The Rose Family has been bread strong ever since our ancestors laid their feet upon this land." Vetti was still wearing dark glasses. Ric thought it was absurd this late at night.

"What's his name?" Ric asked.

"Benavecci Rose."

"That's cool," Ric uncaringly replied. He spotted the bar only a few steps away from the fireplace. Immediately, he raced behind the bar and grabbed the only bottles of booze he could find. Wine. But most likely, it was some good aged shit. He removed the cork out of a full bottle and poured the contents of purple liquid into a lone goblet on the bar counter. When he finished pouring, he looked under the counter and inside the cabinets behind the bar for another cup.

"I don't need any wine," Vetti said to Ric in a stern tone of voice.

"Suit yourself," Ric said back, before chugging the entire goblet of wine. He let out a long sigh of relief and then wiped his mouth clean of any remnants. "Good God, I needed that." He reached inside the side pocket of his robe and pulled out his bottle of pills. He eagerly opened the top, shook out a few painkillers and shoved them in his mouth. To drain the drugs down his throat, he poured some more wine and took a healthy swig, sending the pills to the insides of his body where they will release their serene remedy for pain.

After carefully watching his nephew fill his stomach with toxins, Vetti said to him, "I understand that you have an ongoing problem with addictions, Ric, but tonight will you please keep your head as clear as you possibly can? I need to know every detail of what you witnessed and heard when you ran into Miro Cicello."

Ric took a small sip from the goblet, then shrugged his shoulders and said, "That's more of a reason to get all fucked up, Uncle Vetti. I have to tell you that story and relive that terrible night all over again."

Vetti clasped his hands behind his back and said, "It's important, Ricalstro. Every detail that you give to me will help us figure out the motive behind the order that was given to abduct your father at the Grand Theater. Once we have a clear motive for the attack, then we can start figuring out what our next move should…"

"They want the Relic, Uncle Vetti," Ric cut him off. "It's as simple as that. The Cicello Family wants the Rose Quartet. You and my dad had it figured out before I even went to that deathtrap of a nightclub."

"I see," was Vetti's only response as he paced across the floor, pondering the information he just heard.

Throwing back the rest of the wine in his goblet, Ric quickly poured himself another full glass, and then began to tell his uncle what transpired that unfortunate night. "I was a fool from the very beginning of the night. I never should've taken two of my friends with me, but I didn't want to stick out in the crowd. I figured I could blend in better with some company, but it didn't matter in the end. I was spotted almost immediately."

Vetti stopped his pacing and said, "Really?" in almost a whisper.

"Yea, it was pretty quick," he took a healthy swig of wine. "Then, before I knew it, I was sitting in a VIP booth with Miro Cicello himself, tossing back drinks and talking like we're best friends. He even made up a clever story about how he was hardly part of the Family business and called his dad a retard or some shit. I don't know, Uncle Vetti, I just fell for all his bullshit, and he made himself seem like such a genuinely nice guy. We seemed to have so much in common." He wiped his hand across his forehead, removing the recent buildup of sweat.

"And then what happened?" Vetti stoically asked.

"And then we went to the back of the nightclub, in some shitty VIP room, and snorted the hell out of some powder. Miro was dancing around like some sort of faggot, and then all a sudden, he's blowing my friend's brains out all over the place. I get knocked out for a short time and then I wake up to him in my face, retracting everything he told me about not being a part of his Family. In fact, he's an intricate part of the Cicello Family. He told me everything, except where to find Zasso and who gave his brother the order to attack the Grand Theater."

"What exactly did he say?"

Ric thought for a moment while filling up his goblet with even more wine. "If I can remember correctly, he blabbed on about how Exodus was in for a major change, and how it was critical for the Rose Family to be out of the picture in order for that change to happen, so that's why they want the Rose Quartet. And he also said that my dad was the one man who could give them the information on where it's hidden, because he would put his Family in front of the Relic. But then he mentioned *you*."

Vetti was already giving Ric his undivided attention, but the fact that Miro mentioned him caught his curiosity even more.

"Miro said they wouldn't come after you, because you had too much pride, and rather die than give up the Relic."

Vetti slowly nodded his head, agreeing with the notion. "Go on."

"There wasn't much more. Only the fact that he said that me and my siblings were going to get killed off one by one if dad doesn't give them what they want."

"Was that an immediate threat coming from Xanose himself?" Vetti anxiously asked as he stepped towards the bar.

Ric thought hard on the question. "I don't know. I don't think it was a valid threat. Or I could be wrong. I'm getting kind of drunk from this wine." He glanced at the bottle. "What fucking year is this?"

At first, Ric thought his uncle was going to jump across the counter, but he only leaned across it and smacked the goblet out of his hand, before grabbing him by the collar. "You need to cut the shit and clear your fucking head! Every detail of this encounter is vital to our Family, and your drunk ass isn't helping! I know what your thought process around the rest of the Family is, Ric. You look at everyone else in the room and have the idea that they all think you're just a junky shitbag on the streets. And you know what?" He paused for a quick response, but didn't get one. Ric was in shock by the sudden hostility. "Most of the time that *is* what everyone is thinking about you! Ric Rose. The biggest fuckup to be shot out of Don Maretto's dick!" He paused again, letting that shot sit in. Ric put his head down, apparently hurt by the awful thing his uncle just said. "Yea, Ric. I've overheard someone say that about you before. How does it feel?"

Ric had no reply, besides the tear that formed in his right eye and rolled down his cheek.

"I asked you a question, Ricalstro!" Vetti shouted, shaking the shit out of Ric. "How does that fucking feel?"

"I don't feel anything," he answered in a somber tone.

"Bullshit!" Vetti shouted, then let go of Ric's collar. "I know how it makes you feel. It makes you feel worthless, empty, alone. Your insides twist into a knot and your heart sinks down to the pit of your stomach. Your confidence is ripped out of you and broken into pieces to be served to other people around you. They feast on your confidence, dwindling it down to only a speck of dirt. You thirst to be saved, Ric. Your body aches for someone to come along and mend your pieces of confidence back together. You want to make yourself better, but you don't know how.

"And as much as I don't agree with your lifestyle and the dark abyss it has taken you down into, I understand why you have succumbed to a life of drug and alcohol abuse. It's not easy dealing with tragedy." Vetti waved his fingers in front of his face. "Especially, when it unfolds right in front of your eyes."

"You don't understand me, Uncle Vetti. Nobody does," Ric said, shaking his head, while looking at the ground.

Vetti held up his hand and pointed a finger up. "On the contrary. I do understand you, Ric. I see directly through you. You are dying on the inside, and it's taking you every ounce of strength to wake up and keep living every morning." Ric kept his head down, slightly shaking his head some more as Vetti continued the lecture. "But there is hope, Ric. There is a bright glimmering light at the end of this tunnel of inner destruction. And it's here, in this castle. You are being given a life-changing opportunity to be Blessed by our Family's sacred Relic...That is, if the Rose Quartet deems you worthy of its Blessing."

212

Vetti clasped his hands in front of his face as if he was praying to God that the Relic would Bless Ric.

He finally lifted his head back up and said, "It's a waste of time, Uncle Vetti. I'm *not* worthy of a Blessing."

"You don't know that for sure. A Relic doesn't base its decision on what can be seen on the outside. The strength that lies deep on the inside of a person's soul is what matters."

"Trust me, Uncle Vetti, the Relic won't deem me worthy. And even if it somehow did, I don't want to be given a Blessing anyway."

Vetti's forehead crinkled, his eyebrows slanted, and his face reddened. "What did you just say?"

Ric bent over, picked up the goblet his uncle knocked to the floor, and placed it on the counter to be refilled again. When he grabbed the bottle of wine, he replied, "I said that I don't want to be Blessed."

The lenses in Vetti's glasses were about to shatter from the fire brewing on his face. He seemed livid at Ric's careless attitude toward the sacred Relic. "And why not, Ricalstro?"

Ric guzzled down the entire goblet full of wine, and then answered, "Because the Family Relics have brought nothing but violence and murder into this world. Those things help people who have been overcome by evil and greed. I have seen it with my own eyes, Uncle Vetti. I've lived it. *You* have lived it." He poured himself another goblet full of booze and took a generous sip. He wiped his mouth off and continued, "Most of the people in Exodus treat our Family like we're so noble and great, but there are some out there who know the entire truth of what we're all about. Corruption, revenge, and murder. Shedding blood is what gets everyone off in the Seven Blessed Families. I wouldn't be surprised if some of the Families drank the blood of their enemies like wine." Ric took another healthy gulp, spilling some of it down his shirt. "You know who saw the corruption in this Family, and headed the opposite direction? Melroy. My best friend, Melroy. He became a fucking officer of the law because of the shit he witnessed hanging around this Family. And I witness it all the time too. My girlfriend was raped and murdered in front of me, while I was left for dead by those same bastards. And in the last week, I've been tortured and almost killed twice, because of this fucking Family. So, that's why I don't want to be Blessed, Uncle Vetti. Because that Relic is nothing but a fucking curse!"

It happened so fast, that Ric had no time to react when it did happen. Vetti extended his arms in a pushing motion, and a crimson blast of energy was expelled out of the palms of his hands. The magical blast struck Ric directly in the chest, lifting him off his feet and propelling him backwards. His body crashed into the wooden cabinet behind him, shattering the doors. His limp body slid to the ground.

Vetti performed the same magical blast of energy into the bar counter, and shattered it into thousands of wood splinters. He then walked towards Ric's fallen body and looked down upon him. "You know nothing about our sacred Relic, Ric Rose. And you have no right to speak against its powers, unless you yourself have been Blessed by it."

Vetti reached down and wrapped his strong hand around Ric's throat. Ric tried to resist, but it wasn't even worth trying. Vetti was too strong, and too gifted with his Blessing. He lifted Ric off the ground, and then shoulder rammed Ric into the shelves of the wood cabinet, breaking every shelf and bottle of wine being stored inside. Ric, once again slumped to the floor, but Vetti caught him by the throat before he landed on his backside.

Clenching his throat with a firm grip, Vetti leaned in close to Ric's face, and with a look of detest he said, "One day, you will regret what you have just said about the Rose Quartet…And maybe you're right, Ric. Maybe you aren't worthy of its Blessing."

Instead of letting him go, Vetti decided that another lesson of his strength was in order. He lifted Ric over his head, and flung him like a rag doll across the entire length of the den. He flailed his arms and legs in midair, until landing hard into the stone wall on the opposite side of the room. Vetti wasted no time walking over to his beaten body.

Holding the bottle of wine Ric was drinking, he dumped the rest of it all over Ric's face, burning his eyes with the alcohol. Ric let out a shriek, but it was stopped by a foot being stepped on his throat. "From now on, your intake of alcohol will be regulated and your use of drugs will not be permitted while you stay in this castle. There are no exceptions, and there is no choice of going home, so it will be in your best interest to forget about your precious habits and move on with your life."

Ric lied on the ground in a fetal position as he gasped for air. He was in an excruciating amount of pain. Even more pain than earlier in the evening, but his uncle didn't seem to give a shit. He nonchalantly stepped over Ric's broken body and exited the den without saying another word to his nephew. And if Ric heard his uncle correctly, he was not only going to be in a lot of physical pain, but he about to be in a serious amount of mental anguish as well. His uncle just cut him off from the use of drugs and large amounts of alcohol...*But for how long?* Ric asked himself. *Really? Uncle Vetti just handed me a major ass-whooping, and all I can think of is when I'll have my next fix,* Ric answered himself. *What's the point of being here? The Rose Quartet will never Bless a loser like me.*

Detective Melroy Statz

And the Long Ride Home

It was a long and windy assent up the road to *Skyline Hills*, a lavish, rich neighborhood located in the western hills, overlooking Juna. A congregation of multi-million-dollar mansions, it's inhabited by some of the more prominent citizens of Juna, such as business owners, lawyers, agents, actors, moguls, members of the Legislation, and even a few batball players. But Detective Melroy Statz had no interest in visiting any of them. He was heading towards the most extravagant house in the community, owned by the pompous leader of the Cicello Family, Don Xanose Cicello.

For the past week, Melroy had been vigorously investigating the Grand Theater Massacre case, although the ESFU was supposedly already taking care of it. But he didn't trust them. They worked for the President, not the city of Juna. They weren't interested in finding justice for the Rose Family. They were more interested in creating controversy within the Seven Blessed Families, to prove to the world that the Families were the main source of problems in Exodus, and that the President and the Legislation were going to solve those problems by being in complete control of everything.

At least, that's what Agent Strain told me, Melroy thought as his old-school automobile winded around a curve and into a straightaway. *And maybe they're right. Maybe the world would be better with the President in complete control. Maybe he would make better use of the Relics…Or maybe not. What if he were to exploit his power?*

The ESFU could work whatever scheme they wanted for the time being. Melroy had other priorities. After the impromptu run-in with his old friend, Ric Rose, Melroy was inspired to dig deeper into the murder heard around the world. In their intense conversation down at the municipal building, Ric had pretty much dared Melroy to confront the leader of the Cicello Family to find the answers he was looking for. But Melroy didn't want to just show up at Don Xanose's home with the little information he had. He needed more.

So Melroy went to his superior for help. He met with Captain Riccard at Midway Park, a community park located almost directly in the middle of the city. Melroy spotted the Captain sitting alone on a metal bench eating a sandwich that he'd packed for his lunch. Melroy casually walked towards Riccard and took a seat next to him. There was a period of silence between the two as Riccard chewed a bite of his salami and cheese sandwich. The only background noise was the sounds of birds trying to out chirp one another and the rustling of leaves as squirrels jumped from tree to tree, playing their own version of the game of grab-ass.

"So, what's this about, Detective?" Riccard asked as he gnawed on the fat-ridden meat. "I usually enjoy my lunchbreak in this park alone for a reason. To get away from all the bullshit of our jobs."

Melroy watched as a squirrel crept up behind another squirrel, tickled its ass with its whiskers, and then bolted across a branch and jumped into another tree as the other squirrel chased it.

"I once heard a rumor about a special informant assigned to the Cicello Family," Melroy said, cutting to the chase. "I was just wondering if that's exactly what it was, just a rumor, or if there's actually an officer out there pretending to be in the midst of the Cicello organization. I'm not much of a gambler, Captain, but if I were to bet on which is true, I'd lay down my life earnings on the latter."

Captain Riccard chuckled before he chomped down on the end of his sandwich. He finished the last bite, chewed it up while rubbing the crumbs off his hands, and then replied, "I like to keep my undercover operations as the former. Rumors. Therefore, my snooping detectives won't come to me and ask to talk to one of them, risking the revelation of their identities."

Leaning back, trying to get comfortable on the rigid bench, Melroy said, "Under the circumstances, I was hoping there would be an exception for one of your most trusted officers."

Captain Riccard grinned. "You think I trust you like that, Detective Statz?" he asked. "A young detective like you, who used to run the streets with the Rose brothers?

You're talking to a man who's been in law enforcement for the past thirty-five years. I've lent out my trust to many young detectives such as yourself in the past, Melroy, and many times I've been made a fool. What makes you think I'll give you that special trust as well?"

Melroy reached inside his coat pocket, pulled out a shiny silver badge, and tossed it over to Riccard, who barely reacted in time to catch it in his lap. "That piece of metal means the world to me, Captain. It represents everything I worked so damn hard for in the last couple years. But I'm willing to give it up if I'm not able to continue with my investigation. And in order to continue with my investigation, I need some solid information on Don Cicello that only a man balls deep in his organization can get for me."

Lan Riccard stared deep into the silver shield with the blue letters, JCPD. A ray of sun reflected a bright light off the badge and across the face of Riccard.

"Besides," Melroy went on, "you don't want the ESFU solving the case in their own way and making us look bad, do you?"

Riccard gazed up and down the badge for a few more moments, squinting his eyes. "His name is Detective Broc Hayne, but in the Family, he goes by the alias, Lito Calazari. AKA, Lito 'the Lion'. He has one hell of a mane of reddish-brown hair," he said with a cunning smile.

It was three days later when the contact finally went through. Melroy had been twiddling his thumbs with a piping hot coffee at Crist's Eatery when he got the call. He was to meet the contact under a ruined bridge in one of the eastside ghettos. A shady spot where neither of the Families would suspect a secret meeting between a detective and an undercover agent.

The rain was coming down hard, pounding the roof, windshields, and hood of his car. Melroy clicked off his lights when he spotted the broken-down bridge. There was a lack of moonlight in the sky, but Melroy still spotted an unwanted shadow leaning against the wall of the underpass. He hurriedly unlatched his car door and slammed it shut behind him, then took off running through the downpour. By the time he reached the underpass, he was soaking wet from head to toe.

218

The shadow seemed to jump out to him, grabbing him by the collar and slamming him against the wall in what he thought was an unnecessary violent greeting. *Is this even the guy?* Melroy questioned himself when he was driven into the hard stone. *Or is the jig up before it even started?*

The shadowed man let go of his grasp, then pulled back his hood, revealing his identity. Even in the black of the night, the proud mane of hair was easy to recognize.

"Listen to me, you fuck," Broc Hayne, AKA Lito 'the Lion' spurted out. "The name of the game is this. You get me fucked and then you get fucked by your own accord. I've known a lot of detectives who would sell their souls to get information from undercovers, but who also didn't give a shit if that agent was found floating down the river that next weekend." He pointed a hard, steady finger at himself. "I'm not gonna be one of those sorry, waterlogged sons of bitches, you hear. I'm all about the thrill of the chase, so I like what I do, or I wouldn't be doing it. I get a lot of perks from the Family and from the department, but don't you think for one second that I wouldn't give it all up just to save my ass from getting a bullet between the eyes and then becoming a piece of meat, the fish can nibble on while my wrinkled carcass ends up on the front page of the news. I don't want to be a hero…Not yet."

"You have my word that I won't sell you out," Melroy promised the man he had never met before. "And the Captain has my badge for collateral."

Broc pulled out a revolver from under his coat, pointed the loaded weapon at Melroy, and cocked the hammer. "Your word don't mean shit, detective." Melroy timidly raised his hands, but showed no expression on his face. "I don't trust a fucking soul. You can't trust anyone in my line of work. You can only trust yourself. So, if I even get a hint, a clue, a sniff, a sentence, a word, a fucking letter that has my real name revealed to these assholes, then I'm gonna make sure they make work of you before they even have a chance to get at me." He waved the revolver around in circles in front of Melroy's face. "They'll make dogfood out of you motherfucker. Fresh fucking meat."

The anxious undercover finally released the cocked hammer and put the gun back under his coat. Melroy felt a sense of relief, although his facial expression was still stone cold.

"But this shit going down right now is too important to hide, and I heard your backstory involving the Grand Theater massacre, so I feel like I have an obligation to help you. So, I guess I have a soft spot or something, but don't think I won't put some lead straight up your ass." Suddenly, the hard-ass undercover smiled, reached in his pocket, yanked out a cig, lit it up, and blew out a hefty cloud of smoke. "Now, I'm gonna tell you some shit that's gonna blow your balls away, so keep your ears tuned in tight cause I aint gonna repeat myself when I'm done."

Melroy nodded, and attentively listened to every word Lito 'the Lion' had to tell him...And he didn't need any of it repeated. The info was just too damn good.

Melroy's car pulled up to the metal gate that enclosed the Cicello mansion. There was a guard waiting in a booth in front of the gate. When he saw the car pull up, he immediately stepped outside the booth and confronted Melroy.

"Who the fuck are you?" the guard ignorantly asked. He was around the same age as Melroy. His hair was slicked back and so greased up that it looked like he just got out of the shower. A real fucking grease-ball this clown was.

"I'm here to fuck your mom," Melroy answered back as he flipped open his wallet and held it in front of the guard's face. Inside the wallet was an identification card, displaying his credentials as a Juna Police Detective.

"A detective, huh? Is Don Cicello expecting you? Because he sure as shit didn't mention anything to me about a visit from a police dog."

Melroy closed his wallet and replied, "Just let him know that Detective Melroy Statz is here for a friendly visit. He'll let me through."

"What makes you think that, dog?"

"Because he knows who I am, so make the fucking call, grease-ball."

The guard wasn't too happy, but he still made the call to inside the mansion, and sure enough, Melroy was allowed to pass through the gate.

The driveway leading to the mansion was a long brick road surrounded by tall green hedges that were trimmed with immaculate precision. Once the line of hedges ended, the driveway turned into a large circle that wrapped around a luxurious white marble fountain that shot spurts of water up to twenty lengths into the air.

Melroy parked his car in front of the fountain, stepped out onto the brick road, and gazed upon the home of the Cicello Family. The front door was made of solid black steel, reaching up about fifteen lengths. The rest of the mansion was constructed of cement and brick, nearly indestructible, unless you were to use a massive tank or a slew of helicopters armored with heavy artillery out the ass.

There were no opened windows or balconies overlooking the front lawn and driveway. Everything was sealed tight. Plain and simple, the place was a fucking fortress. The Cicello Family was ready for a war, which made Melroy's suspicions of Don Xanose's involvement in the Grand Theater massacre raise even higher.

It didn't catch Melroy by surprise that the front doors slowly opened with a deep vibrating moan. He had expected not to be allowed access through the mansion. But what he didn't expect, was two gigantic black canines to appear, roaring towards him with vicious barks and displaying their razor-sharp teeth.

It felt like he was in slow motion, but in a state of panic, Melroy reached behind his back for his piece. He wasn't about to get bit in the balls by some dogs that were the size of horses. Those black bastards would rip his dick right off. But in the midst of their galloping, Melroy heard a loud raspy voice yell out to his ravenous guards.

"Boys!" the voice shouted. The dogs skidded to a halt just a couple lengths in front of Melroy, heeding to their master's voice.

Melroy swallowed a lump in his throat, but remained calm and didn't show any fear. He didn't want to give Don Cicello the satisfaction of knowing that he almost pissed his pants right then and there.

A short but stout man with balding black greasy hair casually walked through the entrance of the mansion and out onto the driveway. Don Cicello was wearing a neon yellow dress shirt, only buttoned hallway up, exposing his long chest hairs, and slick white pants and shiny white shoes. A trio of gold chains hung from his neck, and the golden rings on his fingers twinkled in the sunlight as they held a thick cigar, which Melroy thought had the odor of dog shit. But that was only because one of Xanose's dogs just made a hot steamy pile right in front of him.

A fake friendly smile was cast on Xanose's face as he approached Melroy. His bodyguard, Rondo, and a few other Cicello gangsters followed closely behind him.

"Melroy, my boy, Melroy. It's been too fucking long since the last time we spoke," Xanose said, acting as if he was actually happy to see him. But he wasn't. This visit was going to be a pain in the ass for him, and he knew it.

He firmly shook Melroy's hand with both hands, and then patted him on the back like he was an old friend. But he wasn't. No, Xanose couldn't fucking stand him, and Melroy wanted it that way.

"You look good, my boy. You're dressed a little drab, but you still look young and virile," Xanose commented on him with a cheesy grin.

"It's good to see you too, Don Xanose. And might I say, that you don't look a day older since the last time I saw you," Melroy commented back.

"Well, as long as I keep drinking and smoking, the years just keep shedding away," he jokingly said with a hefty laugh that squealed at the tail end. He then placed a hand on Melroy's shoulder, turned around to his bodyguard, and said, "This is one hell of a detective right here, Rondo. A true and genuine officer of the law. Always working for the good citizens of Juna."

Is he being for real, or just being a prick, Melroy quickly thought. *Who fucking knows with this guy?*

"He looks like a pig to me," Rondo mentioned in a deep, hearty tone of voice.

"Well, that's what they call them these days, but Detective Statz is an old friend, so we're gonna keep our stupid shithead comments to ourselves for now, and treat him with some respect. Is that clear, Rondo?" Xanose said with his eyebrows raised. It was more of a direct order than a question.

"Of course, Don Cicello. A friend deserves respect," Rondo replied, not taking his big saucer eyes off of Melroy.

"Good. Now, why don't you take the boys for a walk around the house and then watch over Detective Statz's car while we go have ourselves a private chat. That's a classic automobile he's got there."

Rondo gave only a slight nod to his boss's order. He wasn't very happy about his assignment, but fuck him. Melroy didn't want that big monstrous bastard getting in the way. Things might get a little heated between the two, and the last thing he needed was his investigation getting cut short.

Don Xanose led Melroy through a narrow pathway of elegant flowers and neatly trimmed bushes. Petals from the flowers were scattered all over the stone path as if they were neatly placed there for the arrival of a king, and the bushes were such a sparkling green that they seemed to wink at them with every step. A short breeze picked up as they walked, blowing a couple petals in Melroy's face. It was more annoying than it was graceful.

"I prefer to live my life in style rather than like a pig all cooped up in the middle of the city," Xanose said, breaking the silence as they trekked through his modern garden. "I spend a lot of my hard-earned money keeping up with this property, but it's worth it. I get to spend most of my time smelling fresh flowers rather than fresh piss and shit on the streets of Juna. I always wondered why Maretto didn't get any property outside the city for himself. I guess he loves that fucking trash-hole more than he ever loved the wilderness."

"You're so sure he doesn't own any homes outside of Juna?" Melroy asked, just making small talk.

"None that I know of," Xanose replied after thinking on it for a moment. "When you're the most prestigious man in the world, it's hard to hide your luxuries from the public…But he does hide a lot of his work from the public, so maybe it's not that difficult for him. Who knows what that man has hiding outside of Juna?"

"I certainly don't."

Xanose huffed and said, "I wouldn't imagine you would. The man never trusted anyone outside his own Family, so why the hell would he even begin to trust you?" Melroy shrugged at the thought as Xanose continued, "Just because you were a childhood friend of his boys don't mean shit, Melroy. You're on the other side of the playing field, *Detective*. The opposite side of the law, in which *you* believe to be the correct side."

The tunnel of flowers and bush opened into a spacious chunk of land surrounded by towering pine trees. Right smack dab in the middle was a cement pool with a brick border. The water was crystal clear as the breeze pushed tiny ripples from the shallow end to the deep end. The deep end was equipped with a long white diving board and a spiraled baby blue sliding board. Fancy lawn chairs were scattered around the edge of the pool.

"If we're talking about the true nature of the law, then I *am* on the right side, and you and Don Maretto are on equal sides of the wrong side."

"Equal sides?" Xanose queried with a raised eyebrow, stopping in front of the glimmering waters of his in-ground pool. He took a long drag of his stogie, blew the smoke out the side of his mouth, and said, "I'm on my own side of everything, Detective Statz. Just because he and I decided to make an alliance and share the city of Juna together, doesn't mean that we plan our futures together. We see out of our eyes very differently, he and I. We both have our own plans for the future."

"And what are those?" Melroy quickly asked with half a smile.

A sly smile grew on Xanose's face as he replied, "Well, if I told you that, then I'd have to kill you."

Melroy scoffed and said, "Oh yes, the archaic way of the gangster. Secrecy silenced by bloodshed. How fitting for an old fuck like you."

Don Xanose could've blown up in Melroy's face, or worse, sic his deer-legged dogs after him; or worse than that, call over his big henchman, Rondo, for the lack of respect he was displaying, but instead, Xanose just went along with the punches and shot back, "I may be an old fuck, my boy, but I still hold a higher ground in this world than you could ever imagine. You are a police detective who strictly abides by the law, so you are very much outnumbered in Exodus. Law enforcement wants to quickly point at the Seven Families as the outcasts, but who are you really kidding, Detective? We *do* possess the only accessible magical power in Exodus, you know!"

With his fist to his chin, Melroy chuckled to himself.

Perturbed and annoyed, Don Xanose scrunched his eyebrows and asked, "What seems to be so amusing, Detective Statz?"

With a straighter face, Melroy replied, "You just walked right into the subject I wanted to talk to you about."

Sucking on his cigar a little bit harder, Xanose mumbled, "Oh yea?"

"Yea." He folded his arms across his broad chest. "I had every intention of coming here and demanding answers to where your son, Zasso, is, but I know you'll just deny, deny, deny, and lie through your fucking teeth, but you and I know, that you know exactly where he is and what he's doing."

Xanose spat hard at the ground. "That's bullshit, Melroy! I don't know what rumors are going around the confines of your department building, but you better believe me when I say that I don't have a clue where that skinny prick is hiding! And when I do find out, he's in for a lifetime of trouble."

"My point exactly, Don Xanose. Your lips are sealed and you're covering your son's tracks. I get it. I didn't expect for you to tell me the truth." Xanose was about to open his mouth to lie to him some more, but Melroy beat him to the chase. "But I'll tell you something right now, Xanose buddy, you're not going to be able to deny what I'm going to accuse you of next." A sly smile grew from the side of his mouth. "Nope, the idiotic look on your face is going to give yourself away."

Xanose's eyes became colder, darker. His one eyebrow raised high into his forehead with an exaggerated curvature, while his other eyebrow burrowed down deep into the eye socket. "Try me," he grimly challenged.

Melroy took a couple steps toward Xanose and asked, "Are you going to deny that you have an alliance with Don Maximo Rocca, and that the two of you are trying to infiltrate the other Families in order to find and capture all of the other Family Relics?"

There was no hiding the look of shock in Xanose's eyes. As much as he tried to control his pupils from growing bigger and wider, it wasn't enough to conceal his astonishment. Besides, the pin-dropping silence in the air was a dead giveaway in of itself that Melroy had just caught the leader of the Cicello Family completely off-guard.

A single bead of sweat trickled down Xanose's forehead while his face turned a dark crimson. "Where did you hear such a false rumor?" he said through his gritted yellow teeth.

"False rumor?" Melroy said as if it was the most idiotic statement he had ever heard. "No, I'm pretty sure I was told this information from a reliable source, Don Xanose. You're not the only one in this dark, twisted circle of hell that has secret informants. You should be smart enough to know that, my old greasy friend."

Cigar clenched in between his tobacco stained fingers, Xanose pointed at Melroy and said, "You're making up lies, Detective. I can see it in your eyes and sense it in your tone. The garbage coming out of your mouth has no validity whatsoever. I can smell it on your putrid breath."

"You're the one smoking the cigar that smells like absolute shit, Xanose. So, don't accuse me of spitting up garbage. Your entire life reeks of it."

"Fuck you!" Xanose shouted, his eyes about to pop out of their sockets.

"Very classy response, Don Cicello. Is that how you're taught to speak to law enforcement when you are in the process of being Blessed by your Family Relic?"

Melroy was striking the nerves. He was sliding underneath the skin. Slinking his way through the mind of an elite gangster. Pin-pricking all the nerve cells and fibers, transmitting nerve impulses throughout his body…It was fun. But the fun wasn't going to last. Don Xanose would eventually spoil the entertainment and dismiss Melroy before he lost complete control of his temper.

"Who the fuck are you to criticize how I speak? Like I said before, *Detective*, you are outnumbered in this world. Greatly outnumbered. You are a dying breed. Your badge and your department have no authority over me and my Family, no matter how much you want it to. This world was built on corruption, and my Family's legacy was one of the founding fathers. *You*, on the other hand, were born of a whore mother, knee deep in the excrement of society!"

The entertainment was spoiled as predicted. It was Xanose who had now struck a nerve in Melroy. He didn't care for his mother being labeled as a whore. She had no other choice.

"We breathe the same air, you and I," Melroy said, the pronunciation of the words in nearly a whisper.

Xanose's eyebrows rose and his eyes lit up. "Yes," he said, exaggerating the *s*, "but my air tastes all the finer." He ended the sentence with a devious grin. A grin that said, 'I'm better than you and I always will be'.

Maybe he had a point. The air did smell a little fresher up here in the hills, beyond the city skylights. The air wasn't polluted with exhaust from automobiles, machinery, refineries, and factories. You wouldn't walk around any street corner within miles of this house and see a homeless person taking a shit in public, while masturbating into a discarded smut magazine…No, the air did taste all the finer up in *Skyline Hills*. But Melroy would rather still live in the depths of the city. He was comfortable knee-deep in all the shit.

"You may think you have a point, Don Xanose, but you and I both know that you're not as smart and as tough as you project yourself to be. You're son, Zasso, is a fugitive of the law, and you are hiding his whereabouts, which makes you guilty of harboring a murderer. Hundreds of eyewitnesses recall him bursting into a live theatrical performance and sadistically murdering innocent people. Including Maretto Rose's son, Georgiano."

"Georgiano Rose was not so innocent," Xanose retorted back.

Melroy aggressively stepped forward, looked down upon the balding head of Don Xanose, pointed at his chest, and said, "He was innocent in the eyes of the law! And he was innocent in the eyes of me!" He lowered his pointed finger and took a couple steps back. "Don Maretto Rose deserves justice for the murder of his son, and he's gonna have it, whether it's through law enforcement, or by his own hands. My job is to deliver that justice into his hands, personally. Your son can't hide his face forever, Don Cicello. You don't just commit a heinous crime at a highly publicized event and then disappear forever without a trace, unless you're dead. Sooner or later, he's going to emerge from the little hole he's hiding in, and you bet your greasy fat ass that I'm gonna be the one to nab him when he does."

There was a long moment of silence between the two as they stared each other down. Melroy observed Xanose's facial features as the stare-down drew out. The beady sweat trickling down his forehead. The slanted eyebrows and vampiric eyes. The quivering of his upper lip. Xanose was heated. His internal furnace was on the verge of burning from the inside out like an explosion of liquid hot magma out of a volcano…But then suddenly, his expressions contorted into a look of peace and serenity. Like thunderstorm clouds that had just dissipated and revealed a sunny clear blue sky. He even gave a small grin out the corner of his mouth.

"What?" Melroy asked, his tone harsh and aggressive. "What the fuck are you grinning at you callous prick?"

Xanose's grin grew larger when he answered, "There's a lot in my world to smile about, Melroy. Just take a look around you and feast your eyes on the rewards I get for being such a callous prick, as you say." Melroy's eyes didn't flinch. "Your words don't bother me, Melroy. You can harass and interrogate me as much as your blue-blooded heart desires and scour the lands of Exodus until the engine of your shit-kicker car burns out, but your search for my son will only end up in disappointment…and danger, that you alone, couldn't possibly handle."

"I can handle myself, Don Cicello," Melroy said with a hard look.

Pointing his smoking cigar, Xanose said, "You may think so, Detective. And in many of the ordinary instances in your line of work, I believe that you do handle yourself quite well. But this is no ordinary instance, young man. You don't know what you're getting yourself into. My advice to you would be to stay clear of the dangers lurking around the corners of your investigation. You don't want to get yourself caught up in something that might layout the foundation of your demise."

Melroy swallowed a lump of distaste. "Is that a threat, Don Xanose? Because threatening an officer of the law is a very serious offense. Once that could result in a long ride in the back seat of a shit-kicker car down to the police station." His demeanor was growing past being agitated with the boss of the Cicello Family. He had just about enough.

"A threat?" Xanose said, acting shocked by the accusation. "No, Detective, there's no threat coming from me. I only hold so much power in Exodus."

Confused, Melroy asked, "What are you talking about?"

Wrapping his arms behind his back, Xanose paced along the edge of the pool. Melroy followed closely behind. "The tides of this world are changing, Detective, and I had to make the choice of whether or not my Family would adapt to the change, or if we would be consumed by the tidal wave. The wheels that have been turning, even before my son stepped foot into the Grand Theater, is beyond my control, or the control of any of the leaders of the Seven Blessed Families." He stopped his short walk by the shallow end.

"But of course I can't tell you much more than that, Detective Statz. Like you said before, I follow the archaic way of the gangster. Secrecy silenced by bloodshed, as you put it. And if I reveal too much to a man dedicated to the opposite side of the coin, then it will be my blood that will be shed."

The more Don Xanose talked, the more disturbed and confused Melroy became. He figured that the Cicello leader didn't have the brass to give an order to kidnap Maretto Rose, but it only made sense that he was collaborating with someone who did. Like one of the other Family members. Like Don Maximo Rocca. *They are the ones rumored to be infiltrating the other Families to steal their Relics,* Melroy quickly thought. But if what he's saying is true, then neither of them are handing down the orders, and neither are the rest of the Seven Blessed Families. *But then who does that leave?* The answer was nobody. Or a mystery person. But what mystery person would hold that kind of power? The Juna Police Department has piles of records on all the scum-sucking bastards in Exodus, but they all pale in comparison to the leaders of the Seven Blessed Families, so what the fuck was going on here?

As gentle and as least threatening as he could, Melroy grabbed the sagging shoulder of Don Xanose, and forced him to turn around to face him. With a look of dismay, intrigue, and concern all wrapped into one, Melroy asked Xanose, "Who are you working for?"

From his peripherals, Melroy noticed the bodyguard, Rondo, being forced upon his will through the tunnel of bushes and flowers by the black horses that were supposed to be dogs. He had two thick leashes made of strong leather wrapped around his wrists. The vicious dogs fought and fought to escape his clutches, but they were no match for a beast the size of Rondo.

Xanose's mouth emerged into a devious grin. "That's for me to know, and for you to never figure out, Detective." He stuck his cigar between his lips and took a long drag. The burning end hissed while it glowed a fiery orange. Smoke came billowing out of his mouth while he said, "Oh, but if you only knew, my boy. If you only fucking knew."

Melroy waved the lingering smoke away from his nostrils, then surveyed the big black dogs at the end of Rondo's leashes. Their long-snouted faces stared at him with keen, bloodshot eyes. They snarled and growled while exposing their vicious, salivating white teeth. They were hungry. Hungry for fresh raw meat.

Melroy knew it was time for him to go.

There was no friendly exchange before he entered his car and drove off of the Cicello property. Rondo escorted him to his vehicle, while Xanose watched, standing in front of the gate to the inside of his mansion. He wasn't expecting a goodbye or anything. Not from that prick. Actually, he was surprised that Xanose didn't have his dogs eat him alive before he could make his exit. But Xanose let him go without any violence. Not even a shove or two from Rondo.

Now that his date with Don Xanose was over, Melroy was ready for a smooth and relaxing ride home, so he could forget about all the animosity between him and the Cicello patriarch for at least the next twenty minutes or so. He would dwell about their conversation when he was back in his one-bedroom apartment. The quiet place where he did most of his research. And most of his thinking.

The rich and lavish neighborhood of Skyline Hills was located just north of Juna in a mountainous region overlooking the big city. The drive from the Hills back to Juna took a good twenty minutes on a long stretch of a smoothly paved multi-lane road, surrounded by tall bushy trees and rolling green hills, which was the perfect stretch of a drive needed for Melroy to collect himself before he made it back to the dark and dreary city.

It was getting close to sundown. The sun was lowering into the horizon and the blue daytime sky was now streaked with orange, purple, and red. Melroy leaned back in his seat, using just one hand to drive as he listened to the appeasing tunes of his favorite band, *Afterthought*. He cranked the volume up when one of his favorite songs, *Live to Die for You,* started playing next on his modified sound system.

He slouched ever so more in his seat, zoning out to the melancholic melody of the song. He could drive all night and listen to this music. It put him in a state of nirvana, leaving all of his cares, stress, and worries behind him, disposing all of the negative bullshit from his mind. He was on autopilot, alone on the road, cruising at an average speed, not in any hurry to make it back to his normal life.

Melroy wasn't paying attention to his surroundings. Just the road ahead of him...But he should've been paying attention to what was going on around him, because two black conversion vans with tinted windows hovered closely behind him and landed on the road without him noticing. The black vans quickly caught up to Melroy and separated to opposite sides of the road, diverging on each side of his car. Melroy remained in his own world, bobbing his head to the music, unaware of the dark and strange vehicles keeping pace with him on either side of the road.

His attention wasn't grabbed until a third black van, with boosters shooting blue fire, hovered over top of his car and landed about ten lengths ahead of him. He glanced out the driver's side window and then through the passenger's side, and realized that he was surrounded.

"What in the hell?" he muttered to himself. A moment of panic shot through his body like a bolt of electricity.

The van in front of him lowered its speed, edging closer to the front of his car. The double back doors parted ways and opened up wide. Standing there, with a silver hand-cannon held to his side, was a man dressed in a uniform that Melroy had never seen before.

It was military garb. A suit of armor, mostly black from the neck down, besides the shiny silver chest plate, shoulder guards, elbow and wrist guards, and knee bucklers. The black material the silver armor covered was a thin chainmail, which had a distinct sparkle to its texture. The helmet was also black with a silver outline around the eyes-which were covered by a triangular glass frame-the jawline with a breathing mechanism protruding from the area of the mouth, and a rounded top with a silver stripe lined vertically from the forehead down to the back of the neck, and another stripe lined horizontally from the ear gauges to just above the eyes. The only distinct marking was a bold, royal blue 'L', centered on the left pectoral.

The mysterious uniformed soldier stood motionless in the back of the van, staring in Melroy's direction. His arm slowly raised, the silver hand-cannon aimed at the windshield. Suddenly, the triangular glass eye-frames flashed a bright neon-blue glow.

It was in that moment, that Melroy knew some fucked up shit was about to go down.

Just as the sense of panic was drawing in, the side doors on the vans to Melroy's left and right began to slide open, revealing a second and third uniformed soldier, armed with silver hand-cannons. Their eyes flashed a bright neon-blue, and then the onslaught of gunfire commenced.

"Holy shit!" Melroy yelled.

A hail of bullets shattered the driver side and passenger side windows as more bullets were driven deep into the doors, but to no avail of reaching their way into the car. His old-fashioned automobile was built of bulletproof steel, designed far ahead of its time.

Melroy ducked below the steering wheel as he could feel the wind of the bullets whizzing past his head. A barrage of bullets impaled the windshield as well, but they only became lodged in the bulletproof glass he had personally installed.

The oversized vans to his left and right quickly veered toward his car, ramming hard into the sides, creating a violent rupture of metal on metal. The armed soldiers barely kept their footing as they held on to rubber cables connected to the roof of the vans.

Melroy nearly lost control of his car after the initial attacks from the mysterious soldiers, but kept his composure and sat back up in his seat to steer the vehicle straight ahead.

His car was trapped by a triangular threat of high-tech conversion vans, pinned from the sides and front. For a moment, he thought of slamming on the brakes to break free, but the maneuver could be a costly one at the rate of speed he was going. He could lose control and then really be in some trouble.

As he thought of other possibilities to escape, the van ahead of him inched closer and closer. The uniformed soldier in the back of the van took a step back, and then launched himself in the air. With a loud thud, the man landed on the hood of his car. The soldier crawled toward the windshield, cocked his non-firing arm back, and with a fierce blow, pummeled through the windshield, shattering the glass into pieces. Considering it was bulletproof glass, it took one hell of a punch to destroy the windshield.

The soldier reached into the car, extending his hand toward Melroy's throat, and wrapping his fingers around his jugular before Melroy could react in self-defense. His hand was covered by a black chain-mailed glove with small silver plates on the fingers. The soldier's grip was suffocating. Melroy began to lose air in a hurry.

From behind the soldier's breathing mechanism came a muffled, robotic voice. "Do not resist, Detective Statz. It's time to die."

A verbal response was difficult under the distress his throat and lungs were in, but he mustered up the strength and gurgled out, "The...hell...it...is!"

Even though his air supply was cut off, his face was turning purple, and he was on the verge of losing consciousness, natural instincts still kicked in. His hand fumbled to the inside of his coat to the holstered piece resting on his right thigh. The black and silver pistol was cocked and ready to go in an instant.

"Suck...on...this," Melroy choked out as he shoved the piece into the light chainmail, just under the silver chest plate. Some fancy light armor wasn't going to be enough to protect this guy from hollowed point bullets.

Three rapid-fire shots exploded out the barrel of the gun, followed by three splatters of crimson mist, coating the dashboard and what was left of the windshield. A vibrated grunt expelled from the soldier's breathing mechanism as the impact and mortal wounds from the shots caused the soldier to let go of his grasp around Melroy's neck and fall backwards onto the hood. Melroy took a long breath of air, and then drove his foot hard into the gas petal, accelerating his car. The wounded soldier tumbled off the roof of the car and onto the road, rolling and bouncing off the pavement like a rock being skipped on the surface of a pond.

Melroy's car rammed into the back of the van in front of him, jerking him forward into the steering wheel. When his body recoiled back into his seat, he reached into his coat with his free hand and slung his other piece holstered on his left thigh. Simultaneously, he fired multiple rounds out the driver's and passenger side windows while steering the car with his left knee. The shots completely blew out the windows, and the bullets ricocheted through the interiors of the vans to his left and right, but failed to make contact with the armed soldiers.

The soldiers returned fire, hitting the dashboard, the driver and passenger seats, the steering wheel, and other spots in the interior of Melroy's car, but with luck on his side, Melroy was unharmed again. Melroy knew the luck he was having wasn't going to last much longer. He should be dead by now, so he had to react. He grabbed the steering wheel with both hands, using as many fingers as he could to get a good grasp, while still holding his weapons. With high aggression, he turned the wheel to the left, slammed hard into the van, and then immediately turned the wheel to the right, slamming even harder into the other van. The two vans backed away for the moment, but there was no doubt another attack was imminent.

The van ahead of him tried a new tactic. The boosters fired up and the van hovered off the ground, before turning completely around, so it was now facing Melroy head-on. The grating between the headlights and just above the bumper retracted into the hood and two massive chain guns sprung forward.

"What in the blue fuck is this?" Melroy blurted out to himself as the barrels of the chain guns started rotating.

Melroy knew what was about to transpire, so he ducked below the dashboard and waited for the impending attack.

The rotating barrels produced a whirlwind of gunfire that struck Melroy's car like a destructive wave crashing into a pier. His newly restored white-canvased roof was decimated in a matter of seconds, distorting it into pieces of scrap metal and reforming the car into a convertible.

When the deafening bursts of the heavy artillery stopped, Melroy sat back up in his seat to observe the damage to his car and the road ahead of him as well. He had kept his foot on the gas petal and kept the steering wheel straight, but there had to be a wide turn coming up soon, because Juna was bound to be approaching.

Just ahead, a wide right-handed curve that turned into a downhill stretch was only hundreds of lengths away. It was a stretch of highway all too familiar to the residents of Juna. When the wide curve straightens out, the tallest skyscrapers in the big city of Juna appear in the distance, overtaking the background.

Melroy was outnumbered and outgunned. All he had for firepower against three high-tech conversion vans with armored soldiers and heavy artillery was his two department registered pistols. The odds were not in his favor to survive this attack. It wasn't even close. But Juna was close. If he could just make it into the city, then his attackers might retreat, not wanting to cause a violent scene in such a populated area…But damn if this city wasn't used to murder and mayhem right front and center in the public's eyes.

The chain gun barrels of the hovering van ahead of Melroy began to rotate again, revving up for another heavy attack. But this time Melroy wasn't going to cower below the dashboard. He had to fight back with what he had, so he stood up in his seat and aimed his weapons toward the driver of the van, facing his attacker head on and with no fear. Round after round was fired from his guns. Shell casings were popping out of the chamber like a hailstorm of metal. The hollowed point bullets struck the tinted windshield of the van with precision, shattering the glass and revealing the driver. He was suited up just like the other soldiers. Mask and all.

The driver was struck in the shoulder, spraying a mist of blood onto the metal divider behind him. His reaction was elevating the vehicle higher above the road, not bothering to follow through with the attack. But his hesitation to strike back didn't last long. He maneuvered the front of the van into a downward angle with the tail up, positioned for a direct attack on Melroy himself. The high-speed revolutions of the barrels started back up.

Melroy was about to close his eyes and wait to be decimated into pieces, when fate decided otherwise. A giant green sign made of hard steel loomed over the highway, advising drivers that the exit for the city of Juna was two miles ahead. The driver of the hovering van wasn't paying attention to his rear-view mirror, so the vehicle was on a direct course for a collision with the sign.

Melroy plopped back down in his seat and watched as the hovering van collided tail first right into the center of the overhead sign. The metal on metal collision caused the rectangular mile marker to implode and the back end of the conversion van to crumble inwards, reducing the length of the van in half. There was a fiery explosion, then the van began spinning out of control. Melroy had to step on the gas and accelerate the car forward to avoid being crushed by the falling heap of burning metal.

"Hope that thing has airbags, bitch!" Melroy yelled as he watched the van fall.

An even bigger and louder explosion ensued when the van crashed head first onto the pavement. A smoking fireball rose high into the air as if a fighter jet had just dropped a bomb on the highway.

"Woo!" Melroy exclaimed after witnessing the brutal crash. "No airbag is gonna save you from that."

Only two more miles to go, Melroy thought as his foot pushed the gas petal as far to the floor as it would go. His car was broken apart, but still running at a high speed. The old gal would need major repairs if it survived at all. But that was only if he survived as well.

The vans to Melroy's left and right weren't phased by the other van's demise. They continued to drive alongside Melroy, easily keeping up with his classic automobile. The armored soldiers retreated into the vans, and the side doors slid shut. Then, the boosters on both vans fired up, and they hovered above the ground, flying further ahead of Melroy. The vans turned in mid-air, crisscrossing each other before facing Melroy head-on from a short distance. The front panels on each van propped open and retreated into the hood. Twin chain gun barrels appeared and the rotation toward doom had begun.

"Alright, sweetie," he said to his car while patting the dashboard. "Let's show these assholes what you got."

The chain guns opened fire. A bombardment of high caliber bullets cut through the air. With a forceful jerk, Melroy turned the steering wheel to the right. Bullets hit the road, propelling chunks of pavement as Melroy's car slid into the right-hand lane, narrowly escaping the onslaught. The aggression of the firepower was unrelenting as the vans followed Melroy's every move. He jerked the steering wheel to the left, and the bullets hit nothing but gray pavement again as he moved back to the middle lane, then into the left-hand lane, and back again. Back and forth across the highway he maneuvered, his car only getting struck a few times, taking out his headlights and a couple pieces of the grating. This went on for what seemed like an eternity for Melroy, until the bombardment stopped, and the chain guns had to cool down.

The one-mile marker had passed. Just down the highway, Melroy could see the tunnel leading into the city. He had to survive just one more stretch of highway, and then a few hundred lengths of the tunnel…He was almost home free.

As Melroy shifted in his seat and readied for another hailstorm of gunfire, the two vans made an unexpected move. Instead of continuing the attack, they both veered off in opposite directions and flew away from the highway. It almost appeared as if they were giving up, possibly retreating back to where they came from…But wouldn't they fly off together instead of opposite ways?

"What the hell are they doing?" Melroy quietly asked himself.

His question was answered immediately. He looked back and forth from his left and to his right, and watched as the vans did a one-eighty. They weren't retreating at all. Instead, their boosters powered up, and they burst through the air, heading back towards the highway at an extremely high velocity.

The tunnel was just ahead. Only a hundred lengths away.

Melroy punched it. The gas petal was pressed to the floorboard. Inner electricity flowed through his arms to his fingertips as he grasped the steering wheel with a vice grip.

I can make it, he convinced himself in the back of his mind.

But the turbo-boosted vans were too fast. The one on his left crashed directly through the front of his car, while the one on his right crashed through the back at the same time. His classic automobile became scrap metal in an instant, and the last conscious image Melroy saw was flashes of light from the inside of the tunnel as what was left of his car flipped over and over again before slamming into a concrete wall.

Don Maretto Rose

And the Mysterious Soldier

The tapping of expensive dress shoes on a ceramic floor echoed down a hall that led to the hospital morgue. A bald-headed doctor with thick-framed glasses, garbed in light blue scrubs and white sneakers, escorted Captain Riccard and Don Maretto Rose down the off-white hallway that was alit by tubed plasma bulbs, some of which flickered as if they were having a seizure. Vego Rainze followed closely behind, his eyes covered by his signature shades and a black fedora tilted below his forehead, darkening half his face.

Don Maretto, dressed in a black suit, dress shirt, and red tie, walked with authority next to the Juna Police Captain, who was wearing a navy-blue officers uniform, his white Captain's hat, and shiny gold badge pinned to his left pectoral. Both bore a stoic face, all business as they followed the doctor to the last door on the right at the end of the hall. The doctor swiped an identification card that was clipped to his waste through a scanner to unlock the door.

"Right this way, gentlemen," the doctor informed them before opening the door and stepping inside the room. Maretto, Riccard, and Vego slowly followed him inside, their hands behind their backs as they observed the area.

The morgue was uninviting and morose, dimly lit with a chilling presence. The air was stale and cold, with a slight odor of decay that loitered around the nostrils. There were two walls on the right and left sides of the room which occupied the freezers; metal boxes that acted as drawers to slide in and out dead bodies kept chilled to prevent further rot. A pair of desks with reading lamps and computers were located near the back, squeezed between two tall filing cabinets. Six examination tables were set up in the middle of the morgue, but only one held a dead body concealed with a white sheet.

"The body has begun the decomposition process, so you might want to tighten your breathing if you have a weak stomach," the doctor told the men, apparently unaware of how tough two gangsters and a police captain could really be.

"We'll be fine, Doctor," Captain Riccard assured him. "As a matter of fact, I would appreciate it if I could inspect the body alone with these two gentlemen. We are not here to investigate the cause of death or any other medical discrepancies. We just need some time to inspect the individual himself."

The Doctor seemed confounded by the request. He adjusted his glasses, wiped the sweat from his forehead and said, "Well, um, Captain Riccard, it is common protocol that there is a staff member of the hospital supervising the morgue when there are guests observing one of our admissions."

Riccard gave the doctor a laser-eyed stare and replied, "Do I look like a man who follows normal protocol, Doctor? Does Don Maretto Rose seem like the type of individual to follow the order of a short and weak man such as yourself?"

The doctor swallowed the ball of regret lodged in his throat and looked away as if he was ashamed of himself. "Well, um, okay. I'll just be right outside the door if anyone needs my assistance," he stuttered while pointing to the door. In a hurry, he skedaddled out of the morgue.

With the doctor now out of the room, Maretto, Riccard, and Vego surrounded the examination table with the body. For a few moments, they stood in silence, overlooking the corpse like a group of surgeons about to perform a major operation.

"Where was he found?" Maretto asked Captain Riccard in a deep, solemn tone.

"He was recovered on Route Five, about fifteen minutes from Skyline Hills. From the information I've received, he was traveling towards Juna."

Nodding his head a few times, Maretto then asked, "Was there anyone else recovered, besides our friend?"

The Captain shook his head and answered, "Not anything recognizable."

Maretto rubbed his chin and then pointed to the covered body and ordered, "Remove the sheet, Vego. Let's take a look at him."

With a quick nod, Vego obeyed his boss, lifting the sheet from one side of the dead body and folding it over the other side, covering the left side of the chest just enough to hide the 'L'.

In a heartbeat, the stoic look on Maretto's face changed. He was now puzzled, not expecting to see what he was looking at. *What in God's name is this?* He asked his own subconscious.

Vego took a step back after the unveiling. His eyes were hidden, but the dropping of his jaw gave away his feeling of bewilderment as well. The corpse was dressed in a military garb that neither of the three men were accustomed to. From neck to feet, the person was wearing a black chainmail suit, thin and fitted to the contours of his body. The chest, waste, shoulders, arms, wrists, and knees were protected by shiny silver-plated armor. Even the fingers were protected by thin chainmail and metal guards. But the helmet stood out the most. It completely disguised the individual with a unique mask, complete with glass shields over the eyes and a breathing mechanism over the nose and mouth.

It was a soldier…But from what military?

Maretto didn't want the Juna Police Captain to see the astonishment on his face. A man in his position was not to show any sort of weakness, so he changed his face back into the serious, unfazed look he was conveying when they first entered the morgue.

"What are we looking at here, Captain?" Maretto asked Riccard, hoping that he had the answer to the enigma.

He sniffed, then wiped his nose with his fingers. "I was hoping you would have an idea. I've never seen this type of armored suit in all the years I've been on the force."

"It's a mystery to me too. I would recognize any suit from one of the Families, regimes, gangs, authorities, or military. This is something new, and by the looks of it…dangerous." Maretto glided a hand through his greasy hair, contemplating to himself who or what the hell this individual belonged to.

"I like to gamble, Don Maretto, so I wouldn't hesitate to bet every possession I have in my life that this person is part of some sort of military faction," the Captain surmised.

"He's definitely some kind of soldier," Vego chimed in. "Gangsters and police officers don't sport that kind of armor."

"Well, besides the President's main army, there is no other military in Exodus. Could there be a rogue faction, or rebel uprising we haven't heard of yet?" the Captain asked Maretto and his bodyguard.

Don Maretto slid his hands in his pockets and started pacing around the examination table, studying the mysterious dead soldier.

"There's always a chance for a rogue nation, Captain Riccard. You and I know all too well that citizens of Exodus become unhappy with the way the lands are governed. Whether it's by the Seven Blessed Families, the President and the Legislation, or by authoritative regimes like you and the Juna Police Department, people will feel the need for an uprising…And these days, the threat is higher than ever. The entire nation is fed up with the violence and corruption that goes on in the major cities. Especially, Juna. Did you happen to catch the special news report that Miss Alana Rae produced?"

"If I remember the newscast accurately, it was more focused on the Seven Blessed Families and your line of business," Riccard answered the Don.

Maretto shrugged and retorted, "Be that as it may, the violence in this great city goes beyond just the Families. Just the other day Miss Rae tracked me down after Sunday Service and accused my Family of murdering her father over the sale of the batball team he owned, the Skylarks. Truth be told, Captain, if my Family does own the Skylarks, then I was never informed of the sale. Which means someone in my Family had to go behind my back and purchase the team."

"And?" Riccard impatiently asked.

"And, this person who intentionally went behind my back to purchase the team had to get the permission of the Commissioner of the league in order to complete the transaction. The Commissioner would've known the scam that was in the works, but he obviously only cares about the league and the money that comes along with a major purchase of a batball team. Therefore, the Commissioner is just as corrupt as the individual who used my Family name."

"Your point, Don Maretto?" Riccard asked with an eyebrow raised.

Don Maretto stopped pacing, turned towards Riccard and said, "Even a national sport, focused on teamwork, hard work, and family fun is corrupt in Exodus. We're not the only crooked business in this world of ours, Captain. Even your own department has its issues."

"The men and women in my department don't dress like they're ready to take over the entire city. And even though there are a select few who are crooked officers, we still uphold the law and try to keep the streets clean of thugs and gangsters.

"This individual," Riccard raised his voice, pointing at the dead soldier, "attempted to take out one of my best officers. Detective Statz is clinging on to life by a thread, and now it's my duty to find out why. Why was Detective Statz targeted for an assassination by an unknown military regime, Don Maretto Rose?" Riccard's face turned a shade of red and a pulsating vein stuck out the side of his head.

Crossing his arms, Maretto looked down at the dead soldier and replied, "I don't know, Lan. At one time, Melroy was like a son to me." His eyes became glossy, fighting hard to hold back his tears. "He always will be like a son to me."

"So, what do we do?" Riccard asked. The pressing look in his eyes insinuated that he demanded an answer.

"I say we remove the mask and take a good look at the asshole hiding underneath it," Vego suggested. "Maybe we'll get lucky and recognize the son of a bitch."

Arms still crossed, Maretto looked over at Riccard for a reaction. The redness flushed from his face as he nodded in approval. Maretto then looked at Vego and made a gesture with his hand to give him the okay to remove the helmet and mask.

Vego stood behind the area where the head lied, clutched his hands underneath the helmet, and pulled it off. Although his skin was pale and grey from the touch of death, a handsome young face was unveiled.

The three men bent over and took their time observing the face of the mysterious soldier. Besides his eyes being half-open and a trickle of dry blood protruding from his mouth, he looked rather peaceful and content with death.

Maretto and Vego only stared for a moment before realizing that they had never seen the man before, but Captain Riccard kept on looking as a curious look developed on his rugged old face.

"My God," Riccard prayed. "I know this young man."

Maretto's eyes opened wide, shocked to hear what Riccard just said. "Who is he?" he asked.

"His name is Kelvin Strain. Agent Kelvin Strain. He's a special agent for the ESFU...Or at least he was," the Captain inferred, now confused.

"So, an agent from the ESFU has gone rogue?" Maretto suggested in the tone of a question.

"Either that, or the ESFU has invested in a brand-new uniform for combat," Riccard guessed. "Whatever the case, Juna and the rest of Exodus seems to be in for a big surprise. We're all about to be knee deep in shit if more of these soldiers start appearing around the cities. They obviously have an agenda if they're gonna start by taking out an officer of the law. Who knows who will be next on their list?"

Maretto shook his head in disgust. "First an attack on my Family, and then an attack on Melroy. It can't be just a coincidence."

"But I thought Zasso Cicello was the one behind the attacks at the Grand Theater," Riccard brought up, crinkling his wrinkled forehead in confusion.

"He was, but ever since that night, my Family and I have always agreed that Zasso wasn't the mastermind behind the attack. Someone gave him an order and he followed it to the extreme. And now Melroy was attacked by soldiers we've never seen the likes of before..." Maretto paused before he said, "Wait a second." He took a moment to think to himself. "Melroy went to the Grand Theater that night to investigate the crime scene and to ask my Family questions about what transpired. He promised me that he would do

244

whatever it took to find Zasso's whereabouts. He said he would start investigating the case on his own."

"Yes, I know," Riccard said, as if he was disappointed about the fact. "Even though I warned him not to get himself involved too deep unless we put together a team for the case. But that stubborn young man couldn't wait to dip his feet in the water before jumping into the deep end. It seems as though Melroy cares a lot about your Family, Maretto. As stubborn as he might be, he still is a good young man."

The thought of Melroy risking himself getting caught in the middle of danger for his Family touched him deep into his heart. *That boy always did have a heart of gold,* Maretto thought to himself. *It's amazing considering all the shit he went through as a young child. Please God help that young man pull through.*

"So, Melroy begins to investigate the attack on the Grand Theater on his own and ends up being the target of an assassination while driving on Route Five, on his way back to Juna." Maretto paused for a moment and then took a few steps around the table, looking down upon the dead soldier, whose identity was no longer a mystery. "Route Five is a stretch of highway that connects Juna to Skyline Hills. And who do we know that resides in Skyline Hills?"

Captain Riccard couldn't think of an answer, but Vego was quick on the draw when he answered, "Xanose Cicello. He lives in a fortress up there."

Riccard crossed his arms and then rubbed his gray mustache with his right hand. "You don't think he actually went to the home of Don Cicello and confronted him alone, do you?"

"Was there anyone else in the car with him, Lan?" Maretto asked, raising his eyebrow into his forehead.

"No. Unless someone else drove separate."

"I highly doubt it. Melroy went to Skyline Hills alone, and then he drove home on Route Five alone. And on his way back to Juna, he was attacked by a group of soldiers like that one," he said, pointing an accusing finger towards Kelvin Strain. "The attack on the Grand Theater and the attack on Melroy are connected. And they both lead to one man and his Family." He pointed a single finger upwards to represent the number one. "Don Xanose Cicello." His tone of voice became irritated when he said the name of the Cicello patriarch.

Riccard placed his hands on his sides, and pondered the theory Don Maretto just presented. "Well, if it's true that he was attacked after visiting Don Cicello, then that means he must've uncovered something. Something important. Something that Don Cicello wanted kept a secret from the outside world. I mean, that's how it's done in your line of business, right? If you have a problem, you get rid of it, no questions asked."

Maretto and Vego stayed silent, but they both knew full well that he was dead on. It's the age old way of the gangster. *Secrecy silenced by bloodshed.*

"Am I right or what?" the Police Captain shouted. "This is Melroy we're talking about here! A young man that grew up with your Family! Your youngest son's best friend! One of my best men, who is also like a son to me! Don't just stand there with dicks stuck in your mouths!" His impatience with the tight-lipped gangsters was reasonable. This was not the time or place to be gangsters and cops. Not when someone you care about has only a slim chance of surviving a brutal attack.

Maretto huffed and finally answered, "Yes. If Melroy got critical information out of Xanose, then he would most likely have him killed. The fact that he's a police officer makes no difference. A secret worth keeping, is a secret worth killing for."

The morgue fell silent for a few moments. The only sounds heard were a plasma bulb buzzing from the ceiling, and a constant drip coming out the faucet of an old hand sink, disregarded in the corner of the room. Don Maretto's words were etched in their brains. *A secret worth keeping, is a secret worth killing for.* Melroy Statz had definitely dug up a secret important enough for someone to take to the grave.

"He must've received the information he was looking for," Riccard inferred. "Melroy quite possibly got Xanose to reveal to him the location of Zasso's whereabouts. And he could've been on his way to relay the information to me." He gave a slight shrug, then looked Maretto dead in the eyes. "Or you."

Maretto nodded his head in agreement, and then looked down at the floor, pondering the idea that Melroy discovered crucial information about where Zasso Cicello is hiding…*But where are we supposed to go from here on out? Melroy is on the verge of passing on, which doesn't help solve anything. Damn that kid for risking his life for my Family. He should've come to me for help if he wanted to confront Xanose.*

While Don Maretto and Captain Riccard were searching their thoughts, Vego had the inclination to lift the rest of the sheet from off of the dead soldier's chest. Stamped on the left pectoral of his silver chest plate, was a blocky and bold, royal blue 'L'.

"I don't suppose either of you know of a rebel military group that starts with the letter 'L', do you?" Vego asked his boss and the Police Captain. With his bare knuckles, he gave the chest plate a couple of light knocks. "If not, I suggest we start searching for one."

Both Don Maretto and Captain Riccard stepped closer to the examination table and leaned in for a better look at the 'L'. They then looked at one another, and simultaneously gave each other a look of curiosity crossed with uncertainty.

Captain Riccard and Don Maretto parted ways when their business in the morgue was finished. Before leaving the hospital, Maretto cordially invited Lan over to the Rose Family high-rise mansion tomorrow night for dinner and some drinks, so they could further discuss the source of the mystery military faction they just discovered. Maretto also made Riccard promise that he would keep him updated on Melroy's condition over the next twenty-four hours. With a solid handshake, the Police Captain agreed, and for the first time in his extended career in law enforcement, he would be working alongside a leader of one of the Seven Blessed Families. This was a man who took an oath, vowing to protect the people of Juna from men like Don Maretto Rose, whose business practices were on the opposite side of the law. But ironically, a gangster and a law enforcer had a common cause to work together.

Before Riccard went back to his job at the department, he decided to check on Melroy's condition in the Intensive Care Unit. As he strolled down the hall, he watched as nurses and doctors hustled and bustled their way around the unit, sacrificing hours of their lives and nights of sleep to save the lives of others. To him, the medical field and law enforcement served the same common purpose in society. They both help and protect other people for a living. Occupations that are more than just a job. It's their whole lives.

As he neared the room Melroy was being kept under close observation, he took a deep breath and prepared himself for the painful sight of one of his favorite men, hooked up to a bunch of tubes and machines that were helping him stay alive.

But just as Riccard was about to enter Melroy's room, a solemn voice from behind him said, "Excuse me, Captain Riccard. May I have a word with you?"

When Riccard turned around, he recognized the doctor. His name was Dr. Hill, Melroy's main physician and surgeon.

"Of course, Dr. Hill. What can I do for you?" he asked, polite but businesslike.

Dr. Hill paused, then put his head down. His face was somber, his demeanor sorrowful. He took a shallow breath before he spoke, and Lan Riccard tightened up and braced himself for the news.

The Blessing of Ricalstro Rose

Part Two

A milky white ball of saliva oozed from the corner of his half-open mouth, while his upper lip quivered along with the pulse of his carotid artery. He took in short, rapid breaths as his contracting lungs tried to keep up with his racing heart. His esophagus was swelled from the ongoing sessions of vomiting that has left his breath smelling like a hot pile of dog shit mixed with hot garbage. He couldn't stop the shaking. The twitching of his body parts was out of his control. And the needles pricking him from the inside out made his skin feel like it was on fire, slowly burning him to death.

His left eye was wide open while his right eye was halfway shut. He stared into oblivion. A never-ending black hole of darkness and despair. There was no hope. The last twenty-four hours had been the longest and most aggravating stretch of hell he'd ever been through. He had never experienced so much pain and anguish in his entire life. It was worse than when he watched the love of his life get brutally raped in front of his eyes, before she was shot point-blank in the face. It was worse than all the physical beatings he took and all the near-death experiences he had suffered through and barely overcame.

How pathetic I am, he thought as even the voice in his head was stuttering each word. *Of all the horrible shit that happened in my life, my withdrawal from my drug abuse was the worst feeling yet. I wish it would all just end now. Please God just let me die. I can't deal with the pain of it. All I want is a fix. A dose that would put me into a coma. A coma I would never come out of...Death couldn't possibly be worse than this. I welcome the grim reaper.*

Ric hung his head over the single-sized bed, opened his mouth, and released the bile from his stomach. It burned his throat as he coughed and gagged it all out. He panted, trying to catch his breath while he spat globs of saliva on the concrete floor. His uncle had locked him in a room that wasn't far off from being a replica of a holding cell. The bed was just an old ragged mattress lying on top of a box of rusty springs. The walls were made of brick, cracked and chipped. The air was murky and damp, the smell of mildew lingered throughout the room. An old tin bucket was left in the corner for Ric to relieve himself, but he only pissed in it a few times. He was given just two bottles of water, but the sickness in his stomach had made it hard for him to keep anything down. He drank maybe half a bottle in the last day. Water wouldn't agree with him. Only drugs.

Making it through the night was the most excruciating part. When his body started losing control, the yelling and screaming commenced, followed by long periods of moaning and groaning while he curled up on the bed in a fetal position like a man suffering from a chronic and mortal disease. The yells and the screams brought no relief. He had been left in the room to suffer until the drugs were flushed out of his system. There would be no sympathy or compassion from his uncle. Uncle Vetti had left him to suffer until the agony pushed him to the edge of his pathetic life. The doors had been locked. Locked away from the temptations of the outside world. He was stuck in the desolate room until the first major withdrawal had passed.

Hallucinations were the next phase in the detox process. And they weren't the happy-go-lucky hallucinations brought on by mind-expanding drugs. No, they were the ones of nightmares. Nightmares that could cause a man to go into shock. And if the hallucinations became severe enough, then the heart could give out, unable to pump life's blood any longer.

The first vision he experienced was that of his father, the great Don Maretto Rose. He sat in front of the bed in his throne-like chair, his legs crossed while drinking wine from a golden chalice. He seemed stressed from a long day, his face dejected and worn down. He let out a tired sigh. The same sigh he gave when Ric would disappoint him.

"Look at the man I've let you become," the vision of his father spoke, his voice deep with melancholy. *"I never thought I would fail as a father to one of my sons. I had dreams for you. My youngest. My baby boy. Dreams of you becoming a better man than I."* He took a deep and long gulp of wine. A lot more than he usually drank at one time. *"But you aren't. You've become nothing but a junky loser, and you've brought nothing but shame to our Family name. Sometimes I pray that your destructive lifestyle ends your*

pathetic existence, so you can join your mother in a lonely pit in hell." The color of his father's eyes changed to a deep crimson.

Ric's breathing became erratic, but the rest of his body remained stationary. A single tear ran down the side of his face. "Maybe I can change," he slurred. His words came out slow and nearly incoherent.

His father shook his head. *"No, my son, you can't. You'll never change. You'll always be the screw-up of the Family."* He took another hard drink from the chalice. His eyes began to bleed. The blood flowed down his cheeks and into his mouth. *"The Rose Quartet will reject you and cast you aside, my son. Just like your Family rejects you, you piece of street trash."*

More tears streamed down Ric's face. "Please, dad. Don't give up on me. You never gave up on me before," he cried. "I'm still your son, dammit!"

His father shook his head in disgust as blood dripped out of his nose and from his ears. His entire face was a bloody mess. *"How am I supposed to accept a son who sees imaginary shadows in the dark? There was nobody watching from afar that night, son. You are full of shit. There was nobody there."*

"He was there!" Ric shouted at the vision. "He was there, I swear!" He began to sob. It went on for a few moments, then he calmed himself and said, "I swear to God he was there."

Ric closed his eyes for a brief moment, then opened them back up. The vision of his father was gone, and he was grateful. The hallucinated version of his father was a terrible man. *My father would never say those things to the son he loves,* he thought, shutting his eyes with a sense of relief.

"Oh, he wouldn't, would he?" a familiar voice said. A voice he hadn't heard in a while. A voice he thought he'd never hear again. *"Well then, I guess you don't know our father as well as you thought, little bro."*

Only one of his older brothers ever called him 'little bro'…Georgie.

As Ric opened his eyes, he saw a blurry vision of his deceased brother standing by the side of the bed. He was wearing a blood-splattered suit. A gaping wound ran from his shoulder down to his lower torso. Chunks of flesh spilled from the mortal wound.

"Sure, maybe he wouldn't say those things to your face, but what do you think he says behind your back? He's definitely not telling people he's proud of you," the vision of his brother said with a smirk. *"He's embarrassed of you, Ric. The whole Family is. When are you actually going to come to terms with that, little bro? You make the entire Rose Family look bad. Especially dad, Jon-Jon, Alto, and I. Who the fuck is gonna take dad serious with one of his son's as a junky loser on the street. Who, Ric?"*

The vision of his dead brother was just as hard on him as the vision of his father. And it killed Ric to see him that way. Georgie wasn't just his brother. He was his closest friend. Georgie always had faith that he would turn his life around. He believed in him when no one else did.

"I never wanted to turn out this way, Georgie. I never meant to embarrass any of you. I always wanted to make everyone proud of me," Ric professed, sincere from the bottom of his ill-beating heart.

"Well, Ric. It's not happening. You're fucking it all up, and that's the way it's going to continue to be," Georgie affirmed, a stringent look cast on his face.

From out of the darkness behind Georgie, Jon-Jon and Alto appeared and stood next to their fallen brother. They were both dressed in suits, but Alto had a gaping wound in his chest, which spilled pints of blood, and Jon-Jon had a bullet hole in his forehead, oozing out blood and brain matter.

"You're a fuckup, Ric. And you always will be," Alto said, condescending as usual.

"Don't listen to these guys, Ric. They give you more credit than you deserve," Jon-Jon said in his reserved demeanor. *"You're more than just an embarrassment and a fuckup. You're the worst thing to ever happen to us and the rest of the Family. We all wished that those guys would've just finished you off. How did that guy miss? And why the hell did we get revenge for you?"*

252

"We should've just suffocated you with a pillow in the hospital," Georgie added in.

"You're a fuckup, Ric. And you always will be," Alto repeated.

Ric used all the strength he had in his neck to lift his head. "You're right. All of you. You should've just finished the job. I never asked any of you to help me out. It was my vengeance to fulfill...That was my revenge!" he yelled out, just like he had on so many previous occasions.

Ric closed his eyes and yelled from the depths of his lungs. The veins in his head bulged and were on the verge of exploding. The end of his yell was accompanied by a slight gurgle in his throat. Then he vomited all down the side of the bed, followed by a fit of coughing.

When his fit of rage was over, and he opened his eyes, a new vision had appeared. But this one gave him an immediate sense of peace, along with a feeling of deep sadness...It was Galia. And she wasn't draped with blood like his father and brothers had been. No, she was the beautiful Galia he was accustomed to, wearing an elegant white dress, her blonde hair still shined in the dark.

"Galia? Galia, is that really you?" he asked, wishing it to be true.

"No, I'm sorry my love. It's not really me. But it can be if you want it to."

His eyes swelled with tears once again. "Yes. Yes I do."

"Then it's me," she said with a gorgeous smile. *"But I can only be me for a short time, so what I have to tell you will be brief."*

"Okay, sweetheart. Tell me anything you want." His mouth formed a smile for the first time in the last twenty-four hours.

The vision of Galia stepped closer to the bed as she spoke, *"The road ahead is going to be a difficult one, my love. You will be faced with difficult challenges, hard decisions, and alluring temptations. But you have the power to overcome them. You are strong enough. You are brave enough. And you have what it takes to be Blessed by the Rose Quartet."*

"No. I don't have what it takes."

"Shh," she hushed him with a finger to her lips. *"Yes, you do, Ricalstro Rose. Yes, you do. And when the Rose Quartet Blesses you, you will become a new man, and fulfill your destiny."*

A curious look was now draped across his face. "What is my destiny," he asked in a whisper.

She smiled from cheek to rosy cheek. *"That, my love, will be revealed in time...Take care of yourself, Ricalstro. And remember that I will always love you. But please find someone for yourself. Someone who you love, and in return, loves you the same...Goodbye."*

The vision of Galia disappeared, the hallucinations stopped, and for the first time since he'd been locked in this room of despair, he didn't feel the need for his addictions. For the first time in years, Ric actually thought that he was going to be just alright.

The next morning, Ric awoke to the sound of his door being unlocked, creaking and groaning upon being opened. His Uncle Vetti stepped through the doorway and entered the room. His eyebrows rose above his dark sunglasses when he saw Ric sitting in an upright position on the edge of the bed. He wasn't the distorted mess Vetti was expecting to see. Ric was calm and collected, ready for the start of a new day.

"How was your night?" Vetti asked him, his hands clasped behind his back. He was wearing a blood-red dress shirt and black slacks. The shirt was partly unbuttoned at the top, revealing a thick gold necklace around his neck.

Ric thought for a moment, searching for a good answer. "It was enlightening," he ended up saying.

Vetti's forehead crinkled and his eyebrows scrunched below his sunglasses. "Enlightening?"

Shrugging his shoulders, Ric replied, "I'm just as surprised as you are, Uncle Vetti, but I have to admit that I feel a lot better. I had a lot to think about for the past twenty-four hours, and I can honestly say that it was a good experience for me."

"That's not what it sounded like. I think you awoke all of the dead spirits in this castle with all your yelling and screaming."

Looking toward the ground, Ric nodded his head and said, "I'm not saying it wasn't an excruciating night of hell, but by the end of it all, I realized that there is only one path I can take from here on out."

"And what path is that?"

With a serious look in his eyes, Ric gave his uncle a direct and honest answer when he said, "I'm going to be Blessed by the Rose Quartet, and become the man I was born to become. One of the heirs to my father's kingdom. A true member of the Rose Family."

A proud smile grew from the side of Vetti's mouth. "Good," his response was. Simple and content. "Now, I know it's going to be quite the challenge to avoid the temptations that will follow you on your journey from here on out, but if your mind is clear enough, and your heart is strong enough, then your path to become an elite member of this Family will someday be complete…And you, Ricalstro Rose, will become a great man, who will someday do great things."

An alleviating sense of elation coursed through the inner-sanctums of his body. Uncle Vetti's words were assuring and inspiring. From the moment Ric set foot in the Rose Family castle, there wasn't a doubt in his mind that his stay would be short and he would be rejected by the Family Relic. But now his outlook on the future was becoming more positive. He was truly beginning to believe that the Rose Quartet will accept him with open arms, and his journey to become a made man in the Family will not end in failure.

"Thank you, Uncle Vetti. I truly appreciate all that you're doing for me. There's not many in the Family who believe in me." Ric's words were authentic. His father's brother was a remarkable man and a vital asset in the Rose Family. It was an honor to be taken under his wing.

"Don't thank me yet, my young nephew. You still might want to curse me out and have my head by the end of your journey," he said with a half-smile as he adjusted his sunglasses. "Now, let's get you the hell out of this prison cell and go eat some breakfast. I'm sure you're dying for a decent meal right now."

Breakfast was just what Ric needed. Nourishment was something he'd evaded for the last several years, and a new start to his life meant a new start for his diet. The kitchen staff whipped him up an epic meal. Eggs, sausage, hash browns, toast, and fresh fruit filled his stomach to its capacity. He washed it down with a tall glass of freshly squeezed orange juice, then drank a hot cup of coffee with cream. It felt good to have a normal morning, not rolling out of bed and sticking a needle in his arm to start the day. Maybe he could get used to this lifestyle.

After taking a hot, relaxing bath, Ric dressed himself in a black collared shirt, black pants, and comfortable sneakers. He stood in front of his dresser mirror and used gel to style his hair to look presentable for once. As he looked at himself, he couldn't help but feel sorry for the man on the other side of the mirror. He was a distant shadow of himself, less than half the man he used to be when he was younger and in love. The man in the mirror had aged dramatically. Although still quite handsome, it looked as if he aged about ten years.

What the hell happened to me since I was eighteen? Ric asked the mirror. *The years have gone by so quick and I wasted precious time getting high instead of making a life for myself. This is the prime of my youth. It's about time I started living instead of trying to die.* Ric rubbed his forehead and shook his head back and forth. *Am I really turning a corner here after just a couple days away from my shitty apartment? I'd like to hope so.*

About twenty minutes after Ric was finished getting prepped for the day, his bedroom door swung open and Alessa entered, strutting her stuff like the little temptress she was.

256

"Good day, Ric Rose. I hope last night was as pleasant as you look this morning," she said, sending sweet pleasantries and temptations his way. Her flirtations were not going unnoticed, that's for sure.

Ric was sitting on the edge of his bed, leaning forward with a clenched hand resting under his chin, checking out the beauty that just walked in. "It was very much uncomfortable, to tell you the truth. My night was full of nightmares and restlessness. I didn't get a wink of sleep."

"If you didn't sleep, then how did you have nightmares?" she asked him, acting as if she didn't believe his description of his night.

Ric arose from the bedside and walked a few steps until he was standing directly in front of her. "You don't have to be asleep to have a nightmare, sweetheart. You just have to live a dangerous lifestyle." His words were sly, as was the way they glided off of his tongue.

Alessa's eyelashes fluttered and her lips formed a shy smile. With her fingers, she flung a strand of hair behind her ear. "How dangerous do you live, Ric Rose?"

He bent his head down to her level, nearly close enough to lay a kiss on her lips. "As dangerous as I can, sweetheart." His bad-boy demeanor caused her face to flush. She looked like a little school girl who was in love with her handsome and much older teacher. "So, is there a reason why you came to my room looking so delightful?"

She let out a playful laugh, then replied, "Your uncle, Mr. Vetti, sent me up here. He wants you to meet him down by the Blood Fountain. I'll escort you down there so you don't get lost. Follow me."

Ric followed Alessa down the maze of hallways and stairs, checking out her backside all the way to the meeting spot at the Blood Fountain. He should've been paying attention and memorizing the way there, but it was hard to concentrate when a beautiful woman with an amazing behind was strutting her stuff in front of him, while she occasionally looked back at him with a seductive smile. She knew what he was looking at. That tantalizing ass.

There was no doubt in his mind that he needed the satisfaction of a woman before he burst in his pants, and if Alessa kept on putting herself out there like she had been doing, he was going to have to disobey his uncle and make the move on her. He'd feel a little bad ravaging his cousin Veno's future bride, but hell, he didn't really give a damn about that shmuck anyway. The poor fuck would probably never find out about it. Alessa seemed the type to keep her sexual escapades to herself.

Uncle Vetti was sitting on the edge of the circular marble base of the fountain with his arms crossed. The stringent look on his face meant that he was all business, so Alessa went away as soon as they entered the grand hall, leaving Ric and his uncle alone.

Ric glanced up at the father of the Rose Family, the constant flow of blood-like liquid spewing from his orifices and hand. Ric was still transfixed by the awesome visual that was the great Blood Fountain.

"Today I'm going to give you your first research assignment, in which you'll have to travel back to the Archive Building in order to complete, but before I send you off, there's something I want to show you. Something significant and vital to every member of the Rose Family whose been Blessed by the Rose Quartet." Vetti stood up straight, adjusted the collar on his shirt and brushed a speck of dust off the shoulder.

"Wait a second," Ric said before his uncle took him anywhere. "You're giving me a research assignment? And I have to go to the Archive Building with all those people studying and reading and all that other book shit?"

Piercing his eyes through his dark sunglasses, Vetti replied, "Do you have a problem with that?"

His uncle's intimidating stature shrunk Ric back a little. "Umm, no, I don't have a problem with that. I just thought being Blessed had to do more with magical powers, hand to hand combat, and other cool stuff, not research assignments. I feel like I'm in school right now, getting homework from my teacher."

Vetti cracked a smile and said, "Trust me, Ric, this kind of schooling you can't learn in a classroom full of nose-picking shitheads and ugly fat-assed teachers. What you will learn today is about the heritage of your Family. The most powerful Family in the entire nation of Exodus. So cut the kindergarten shit and do exactly as I tell you today."

Ric rubbed his chin and nodded his head in agreement. "You're the boss, Uncle Vetti. And I'll do whatever you want me to do, so show me the way of the Rose."

Vetti gave Ric a quick nod, then said, "Follow me."

Behind the master spiral staircase was a set of iron doors, sealed into the stone wall to appear inaccessible and useless. But when Vetti walked up to the doors and placed his palms against the surface of the metal, his hands began to glow a bright crimson, and intricate patterns of light expanded from underneath his palms, branching out across the doors. When he took a couple steps back, the iron doors let out a deep vibration, then grinded along the stone, unveiling a dark chasm, alit by burning torches on either side.

Ric shook his head in disbelief, then made a hand gesture toward the chasm. "Fucking torches? I mean, I know this place was built around the same time fire was discovered, but couldn't you guys install some modern lighting fixtures or at least an oil lamp or two?"

"The ancient style of the underground passageways, chambers, and halls is what keeps Heritage Castle authentic. Why change a masterful piece of historical art just to go along with modern times? It defeats the purpose of what this structure represents."

"Yea, but it's fucking morbid," he said, taking a peak at the dark chasm over his uncle's shoulder. "I feel like I'm about to walk down into an ancient dungeon or some shit."

Vetti lowered his head in frustration. "Just grow a pair of balls, shut the hell up, and stay close behind me."

Ric adhered to his uncle's instructions and followed closely behind him as they entered the shadowy chasm. The torches emitted a faint orange glow that barely illuminated the hard-stone walls and pathway that led to a descending stairwell, which was alit by flaming torches as well. The stairs were a nuisance, as you had to watch your footing while you stepped on cracks and pieces of chipped stone. And besides that, the staircase was never ending. If they had been barefoot their feet would've been a bloody mess by the end of their decent.

"Where do these stairs lead to? All the way to hell?" Ric asked in a sarcastic way.

Ric couldn't see his uncle roll his eyes behind his dark glasses. To think of it, Ric wondered how the hell his uncle could even see the steps in front of him.

They came to a flat platform, which was just a brief tease before the passageway turned right and an even longer stairway ensued. By the time they reached the bottom of the stairs, Ric's legs were cramped. He was in terrible shape from years of abusing his body with alcohol and drugs. He couldn't remember the last time he had a genuine workout. It must have been years since he hit the gym or participated in a sport in which good cardio was essential.

To Ric's surprise, the door at the end of the stairwell wasn't dark and morose like the rest of the passageway. It was about seven lengths high and four lengths wide, and made of solid gold. Gold that was smoothed to perfection and glistened in the pale glow of the torches. There were decorative patterns of stemmed roses that bordered the door, but the ornate design crafted in the center was the real luxury. A unique sword with a curvature at the end of the blade was sketched with professional precision, and the word *Familia* was etched below the grip of the sword.

Again, Vetti used the Blessing of magic and placed the palm of his hand against the gold surface of the door. A red glow engulfed his hand. The magic flowed through the sketched sword, illuminating the crevices into a yellow gleam so bright that Ric had to shield his eyes. The gold door rumbled and shook, and rose into the stone ceiling from the bottom up.

Vetti stepped through the open passage as soon as the door was lifted, but Ric was hesitant to follow. These magical shenanigans had his mind racing in different directions. Although Ric had grown up with a Family full of magic users, he never saw the powers being used in such a mystical kind of way. It was unearthly. His uncle was opening doors and unveiling hidden passageways by unleashing inner energy from his palms and

260

fingertips. It was a far cry from the destructive use of magic that he had been accustomed to. This was far more mysterious.

Can my brothers use their Blessings in the same manner? Ric thought as he stood motionless in front of the open passage. *Can they use their powers in the form of wizardry?*

Noticing that Ric wasn't following him, Vetti turned around and asked, "Are you coming?"

Staring through his uncle, Ric replied, "I don't know. What's in there?" He felt afraid. A different fear from the one he felt when he was on the verge of death…It was fear of the unknown.

Vetti could see the fear in his nephew's young eyes. "It's alright, Ric. There's nothing in the next room that can hurt you. Only things that will educate and inspire you," he explained. His voice was comforting rather than displeasing. "You need not to be afraid of what you are about to see."

Upon taking a deep breath and slowly exhaling, Ric nodded and said, "Okay. I'm ready."

Ric and his uncle walked through the passage and entered a chamber that was a contradiction to the murky stone staircase they just traversed. Ric's mouth hung low and his eyes lit up like he was just hit by a bolt of lightning. The chamber was spacious and extensive. The floors, ceiling, and walls were made of glimmering black marble, the surface smooth and polished. As Ric took a few steps across the floor, he noticed that the sections of marble were bordered by an inlaid of sparkling red gemstones. There were four cylindrical pillars located in the middle of the chamber, which extended from the floor to the semi-high ceiling. Those too were strewn with gemstones, but the bases and the tops were coated with polished gold. They were connected by a transparent red force-shield, but Ric only saw an altar-like platform in the confines of the four pillars.

The light sources and heat in the room came from a collection of fire-burning stone braziers located in the four corners of the chamber, a number of torches attached to the walls, and lamplights hanging from the ceiling.

But the main attraction of the chamber wasn't what the style of stone which it was constructed with. It was the objects that were on display. The majestic swords that were enchanted with magical powers. The main weapon of a Blessed Family member, who has mastered the art of their Relic's Blessing.

Ric took a stroll around the chamber, not uttering a word to his uncle as he was immersed in the exposition of master weaponry. He was in awe. In his own world like a little kid roaming around a toy store.

Most of the swords were displayed along the walls. They were hovering above marble platforms, and engulfed in red auras of energy. Sealed on the surface of the platforms were rectangular gold plaques, etched with the names of the Family members who had possessed them.

Ric stopped in front of a specific sword he was interested in. He observed the blade. It was shiny, jet black, and the edges were razor sharp. The surface was polished and smooth, with an indented fuller that was a lighter shade of black. The hilt had its own unique qualities, as did every other sword in the chamber. This particular one had a silver cross-guard with a shimmering red ruby in the center. The grip was wrapped in a blood-red leather, and the pommel looked like a small oval knob of clustered diamonds.

He read the plaque attached to the platform. *Anto 'Menace' Rose*, was etched in the gold. The name brought a grin to Ric's mouth. "His nickname was *Menace*," Ric told his uncle, who was loitering around him. "He must've been a real badass for that name to stick."

Leaning against one of the pillars with his arms crossed, Vetti grinned and said, "He *was* a badass. He was the bastard son of one of your great uncles from the Industrial Age. A simpler time when there were no fancy flying vehicles or video monitors, cell phones, or computer technology." He paused for a moment, thinking back on history. "It was also an extremely violent time. The Seven Blessed Families were at war with one another, fighting over the new advancements in technology. The automobile, steel, and oil industries were the hot ticket back then, and everyone was ready to shed blood to get their hands on them." He paused again, looking down at his feet. The marble floor was so polished that he could see the reflection of his shoes. "A lot of blood. Your distant cousin, Menace Rose, was one of the most ruthless soldiers on the streets for the Rose Family at that time. He used a special kind of submachine gun to do his handiwork. The *Regal 220*, nicknamed 'the street sweeper', or 'the Juna cheese grater'. It made mincemeat out of its victims.

"And although Menace Rose was considered to be a merciless thug on the streets, he was highly regarded in the upper-echelon of the Family for his undying loyalty. So, when he was ready, he was taken to the Rose Quartet to be Blessed. And low and behold, a street thug was changed into a Blessed Family member. A bastard child. It was unheard of back then, and is still rare to this day.

"So, upon being Blessed, he was given that sword."

Intrigued by the story, Ric studied the sword from blade to hilt one more time. The ruby in the center of the cross-guard glimmered in his eyes, and the aura of energy caused him to squint.

"Every man who is Blessed by the Rose Quartet is given their own sword as a gift. These swords contain special characteristics and magical powers. They are beyond lethal in combat, both offensively and defensively. The blades can repel bullets, and slice through pretty much anything it encounters."

"What is it made from?" Ric asked. His curiosity had been captured like a ray of sunlight in a glasshouse.

"Obsidian. A shiny black stone that can be cut, sanded, and polished into a deadly knife-edged weapon."

Ric was puzzled, so he asked, "How can a sword made of stone cut through pretty much anything? I mean, it looks sharp enough, but stone doesn't cut as well as metal."

"The obsidian is mainly used for its durability and ability to stop bullets," Vetti replied, "but the stone blade isn't what cuts through objects with such precision and ease…It's the magical force that surrounds the blade when it's used. A special power given to the sword when someone who is Blessed by a Relic holds it."

Ric nodded but still looked confused.

"Did any of your brothers ever show you their swords?" Vetti asked, as he uncrossed his arms and took a step forward.

"No," Ric put his head down, lowering it in shame. "Jon-Jon was never one to brag, so he never showed it off when he was Blessed. And by the time Alto and Georgie got their Blessing, I was already on the streets, up to my neck in drugs.

"I never wanted to see one back then anyway. I didn't really give a shit about their Blessings. It would only remind me of how much of a failure I was. Besides, my dad never showed me his when I was younger, or as I got older, so I guess I just thought I wasn't allowed to."

Vetti huffed and said, "He never showed you his sword because he didn't have it with him. He keeps it down here."

Ric took his eyes off Menace's sword and turned around to face his uncle. "He keeps it down here? What's the fucking point of that?"

Vetti let out a modest laugh. "That's a good question. For some reason, your father doesn't believe in keeping it on him. He's kept it hidden down here for a very long time."

"And you don't know why?"

Vetti shrugged and replied, "I have my theories. Your father's been through a lot. He took over the Family at a very young age, your mother died before her time, he has to beat guys with a stick away from his beautiful twin daughters, and his youngest son was killing himself with drugs for a number of years."

Ric gave his uncle a sarcastic smirk.

"Whatever the reason is," Vetti went on, "it must be a good one. Because I never keep mine very far from my side."

Ric nodded and said, "I see." He turned back toward the sword of Menace Rose and made a hand gesture at it. "Can I hold it?"

Vetti crossed his arms and answered, "Go ahead."

For a moment, Ric just stared at Menace's sword, hesitant to put a hand anywhere near it. But then he mustered up the courage to extend his arm forward, and with a timid, shaky hand, he reached into the aura of energy keeping the sword afloat. Wrapping his fingers around the hilt, he slowly removed the sword from its position. As soon as the sword was free, the energy dissipated.

Ric held the sword in front of his face and glared at it like it was a hidden treasure from an ancient world. And to him it was. He had never seen anything up close that was so invigorating. He squeezed the hilt ever so tight to feel the presence of his ancestor's past. With his other hand, he slid two fingers down the obsidian blade. It was so smooth and clear that he could see his own reflection in the slick stone. It was like a glossy black mirror.

As he rubbed his fingers over the sparkling ruby stone on the cross-guard, Ric asked, "Where does this magical source that surrounds the blade come from?"

Vetti held out his hand and motioned for Ric to hand the sword over to him. Ric complied, and as soon as Vetti wrapped his fingers around the grip, a crimson flow of magic engulfed his hand, then coursed up the hilt and into the blade. The red glow of power surged around the edges of the blade until it was completely surrounded by the awesome energy of light.

Ric watched in amazement as the crimson glow reflected into his eyes. He was intrigued by the raw power of the sword. And now, he had an even greater respect and admiration for his uncle.

"That might have been the coolest fuckin thing I've ever seen," Ric admitted with a childlike smile.

Vetti let out another modest laugh, then placed the sword back to its original position. The aura of energy commenced, and Menace's weapon was now fastened securely above its marble platform.

"How about I show you something even cooler," Vetti suggested.

"Sure," Ric agreed, his interest expressed by the look in his eyes.

Vetti turned around and approached the pillar stationed behind him. With his fingers, he pushed a specific spot and a hidden panel slid open, disclosing a secret keypad. He pressed a code of numbers, and then the panel slid back to its original positing. The crimson force-shield dissipated in an instant.

The moment the force-shield disappeared, Vetti entered the confines of the four pillars. There was a loud click, and then the surface of the alter-like platform retracted below the floor. Rising out of the ground like a hallowed spirit arising from its grave, was the statue of a woman, sculpted out of pristine white marble. The woman was shrouded by a hooded cloak, two blue sapphires produced a sparkle in her eyes, and a large red ruby was inserted in the area of her heart. Her arms were extended outward, as if she was praying over a congregation of followers, and hinged on either hand, were the hilts of two more magical swords with the blades pointing down, each with their own distinctive features.

Ric stood next to his uncle and gazed upon the sculpture of the woman. He examined the opposing swords. The one held in her right hand had a black leather grip, a blood-red cross-guard with triangular spikes, a chape was a vignette of a rose, and a shiny silver pommel. The obsidian blade was curved until it reached the point, and the indented fuller was painted red. The sword appeared to be aged, crafted during a simpler time.

The sword held in the left hand was crafted in a flashier, more modern style. The entire hilt was draped in pure gold, both sides of the cross-guard were shaped like an eagle's wings. The grip had no leather wrap, but was strewn with shimmering diamonds. The pommel was a rounded black gemstone that glimmered like a starry night. And the chape was in the shape of a crown with three red amethysts, small enough to fit inside the tiny replica of a king's headwear. The curved blade was fine-edged, and the indented fuller was painted in a sparkling gold.

"Who do these belong to?" Ric asked his uncle.

"The elder sword, held in the right hand, belonged to the First Don of the Rose Family, Ulozio Manazotti. The statue holding the swords is a depiction of his wife."

"Interesting," Ric responded in truth. "And the other one?"

"That sword belongs to your father."

Ric huffed and asked, "Is there a reason why he keeps it next to the First Don's sword?"

With a subtle grin, Vetti replied, "Because Maretto Rose is the 'Father of Gangster', and what better place to keep his sword safe than hidden next to the sword once possessed by the founder of the Rose Family."

"Makes sense, I guess," Ric kind of agreed. "But with all the bullshit going on recently, you'd think he'd come here and scoop it up. Zasso Cicello attacked him and tried to capture him in front of a crowd of people, for God's sake. And Georgie was killed because of it." Ric shook his head in disgust over the thought of his dead brother. "He needs to protect himself. He may be called the 'Father of Gangster', but he isn't fucking invincible, ya know."

"You're right," Vetti admitted. "Maybe *you* should be the one to tell him that."

Ric exhaled a deep breath out of his nose, scoffing at the idea.

"Or not," Vetti said with a grin.

They stood in silence for a few moments as Ric gaped at the two swords. He was mesmerized by their presence, as he was by the entire collection of them in the concealed chamber. They were mementos from the past. Memorials for the honored men who lived and died for his Family name. And for the first time since he was a little boy, when his father was his biggest hero, he felt the desire to be just like him. A true member of the Rose Family. An *elite* member of the Rose Family.

I want to hold my own sword, and feel the power surging through my hand and into the blade, just like Uncle Vetti showed me, he thought in the back of his mind.

"What's this research assignment you want me to do?" Ric asked his uncle, ending the silence.

Vetti clasped his hands in front of him and lifted his chin. He seemed proud of his young nephew taking the initiative and asking what he needed to do in order to continue on.

"The history of our Family wouldn't be possible if it wasn't for the history of Exodus itself. Before the original members of the Seven Blessed Families discovered the full potential of powers within their Relics, there were three kings who ruled the lands of Exodus. Before Ulozio Manizotti destroyed the last king of Exodus, the three kings went to war against one another. I want you to research the names of these three kings, give me a brief description of their families, and the specific reasons for their conflict. I want to know why the peace between the three kings was broken, and how the last king of Exodus was victorious."

Ric thought to himself for a moment and then said, "Damn, I should've paid more attention in my history classes."

"This is not information that would've been taught in the schools you attended," Vetti explained. "You were only taught about the glory and prosperity of the Seven Blessed Families. Not about the history before they came to be.

"Knowledge is power in of its own, Ric. And the more you know about this wonderful world we live in, the more powerful you could ultimately become."

Ric's eyebrows raised after the explanation from his uncle. "Alright, sounds fair enough."

"But that doesn't mean that knowledge of the Seven Blessed Families isn't equally important. I want you to also give me the names of the Seven Families, descriptions of their Relics, and the powers that they possess.

"You will travel back to the National Archive Building and research your answers there," Vetti ordered his nephew. "And be mindful of other citizens who are attending the facility." He cast a guileful smile on his face. "You never know who you'll meet."

Two hours later, Ric was sitting by his lonesome at an elongated table, surrounded by rows upon rows of bookshelves. He was nose-deep inside an old text he had found through the computer database system. All he had to do was type in the keywords *three kings of Exodus*, and the database provided him with the call number and section of the most popularly used books on the subject. While there was a whole entire section of the Archive Building that was supplied with modern high-tech computers for electronically downloading books, Ric rather enjoyed doing his research the old-fashioned way. He hadn't been in a library, with stacks of bound texts enclosed around him, since he did his final research project his last year in high school.

Giving his eyes a break from scanning the endless chapter on how King Leroy's wife, Queen Annabella, gave herself over and over again to King Vera's entire Elder High Council, Ric took a few moments to observe the scenery around him. He was seated in the archaic section of the Archive Building, an old rendition of how libraries looked and functioned in the days before technology simplified the way people did research.

There were about a dozen long tables in the center of a massive hall lined with endless shelves of books. The bookshelves were stacked with modern and ancient texts, and seemed as tall as skyscrapers when standing next to them. The walls and floors were made of a bluish-white marble, adding a cheerful kind of atmosphere to a solemn place of study. And the domed ceiling was constructed in a three-dimensional effect of layered solar panels depicting a feathered pen writing on a sheet of parchment. It was an architectural designed masterpiece.

The patrons of the library were mostly older men over the age of fifty, dressed in casual attire, and minding their business while browsing around the bookshelves. There were a few others sitting alone at different tables, transfixed into their reading materials, but there was one individual in particular who stuck out from the rest like a homeless man would at a fancy dinner party. And that's because she was a young attractive woman, around the same age as Ric.

She was sitting at an adjacent table, all alone, with her legs crossed like a lady and smiling as she was deeply involved in the opened text in front of her. Her face was a thing of beauty. Not the type of face you would see posing for a magazine or a commercial on a video monitor. She was the girl next door type. A wholesome and natural beauty with shoulder length brown hair that was wavy and conditioned. Her eyes were the color of a tropical ocean and her lips were pouty but not too full. She didn't bother to wear makeup, because she didn't have the need to. Her breasts were concealed in a tight black shirt, but Ric could tell they were nice and firm. And her hips, thighs, and legs fit snuggly in her dark blue jeans.

Ric was attracted to this woman the moment he laid eyes on her, and he didn't hide it. He kept taking short glances at her every few moments, until she noticed him. But little did he know, she had noticed him sitting there before he even knew she existed. Finally, after a couple quicker looks from his table, she made eye contact with him, and they shared a smile. It was a mutual connection.

After a few more minutes of eye to eye flirtation, the woman closed the book she was reading, slowly stood up from her chair, and made a move toward Ric's table. He pretended like he didn't notice her coming his way, but when she stood directly across from him and leaned forward on the table, there was no denying her presence.

"Hi there," she said with a smile, her teeth whiter than a piano key.

"Hey," he replied, smiling back.

"I'm Dada. Dada Flace," she introduced herself, extending her hand toward him for a friendly handshake.

He accepted the handshake and introduced his own self. "I'm Ric."

When they let go of each other's hands, she asked, "Aren't you going to tell me your last name?"

"It's not that important," was his response. He instantly felt wrong for denying her that information. It was rather rude of him and he didn't want her to think that he was an asshole from the get-go, but she didn't seem fazed by the response.

"Well, that's ok if you don't want to jump out and tell me who you are. I understand."

"You do?"

"Of course, I do. Because I already know who you are. I recognized you from seeing you on the television. You're Ric Rose, the youngest son of Don Maretto Rose," she said, her pleasant smile never failing to accentuate the beautiful features of her face. "So, in actuality, your last name is very important. Far more important than any other person in this entire building."

Ric looked down at his opened book and said, "I wouldn't go as far as saying that, Miss Flace."

"Please, just call me Dada."

"Okay, Dada," he said with a pleasant smile of his own. "Would you like to have a seat," he asked her, gesturing to the chair on the other side of the table, "or are you too busy reading whatever it is you're reading over there?"

Without hesitating, she slid the chair from under the table and plopped herself down on it. "I'm never too busy to talk to someone famous."

Ric huffed and said, "Trust me, I'm not famous. You have to do something significant with your life in order to be famous. And I haven't done shit."

She let out a cute laugh and said, "That's not always true, ya know. Some people are just born famous. Like a princess from the Elder Age, born into a life of luxury, pampering, and popularity, without even uttering a word. Or someone like you, the son of the most famous man in Exodus."

"It's funny that you mention a princess from the Elder Age," he said, ignoring the fact that she mentioned him in her statement. "I just finished reading about a princess who left her family heritage to live down in the Deep South and care for those who were less fortunate. It was kind of inspiring, to tell you the truth."

"Oh, yes, Princess Tulsa, the youngest daughter of King Vera. She was a very special woman. So generous and so kind-hearted. It's too bad there weren't more members of the royal families like her back in the Elder Age. Such a shame that she was brutally murdered at such a young age."

"She was?" Ric asked, sounding surprised.

"Uh huh. She was beaten and stabbed to death by a drunken pirate for just five gold coins," she somehow explained the morbid story in a cheerful manner.

Ric rolled his eyes in disappointment. "Well, I was inspired for a moment, but now I'm just depressed."

Dada let out a high-pitched giggle, which Ric thought was cute. "So, Ric Rose, why are you reading about Exodus's historical past? Do you have a test or something?"

Ric shrugged and replied, "Yea, I guess you could say that. My uncle has me doing all this research, so I don't end becoming the Family's biggest dumbass." His answer made her giggle some more. "But it's for a good cause, so I have no problem sticking my nose in a few books for a couple hours. As a matter of fact, I'm finding the story of the three kings of Exodus rather interesting."

Her eyes lit up like a pair of fireflies on a moonless night. "You're going through the Family ritual to get Blessed by your Relic, aren't you?"

Ric was taken aback by her correct assumption, but he was also impressed. "How could you possibly know that?"

"Because I saw your brother doing the exact same thing a couple years back. I even had the chance to talk to him for a bit while he was studying here one day. He seemed quite interested in my research, which surprised me a little." She took a moment to look deep into Ric's eyes. "You look a lot alike, you and him. You both have those honest eyes." Her smile quickly disappeared when she said, "It's very unfortunate that he...ya know..."

"Died?" Ric finished for her. "It's okay to acknowledge that he died, Dada. If people don't acknowledge his death, then he would've died for nothing."

Her beautiful smile returned in no time. "You're very right, Ric Rose, and that's a very insightful statement. There's no doubt in my mind that you won't end up becoming the Family's biggest dumbass."

They shared a playful laugh together, followed by a moment of passionate eye contact that was obviously flirtatious. They weren't hiding the fact that they were attracted to each other.

Ric repeatedly blinked his eyes, and snapped out of his gaze into her eyes. "So," he said, ready to change the subject, "enough about me. Let's talk about what you do. What's this research that you do that had my brother so interested?"

She too had to snap out of the trance she was in to answer his question. "Well, ever since I was around fourteen or so, I've been doing extensive research and studies on the seven Relics of Exodus."

"Oh, good. The second part of my assignment has to do with the Relics of the Seven Blessed Families. You can definitely help me out with that."

She smiled, tilted her head and said, "Yes, I could. But my research is a little more complicated than that. My older brother and I started this group a few years back based on the information we have gathered ever since we started making daily trips down to the Archive Building. You see, this building has a lot of books tucked away that haven't been read in centuries. Books that were hand-written by men and women who share the same beliefs about Relics that we do. Many of the texts we've found don't even have the modern day calling card system, and are not recorded in the library database. We like to call those texts, *ghost books*.

"I personally believe that these *ghost books* have been hidden away for a reason. Modern day historians and theorists have been forced to hide the complete truth about the seven Relics of Exodus. A truth, if unveiled, that would flip the minds of every single person who inhabits this nation. It would cause a revolution throughout Exodus. A revolution that my brother and I have secretly begun."

Ric was intrigued to say the least. *If this woman and her brother are starting a secret revolution,* he thought, *then why is she sharing this information with me? Maybe I'll ask her after she tells me a little more.*

"So, what do you believe to be the truth about the seven Relics of Exodus?" he asked, not pushing the envelope too hard...yet.

"I believe that the Relics possessed by the Seven Blessed Families aren't the only living Relics that exist. There is another world out there, beyond the lands of Exodus, which contain numerous other Relics. An abundance of them. Hundreds, maybe thousands more that never made it to our world," she explained, her heart deeply entrenched in her beliefs by her enlightened passion on the subject.

Ric's mind was completely blown. Growing up as the son of the great patriarch of the Rose Family, he had never heard even a whisper behind someone's back that there was anything but the Relics of the Seven Blessed Families. And he especially never heard about some world outside of Exodus. It was an impossible notion for him to wrap his mind around. *So, why is this random girl suddenly telling me this? Uncle Vetti was right. You never know who you'll meet down here.*

"I have to admit," Ric said. "That is one crazy notion coming from someone I just met a few minutes ago. You definitely have sparked my interest in the matter."

A flattered grin projected off of Dada's face. "Have I?"

Smiling, Ric answered, "Oh yes, you have. I've never met someone so forthcoming about something that is supposed to be kept a secret. In my life, and in my Family's culture, everything is so secretive and kept silent. But that's what you get when you mix loyalty and fear. It's all part of a code of silence that the Families follow...Or try to follow. A lot of men break that code at their own risk." He leaned back in his chair, stretching his arms back and clasping his hands behind his head. "I can't believe I just told you that. You're already starting to grow on me, I guess."

She let out another cute little giggle and said, "Well, maybe that's a good thing, Ric Rose. And I give you my word, anything you let slip off your tongue that you shouldn't, I'll keep between just you and me."

"As will I, Dada Flace," Ric assured her.

"Deal," she said, extending her arm across the table for a handshake to seal the compromise.

Ric accepted her handshake and felt a tingling sensation throughout his body when touching her soft and smooth skin. It was amazing how turned on he was from just a simple shake of her hand.

When they let go of their gentle shake, Ric said, "So, I'm a little curious. If you're involved in a secret group that wants to start a revolution in Exodus, then why would you trust me enough to tell me about it?"

She innocently shrugged her shoulders, smiled, and replied, "Like I said, Ric Rose. You have those honest eyes like your brother."

"Did you ever tell him about your secret group?" he asked, hoping that he would receive the answer he desired.

With a flutter of her eyelashes, she answered, "No, I didn't."

He got the answer he wanted, and for the second time, a moment of passionate eye contact passed between them. Ric could feel the chemistry between the two. It was real. She was real. And for the first time since he lost Galia, he felt true sensuality with another woman. An attractive woman with intelligence. A brain and a beauty.

"Well," she said, rising from her chair, "I should get home before my brother starts to worry. He's still not a fan of me coming downtown alone. He's kind of protective of me. Actually, he's really protective of me."

"Then, he's a good brother."

"He sure is," she said with that cute smile that Ric would be thinking about for the rest of the day. "It was a pleasure to meet you, Ric Rose. I sure hope I see you again soon."

"I'm sure you will," Ric said, his tone pleasant and his words genuine. "And it was a pleasure meeting you, Dada Flace."

She gave him a wink, turned her petite body around and started walking away from his table. But before she left, he wanted to ask her one more question.

"Hey, Dada." Her attention was caught as she stopped in her tracks and turned around to face him. "What's the name of the group you and your brother started?"

She thought about her answer for a moment and then replied, "Maybe that's one piece of information I'll keep a secret from you for now. I think I told you enough for one day." She smiled and flipped her hair as she skidded out of the grand library.

It was a playful rejection, and all Ric could do was smile to himself about it as he got back to his studies. It was time to cram the books for a couple more hours before he reported back to his uncle.

Dusk was breaking. As Ric stepped out of the revolving glass doors and back into society, he took a long gaze up at the orange sky. Stratus clouds cluttered the atmosphere like a teacher's scattered lesson plan on a chalkboard. It was a picture-perfect view from the earth, and reminded Ric of how vast the world really was. Could the things Dada Flace said about a world outside of Exodus be true? While looking up at the endless sky, it didn't seem too farfetched.

Rapidly blinking his eyes, he snapped out of his trance and scanned the neighborhood around him. The sidewalks were crowded with citizens of Juna walking home from work or leisurely strolling about the city. Cars were zipping down the street. The city was always in a hurry. But Ric wasn't. He took his time making his way to the phone booth around the corner, which was his secret way back to Heritage Castle. In a couple minutes, he would be ascending down a hidden elevator shaft and then whisked away through an underground tunnel by a high-speed train.

As he rounded the corner of the Archive Building, he spotted the phone booth. With his eyes, he traced the block surrounding him, searching for unwanted guests in the area. He saw nothing out of the ordinary, so he made the quick walk to the booth. As he approached his destination, he noticed a man stepping out of the doorway of a building near the opposite corner of the street. The man was not a threat to spot him as he was behind a sheltered bus stop and looking the other direction.

Ric paid no mind to the man at first, but when he stood next to the phone booth, ready to enter, he had the inclination to take one more glance at the man across the street. He could see the man better now that he was standing just off to the side of the bus stop. For a moment, he didn't believe his eyes. He thought they were playing a trick on him like eyes from a man withdrawing from hard drugs would do. But they weren't. He recognized the man. Oh, did he ever recognize the sleazy son of a bitch, standing near the street corner, taking hard drags of his cig like he was the coolest cat in town. Wearing a shiny silver polo, tight white pants, and sunglasses that seemed to cover half of his face, was the man Ric was hoping to track down again ever since they had their hellish encounter. Miro Cicello.

In an instant, Ric hid behind the phone booth, peering around the edge of the glass framing, eyeing his nemesis from a safe point of view. Miro had no clue about Ric's presence across the street, and he needed to keep it that way, so when Miro started walking away from his location, Ric stepped out of his hiding spot and scurried across the street, remaining incognito.

Miro took a right at the next block, strolling down the sidewalk like he was the cat's pajamas. There was no care in the mind of that asshole. He was exposing himself in public as if there was no threat to his whereabouts, and Ric was ready to take full advantage of it. Block after block, Ric followed Miro at a safe distance, patiently waiting for him to arrive at his destination, which Ric hoped would be a spot where Miro was hiding out at, or a place he would frequent from time to time.

Then, Ric got his break. Miro stopped in front of corner tavern with a large, unconcealed window in the front. The place was called *Marty's*, a bar located in an irrelevant spot in town, surrounded by closed businesses and abandoned apartment buildings…It was perfect.

Miro stepped through the entrance of the tavern and disappeared from sight. But that's exactly what Ric wanted. As soon as Miro was inside, Ric hurried across the street and leaned his back up against the brick wall next to the wide-open window. After taking a deep breath, he peaked his head around the edge of the window and looked inside. With a spark of fire in his vengeful mind, he watched as Miro strutted his shit to the bar area, and shook the bartenders hand like they were old chums. He took a seat at the counter, and the bartender made him a drink without even asking for his order.

Ric closed his eyes and exhaled a breath of satisfaction. Miro and the bartender's interaction meant that he frequented the bar often. He appeared to be a reoccurring and preferred customer, which was the golden ticket for Ric. Marty's Tavern had just placed a cold dish of revenge in front of him. He could feel a tingling sensation throughout his nervous system. The loins in his muscles ached for the satisfaction of payback. And he couldn't wait to get back to Heritage Castle and tell his uncle.

The train ride back to the birthplace of the Rose Family felt like an eternity. He was so anxious and eager to reveal his discovery to Uncle Vetti. His uncle would be proud. The fuckup that was once Ric Rose was turning a sharp corner heading toward a straightaway into redemption. A redemption that could propel him from being the boy who flushed his life down the toilet, to a man who would become a respected member of the Rose Family.

As soon as Ric hopped off the train and onto the wooden planked dock station, he started jogging his way up the stone road toward the entrance of Heritage Castle. In front of the entrance gate, stood Vetti Rose, already waiting for his return.

Ric jogged harder up the road, and when he was just about twenty lengths away from the gate, he yelled to his uncle, "Uncle Vetti!" When he was finally just a few lengths away from him, in a lower tone he said, "You're never gonna believe who I just saw…" Ric cut himself off from finishing the rest. Something was wrong. His uncle had his head down and removed his dark glasses, before wiping a trickle of sweat from his forehead. His demeanor was solemn. A hard, but saddened look was draped all over his face. "What?" Ric asked in a panic. "What is it?"

His uncle looked him dead in the eyes and said, "There's no way to sugarcoat this Ric, so I'm just going to tell you straightforward…Your friend, Melroy Statz was involved in a vicious attack. He's dead."

The day had been so good, so refreshing, and so promising. And in the flash of a lightning bolt through his chest, Ric's day had turned to dread. His face sagged, his mouth hung open, and his eyes stared off into the space between spaces. Instantly, he had a vision. A vision of him and Melroy, running down the streets of Juna, laughing and playing. They were having the greatest time of their lives…just being kids.

Alana Rae

And Her Night with a Prince

She peered out the window, looking down upon the street below. A black stretch limo was parked by the sidewalk in front of her apartment building. She watched as the limo driver walked around the limo and opened the back door for his passenger. Out stepped the most handsome man she had ever met in her entire adult life. Jonero 'Jon-Jon' Rose was dressed in a fancy black suit with a red dress shirt and black tie. In one hand, he held a bouquet of red roses, and with the other, he adjusted his tie. Giving the limo driver a nod of gratitude for his service, Jon-Jon stood by the limo, awaiting for her to make her way down to the curbside service.

Before Alana Rae left her apartment, she took a few more moments to stop in front of the wide mirror next to her dresser and look at the woman on the other side. She was wearing a black dress that was as fancy as it could be for being so revealing. It had straps around the shoulders and was low cut, exposing a great deal of cleavage. The skirt was short and skin-tight, leaving nothing to the imagination about how sweet her ass was.

She took a close-up of her face. She wasn't wearing an extreme amount of makeup, but her eyeliner was a little heavy. Her lip gloss was clear, but sparkling, and she checked the corners of her mouth for any gunk buildup and her perfectly white teeth for any black or green specks hiding in the crevices. There was nothing. *You look amazing tonight,* she told herself. *Now, if I can continue this good self-esteem throughout my date and try not to think about getting raped by my ex the other night, then the night should go well for me.*

She also had an assignment for herself tonight, just as she did any time she went anywhere. She was a journalist to boot, but tonight was exceptionally more personal. She wanted some answers. He father was murdered and thrown away like a used hamburger wrapper out the window of a moving vehicle. And it was over the ownership of a batball team. Her father refused to sell the team to what she thought were members of the Rose Family. But her confrontation with Don Maretto Rose had her doubting the rumors that she had heard and evidence she had obtained over the years. The Father of Gangster was adamant that his Family was not in ownership of the team. And the Don could be convincing. His intimidating presence has swayed her to look in a different direction…And that's where Jonero Rose comes in. He assured her that on this dinner date, they would discuss what really happened to her father.

When she was finally ready to go on the date, she locked up her apartment with an extra lock she had installed to keep unwanted visitors out, and then ascended down the stairwell and stepped out of the building. Immediately, Jon-Jon approached her with a handsome smile and presented the bouquet of roses to her. The type of flowers were very fitting for the heir to the Rose Family throne.

She accepted the roses with an appreciative and heartfelt smile, then was kissed on the cheek by the handsome son of the Rose Family patriarch. He led her into the backseat of the limo, and they were off to their destination.

Their dinner date took place at a fancy, old fashioned restaurant, designed in the décor of the Industrial Age, and has been a running establishment for over a hundred years. The tables were round and draped in a white satin cloth with a triad of lit candles for a romantic mood setting. And by the look of silverware, plates, and glasses, she guessed that the expense of one table setting probably cost more than a month's worth of her salary at the news station.

At first, their conversation was small talk. He asked personal questions about her life and her job, and made some jokes, but anything she asked him about his Family business, he just shrugged off and changed the subject. But that didn't bother her so much. What she really wanted to know was the truth about his Family's involvement with her father and his batball team.

So, when they were finished eating a gourmet pasta entrée, and were poured their second glass of a decadent red wine, she jumped right into the matter she was eager to discuss.

"So, did you find anything substantial about my father?" she asked, her demeanor dramatically changing from sweet to hard and edgy.

Jon-Jon leaned back in his chair, took a sip from his glass of wine, and answered, "Yea, as a matter of fact, I did come across something rather interesting."

She was all ears.

"I had one of my men look into it, and he brought me a number of receipts and contract agreements from the head office of the Skylarks organization. And on every single documentation I was handed, was the signature of my father, along with a stamped seal of the Rose Family emblem."

Okay, that fairly incriminates the Rose Family, she thought.

"But there's a problem with the signatures," he continued. "They're all forgeries. Every single one of them."

Holding up her glass of wine in a nonchalant manner, she said, "And you know this because you're a handwriting expert?"

"You don't have to be an expert to notice the differences in the signatures. My father has a very distinct way of writing out his name. And the signatures I saw weren't even close to matching his."

She took a sip of her wine and asked, "So where are the documents? I want to see them. I have to see proof in front of my eyes if I'm going to believe any word coming out of a gangster's mouth."

Jon-Jon squinted his eyes and said, "Now those were some pretty harsh words. But I guess you can expect that kind of attitude coming out the mouth of a journalist trying to vilify my Family."

She gave a half-smile and said, "I only tell it like it is, Jon-Jon Rose. You're not part of a group of humanitarians. Your Family, especially your father, has a vilified reputation that has been tainted by the evil doings of your businesses. Killing other men isn't supposed to be part of a job. Normal people don't live their lives using murder as a means to solve business issues. And the only reason I'm out with you on this date is to get answers about my father. Even though you're extremely handsome, I would never go for a man whose life is based on crime."

Jon-Jon had no reply at first. Instead, he wrapped his fingers around his glass of wine, lifted it close to his face and swished around the contents before smelling its sweet fragrance. "You don't know me, Alana Rae," he said, then took a healthy sip of wine. By the way he snapped his lips, you could see how much he enjoyed the taste. "You don't know me at all. I've never personally harmed a soul, and if the Family were in my hands, the violent ways of doing business would come to a complete end.

"And my father may be called the Father of Gangster, but as he has gotten older, his business practices have become more legitimate and less corrupt. That's why I couldn't believe when you accused him of having your father killed, or thrown away like a piece of trash, as you put it. His interest isn't in the sports industry. It's in the mega corporations of oil, natural gas, the auto industry, and land ownership that he wants to control. He wants businesses that produce resources that the world will forever need and use. And that's how the Rose Family is powerful. The other Seven Blessed Families can fight over the entertainment and sports industries. They mean very little to us."

Staring directly at the man sitting across from her with her piercing eyes of jade, she said, "You can explain to me all you want about how your Family isn't as evil and corrupt as I presented them to be in my special report, but I still have yet to see any proof that you and your father are telling me the truth about the death of my father."

Without a moment's hesitation, Jon-Jon reached into the inside pocket of his suitcoat. He pulled out a white envelope, then tossed it across the table. It slid and came to a rest directly in front of Alana.

"Open it," Jon-Jon instructed her.

Alana picked the envelope up off the table, fiddled around with the tab, and then removed the contents. It was a folded piece of parchment, which she unfolded and examined.

"That right there is the secondhand copy of a certificate of ownership for the Southside Skylarks," Jon-Jon explained, "signed by two individuals of whom I've never heard of, and by the commissioner of the Exodus Batball League himself. The final signature on that document is yet another forgery of my father's name, and a stamped seal of the Rose Family emblem."

As she examined the certificate, high emotions went through her mind. Feelings of intrigue, curiosity, and confusion intermixed, sending her thoughts into a tailspin.

"You're positive that you don't know the name of these individuals who signed on as the owners," she pressed, wishing that he knew exactly who they were, so she could confront them herself.

"Never in my life," he assured her, sounding adamant about it. "And neither has my father. And we know everyone of importance, Alana. My guess is that these two names aren't real. They're fake or they're some sort of aliases. And what really bothers me, is that the identities of the real owners of the Skylarks have been hidden for this long. Someone is helping them stay anonymous, and that's why you and the rest of the Exodus Batball League have been led on to believe that my father took on ownership of your father's team. Because his fake signature is found on everything. Each document, contract agreement, and even the paychecks for members of the front office.

"So, what I'm going to do now, is put together a full-out investigation of the Southside Skylarks, and find the identities of the two men on that certificate. How does that sound to you?" he asked, a serious look of confidence projected off his face.

She had lied to Jon-Jon. Her attraction to him was so intense that it didn't matter to her whether or not he was involved in a crime syndicate. And now, as she stared into his big brown honest eyes-and listened as he offered to use his Family leverage to assist her in figuring out the truth about her father-the yearning for her naked body to be wrapped around his virile physique was going to culminate into her letting him ravage her repeatedly, until her skin was torn away from her bones.

"That sounds wonderful," she replied, showing him a sincere smile of appreciation. As she stared deep into his eyes, she couldn't hide the lust in hers.

A long moment of comfortable silence drew on between the two, and when Alana wouldn't take her eyes off of his, Jon-Jon asked, "What are you thinking right now?"

Without even thinking about the consequences of having an affair with a man who was engaged to be married and the heir to most powerful crime Family in Exodus, she answered, "I think I want to go back to my place and make love to you."

Jon-Jon's mouth formed a grin of desire. "Then let's finish our wine and get the hell out of here."

Alana led the Rose Family prince to her bedroom as soon as they entered her apartment. There was no hesitation. Their lips were suddenly connected, their tongues wrestling in the inside of their mouths. Arms were vigorously wrapped around each other's backs, sliding down the spines, venturing lower and lower into body parts with more curves. It was only a matter of seconds until Jon-Jon reached underneath her skirt, grabbed a couple handfuls of fabric, and lifted her dress above her waist, until it was completely over her head and tossed to the floor.

After he tossed his suitcoat behind him and unfastened his tie, she ripped his dress shirt open, exposing his broad chest. She then undid his belt buckle, unzipped his pants, and reached down inside, grabbing a handful of what she had been yearning to feel. She moaned as she stroked. He tilted his head back, taking heavy breathes from the pleasure.

Not wanting to wait any longer for him to be inside her, Alana unfastened her bra, exposing her luscious breasts, then stripped herself of her panties and laid herself on the bed with her back arched. Jon-Jon tore away whatever other clothing he had on, and threw himself on top of her. She groaned as he sucked and licked her neck, his mouth making its way down to her breasts. His hand began to rub and squeeze her waist, until it began to slide further below.

A single beam of white moonlight shone through her bedroom window and partially lit the right side of her naked body. And just as she felt like she was about to let out a scream of sensation, the passion abruptly stopped.

Jon-Jon backed off her and stared at the moonlit part of her body. "What happened to you?"

In the heat of the moment, she had forgotten. The mood was so intense that she had forgotten about the bruises around her waist and private area.

Breathing heavy from the sexual tension, she replied, "I shouldn't tell you."

He caressed the bruising on the surface of her skin in a delicate motion, then said, "You have to tell me. Or this has to stop."

That was the last thing she wanted to happen at the moment, so she immediately confessed, "I was taken against my will the other night. By an ex-boyfriend. He broke into my apartment, then assaulted me when I came home."

In the blink of an eye, Jon-Jon's facial expression went from concern to pure anger. "Who is he?"

Alana confessed. She told him everything. His name, his line of work. Everything. She wanted him inside her so bad, so she came completely clean to satisfy him. And when she was done confessing, she grabbed him around the waist, urging him on top of her again. And in one satisfying gyration, she finally had what she wanted.

Salic Stone

And the Welcome Home Party

It had been a long time since Salic Stone had gazed out the window of a moving vehicle and watched as the neon lights of the Vena Strip passed him by. He was a loyal member of the Rocca Family back then, asked to do a dangerous job for their cause. A job that he had a slim chance of surviving if the truth of his mission was ever uncovered by the Jovani Family, led by the Don of the Deep South, Calio Jovani. He was a man Salic began to love and respect more than any other man he had known since the first time he could remember. He respected him more than his boss, Don Maximo Rocca. He even respected him more than his late father, a man he had grown up idolizing.

But things change you. Life changes you. Experience changes you. And by the end of six months infiltrating the Jovani Family for the main purpose of finding their Family Relic, Don Calio didn't have to uncover the truth of Salic's mission. Because Salic told him the truth himself. He came clean to the man he loved and respected most, risking his life in the process. It was a bold move. A move that no one in this business survives.

But Salic did. And not only was his life spared, but he was now one of Don Calio's right hand men. He was an underboss to the Don of the Deep South. A former grunt for the Rocca Family, who in actuality, *did* complete his assignment. Salic Stone was shown the hidden location of the Triad; the Jovani Family Relic.

And now I'm back again, Salic thought as the multicolored lights flashed across his face. *I'm back to report the success of my mission. I'll be taken in by the Rocca Family like a hero. But then I'll be spit out like a wad of phlegm in their throats.*

Salic knew the drill. He had seen it happen to many men in his line of work. The Rocca Family was going to welcome him back with open arms, hugs, and kisses. There would be a celebration. And when he was distracted and least expecting it, they would dispose of him. To the Rocca's, he was expendable. Replaceable. He would be recycled like yesterday's newspaper...Although, there was a chance of him being promoted to a higher rank in the Family. His information *was* invaluable.

But whatever the situation, Salic Stone and Don Calio Jovani had their own plans for his return.

Along with a few of Don Maximo's henchmen, the overseer of the Classic casino escorted him up to the private quarters. The overseer acted like he was a complete gentleman and one of the legit personnel of the casino, but Salic knew the truth of the man. He was the Family's High Consultant. The main advisor to Maximo. For some odd reason, Maximo kept him a secret from other Families. Who the fuck knew the real reason behind it? But Salic couldn't stand the guy. Especially his fucking blond ponytail.

The overseer punched in a code to retract the light blue beams that guarded the double white doors, then yanked on the golden handles and led Salic inside. Immediately, Maximo rose out of the chair behind his glass surface desk, flashing a big triangular smile on his face. There was a group of other men in the room accompanying him, including his son, Lucius, two of Salic's closest friends growing up-who joined the Family from the bottom with Salic-and none other than Don Xanose Cicello and his bodyguard. He was drawing a blank of what the bodyguard's name was. *I think its Ronda or Rondo,* he thought. Anyway, it didn't matter. He just knew him as a big and cocky asshole.

"There he is, there he is," Maximo repeated himself as he made his way around his desk and walked toward Salic. His eyes were bugging. He was definitely hopped on powder. "The man of the hour. The guy who conquered the Deep South. The one member of this Family who has both balls and brains." He placed his hands on Salic's shoulders and pulled him in for a tight embrace. "You did well, my boy," he said, patting his back and then kissing him on the cheek. He pinched his cheeks with both hands and gave him a light slap of affection.

"Thank you, Don Maximo. It was my honor to serve the Family to the best of my ability," Salic lied.

Maximo gave a light chuckle and said, "Come on now, Stone. Enough with the formal talking bullshit. This is a business meeting and a celebration, so relax a bit. You

288

want a taste of some of the finest powder in the land? My oldest likes to call it White Lightning." Maximo returned to his desk.

"No thanks. I'm trying to cut down after nearly snorting my nose off when I was down south." He wasn't lying. "So, where is Augusta? I haven't seen him in a long time."

With a wave of his hand, he sat down at his desk and replied, "Eh, I think he's up in Juna running his product around the streets." He stuck a short metal tube up his nose and snorted a long line of powder. After rubbing some of the remnants on his teeth, he continued, "He's gotta be making some good coin up there with this shit. My God is this a mind blower."

"Why don't you ease up on that shit, pap, before you blow your heart out?" Lucius Rocca said to this father.

He pointed a finger at his son and said, "Why don't you just shut the fuck up? I know what I'm doin here."

"Whatever, motherfucker," Lucius said under his breath.

Maximo burst off his seat and shouted, "What did you say to me!"

"Alright, alright," Don Xanose stepped in. "Let's cut the father-son bullshit and concentrate on our friend here, who sacrificed himself for our Families." He came to Salic's side and put a hand on his shoulder. The feeling of his stubby sausage fingers made Salic cringe. "We want to hear all about your trip to the Deep South, but first, let's celebrate with some champagne and cigars."

And that's exactly what everyone in the room did. They all toasted to Salic Stone, the new hero of the Rocca Family, who was the first of their spies to come back home with his mission accomplished. Everyone except for Rondo. That asshole stood off to the side, looking and acting like a little bitch who thought he was too cool for a party.

Salic was surprised to see Xanose Cicello in the room when he arrived, but he was even more surprised to see his two friends, Ander Lucille and Vennie Vaccio. They grew up on the streets together, running quick errands for this gangster who called himself *The Ripper*. He was a ruthless hitman for the Rocca Family, but was also involved in sports

289

betting. He loved the shit, and he would have his three sidekicks run all over Vena placing bets for him. Even though he was a sadistic killer, Salic always thought The Ripper was a good guy. He was funny as hell and tough as nails. But one day, he was found with his head cut off and his dick stuck in his ear. Poor Ripper. Salic never did find out what he did to deserve that kind of treatment in death. He probably did a lot of things. That man murdered a lot of other gangsters.

So, right when the champagne was poured and the cigars were lit, Ander and Vennie paid their respects to their old friend with hugs and kisses on the cheek and pats on the back. They seemed genuinely proud of Salic and happy to see him. *But are they?* Salic thought as he smiled and took in the moment of fake pride. *Fuck if I can't trust anyone anymore. Especially two goons I used to roll with in the Rocca Family.*

"So, tell us man. How were the bitches down in the Deep South?" Ander asked Salic. He was the taller of the two and stalky as well. He had a shaved head because his hairline was receding, but he always wore a white fedora to cover up his hairless cranium.

"They'll ride you into the night and then slit your throat at the break of dawn, my friend." The embellished statement received a chuckle from both his friends.

"That's what I'm talking about," Ander said, dapping Salic up.

Vennie pushed Ander out of the way and plopped a hand on Salic's shoulder. "Seriously though, bro. What was it like being so close to the Don of the Deep South? I heard that guy is one fucked up cat." Vennie was the good looking of the two, but shorter and scrawnier. Still, he could pack a hard punch during a fight.

Salic thought about how to describe Calio Jovani to these guys without sounding as if he admired the guy, but also not sounding like the man was a complete jackass.

"Well," he hurried to think, "Don Calio liked to have a good time, that's for sure. But when it came down to business, he didn't fuck around, and he didn't like to be fucked with. But damn if he sure knew how to throw a good boat party." Salic smiled as he thought back on the good times he had down there. But he shouldn't have.

"What? Did you like the guy or something?" Vennie asked, always the perceptive one.

Salic lost the smile and quickly thought of a good rebuttal. "Nah, are you kidding me? The guy was fucking crazy. But there's nothing wrong with having a good time while I was down there, don't you think?"

Vennie's mouth formed a cunning grin when he answered, "Of course not. That's what it's all about, bro." He dapped Salic up and gave him a bro hug.

"A salute!" Maximo silenced the celebration for the moment by shouting out. He raised his glass of champagne and said, "To the man of the night, Salic Stone. From what I've heard, he brought back a video that will lead us straight to the Jovani Family's Relic, The Triad. That's one hell of a job if you ask me, and one hell of a risk he took for our Family. And if this video is the real deal, then you're all looking at a new boss of the Rocca Family."

Everyone in the room raised their glasses and yelled, "Salute!" They all drank to his accomplishment and gave him pats on the back, hugs, and handshakes. Whether it was genuine or not, has still yet to be determined. But Salic was always a step ahead. If this was some kind of bullshit celebration, then he would be ready for the aftermath.

Maximo had his son set up the disk player for the flat-screen video monitor. When it was turned on, the twenty-four-hour news station channel was broadcasting footage from a scene of an accident on Highway Five. A Juna Police Department detective was involved in the incident and had been declared dead. His name was Melroy Statz. *Never heard of him,* Salic thought in the back of his mind. He then took a glance at Xanose Cicello, who upon seeing the news footage, scratched his cheek, turned, and took a quick look at his bodyguard. The big bastard gave him a little shrug with his shoulder.

Salic squinted his eyes. *Did that son of a bitch have something to do with that accident?* Salic wondered. *Oh well, it's none of my business.*

Reaching into his pocket, Salic pulled out a small rectangular disk with a silver tab. Propped in between two of his fingers, he held it up so everyone in the room could see. The silver tab sparkled in the spotlight.

"This right here," Salic said, "is footage that I personally took on a boat ride out to an island that inhabits the Triad Relic." He tossed the disk across the room and into the hands of Lucius Rocca. "Access to the boats is rather simple with minimal security, and the coordinates to the island have been recorded in the disk's database."

Lucius inserted the disk into the player, and Salic's footage started showing on the video monitor. The hidden camera was inserted into a charm hanging from a thick gold necklace he was wearing that day he went out to see the Triad Relic. It was actually the second trip he made out to the island. And little did everyone else in the room know, the secret footage they were about to witness was a setup.

The video was watched with keen interest as it showed the specific dock to take a boat out, the route taken out to sea, and the exact island in which the Relic was hidden. Once on the island, the footage captured Salic following Don Calio and Petro through a pathway of palm trees until they came upon the dark cavern that held the Relic. And after the shield of flames was dissipated, the jerky footage broadcasted the image of the fiery triangular Relic, called the Triad.

The men in the room were at the edge of their seats witnessing a Relic they have never had the privilege of seeing before, but Salic didn't have to watch the video to remember its almighty presence. He was a nonbeliever and a skeptic about the powers of Relics. But after he was up close and personal-and could feel the tips of the triangle warm the inside of his body, while an eye opened in each corner, staring deep into his soul, trying to figure out who this human was and why he was in its presence-he instantly became a believer and a follower of the Triad. His Family was the Jovani's. Not the Rocca's. He couldn't even remember the name of their fucking Relic as it meant nothing to him.

When the video was over, and Don Maximo and Don Xanose looked at each other as if they were satisfied, Maximo stood up from his chair and declared, "There it is. Absolute proof that Salic completed his mission. We now have direct access to the Jovani

Family Relic thanks to him and him alone." There was an eruption of clapping hands directed toward Salic, then Maximo raised his glass of champagne for another salute. "Let it be known to the men who are witness to this night. Salic Stone, you will be made into a boss, starting with your own crew that has joined you here tonight." More hands clapped. "And let it also be known, that on the day of the President's speech, when the entire world of Exodus is tuned into or attending the event, the Triad Relic will be retrieved and brought to its knew home. The great alliance of the Cicello and Rocca Families has begun!"

"Salute!" the room shouted, then drank from their glasses. Salic joined in, trying to look as excited as the patriarchs of the newly formed alliance. Salic was going to be made into a boss now. He would have his own crew, starting with his two friends growing up.

But I don't even like Ander and Vennie anymore. Not like the old days, Salic thought. *And as far as this new alliance goes, Maximo and Xanose are making a bold move tonight. First it was the attempted abduction of Don Maretto Rose, and now the stealing of a Family's coveted Relic? They've got a lot of balls, those two.*

Salic was lost in thought, wondering whether or not Don Maximo was going to go fetch the Triad himself. He was the patriarch of the Family, and supposed to be the most powerful Rocca, so he should trust no one else to carry out the heist. Salic was sure of it. Maximo was going to travel down to the Deep South, and take a boat ride out to that island.

"So," Ander interrupted Salic's thoughts, smacking him across the back, "me and Vennie have a little surprise for you tonight. We're taking you to the finest gentlemen's club on the strip, and we're not taking 'no' for an answer. So how about it, boss?"

Salic wasn't going to lie to himself. It felt good to hear someone call him boss. He'd been waiting for this type of respect ever since he was doing smalltime jobs for the Rocca Family.

But things have changed now. I'm a new man. Reborn into a new Family. A Family who respects me. A Family who loves me...A Family I can trust.

"Well, if you're not gonna take 'no' for an answer, then I guess I've gotta go," he replied with a fake smile, knowing damn well he didn't want to, but had to.

Maximo walked up to the new crew trio and put his arms around Salic and Vennie. He looked blitzed out of his mind. "You boys go out and have a good time on me." He reached into his pants pocket, brought out a wad of cash, and tossed it across the way to Ander. "You're in charge of the money, you husky bastard. And if I hear that my man, Salic here, didn't get a lap dance from the finest piece of ass in the club, then I'm gonna make sure you pay my ass back." He let out a sinful laugh and smacked Salic and Vennie right on their asses. "Go have some fun boys!"

Salic and his two boys were picked up in front of the Classic casino by a black stretch limo. A plethora of drinks were provided inside the vehicle, along with a mound of pure white powder. Salic didn't partake in the wide-eyed wonder, but Ander and Vennie were hitting the lines hardcore. Along the way to the strip club, they reminisced about the old days when they ran around the streets together collecting money for The Ripper. *Damn those days were fun,* Salic thought back. *But those jobs were petty compared to what I'm involved in now. The Ripper would be proud that one of his boys was getting his come-up...Or maybe not. I'm breaking one of the cardinal rules of the business. I'm backstabbing the Family who brought me off the streets...Oh well. Fuck them.*

They arrived at the *Panty Dropper*; a low-key strip club off the main strip of Vena, which delivered some of the finest dancers in the city. A personal valet, dressed in a traditional red vest with black slacks, opened the back door upon their arrival and escorted them into the club without having to go through the bullshit of security or a cover charge. Even the owner of the club was waiting for them when they passed the velvet ropes on the inside. He was short and fat, with long black hair and a porno mustache, but he was dressed in a fancy white suit and sported a thick gold chain around his neck.

The owner led them into the dance lounge where the main stage was dark, but lit by poles with flashing colored lights and blinking white lights around the edges of the dancing platform. Gangsters from all over town were throwing their money at the blonde with big tits, shaking her ass to a hard rock song from a decade ago.

Salic, Ander, and Vennie were then taken to the bar where they were served a round of drinks on the house. For about an hour they sat at the bar and bought drinks until they were all feeling a nice buzz. Then, Vennie stood up from his bar stool and grabbed one of the scantily clad ladies walking by. He whispered something in her ear, and she gave him a smile while nodding her head.

Vennie turned toward Salic and yelled through the loud music, "Well, soon-to-be boss. We have a very special treat for you. We're not the type to disobey the patriarch of our Family, so in a moment, you're gonna be taken back into one of the private rooms and feast your eyes on the best prize in the club. She's gonna rub her ass and cunt on you until your dick falls off, my man." He let out a laugh that was cross between sinister and joyful.

Salic chugged the rest of his mixed drink and said, "Well, that's what I came here for, so bring it on, bitch."

In actuality, he came because he had no other choice, but if he was going to see some bodacious tail, then why the hell not enjoy himself while he was here…Still, he had to keep a close eye out all night long. You never know if something were to go down tonight. He had to keep his guard up at all times.

Two big and bald security guys with beards and sunglasses, dressed in all black suits, took Salic over to the area with the private dance rooms. One of the men opened a black curtain and waved him inside. The dark ominous room had but a single wooden chair with a red cushion for a little comfort. The big and bald security guy told him to have a seat and the show would start in a moment.

Salic took his seat, and almost immediately, a bluish spotlight shone over top of him. A slow and groovy dance song started playing in the background, and out of the shadows came a tasty blonde treat dressed in nothing but a silver bikini. She was smoking hot. The kind of woman he was used to seeing on the beaches down in Sonia, but this one had a city girl edge to her.

The luscious blonde had a sultry walk on her way toward Salic's spot in the middle of the room. Upon closer look, she had a perfectly round set of perky tits, a flat stomach with her naval pierced with a diamond stud, and legs that he would love to have wrapped around his head for the night. At first, she danced slow and seductive, rubbing her tits across his junk and up his torso, until she straddled him, grinding him with her tight ass. Salic was turned on big time, and she hadn't even taken off her clothes yet. But that was soon to come.

As the groove of the music became more sensual, her dance moves became more provocative. She then dismounted from his lap and removed the silver bikini, tossing the top and bottom to the side, revealing everything she had. Her naked body sent a tingle through his body. He couldn't wait until she was grinding him with that perfectly shaved pussy. And moments later, she was doing just that. Riding him like she was in the rodeo and breaking all sorts of national records. He was starting to get aroused, and the hot blond stripper could feel it.

She slid her way down his body, until her face was in his crotch. She motioned her head back and forth. He was on the verge of poking her in the face...And then she did something strange that Salic noticed right away. She reached under his chair and grabbed something. It had to be some kind of object, because he heard a slight clink when she did.

When she was done rubbing her face in his crotch, she slid herself back into a straddling position and said, "Just put your head back, close your eyes, and I'll give you the best ride of your life."

Salic complied with her request, but kept his eyes half-open. And once the stripper thought he wasn't paying attention, she brandished a sharp, silver knife with a gold grip. With a sudden look of fury and evil, the stripper lunged the knife forward, but Salic caught her hand just before she could stick it into his heart. He then lifted his head and saw the shocked look in her hazel eyes. He squeezed her wrist with a tight grip, then with his other free hand, he grabbed her throat and wrapped his fingers around it so tight that her eyes began to bulge an inch out of her head.

Salic stood up from the chair, standing her up as well. He leaned in toward her face and said, "Those pieces of shit should've been smarter than this." With a snap of his hand, he broke her wrist with ease, causing the knife to fall out of her hand. She tried to scream when her wrist snapped, but there was no air in her lungs to let out the slightest peep. And then he took both of his hands and grabbed her by the cranium, and with a violent jerk, twisted her head, breaking her neck and killing her instantly. After the deed was done, he shoved her lifeless body to the ground.

The seductive song was over, so that meant the private dance was over as well. One of the big security guys opened the curtain and walked into the room. He was absolutely stunned when he saw the stripper's corpse on the ground. "Oh, fuck!" he shouted. And then he was taken by surprise when Salic came jumping out of the darkness and shoved the knife into the man's heart, killing him before his body hit the floor.

The Rocca Family had betrayed him, just as he thought they were going to do. And what was even more degrading, was the fact that they sent a dirt-bag stripper to carry out the deed. *What a fucking insult,* he thought. *And what a stupid fucking move.*

Payback was going to be a bitch for the Rocca Family no matter what, but Salic wanted to get a little of his own tonight, so he reached down to his pant leg and removed a loaded piece he had strapped to his calf. His so-called friends were about to get what was coming to them.

Salic flipped open the black curtain and locked on his targets across the lounge, still drinking at the bar and waiting for the message that his heart had been stabbed. But when Salic made his way back over to the bar area and tapped the back of Vennie and Ander's shoulders, you would have thought they saw a ghost when they turned around and realized their plan had somehow gone awry.

"Fuck you both," Salic stated, before he pointed his piece at Ander's forehead and pulled the trigger. The gun exploded, and a giant cloud of pink mist came out the back of Ander's head. Vennie tried to run, but Salic fired a shot that caught him through the neck. Vennie opened his mouth to scream, and then was shot again through the back of his head. The shot took most of the middle of his face off and blood sprayed all over a stripper standing next to him. She screamed, but no one else in the building made a move. They were too scared. A madman had just shot two men point blank in the middle of the club.

Zasso Cicello

And the Calm before the Storm

He stood above the world, his foot propped on a cement ledge as he overlooked the city with his sharp silvery-black eyes. The altitude was high, the air was cool, and the light breeze carried the stench of smog into his nostrils. The city looked small from his point of view, atop a skyscraper built hundreds of lengths up from the ground. The gray structure made of solid cement and steel stood among its siblings, creating a metropolis like none other in the world of Exodus…And it would be his. All his. The great city of Juna would be owned by Zasso Cicello. That's what he wanted. That's what he always wanted. To be the king of his city. Not just a prince. The king. The man in charge. And not just the patriarch of the Cicello Family. He wanted to be the patriarch of Juna.

That's what he had been promised. The key to the city. The only key. All he had to do was one simple job…But it wouldn't be that simple. It sounded like an effortless mission the time it was given to him, but on his first attempt, he realized that it would be more difficult than he was led by himself to believe. There were many men ready to die for the man he had attempted to capture. Especially a son, who gave his life in order for his father to stay safe, in which also protected the safety and sanctity of the most coveted Relic of the Seven Blessed Families. The Rose Quartet.

But there would be a redemption. Zasso was given a second chance to prove himself, and to show the world his glorious ascension into the hierarchy of mankind. The citizens of Juna would soon be accepting him as their ruler. And the entire world would soon be groveling at the feet of a new leader. A leader who exemplified the meaning of godliness. Exodus would be underneath him. And the Seven Blessed Families would be kissing the rings on *his* fingers…If they survived at all.

The sun was beaming rays of iridescent orange light as it began to set on the distant horizon. Zasso squint his vile eyes as he stared directly into the sunlight and thought about the events that would transpire two days from now. *All I have to do is succeed this time around, and then my time in the sun will be within reach. I will not only rule over the city I was raised in, but I will wreak chaos among those who try to defy me. And I will salivate over every drop of blood I shed.*

"Our contact should be arriving soon, prince of the city," Razo notified Zasso, as he stood next to his boss atop the roof of one of the tallest skyscrapers in Juna. It was the General Steel building, which the Cicello Family owned. It was just a block away from the spot the President would give his speech in two days.

Ignoring Razo's heed of the contact's arrival, Zasso said, "Can you feel it, Razo? Can you feel the energy from the sun as it beams through your skin? That's the feeling of everlasting life. An eternity of natural energy giving life to a world lost in the universe of forever."

"I see whatever it is you see, Zasso," Razo replied. He wasn't much for his own opinion. He was a follower. A follower of Zasso Cicello and any endeavor he embarks on. A follower until death.

"You can be so boring with your point of views, Razo. But it's better to not have an opinion than to have one that would anger me, so keep up the good work."

"I do the best work I can," Razo retorted.

"Yes, you do, my friend. And I'll need you to be at your very best when we attempt to accomplish what we started. My father believes that it was an idiotic idea to attack Maretto Rose in public, but he just doesn't get the fact that it's nearly impossible to get to him when he's locked up in his sky-rise mansion. Vego Rainze is always by his side. I hate that man. When I was growing up, he always treated me like I was the excrement of my Family. He once told me that my brothers and I would fail taking over the Cicello Family when my father was gone."

"He knows nothing, Zasso."

"Of course, he doesn't. But he's still dangerous for a man who doesn't possess the powers of a Relic, and I want him dead. It's a given that he will be stuck to Maretto's side like a lowly fly on shit during the President's speech, so your main goal, Razo, is to take him out when the moment presents itself," Zasso instructed his protector.

"I will do what I must to spill his blood. Vego Rainze will breathe his last breath and we will celebrate his death when it is all said and done."

Zasso's mouth formed a cunning grin. *Just the thought of Vego Rainze's death makes me smile. If there was one glass of blood I would love to drink down, it would be a vial of his. It would taste sweet and satisfying. I would savor the flavor. Just like my favorite aged wine.*

Just as Zasso's twisted thoughts were taking over his mind, a thunderous roar and a swirling wind developed behind him. The ends of his silvery-black hair began to ruffle as he turned around to see what the ruckus was all about. He removed his fedora, so that it wouldn't blow off his head, and gazed unto the flying machine hovering above the roof.

The flying vessel was three times the size of an extended SUV, the base was rounder and longer with elongated wings extending from the sides. The solid steel exterior was all black. The windows of the cockpit and passenger sides were all tinted, making it incapable of seeing inside the vessel. Hydraulic boosters were attached to the wings and in the center of the undercarriage. The tail of the flying vessel had an array of flashing blue lights and mini-boosters. There was no name or logo identifying the large aircraft, but Zasso didn't have to see any identification to know who was riding inside. The contact had arrived.

Zasso and Razo shielded their eyes from the dirt and other debris kicked up from the vessel landing on the roof. When it came to a halt and the boosters cooled down, Zasso brushed the dust off his royal blue suit coat while Razo wiped his silver one clean.

Below the cockpit, an automatic hatch slid open and a metal walkway extended to the ground. From the inner depths of the vessel came a group of what appeared to be armored soldiers, strapped with hand cannons that looked mighty lethal. From Zasso's advantage, the soldier's uniforms were all black with silver armor in select areas of the body. They were also wearing helmets and masks with breathing mechanisms.

Then, as the soldiers formed a line on each side of the walkway, two more individuals came striding out. One of the men Zasso was expecting. The other he was definitely not. The contact was wearing a black suit, black fedora, pink dress shirt, and white bowtie. His crisscrossed scars on his face were still visible from a distance. And the individual walking next to him was dressed completely different. His attire was something out of the Golden Age of Exodus, in the times of kings and royal families. He bore a black velvet cape with ornate silver patterns embroidered on the fabric, and the edges were hemmed with gold linings and tassels. His torso and arms were covered by a black tussled shirt and a silver sash wrapped over his shoulder and diagonally down his chest. His belt was of a shiny silver fabric as well and a black kilt hung down to his metallic boots. A slithery black hood was draped over his head to complete his dark attire.

But the most the most intriguing part of his outfit was the masklike form that covered his face. It wasn't necessarily made of any type of material. It was as if his face was plastered with a digital computer program with numbers and symbols constantly running parallel, projecting a bright bluish glow. The mask was in the shape of a masculine face with a hard jawline and slanted, forbidding eyes. There was no way of identifying the true appearance of the man hiding behind it, but Zasso knew the disturbing truth. It was Thy Master; the dark organizer behind it all. The man Zasso Cicello was vigilantly following, although he had never met him before. But that's because he was called upon by Thy Master through an unnatural dark force.

As Solace Volhine and Thy Master approached Zasso, his legs began to tremble. Never in his life had he feared a man. But Thy Master wasn't any ordinary man. He wasn't the grease-ball gangsters Zasso was used to dealing with. No, this man was special. He was above the lifestyle of organized crime. He was above the Seven Blessed Families.

"These are the two young men sent to do your bidding, Thy Master," Solace said, a heartless smirk forming at the mouth.

Thy Master's digital eyes moved back and forth between Zasso and Razo. His stare dug deep into their hearts, studying their souls. His mouth never moved.

"They are the ones responsible for the mishap at the Grand Theater," Solace continued. "They broke in like madmen, creating a stir, murdering innocent people, then slaying Don Rose's son."

Zasso immediately dropped to one knee, bowed his head, and said, "I'm sorry for the failure I have committed, Thy Master. I promise it will never happen again."

Thy Master took a hard step forward, looked down upon Zasso and said, "Rise, my child. Do not grovel at the behest of a man you have never laid eyes on before. And do not make a promise that could end up out of your control."

Zasso lifted his head, but did not look Thy Mater in the face. He was too nervous. The man's tone of voice was so sharp and elegant, but yet so vicious and deep. It was unrelenting on the ears, but in a good way. You wanted to hear him speak again, but felt like crying when it was heard. It wasn't a true man's voice. It was artificially made through his computer animated mask.

Rising back to his feet, Zasso straightened out his suitcoat and looked over at Solace. Solace shared the look with him and with the same smirk on his face, said, "Don't look at me, kid. I'm not the one calling the shots here. You and your friend have the privilege of meeting Thy Master because he chose *you* to do the work he cannot in the public's eyes. I would try to talk him out of using a couple of punks like you, but he insists that you are the right men for the job."

"Take it easy on them, Solace," Thy Master cut in. "They are but young cubs wanting to play among the wolves. But they have to learn to play smart instead of acting savage, in order to accomplish what I have asked of them to do. The Grand Theater mission was done sloppy and errant, but that fault lies on my shoulders. I should have made my presence known to them first, before I sent them to do my bidding."

"Do not blame yourself, Thy Master, for the faults of the young and inexperienced," Solace said. "They should've adhered to your calling more appropriately. But what can you expect from a Cicello thug?"

The comment blew a sudden fuse in Zasso. "I'm not just some thug, asshole! I'm the heir to the Cicello throne! I'm the prince of this city!"

Zasso's outburst had no effect on Solace. Instead, he just turned his head and looked at his superior. Thy Master's digital eyes became more solemn and less forbidding. "Good," he said as he stepped directly in front of Zasso. "There is much aggression in you and you don't let others belittle you. I like that…But you are not the heir to your Family's throne and you are not the prince of this city. No, Zasso, you are much more than that. From this day on you will begin to realize that the Seven Blessed Families and their way of life is beneath what my purpose in this world will become. They are pathetic, and I will show you first hand that my powers far exceed any of theirs." He made a gesture with his gloved hands towards Zasso. "Remove your sword," he commanded.

Hesitant at first, Zasso reached over his back shoulder, then unsheathed his personalized Blessed sword. The obsidian blade was bordered by a transparent yellow force of energy.

"Good. Now attack me with it," Thy Master ordered.

"No," Zasso boldly said back. "I will never."

"You will do as I say, or you will experience pain like you've never felt before!" Thy Master commanded in a thunderous roar. "Prove to me that you deserve to be the ruler of this city! Prove to me that you are more than just a Cicello thug, destined to be a rat on the rotting streets that you have walked on since birth! You will never amount to anything, since you were born of a whore mother, who abandoned your inept father, because he could not satisfy her the way she wanted. And you could not possibly be the prince of a city that had four princes in line ahead of you with the heralded name of Rose."

Suddenly, the rage deep inside Zasso's body and mind reached a point that couldn't be contained. Thy Master's words struck a nerve that couldn't be pacified. *Damn the Rose brothers!* Zasso thought as angry blood rushed into his head. *I destroyed one of them and I can destroy them all! They will never hold the power I possess! Fuck you, Thy Master!*

Lifting his sword in the position of an attack, Zasso used the rage boiling inside of him to take a mighty hack at Thy Master's head. But Thy Master simply raised his hand, and stopped the glowing blade short of striking its target. He then grabbed the hand Zasso had wrapped around the grip of his sword.

Zasso's hand became completely stiff, and then his skin began to glow a bright blue. The pain was instantaneous and brutal. It felt as if he just stuck his hand inside an ice-fishing hole. It was freezing cold. The type of cold that gives you instant frostbite.

Zasso wanted to scream in agony, but he didn't want to show weakness in front of Thy Master, so he gritted his teeth to the point of shattering his molars and channeled the pain through the blood in his veins. His eyes were on the verge of bursting out of their sockets when he looked down at his sword and witnessed the transparent yellow glow bordering the blade being overtaken by a fierce transparent blue. At that moment, Zasso realized that the sword wasn't his anymore. Thy Master had taken possession of his personalized Blessed weapon.

But it didn't end there. Thy Master gripped Zasso's hand even tighter, and the bright blue glow in his hand surged up his arm and unto the other extremities of his body. The pain was so excruciating that he couldn't help letting his vocals express it, but in a matter of seconds, his throat and mouth were succumbed by the powers infused into his body, and his agonizing scream was cut off just before he let it out.

He was frozen stiff, unable to move a muscle. His facial expression and position was stuck in limbo like a mannequin posing in the front of a clothing store window. The pain seared through his body like an electrical charge through a wire. But there was nothing he could do about it. He was now Thy Master's possession, paralyzed to defend himself.

"What did you just do to him?" Razo had the brass to ask Thy Master as he took a couple steps toward him.

Without looking in Razo's direction, Thy Master waved a hand at him, spewing a bright blue force of energy over his entire body. In an instant, Razo became an ice sculpture, stuck in a walking pose with icicles hanging from his face and arms.

Thy Master began to walk back and forth in front of a frozen Zasso with his arms clasped behind his cape while he said, "In two days, the President will give a nationally televised speech to the entire world of Exodus. The speech is supposed to be one of the most publicized events in the history of our great nation, which means that all of the important figures in Exodus will be attending. Including our friend Don Maretto Rose." He stopped directly in front of Zasso, stared into his wide, frosted eyes and continued, "*He* is our target. His capture means everything for our future and the future of this world. Without the Rose patriarch in our clutches, our mission is going to be a failure. Vital information in his brain holds the key to our success, so it is imperative that you and your frozen friend over there accomplish your assignment. Failure is not an option this time. The Grand Theater massacre was a sloppy mistake on every level. And even though one of the young Rose brothers was eliminated, he was not our true target.

"Don Maretto Rose is the one we need. He is the one member of the Rose Family who can tell us the exact location of the Rose Quartet. And he will indeed tell us, because he would rather sacrifice the Family Relic, instead of sacrificing his children. And that is the ultimatum that will be given to him once he is captured.

"Soon enough, the Rose Quartet will be in our clutches. The most prized Relic of all the Seven Blessed Families. Do you know why the Rose Quartet is so powerful, young Zasso?" He asked the question knowing that he wouldn't get a response. "Of course, you don't know, because the Rose Family have very tight lips. They would never reveal the deepest secret of their precious Relic." His digital mouth made a computed smile. "But I know the great power hidden inside the Rose Quartet. Yes, I know the secret ability their Relic possesses. An ability that trumps each and every other Relic.

"And how did I come across this monumental secret of the Rose Quartet, you may wonder? Well, you could make an educated guess that an important member of the Rose Family happens to be on our side. But I think I'll keep that person's identity a secret of my own." Thy Master chuckled to himself, obviously proud of his devious ways.

"So, my young friend, I sure hope that you and your shotgun wielding confidant have a good plan after the President's speech, because when he delivers his new plans for the future of Exodus, there will be a bit of chaos that ensues on the streets, which will be the perfect opportunity to get to Maretto Rose. His mind will be focused on what his Family must do after the details of the speech, so you will most likely be able to catch him off guard."

Thy Master stepped even closer to Zasso's frozen body, placed a firm hand on his shoulder, and asked, "Do you understand me, young Zasso?"

Of course, there was no response, but Thy Master persisted. He put a tighter grip on Zasso's shoulder, which sent a wave of heat throughout his body. Zasso's body went limp, and he collapsed to the hard cement ground, cracking his head. Blood trickled down the side of his temple as he coughed and hacked, desperately trying to fill his lungs with healthy air.

"I asked you a question, Zasso Cicello. If you want to rule over this city when I rule over every soul residing in Exodus, then I suggest you do not fail the bidding I have bestowed upon you." Thy Master used the tip of his metal boot to lift Zasso's head off the ground. "I'll ask you again, my child. Do you understand me?"

Panting for breathes and groaning from the pain, Zasso used all the strength he had left to answer, "Yes, Thy Master."

With a shove of his boot, Thy Master discarded Zasso's head to the side.

"Very good." With a flick of his wrist, a wave of heat engulfed Razo's body and he collapsed to the ground coughing and panting as hard as Zasso had.

"It's been a pleasure meeting you, gentlemen. I will pray that the next time we meet, we will be celebrating a monumental victory." Thy Master's long black cape flapped in the breeze as he turned around and headed back to the high-tech flying vessel.

Solace Volhine stayed behind for a moment and looked down upon the suffering men Thy Master just had his way with. He smiled, a foul and devious grin when he said, "You better not let him down, boys. The pain you are experiencing now will be nothing compared to what he will have in store for you if you fail him once again." His smile disappeared and was replaced by a serious scowl, which enhanced the crisscrossed scars on his face. "But I really do want to be friends someday, so I'll be giving you the benefit of my company during the President's speech. Maybe with a little help from me, you won't be so prone to screwing things up." Solace tipped his fedora and said, "Good day, gentlemen."

Zasso and Razo lied on the ground, helpless to move a muscle for the time being. They continued to try and catch their breath as they watched Thy Master, Solace, and soldiers board the flying vessel and take off into the dimming sky.

The Blessing of Ricalstro Rose

Part III

Ric stood by his lonesome in the center of the grand hall staring up at the Blood Fountain, watching in awe as crimson liquid spewed out of the statue of the founder of the Rose Family. His eyes were open wide, but they felt tired. His mind was tired as well. It had been a long week of recovery, which meant that the nights were restless. It was getting harder and harder for him to sleep. Drugs and alcohol had always been the aid that put him down for the night, but ever since his Uncle Vetti saved him from a slow and torturous death and brought him to Heritage Castle, he has respected his uncle's rule of no hard drugs and limited amount of booze. It was the least he could do for his uncle. The man went out of his way to rescue him from an impending doom and begin the process of being Blessed by the Family Relic.

And his time had almost arrived. For a blood member of the Rose Family to become fully Blessed with powers, he or she has to receive the Blessing by the Rose Quartet first. But not everyone is righteous enough to receive this Blessing. The Rose Quartet decides whether you are worthy of it.

That had been the question Ric was asking himself over and over since he had arrived at Heritage Castle. *Am I truly worthy of a Blessing from the world's most powerful Relic? I've done nothing but live in the gutter for the last four years, injecting garbage into my veins, filling my body with poisons, and banging skanky broads to make up for the love I lost that one fateful night...Fuck that life I lived. I can become a new man. A man of values and strengths. Something this Family doesn't always have.*

Ric heard a wooden door open and then close down one of the adjacent corridors to the grand hall. The distant echo of heavy footsteps raptured off the walls. It was as if his uncle could hear the private thoughts in his head.

Vetti appeared out of a corridor like a ghost out of the darkness. The chandelier lights hanging from the ceiling reflected off of his shiny bald head as he made his way toward Ric. He straightened the dark glasses covering his laser eyes and brushed a speck of dust off the sleeve of his red button-downed shirt.

"It never gets old, does it?" Vetti asked his nephew, referring to the Blood Fountain.

His eyes still captured by the constant flow of the bloodlike liquid, Ric replied, "How does it work?"

Now standing next to Ric and gazing up at the fountain as well, Vetti answered, "How does anything that defies the physical and visual laws of nature work? There are powers involved. Mysterious forces not understood by an ordinary human being. Only those who are Blessed by a Relic's power can comprehend what has been erected in front of you. It is said that if you stare at the Blood Fountain long enough when you are searching for answers in your life, Don Ulozio will speak to you and give you the answers you are looking for."

Ric blinked his eyelids a few times and looked away from the statue. "You speak of the Relic and of this statue as if they represent moral values. But you and I both know that what our Family does is not moral at all. I understand the greatness of our Family, Uncle Vetti, but I've seen the corruption that we and the rest of the Seven Blessed Families have caused in this world. We project ourselves as glamorous. But bloodshed and murder isn't glamorous. It's wrong, Uncle Vetti. And I shouldn't be one to talk, because I've committed more than my share of sins in my life, but I guess that's why I want to be a part of our Family so much now. Because deep down inside, I lack morals as well." Ric lowered his head. "In fact, I know I do. I royally fucked up everything in my life."

Vetti looked upon his nephew and just smiled. A rare kind of smile. One that Vetti's mouth doesn't display too often. It was personable.

Ric took notice of the smile and asked, "What? You're just gonna smile at me? My words don't anger or trouble you?"

"Not at all," Vetti replied. "I think it's good that you question the morality of our Family and the Family Relic."

"Really?" Ric responded in a confused tone of voice.

309

"Of course." Vetti took a couple steps forward and looked up at the statue. "When Don Ulozio founded this Family, do you think he intended for it to be involved in organized crime forever?"

"I don't know. Was the Family deeply involved in organized crime back then like it is now?"

"What has your research taught you?"

"That Ulozio Manazotti conquered the last remaining king of Exodus and basically took over the world. Except he didn't crown himself as a king. Instead, he changed the Family name to Rose and selected three candidates for a President in which the people of Exodus would vote for."

"And why did he do that most honorable gesture?"

Ric rolled his eyes and smiled about the phrase *honorable gesture*. "He wanted an authoritative figure to hide his Family behind, so they could get away with all the dirty business they were involved in. The Rose Family *was* corrupt, even back then. The President was just a front for the Rose Family. He would govern the world of Exodus, while Don Ulozio would rule over it with riches and power. It was a simple yet effective method of doing his business."

"Yes, his method did work in our Family's favor. But that's the way in which you build an empire. When you become the most powerful Family in the world, bloodshed is inevitable. But that doesn't mean Don Ulozio wanted the Rose Family to be forever linked to organized crime." Vetti turned toward Ric, clasped his hands behind his back, and continued, "Near the end of his astonishing life, Don Ulozio wrote a personal memoir on five pieces of parchment paper in which he explains his theory that the Rose Family name would be related to peace instead of violence. Four of those pieces are locked and sealed in a glass case in a secret chamber in this very castle. But the fifth page has been missing for hundreds of years. Rumor has it, the fifth and last page reveals a prophesy of some sort. A prophesy which foretells the bringer of this so-called peace in our Family. And there are also rumors that the missing page is hidden somewhere in the National Archive Building."

Ric nodded his head and said, "And I suppose you want me to take a trip downtown and find this missing page."

"You have four hours to accomplish something nobody else in the history of our Family has," Vetti explained, his chin up and his eyes looking below his dark glasses. "Find the missing page, and I can almost guarantee you that the Rose Quartet will give you its Blessing. But if you fail, like everyone else has, you will still go in front of the Relic tonight, and your fate will be decided just as we had planned. This research assignment is a special one. One that does not need to be finished." Vetti grinned, then finished, "But it sure would be something if it was a success."

Vetti patted Ric on the shoulder as he brushed past him and said, "I'll see you when you get back, Ric. Tonight, is the night."

Four hours to complete an assignment that has never been accomplished. It made Ric wonder if he should even try. *What's the point if I'm just gonna fail anyway?* Ric asked himself. *I might as well take the time to relax and think about what might happen tonight. Am I going to be Blessed by the Rose Quartet, or will it reject me? I'll feel some kind of way if I'm rejected, but if that's how it's supposed to be then I just have to accept it and move on...Damn that's gonna be a long time to think about it. I sure hope I bump into that girl one more time. She fascinates me for some reason.*

The girl. Dada Flace. Since the first day Ric met her, he had thought about her day and night. Even more than his future encounter with the Rose Quartet. Throughout the week he had gone down to the National Archive Building, and she had been there, cozied up inside a text at the same spot. It was as if she was expecting him to show up. Waiting for him every day so they could talk for a while. And she was so damn interesting to Ric. Her theories about Relics beyond the lands of Exodus, her secret club that she and her brother organized together, and her views on life and the everlasting pursuit of happiness. But what got Ric's attention the most, was the way she acted around him. She put out a vibe. A good vibe that clearly showed that she liked him. Whether as just a friend, or something more, Dada Flace had a strong liking for Ric. And that just simply made him happy.

So, when Ric stepped foot inside the library of the Archive Building and saw her sitting in her usual spot, his heart started beating a little faster, and good vibrations flowed through his insides. She was waiting for him once again, which made Ric do something he hadn't done in a while. He smiled. But not just any ordinary smile. This one was genuine. He was genuinely happy to see her...*My God does this feel good,* he said to himself as he rubbed his chest like he was trying to massage the tender feeling out of his heart. *I think I could really fall for this girl.*

But through all the mushy, gooey feelings he was having at the moment, an idea came to his mind. *This girl knows a lot about everything in this building. Maybe she can help me actually find the lost page of Don Ulozio's memoir.* Most likely she wouldn't have a clue, just like everyone else for the past hundreds of years, but hell, it was worth a shot.

"Hey there," Ric greeted Dada as he approached her from the side.

When she looked up from her text, her mouth grew an instant smile. "Hey, you. I was just wondering if I was going to see you today...Or ever again."

The comment caused him to squint his eyes and wonder. "What's that supposed to mean?" he asked, smiling right back at her.

"Well, I don't know," she replied in a shy manner. "You're getting trained to be Blessed by your Family Relic. You never know when your research assignments will come to an end, and you won't have to come visit the Archive Building anymore. And when that happens, I'm gonna miss talking to you every day. I guess I look forward to it when I wake up in the morning." Her smile made Ric's heart skip a beat or two.

"Well, if that isn't the nicest thing anyone's said to me in a while, then I would be a cold-blooded liar."

Dada giggled, then flung her hair back with a quick swipe of her hand. "So, what kind of assignment do you have on your agenda today?"

"Actually," he replied while taking a seat across from her, "I was gonna ask you if you could help me with something. It's my last research assignment before I go in front of the Family Relic tonight, and according to my uncle, it's an impossible one to accomplish. No one in the history of my Family has ever completed it."

"Okay," she said with a smile. "Sounds like fun. What is it?"

In almost a whisper, Ric began to explain, "The founder of my Family, Don Ulozio Manazotti, wrote a five-page memoir just before the time of his death. From what my uncle told me, it's something like a prophesy, explaining how there would eventually be some kind of peacemaker in the Family. A leader who would bring peace to the Family name, rather than use organized crime as a way of doing business. But the last page of the memoir went missing hundreds of years ago, and nobody has seen it since.

"My uncle told me that there have been rumors floating around for years that the fifth page is hidden in this very building, but I can't imagine it's just lying around the library on a shelf or inside some old text. It's gotta be hidden in some more obscure location, or it would've been found by now."

Dada was quiet for a moment as she thought. Then, her sparkling eyes got real big and she said, "There's an old underground chamber that's restricted to visitors. It contains some of the rarest books and documents ever written. Most of them are hand-written with a quill and inkpot on sections of parchment paper."

"That's exactly what Don Ulozio's memoir was written on. But I can't imagine that the chamber has never been searched before. After hundreds of years, I'm sure this building has been combed from top to bottom."

Shrugging her shoulders, Dada said, "Well, maybe everyone else weren't looking in the right spots. Maybe they missed something right under their noses."

"Well, it wouldn't hurt to try. Show me this underground chamber."

Ric followed Dada's lead as she took a brisk walk to the back corner of the library where there was a fireplace surrounded by a long wooden table and a set of leather chairs. About ten lengths down the wall was a random wooden door with a rusty iron knob. 'RESTRICTED AREA' was painted in black across the middle of the door. Dada stepped in front of the door and looked both ways to see if anyone was watching. The library was rather bare for the time being, so Dada twisted the knob and opened the door. The old wood creaked something awful, but it wasn't loud enough to signal any security guards for unlawful entry. She stepped through the doorway, and was immediately greeted by a massive cobweb in the face. She let out a shriek of terror, but Ric closed the door before it was heard throughout the entire building.

Dada continued to shriek as her high-pitched squeals bounced off the walls like a superball. Ric held a finger to his mouth while making shushing sounds as he helped her rip away the sticky web.

"It's just a cobweb. You're fine," he told her in a low-pitched tone. "I don't even see the spider on you. It must be away from its home."

With a look of disgust, she said, "Don't even say the word *spider*. I hate spiders. They are so gross."

He brushed the last remnants of the web off her cheek and said, "My goodness, for someone who wants to travel outside the lands of Exodus, it's a little surprising that you're afraid of a little spider."

"Whatever made this web can't be little," she said, wiping her chest free of any web stragglers. "And I didn't say I was afraid of them. They just creep me out a little with their long, furry legs and jumbo eyes."

"I see," he said, then searched the area with his eyes. But it didn't do him any good. It was complete darkness. "We'll talk about your arachnophobia another time. Right now, we need some light."

Without a verbal response, Dada reached into her pants pocket and pulled out a cellular phone. She slid her finger a couple times then pressed the screen once and a bright white light beamed out of the phone. It was good for up to twenty lengths ahead of them.

She held out the phone turned flashlight in front of her and said, "There's torches and candles to light in the chamber, but this will have to do for now, until we get there."

Side by side, they made their way down a narrow hallway until they reached a wooden staircase that led to the depths of the building. Together, they took careful steps down the stairwell. Dada hooked her arm underneath Ric's for extra leverage, or maybe because she wanted to be as close as possible to him and feel his touch. At least, that's what Ric was hoping.

When they reached the bottom of the stairwell, Dada shined the flashlight phone ahead of them, and spotted an old rusty door with an old-style sliding latch. The door was surrounded by a cement wall, which had tiny cracks that oozed brown water droplets.

"This is the entrance to the chamber. Hold my phone," Dada instructed him. She handed him the phone and he shone it at the latch on the door. With a mild grunt, Dada slid the latch over, creating a loud clank that echoed up the stairs. She yanked on the door handle, and with a creak and a groan, the door opened.

Ric took the initiative to walk through the doorway first, so Dada wouldn't get a face-full of cobweb again, but the room he walked into wasn't as dusty and web-ridden as the hall and stairwell. It was also not as dark. Dada turned the flashlight on her phone off, and followed behind Ric as they entered the chamber. The hardwood floor was smooth and glossy and there were braziers, candles, and a pair of lit torches lining the walls. Someone had been down here.

"I thought this place was restricted," Ric said. "To me it looks like its wide open for business."

"It's restricted to visitors of the Archive Building. But there are many professionals like historians and professors who are allowed access to this chamber." She took a look around the room. "They have certain workers who have to keep this place up to par every day, just in case the chamber is to be used."

"Then why the hell don't they keep up with the hallway and stairwell?"

"To keep the visitors away, I guess."

Ric shrugged his shoulders and said, "Makes sense."

The chamber was long and linear, but the ceiling was low and claustrophobic. Old wooden cabinets with protective glass doors, stood along the cement walls, and were stocked with ancient texts and documents, which were laminated for their own protection from greasy hands. There were a dozen small desks strewn throughout the room with their own lamps and magnifying glasses resting on the wood surface. Ric guessed to himself that the magnifying glasses were for maximum advanced research of every single detail of the hand-written text being analyzed.

"I have to be honest with you about this room. I'm not all that impressed," Ric confessed.

"What did you expect?"

"I don't know," he replied with a shrug. "Some lavish room with golden bookshelves and diamond floors. Naked virgins with big breasts serving you drinks. I'm sorry but I expected more from a place that holds the rarest books in Exodus."

Dada rolled her eyes and said, "You've been to too many strip clubs."

"I don't know what strip club you've been going to, but I've never been to one that has virgins," Ric said back with a smirk.

Dada giggled, then took a stroll about the room. As she passed by the wooden cabinets, she peaked inside each one. "Most of the documents kept down here are from the Golden Age of Exodus, when print technology was non-existent and books were written and copied by hand. By the time the Seven Blessed Families took over Exodus, technology was more advanced, and books were mass produced by a printing press."

"So, what you're saying is that the page I'm looking for probably isn't down here," Ric said as he began to walk through the chamber.

"No, not exactly. Your Family was founded during the end of the Golden Age, which means that Don Ulozio's memoir would not have been mass produced, unless it fell into the hands of a historian or publisher many years later. But if your uncle says it hasn't been seen or read in hundreds of years, then there's the strong possibility that it isn't even hidden in this building. Every document in the Archive Building is accounted for."

"Then I'm just chasing after a ghost," Ric surmised as he headed toward the end of the chamber.

"Sorry to say, but most likely," Dada finalized.

"Well, that sucks." Ric felt disappointed that he wouldn't accomplish the impossible. He wanted to make an everlasting impression on the Rose Family if he were to be Blessed, and finding the fifth page of Don Ulozio's prophetic memoir would've been one hell of a start. Instead, he would be just like all the others before him.

As Ric approached the back wall of the chamber, he caught sight of an interesting object that stood out like a tree in a desert. It didn't quite belong. *What the hell is this thing doing here?* Ric asked himself as the object drew him closer. It was a tall mirror, imbedded into the wall. But it wasn't the normal kind of mirror you would see this day and age. It was an ancient mirror. The kind that was a bit blurry and made you look wide and droopy.

Ric focused his eyes on his own distorted reflection as he stepped closer and closer toward the mirror. The reflection didn't look like him. As a matter of fact, it wasn't him at all. For a split second, he thought he saw an image of Don Ulozio himself, so he squinted his eyes and gazed even harder into the reflection.

"What the…" Ric started to say, before he tripped over a metal handle sticking out of the floor. He lost his balance and stumbled forward, crashing head first into the mirror. He put his arms up in front of his face just before he broke through the glass. Ric was expecting to be met by a cement wall behind the mirror, but instead, he just kept on falling through the wall and went into a somersault as he landed on the other side. The ancient mirror had been destroyed, shattering into hundreds of glass shards. But it was for a good reason, because Ric had just stumbled into a secret room.

Dada came rushing down the chamber to see what had happened to Ric. "Ric!" she yelled as she peered through the broken mirror. "Are you okay?"

Ric rolled over and sat up. "I'm fine, I think," he answered, brushing some of the shards of glass off his shirt. He took a look around, but it was too dark to see anything. "Go grab one of those torches. I think I found something that I shouldn't have."

Dada hurried as fast as she could to the nearest torch, yanked it off the wall, and ran back to the back of the chamber. She took a timid step through the shattered mirror and held the torch out in front of her, so they could both see what lied inside the secret room.

There wasn't much to the room. It was condensed and not very wide. There were layers of dust on the hardwood floor and large cobwebs hanging from the corners of the ceiling. The secret room was pretty much empty, except for one significant object placed in the far corner. A small wooden desk with a drawer slightly cracked open.

Small clouds of dust puffed out of Ric's clothes as he brushed himself off and slowly rose to his feet. "Follow me," he told Dada, then started walking toward the lonesome desk.

They casted eerie shadows of themselves on the wall as the orange glow of the torch flittered above the desk. For a quick moment, Ric and Dada glanced at one another like two school kids about to get themselves into trouble, before Ric extended his hand and grabbed ahold of the slightly opened drawer. There was a low scraping sound when Ric pulled the drawer open, and a flurry of dust wafted into the dry air. And when Ric saw what was lying inside the drawer, a rush of excitement tingled through his body.

It can't be, he told himself.

But it was. A brown, crusty piece of parchment had been revealed right in front of Ric and Dada's eyes. The parchment was old and worn, and looked so brittle that just a light touch of the paper could dissipate it into thin air. But there was a clear hand-written paragraph on it in black ink. The writing was in a fancy cursive style, not used very much in modern times. And so was the language it was written in as well.

Dada reached into her pocket and pulled out her phone. After a couple of taps on the surface, the bright flashlight beamed out of the end. She shined the light directly onto the parchment and leaned in for a closer look.

"It's written in the Old Language of the Seven Blessed Families. Do you think this could be the page you're looking for?" she asked Ric.

318

Ric knew it was the lost page the moment he saw it lying in the drawer, but for direct proof, all he had to do was read the signature at the bottom of the paragraph. "Look," he said, pointing to the flamboyant signature.

Per Sempre Benedetto,

Don Ulozio Manazotti Rose

Dada's eyes widened as she gazed at the signature. "My goodness, Ric. You found it. You actually found it. What made you crash through the mirror?"

Ric shrugged, then replied, "Nothing really made me. I just tripped over a piece of metal that just so happened to be sticking out of the ground. It's almost as if it was there for a reason."

"It was," she said in a ghostly tone. She squinted her eyes and analyzed the signature even harder. "I wonder what *Per Sempre Benedetto* means?"

"It means *Forever Blessed*," Ric answered her right away.

She looked at Ric, her eyes curious and confused. "How do you know that?"

His mouth formed a sly grin. "You might be a little surprised by this, but I know how to read and speak the Old Language. My father made me and my brothers learn it when we were all kids. He told us it was out of respect for our ancestors, and that there would be a day when we needed to know it." Ric paused in thought for a moment. "Huh. Who would've fuckin figured?"

Dada looked impressed, and she gave Ric a big smile to show it. "So, I guess there's only one thing left to do. Read it to me."

Ric bent down closer to the parchment as Dada shined the flashlight over the entire paragraph, enhancing the fancy lettering. The parchment had cracks and creases, but it was still completely legible, so Ric translated it for Dada. Word for word.

So, as I near the end of my grand and fortuned life, I will endow upon thee the great destiny of the Rose Family, the Rose Quartet has foretold me in my most recent Blessing. In many far years to come, the future of the Seven Blessed Families will be in danger of

319

being eradicated from their positions of power. During this time, there will be a great leader of the Rose Family, who will be called 'Father' by the people who love him. This leader will have four heirs beneath him, all with their own special traits and powers. The night of one's demise by the hands of an ambitious young foe, will begin the downward spiral of the relationships between the Seven Families, and commence a new darkness that the world of Exodus has never seen the likes of before. The only light to contrast this darkness will be the youngest of the 'Father's' heirs, who will lead the Rose Family into a time when peace has overcome the Family's violent past.

After reading the page out loud, Ric read it one more time to himself. He couldn't believe what the passage had said. He must've made some errors in the translation, because nearly every word Don Ulozio wrote was completely accurate. It couldn't have been written hundreds of years ago. Ric didn't believe in fortunetelling or prophesies. The fact that a Relic could give a person powers beyond the realm of nature was far-fetched enough. Predicting the future was just outright ridiculous.

"Ric," Dada whispered. "If what you just translated is correct, then this prophesy was written about you." By the look in her eyes, Ric could tell that she was beyond mystified. She seemed pretty spooked.

"It can't be. This can't be right," Ric whispered back. There was no reason for them to whisper, but it felt like the right way to talk at the moment. "I'm nobody, Dada. There's no possible way that a prophesy written hundreds of years ago is about me. I'm just a junky."

"You're a what?" Now she looked confused.

"I'm a junky, Dada." It was a good time for Ric to be honest with this woman. He didn't want to hide anything from her. She was special to him. "Before my uncle started getting me ready for my Blessing, I was shooting up smack, snorting powder, and drinking heavily. I'm a loser. I have no right being Blessed by my Family Relic, let alone being mentioned in a prophesy. I'll never be able to bring peace to anyone or anything, and I'll never be the leader of my Family. It's just not in my blood." In an anxious action, he ran

320

his fingers through his wavy hair. "Besides, in order for me to become the head of the Rose Family, my father and my other two brothers would all have to die. And that's not gonna happen. They're all much stronger than me."

Dada lowered the torch, along with her head. She took a deep breath and a moment to think to herself before she said, "I don't know, Ric. I feel like you're wrong about yourself. You've been impressing me since the first day I met you. So much so, that I find it hard to believe that you're just some loser junky who doesn't deserve to be Blessed. You're something much more, Ric. I can see it in you. No matter what kind of bad things you did before we met."

Ric placed his hands on his hips and shook his head. "You just don't get it, Dada. You don't know me like you think you do. You don't know the things I've done in my life. I'm not the man you think I am."

Dada took an innocent step toward Ric, and then another one. Her body was getting closer to his. It made his heart beat faster. And as she crept up to him, she placed a gentle hand upon his chest. "I might not know everything about you, Ric. But I do know one thing." She gazed into his eyes. A deep, passionate gaze. "You're a great guy, Ric. And even though you probably have done some wrong in your life, you're still a good person at heart." She placed her other hand upon his chest, then slowly moved her hands up to his shoulders. "You have to be strong, Ric. You have to be strong not only for your Family, but for yourself. And I believe that you will be. Call me crazy, but I believe in what the founder of your Family wrote on that piece of parchment...But you must be strong. Stronger than you've ever been before."

As their eyes were connected and her hands were gently rubbing his shoulders, Ric had his best opportunity to go in for a kiss. But when he started thinking about what Don Ulozio's memoir said, the urge to make a move on the beautiful woman was overcome by fear and anxiety. *I can't suck this girl into my heinous life just yet. I still have a lot to overcome before I let her in. But maybe, just maybe, it could happen sometime soon.*

"I'll try to be strong, Dada," he said, then placed his hands over hers. "I'll try my best."

The train ride back to Heritage Castle felt longer than it actually was. There were so many thoughts running through Ric's head that he thought he was going to have a brain aneurism. Should he tell Uncle Vetti about the prophesy? He wasn't sure if he should. He had already decided to let Dada hold onto the fragile piece of parchment. She promised him that she would keep it safe, because now that the antique mirror was broken and the secret room had been revealed, he didn't want some random historian or professor finding the page and displaying it to the public. It was his Family's heirloom. Not the outside world. But he also didn't think it was the right time to hand it over to his uncle. It was too cryptic for anyone else to see at the time being.

As he stepped off the train, Ric took a deep, exasperated breath, before making the last walk up to the castle before he would finally be face to face with the Family Relic. Discovering the lost page of Don Ulozio's memoir was a sure sign that he was destined to be Blessed, but there was still a nagging thought in the back of his mind that he would be rejected. But all his thoughts dispersed when he saw his uncle standing at the front gate.

Uncle Vetti was standing alone. He was stone-faced with his hands clasped in front of him. His attire consisted of a black tuxedo with dark red pinstripes, a dress shirt that was the color of blood, and a tie as black as a starless sky. The bulb of a fully bloomed Rose was pinned to the left flap of his tuxedo coat. He was the archetype of a high-class gangster. A man who defined the upper-echelon of the Rose Family.

"Did you succeed in your assignment, my young nephew?" Vetti asked Ric as he approached him.

The time was now to reveal the truth. There was no turning back if he told his uncle what the lost page had said. It would change the course of the Family's direction into the future forever.

Ric lowered his head and gazed upon his uncle's shoes. They looked like they were made of black glass. "No," he answered.

Vetti nodded his head, then placed a hand on Ric's shoulder. "There is no shame in failing the assignment. The lost page will be found when it is meant to be found, so keep your head up."

Ric lifted his head and looked at his uncle's somber face. He wondered if his uncle knew he was lying, but he couldn't read his eyes behind the dark glasses.

"The moment has arrived, Ricalstro Rose. Are you ready to step in front of the Rose Quartet and perhaps receive its Blessing?"

"Yes," Ric answered without a second thought. He was tired of the waiting. The suspense had been eating him inside all week.

"Good. But before you encounter the Relic, you must take an oath and swear your loyalty to the Rose Family." Vetti turned and faced the front gate. Using his magical powers, the gate opened. "Follow me inside," he instructed.

The grand hall was darker than usual. The lighting had been reduced to a tunnel of golden candles stands with red wax candles alit by small dancing flames. A long red carpet had been placed down the middle of the tunnel of candles, leading to the Blood Fountain. And to Ric's surprise, standing in front of the fountain, in the exact same attire as his uncle, was Ric's father.

Vetti stopped in front of the red carpet and made a gesture with his hand for Ric to proceed through the tunnel of candles. He complied, and took trepid steps down the red carpet, until he stood directly in front of his father. Don Maretto Rose gave his son a stoic look, then placed a hand upon his right shoulder.

"Kneel on one knee, my son," Maretto ordered.

Ric followed orders and dropped his left knee to the ground, resting his right forearm on top of his right knee. The hall was completely silent, except for the placid sound of water flowing out of the statue and dripping into the base of the Blood Fountain.

Maretto took a loud step forward, and stood over his son. He clasped his hands behind his back and said, "Before we give you the honor of stepping in front of the Rose Quartet, you must swear your allegiance to the Rose Family. Your undying loyalty to our Family is essential if your eyes are to gaze upon the Family Relic. Will you take this oath, my son?"

Ric nodded and answered, "I will."

"Very good." Maretto extended his right arm and put a firm grip on his son's shoulder. "Until the end of time, until the lust for revenge no longer imposes, the Family will forever stay strong and yearn for the smell of blood and roses."

Ric recognized the saying from the Blood Fountain.

"This is the motto of our Family. A Family founded by the great Don Ulozio Manazotti. He was given his Blessing at a time when a self-righteous king tried to scour the lands of Exodus with his tyranny and prejudice. But Don Ulozio used his powers to relinquish this tyrannical king and brought prosperity to his Family and the rest of the Seven Blessed Families. To show his respect and admiration for the Rose Quartet, he changed the Family name to 'Rose', and began a legacy that would forever be forged into the history of Exodus.

"The Family legacy has been passed down from generation to generation, and each member of the Rose Family has lived a lifestyle we hold sacred and sanctimonious. And when it comes to the Family business, we have all taken a vow of silence. To break this vow of silence, is to break the souls of our ancestors who came before us. Do you understand, my son?"

"Yes," Ric replied. *Yes, I understand that I'll be killed if I break this vow of silence,* was his real response in his head.

Maretto gave a slow nod with his eyes closed, then continued, "Will you, Ricalstro Maretto Rose, give your undying loyalty to the Family that has given you birth?"

"I will."

"Will you forever keep the sanctity of the Rose Family name?"

"I will."

"Will you forever hold the secrets of the Rose Family name, or pay the ultimate price for your betrayal?"

"Of course I will," he answered in absolute truth. *I would never betray my Family. Not for anyone or anything.*

324

"Would you, Ricalstro Maretto Rose, die for the Family that has given you birth?"

"I would."

"And would you kill for the Rose Family name?"

There was the slightest hesitation from Ric to answer such a bold and morbid question. But when it comes to his Family, Ric would do whatever he had to do, so he answered, "I would."

Maretto let out of breath of relief, then opened his eyes and removed his hand from Ric's shoulder. "You may rise, my son."

Ric rose to his feet and straightened out his shirt, before slicking back his hair. He stood straight with his chin in the air. He felt a sense of pride after taking his oath. He was now one step closer to becoming a Blessed member of the Rose Family. It was quite the honor.

"You are now ready to stand in front of the Family Relic, Ricalstro Rose. As I look at you right now, I truly believe in my heart that you will be Blessed by the Rose Quartet. And if you are chosen to be Blessed, then we will complete the ritual we have started today and you will continue your training with the new powers bestowed upon you." Maretto embraced his son, patted him on the back, then grabbed his face and kissed him on the cheek. "It is time." He peered over Ric's shoulder and gave Vetti a nod. Vetti nodded back, then proceeded to walk down the red carpet.

Together, Maretto and Vetti escorted Ric around the Blood Fountain, until they were directly behind the statue of Don Ulozio. Don Maretto stepped toward the marble foundation and pushed a slab of the stone forward. Underneath the piece of stone was a red button. Maretto pressed on the button with his index finger, then took a couple steps back. He stood next to his son, patted him on the back, and with a pompous grin said, "Watch this."

There was a loud click, followed by an ear-piercing clang of metal on metal. Abruptly, the flow of crimson water out of the orifices and hands of the statue stopped, and the large basin full of the red liquid drained and emptied in a matter of moments. The fake blood was replaced by beams of red energy, streaming out of the statue as if Don Ulozio was alive and casting magical spells at the ceiling. Then, there was a sudden tremor underneath Ric's foot, followed by an ongoing vibration that was strong enough to make the roots of your teeth hurt.

The sound of stone grinding on stone enveloped the grand hall as the statue turned a hundred and eighty degrees, so the front depiction of Don Ulozio was now facing Ric, his father, and his uncle. Not a moment later, the base of the statue rose from the bottom of the basin, revealing a metallic cylinder, large enough to hold about four or five grown adults. The front of the cylinder was embedded with a door and a circular glass window. There was a hydraulic hiss, and then the door slid open.

"Nice touch," Ric said about the spectacle that just unfolded in front of him.

"Thought you might like that," his father said back.

Ric followed his father over the wall of the basin. They stepped on the remnants of rose bulbs and petals as they made their way into the metallic cylinder. Vetti followed their lead, and once they were inside, there was another hydraulic hiss, and then the door slid shut. A second later, the cylinder dropped through the floor at a rapid rate of speed. Ric's balls ended up in his throat as the cylindrical elevator kept falling and falling. He braced himself against the wall, hoping that the ride would stop at any moment. But it didn't. It just fell deeper and deeper underground. How far they were going, Ric had no way to tell.

Maretto and Vetti both had shit-eating grins on their faces as they watched Ric cling to the wall. They've experienced the ride plenty of times before, so it was of no bother to them, and they were enjoying the sight of Ric freaking out.

Not a moment too soon, the cylinder came to an abrupt halt, then lowered about twenty lengths more at a much slower rate, until it came to a complete stop. And when the hydraulics hissed, and the door slid open, Ric ran out of the claustrophobic cylinder, dropped to his knees, and let loose a shitload of vomit. He coughed and gagged as he spat out the bile that had burned his esophagus on its way up from his stomach. His father and uncle chuckled as they came from behind.

326

"One hell of a ride, isn't it?" Maretto joked.

He coughed and spat some more. "My God, that was so bad. That was so fucking bad."

Maretto and Vetti laughed at Ric some more as they helped him to his feet.

"Why the hell did that thing have to drop so fast?" Ric asked, then looked around at his surroundings. "And where the hell are we?"

The area surrounding them was vast, and the atmosphere was dark like a nighttime sky without the stars. The surface was soft. Ric dug his feet into the ground and it felt as if he was standing on fresh grass. But it was hard to believe there was fresh grass so far underground. There was no sunlight to help the grass grow, so it had to be artificial turf.

Ric observed the areas to his left and right, and noticed that although this place was expansive, there were stone walls that barricaded it. He couldn't see too far ahead of him though, as the darkness overcame the ability of sight, but when his father and uncle walked on ahead, a new path forward would be unveiled.

As soon as Maretto and Vetti stepped off the grass and onto pavement, one after another, tiny rectangular light fixtures embedded into the ground became alit on opposing sides, and a linear walkway forged the way ahead. And at the end of the lighted path, stood a prodigious structure made of glass.

Ric made his way forward and stood behind his father and uncle. "It's a greenhouse," he assumed, although he wasn't quite sure.

Maretto turned to his son and said, "The strongest and most high-tech greenhouse ever built to inhabit the most beautiful flower in the entire world. The Rose Quartet."

Ric gazed harder at the massive greenhouse. It had to be at least thirty lengths high and just as wide. The perfect geometric cube of solid glass. He noticed there wasn't a door, but just a small opening at the end of the path that led inside.

Maretto placed a comforting hand on the back of Ric's shoulder and said, "We cannot take you any further, my son. You must venture into the greenhouse on your own.

327

Inside, the Rose Quartet will be awaiting your presence. Your uncle and I will wait here for your return. We will pray that you come back to us a Blessed man." He took his hand off of Ric and used it to nudge him forward. "Go on, my son."

Ric took a step forward, then looked back at his uncle for reassurance to go on. His Uncle Vetti gave him the nod of confidence. Ric trusted his uncle more than anyone in the Family, so there was no more hesitation to move forward.

Each step felt like it was in slow motion. Time was standing still around him as the modern greenhouse grew larger and more magnificent the closer he approached it. He thought about looking back one more time to see if his father and uncle were still standing there, but he didn't. He had to be a man and go forward without being afraid. He couldn't act like an immature child anymore. His destiny was to be a powerful Blessed member of the Rose Family. The Family he was born into. One of the four heirs to the throne his father sits on…And if the prophesy he read was true, he will be the one who leads the Family into the future…In peace.

But it couldn't possibly be true, Ric thought about the prophesy as he walked toward his destiny. *If I'm to lead the Family, then that means my father and brothers will have to either die or relinquish their right to their inheritance. But that will never happen. Even when my father takes his last breath as an old man, Jon-Jon will take over the Family. They can't die and they won't die. They are too smart and powerful…Well, maybe Alto's fiery temper could get the best of him, but Jon-Jon is just like my father.*

When the thoughts about the future cleared Ric's head, he was already standing at the entrance of the greenhouse. On the outside, the panels of glass were clear, but because of the surrounding darkness, the glass appeared to be tinted.

He peered through the entrance. He saw nothing. From the outside, the inside of the greenhouse looked to be just a large empty space. But Ric knew it wasn't empty. The Family Relic was waiting inside. The Rose Quartet was just a short walk away.

Ric took a deep breath of courage, then stepped through the entrance. As soon as both of his feet were inside the glass structure, a red force field enveloped the entrance. The borders around the entrance sparked and crackled, sealing Ric inside.

"Well, shit," he said to himself. "I guess there's no turning back now."

The moment Ric took his next step forward, the square panel of glass underneath his feet lit up around the edges. One after another, each panel of glass began to light up, until the entire floor was a spectacle of squares outlined in bright white lights. The effect spread all the way to the back of the greenhouse and up a wide glass staircase with columns on either side that stood tall up to the ceiling. And at the top of the staircase, resting still between the two columns, was the object Ric had been waiting twenty-two long years to see in person. The Rose Quartet.

Four fully-bloomed roses, about the size of human heads, were settled in the shape of a diamond, and were attached to one thick stem that was planted to the floor. The red hue of the rose petals was crisp and dynamic, creating an aura of crimson in the background. The stem was bright green with large thorns the size of railroad spikes. The Relic was tall. About the height of an above average adult male. And its fragrance was exhilarating, soothing the nostrils and tickling the esophagus.

Ric was still a good walking distance away, but he could feel the Relic's presence surging through his body. His insides felt warm. Like he just injected a healthy dose of the best smack he ever had. But he wasn't on any drugs whatsoever. He'd been totally clean for the last week. This was a natural high. One without the consequences of feeling like shit the next day or overdosing into a coma until death eventually puts its dark hands over his heart.

His steps toward the Relic were hesitant at first, but as he got closer, confidence and courage filled in the gaps of apprehension and fear. *This is it,* Ric told himself as he approached the Rose Quartet. *I couldn't even run away if I wanted to. I'm being drawn into its energy. I feel so damn good inside. Hell if this isn't the best drug I've ever had. And it's not a drug. It's a magnificent natural object.*

The moment Ric was only a few lengths away, the bulbs of the roses began to steadily open, revealing a woman's face in each rose. The faces were mesmerizing and beautiful. They had catlike eyes, button noses, and pursed lips, and their expressions were pleasant and serene. Their mouths suddenly opened, and all four of the roses let out a pleasing melody full of *Ahs* and *La La Las*.

The Rose Quartet was singing to him. Singing a song of welcome. A harmonic melody to give Ric a sense of comfort. Comfort he needed to stand firm in front of an object with great power.

Ric waited in angst as the serenade continued. It was the most pleasing song his ears had ever had the pleasure of hearing. He closed his eyes and let the melody sink in. It was so smooth and delightful, like a lullaby being sung from a mother to her child. It was so soothing that he almost fell asleep standing up. But after a few more moments of the harmonious music, the Rose Quartet suddenly stopped.

"We are gracious of your presence, young one," the rose at the top spoke.

"We have been patiently waiting for your arrival," the rose at the bottom then spoke.

"You are a lost soul. A child that needs an awakening," the rose on the left took its turn.

"And we are here to awaken your soul, and provide you with the powers you need to grow," the rose on the right concluded the welcome.

Ric was stunned. They were speaking to him. The Rose Quartet was communicating with him using his language. How could an object speak like a human?

"You can talk," Ric said to the Relic. He didn't know what else to say to them.

"Of course, we can talk," the top rose replied. *"We are living beings just like you, and we have adapted to your way of communicating. But let's not divulge in the manner in which we speak to you. Such information can be too complicated for your mind at this time. You are here for a reason. For us to bestow our great Blessing upon you."*

"But before we begin," the bottom rose took over, *"you have an ongoing dilemma in your mind. One that has to do with morality. You question the morals of your Family*

and of us. None that have received our Blessing thus far have questioned this before. Why are you so different from everyone else?"

For a moment Ric thought about the pressing question. Why *was* he so different from the rest of his Family? His answer was going to have to be nothing but the truth.

"I guess I just don't understand how a prestigious Relic could give such a wonderful gift to a Family who commits acts of violence. It's as if you condone the way of organized crime."

"We don't condone anything but the never-ending loyalty to the ones who rescued us and protect us," the left rose replied. *"We find it a great honor to Bless those who believe in our powers and strengthen the bond of family."*

"We would be nothing but an inanimate object if it wasn't for our discovery by your ancestors, so who are we to judge how are Blessings are used in this world?" the rose on the right stated. *"The blood of the Rose Family is strong, and our powers have been unmatched thus far. There is an undying bond between us and your Family, and unless interrupted, it shall continue until the end of time."*

The explanation was satisfactory enough for Ric. Who was he anyway to question the moral standards of the Rose Quartet? He was nothing but a loser who happened to be born a Rose.

"Something else troubles you, young one," the top rose pointed out. *"A matter that must be quickly discussed before you are to receive our Blessing."*

It was as if the Rose Quartet was reading his mind. And Ric knew exactly what the Relic was speaking of. "The fifth page of Don Ulozio Manazotti's memoir. He wrote about a prophesy that was given to him by you. It said that there is to be a patriarch who will lead the Family into a time of peace."

"Yes," the bottom rose agreed, *"we are aware of what we told the man who rescued us."*

"So, is the prophesy true?" he asked in an unsettling tone.

"The prophesy is what a prophesy is. A foretelling of future events that was seen in a clouded vision," the left rose answered. *"But the future can never be accurately predicted. Events have to unfold in a certain way in order for a prophesy to become true."*

"So, there's a chance the vision you saw might not even happen," Ric said to the Relic instead of stating it as a question.

"Future events must not concern you," the right rose responded. *"The present time is all that should matter."*

"Easy for you to say."

"The time for discussion is over," the four roses said in unison. *"Communicating with the human kind drains great amounts of energy. We shall now give you your Original Blessing, for you have earned our respect and are ready to receive our gift. Please stand still, tilt back your head, and extend your arms as if you are about to give us a warm embrace."*

Ric did as the Rose Quartet instructed. At first, he felt ridiculous standing that way, but then realized he must do what he has to in order to be in the good graces of the Relic.

The petals of the roses opened wider and the redness of their silky texture casted a brighter hue. The four roses separated a length apart from each other, dismantling their diamond shape. From the center of their separation grew four slippery green vines, which squiggled their way toward Ric. One vine wrapped itself around Ric's right arm, another wrapped around his left arm, while the other two did the same to his right and left legs. The pressure of their squeeze was intense, causing Ric to resist and pull away, but resisting them just added pain to the pressure, so he stopped resisting and gave into the Relic.

The feminine faces on the roses opened their mouths and let out a harmonizing hymn. The Rose Quartet glowed even brighter as traces of red beams emanated out of the petals. There was a low vibrato, then Ric felt himself being lifted off the ground. He hovered ever so lightly into the empty air, feeling a sense of euphoria as the Relic infused his body with its tantalizing energy. His body was raised and then titled back, resting in the air as if he was sleeping on a bed of empty space.

The voices of the four roses drew a higher tone, and then suddenly, rays of crimson energy beamed out of his eyes, mouth, and hands. He couldn't see real life anymore. He saw visions. Visions of open fields of tall grass strewn with wild flowers of all different types and colors. Visions of rolling hills met by a running bluish-white river that ended with a waterfall crashing down upon jagged rocks. There was a dark-green forest with trees that grew up into the heavens, and in the middle of the forest was a single cabin. Outside the cabin was a man. A man with an axe chopping planks of wood.

Then the visions suddenly disappeared and was replaced by a never-ending vortex of red. Ric let out a relieving gasp as the Rose Quartet infused more of its energy into his body. It was the greatest sensation that he ever felt. Almost too euphoric for his mind and body to handle. *My God does that feel good,* he thought to himself as the powers of the Relic flowed through his veins. *I want to feel this sensation for eternity.*

When it ended, Ric found himself lying on the glass floor, his arms and legs spread out like he had just been laid out for a sacrifice to the gods. He opened his eyes, blinking them repeatedly. Then he sat up and gazed upon the Rose Quartet. The petals had closed, hiding the faces of the four singing women. It was over. His Blessing was complete…He could feel the power they had given him. The gift of the Rose Quartet was now his.

His father and uncle were waiting for him at the end of the path outside the greenhouse. Their faces were stoic, waiting for the news of whether or not he had been given the gift of the Blessing. Ric approached them in a calm demeanor. He lifted his arms and opened his hands, retracting his fingers in and out from his palms.

"I can feel it," he said in almost a whisper. "I can feel it inside me."

Maretto's mouth formed a proud smile. "Now you know what it feels like to have the greatest gift in the world. And now that you have received your Blessing from the Rose Quartet, it is time to officially become a member of the Rose Family." His smile disappeared in an instant. A more morbid look formed on his face. "You took an oath for the Family. An oath that declared your loyalty. Now it is time to prove yourself by obeying one of the oaths you have taken."

Ric stared into his father's eyes. The eyes he always mistook for kindness. But deep down his eyes were dark and coldhearted. He then looked over at his uncle, who stared at him with those same cold and deadly eyes. "I will do as the Family wants," he said to his father.

"The son of one of our enemies took your brother from you, and another one of his sons tried to eliminate you as well. I have been told that you have located the whereabouts of the man who murdered your friends and tried to kill you." Maretto waited for an answer and was given one by a slight nod from Ric. "Then tomorrow, during the President's speech, you will track Miro Cicello down, and get your revenge."

The President's Speech

The day had arrived. The millions upon millions of people who reside in Exodus had been waiting for this memorable moment in history. The President of Exodus. The man who, along with the Legislation, governs the lands only as a facade to the Seven Blessed Families, was going to deliver a speech in front of the entire nation.

But it wasn't going to be just an ordinary speech addressed to the people of Exodus. The rumors have been swirling around like debris inside a whirlwind. Rumors that the great President of Exodus was going to finally come down hard on the Seven Blessed Families. That the government was fed up with the criminal activity and violence the Families have brought to the forefront of the nation. The time for change was now. The time for a new age of rule was inevitable.

A sky-coaster flew low above the crowded streets of Juna. It captured footage of the hordes of people filing into the streets just hours before the President was scheduled to deliver his speech. Thousands were already in attendance, flooding the streets like an over capacitated river. Some of the mobs of people were calm, patiently waiting for the moment to arrive. But most of the people were enigmatic and in a frenzy, hooting and hollering negative slurs against the Seven Blessed Families. Many people held signs that were anti Seven Blessed Families. There were also groups that were for the Families, but not many. It was a unanimous belief that Exodus's problems stemmed from organized crime.

The media was everywhere. Film crews were set up on every corner, recording their reporters who were giving detailed updates minute after minute. They were interviewing citizens on the streets of Juna. Innocent bystanders to the madness, who gave their opinions of what they thought of the President and the speech he was about to give.

A male reporter with slick black hair, dressed in a gray suit, held a microphone in front of the face of a middle-aged man with a white shirt with the phrase *No More Relics*, and asked him, "Can you please explain the meaning behind your shirt, sir?"

"Well," the man started to say, "I believe that Relics are an abomination to our society. They are possessed by the scum of this world, who use them for murder and corruption. We as a nation have to take a stand once and for all against the Seven Blessed Families, and I believe the Relics should be destroyed. They are unnatural and a curse to all of us hard-working people."

The next block over, a blonde reporter in a tight red dress stopped a man walking by her. Microphone in hand, she asked the man, "Sir, what is your opinion on the Seven Blessed Families? Are you for or against them?"

The man gave her a disdained look, then just shook his head and walked away as fast as he could. He was too afraid to answer a question of that caliber on a live video feed.

Closer toward the Capital Building, Alana Rae was surrounded by a film crew and a group of bystanders. She was wearing a royal blue dress, exposing an ample amount of cleavage and leaving nothing to the imagination with her curves. Holding a microphone, she began her report by saying, "Good afternoon everyone, this is Alana Rae reporting live from our nation's Capital. Today marks a memorable time in our history. The President, yes the President of Exodus will be addressing the nation in is what to be rumored as the most important speech of our time. The contents of the speech have been kept behind closed doors, but there have been leaks and disclosed sources who have confirmed that the subject will be about the Seven Blessed Families, and the reign of terror they have brought to our world. If this is true, then the President is making a bold and dangerous move, speaking out against the Families. No President before him has even thought about taking a stand against organized crime, but today's world is different from the past. The citizens of Exodus are tired of being ruled by an empire of criminals, and by the look of the crowd down here so far, the people will be making a statement that says that they aren't scared anymore. It's time for a change. Even if this change will put lives in danger..." She stopped her report, lowered her microphone, and stared beyond her film crew.

With his hand, the cameraman motioned for her to keep talking, but Alana was frozen. She could see someone walking around aimlessly in the crowd. Someone she recognized. It was Ric Rose. Jon-Jon's youngest brother, leisurely walking through the crowd by himself. *What the hell is Ric Rose doing walking through the crowd alone? Has he lost his mind or something?* Alan asked herself as she followed Ric with her eyes.

Ric Rose side-stepped his way through a group of loitering bystanders. The streets were crowded, which worked to his advantage in tracking down his target for the day. He was making his way toward the apartment complex down the block from the National Archive Building. Just the other day, Miro Cicello appeared out of the blue, exiting the apartment complex. It was his hideout for the time being. He was hiding from the Rose Family. The second Cicello son that went into hiding. But Miro's secret was out. Ric had found him. And the day had come for Ric's revenge.

The National Archive Building was just a few streets down from the Capital Building; the site of where all the action would be today. The gathered crowds of people would be distracted by the President's speech, making it easy for Ric to follow his target without anyone getting suspicious. And Miro would have no idea he was being followed, because Ric was going to blend in with the crowd, hunt him down, and then strike when he was alone and comfortable.

Two drunk guys bumped into Ric as they shoved their way through another group of bystanders. It was going to be chaotic in the center of Juna. But a good chaotic. It was the perfect scene for a murder. People's focus was going to be on the President. Not the violent display Ric was about to put on in a corner pub.

As Ric sifted his way through more rambunctious citizens, he looked down the street to his right and could see the Capital Building looming in the background. For a moment, he thought about his father. He was going to be front and center during the speech, protected only by Vego Rainze and a handful of bodyguards. None of his sons would be there by his side. His father didn't want any of his sons in today's public event. It was a dangerous atmosphere for the Rose Family to be out in the public's eye, and he couldn't afford to lose another son. He had a gut feeling that Zasso Cicello would be nearby, planning another attack.

Don Maretto Rose gazed out the window of his black stretch-limo, watching as hordes of people lined the streets, hoping to get as close as possible to the President's public address to the nation. The people of Juna had hungry looks in their eyes. Hungry for a day of drama. They seemed to have the urge to be a part of this so-called historic speech that was about to be given by the modern-day President. A man Don Maretto thought could be at least slightly trusted to give him fair warning about the subject matter in his address. But the President didn't contact him once. Not a phone call. Not a letter. Nothing. He was going about the speech without consent. *But I guess he has every right to do so. He's the President of Exodus,* Maretto tried to compromise in his head. *But my Family is the true leader of this nation. The President doesn't hold the power I do. I possess the Rose Quartet. Not him!*

The limo took a right turn and headed down a side street just a block over from Capital Way; the main street leading to the Capital Building. His driver was taking him the back way to the where the speech was being held in order to not draw too much attention to themselves. There was going to be madness out on the streets of Juna, and Don Maretto Rose wasn't going to be a welcomed party member to the scene.

Vego Rainze sat next to his boss, sporting his special sunglasses, equipped with a high-tech targeting system. He was dressed in an all-black suit with no tie and his pistols were strapped to his sides. Leaning over close to Don Maretto, he said, "I still think we should've brought more men. Without your sons here, you're an easy target."

"I already told you why I didn't want my sons to come and that decision was final. Danger might lurk from every building in a mile radius, but that is why I have you, Vego," he said with a grin.

"Sure, I can waste away a bunch of street thugs, but a man Blessed with powers is an entire different story, Don Maretto. Bullets can be stopped by an obsidian sword. And you haven't carried yours in years."

"And I will continue to not carry it on me. My own defensive powers will protect me if need be, my friend. You just make sure your sunglasses are on target today."

"They always are, boss. They always are," Vego said as he sat straight up with his eyes looking forward.

Maretto looked back out his window, and as the limo took a left onto a side street leading directly into Capital Way, he could see a massive crowd gathered in front of the Capital Building. It was an impressive sight indeed. There were waves of Juna citizens from the front of the Capital Building all the way down Capital Way. It looked like a crowd that was packed inside a batball stadium. Thousands and thousands of people waiting for the first pitch to be delivered by the President of Exodus.

It was impressive, but yet very troublesome. A crowd this size could hide many dark faces within. There could be a few surprises waiting this afternoon, and Don Maretto believed deep down inside that Vego may be right. They didn't have enough men for this. They were heading directly into a danger zone. The Cicello Family would be in attendance, whether it was Don Xanose and his gay son, or his other two murdering bastards who went into hiding. This was the perfect scene for Zasso Cicello to reenact the performance he put on at the Grand Theater. In fact, it was even more perfect than that fateful night.

Zasso Cicello and Razo Malvagio were standing at the edge of the roof of the General Steel building, overlooking the gathered crowd down below. Zasso had never seen so many people gathered in one place before. It was bigger than any sporting event or presidential rally in the long history of Exodus. The streets were flooded with Juna's people. But all Zasso saw were flocks of followers that would someday bow down to him. Future slaves of his, doing whatever his bidding was for them to do.

He felt a warm sensation course through his body. A sensation that would make him erect if he weren't standing next to another man. Just the thought of owning the lives of millions of people nearly caused him to explode in his pants…But then the moment was ruined when he heard the clicks and clacks of someone walking up from behind them.

"A sight to behold, isn't it?" Solace Volhine said as he approached the two men. "Can you believe that so many citizens of Juna have gathered together just to hear some old man talk some shit against the Seven Blessed Families? Man, are those assholes hated these days," he said, shaking his head.

Solace grasped the back of Zasso's shoulder. "And to think that you are a high member of one of those Families. What a fucking shame."

"You shouldn't touch me like that," Zasso said with a scowl that couldn't be seen by Solace.

"And why's that?" Solace replied.

"Because I don't like being touched like that. And one day, when I'm stronger than you'll ever dream of being, I will rip your fucking arm off for touching me at all."

Solace didn't back off. Instead he grabbed his shoulder with an even fiercer grip. "Well, I'll be waiting for that day you young piece of disrespectful shit."

Zasso's hands were shaking with the urge to reach back and unleash his Blessed sword, but the consequences of killing Thy Master's confidant would be fatal. There was too much at risk to slaughter this measly pile of dog excrement. If he accomplished his mission today, then the future of Juna was going to be under his rule. He couldn't screw it up. Not this time around.

Solace finally released his grasp, then gave Zasso a shove. "But let's not get carried away with our emotions today, young Zasso. You have a job to do and it won't be long until the President takes center stage. Look," Solace instructed as he pointed toward a section off to the right of the Capital Building staircase. "Your target has just arrived, and not one of his boys is with him."

Zasso gazed over the ledge of the roof toward the area where Solace was pointing. Next to a black stretch-limo stood Maretto Rose and his entourage of bodyguards. None of which were his sons...But another dangerous individual was with him as usual.

"No sons. But Vego Rainze will be attached to his side like glue," Zasso told Solace.

"Vego Rainze? A bodyguard with no Blessed powers? That's who you're worried about?" Solace said in a laughable tone.

"Trust me. That man has taken out more of my father's men than you could count, Volhine. He has a special gift of aim with the pistols he carries. The man is as dangerous as his sons."

"That man's bullets can be stopped by your Blessed sword," Solace pointed out. "If a man with guns is who you fear, then this day will end in another failure."

"I will not fail!" Zasso lashed out as he whipped his head around to face Solace. "And I don't fear anyone! But the man *is* a threat, and I'm going to treat him as one."

A vile grin was cast on Solace's face. "Treat him like your prom date for all I care. Just get your job done today. Thy Master is counting on you…And he will be watching very closely."

The Capital Building was the centerpiece of Juna. The architecture of the ages, built hundreds of years ago by the bare hands of ancestors. The pristine white stone has held strong for centuries, unfazed by the weathering of Father Time. It was a rectangular building, ten stories high, topped with its signature golden dome-which was in itself a wondrous marvel, reaching thirty lengths to the heavens, with a statue of what the government calls *The Penitent Man*, a robed figure holding out an unraveled scroll.

A platform of black marble was laid out in front of the Capital Building which lead to a white marble staircase descending down to the sidewalk. A stage and podium had been placed in the center of the platform, near the edge of the staircase. It was the location of where the President would be giving his speech. An entourage of government officials from the Legislation would be standing on each side of the podium in support and out of respect for their President…The Legislation. The government of Exodus. They were more crooked than a question mark.

Ric Rose stood across the street from the apartment complex, waiting patiently next to an empty newspaper box that at one time had a picture of the President on the front page, building the excitement for the speech that could start at any moment. And as a matter of fact, he heard an eruption from the crowd down the street, which meant that either a chaotic scene of violence had broken out, or the President himself was about to take center stage.

It was neither here nor there for Ric. He was patiently waiting for another's arrival. The man who had murdered two of his close friends right in front of him in an inhumane sadistic style. Ric would have been next if he hadn't had the wits and skills to escape with his life. And now it was revenge time. Payback for the horrific night he experienced at the hands of Miro Cicello.

And just as Ric was thinking back on that dreadful night at the club, Miro Cicello came strolling out of the apartment complex, clueless that he was about to get stalked and murdered.

Maretto and Vego took their seats near the platform and stage of the Capital building. Front row seats to the biggest speech of the century. Don Maretto was interested in hearing what the President was going to talk about. *Was he actually going to tell the people of Exodus that the Seven Blessed Families were the root of all evil? Or would the subject of his speech veer off the Families as they should?* Maretto thought as he waited in his seat, eager for the speech to begin.

And then the golden double doors drew open, and the eruption of the crowd began. The grand spectacle of the President's speech was about to take its place in history.

A dozen older men, dressed in long black robes with silver sashes, came strolling out of the Capital Building, all with their hands tucked into their robes. Their faces were stoic, all business as they marched across the black marble toward the stage. Half stood on one side of the podium while half stood on the other side, all facing the large crowd of Juna's people. The crowd erupted in cheers as the robed men gathered on the stage. It was a lively roar for the members of Juna's government...The Legislation.

Don Maretto watched as the crowds shifted in waves and let out a tremendous ovation for the first twelve members of the Legislation. He sighed and shook his head. "They cheer for a government they used to pay no mind to. A government the people never respected," he said to Vego. "But now they cheer them as if they are vigilante heroes who save us from the dangers in the night. This is a travesty already, and it has only begun."

Vego nodded toward his boss, and then they watched as the thirteenth official of the Legislation made his way out of the Capital Building and onto the marble platform. He was a tall and lanky man, walking with prominence and pride, his hands interlocked in front of him. He had dark, beady eyes, enhanced by a pair of black-framed spectacles. His cheekbones were sunken in and his head was shaved to the skull. The man appeared to be older than he actually was.

The thirteenth member of the Legislation approached the podium, then bowed to either side of the stage. When his fellow Legislation members bowed back, he stepped up to the podium and put his mouth close to the microphone attached to it. "Good afternoon, ladies and gentlemen. I am Pontius Vius; the High Inquisitor of the Legislation."

The crowd erupted in cheer and clapping. The High Inquisitor raised a hand in acknowledgement to their warm welcome. "Today will be a historic day. The world as we know it is on the verge of change, and today that change will be seen right in front of your eyes. In a few moments, the President will grace us with his presence and share with the nation, his beliefs and ideas of a new Exodus." The crowd clapped and cheered again. Louder this time.

"I have the distinct honor of standing by this man every day, and now I have the distinct honor of introducing him to the world on this historic day. Ladies and gentlemen, he is the unanimously elected President of Exodus! *PRESIDENT PALTRIC UNIASIS PAYNE!*"

The crowd went into immediate hysterics. The roar was deafening. They were all screaming and shouting for the man they call their President. The man who had always hid in the shadows behind the Seven Blessed Families…Until now. Now, he was stepping out of the shadows and onto a platform in front of thousands of people, ready to deliver a speech that would somehow change the nation.

President Paltric Uniasis Payne stepped out of the doorway of the Capital Building. He walked with a prideful, all-knowingly stride, like a king who had already conquered an entire nation. He was followed by two ESFU agents as he made his way onto the marble platform. Waving an inviting hand, he sent the crowd into a frenzy when they saw him in the flesh.

President Payne had flowing silver hair, an almost square-shaped head with puffy cheeks and a bulb-shaped nose. His jawline was hard and rigid, his lips thin and concentrated. He had gray eyes topped with bushy eyebrows that were the same silver hue as his head of hair. The President was tall and bulky, dressed in a loose-fitting crystal white robe, complete with a royal blue waistband and a silver sash with gold bordering. A royal blue cloak wrapped around his neck and draped down his back until it was close to dragging on the ground behind him. The President's fashion was that of a ruler from centuries ago, but it caught the attention of the people of Exodus as they yelled and howled when he stepped onto the stage and took his rightful place behind the podium.

The crowd continued to cheer in raucous fashion as President Payne continued to wave at his enduring fans. Don Maretto Rose gazed upon the crowd from where he was standing. He watched as the waves of people went hysterical in the presence of the President. "They welcome him as if he is a conquering king," he said to Vego. "This is not good for us. This is not good at all." The leader of the Rose Family and most prominent figure of the Seven Blessed Families was downtrodden and shaken. In all his years of life, the President was never taken in so well by the people of Exodus. Something big was on the horizon. He could feel the imminent arrival of an uprising in the future.

After the President finished waving to his people, the crowd calmed to a dull roar as they waited for him to speak. "Good afternoon," President Payne addressed the crowd, but was barely heard under the still frantic scene. "Good afternoon," he repeated after clearing his throat. The crowd became silent as they keened in on the beginning of his speech.

"I am delighted and much honored by the number of citizens who have graced me with their presence on this beautiful day in Juna, the Capital of Exodus." The crowd began to cheer, but the President quickly shut them down with his stern, forceful voice. "I stand here a proud man. Proud of my position as your President, and proud of my people. Today I will not only address our nation of a dramatic change to our society, but today I will also be completely honest with my people."

The President paused while the crowd reacted with cheers, then continued, "I will admit to you today that my position as President has not been an honest one. There have been lies. Lies covered up by our government to satisfy the average citizen of Exodus. But I can assure you that today I will repent my dishonesty, and the dishonesty of the Legislation, in order to gain your trust as I always have wanted to do."

The crowd simmered down, everyone questioning what the President was leading towards. "The people of Exodus were drawn into believing that they unanimously elected me as their President and leader…But that, I'm sorry to say, is not the truth." The faces in the crowds were stunned. "I was given my Presidency by the Seven Blessed Families. Yes, they were the ones who voted me into office."

The enormous crowd let out an amplified melody of boos, letting the President know they were unhappy by the revelation. A mob scene would surely escalate if the President wasn't quick with an apology.

"Yes, my people. I understand your anger and frustration. A farce had been committed. A farce that a highly regarded figure was elected by the free people of Exodus." Boos and yells grew louder, more agitated.

Don Maretto looked dumbfounded. "I can't believe he just revealed that to everyone," he said to Vego. "No citizen of Exodus was to ever learn that information."

President Payne waved a hand to try to silence the crowd, but the people were unrelenting. "I want to apologize on behalf of myself and the Legislation," he raised his voice over the disgruntled yells. "Yes!" he shouted. "I understand your anger! I am angry as well! Angry at myself for going along with the dishonesty! Angry for trusting the Seven Blessed Families, and for allowing them to continue to rig the elections! And angry that I have been a weak President of this beautiful nation we call home! But that ends now! The Seven Blessed Families will not control me from here on out!" His voice was heard, for the crowds quieted down and listened to the President's reconciliation.

The President recollected himself after his forceful apology. "I, like you, the wonderful citizens of Exodus, am sick and tired of what I see out my office window every single day of the week. I see a great city that has been overrun by crime. I look further upon the land, and see a great nation that has been controlled by organized corruption for far too long. And then I look further into the future, and see us as a whole, changing Exodus forever and ridding the streets of senseless violence, drug addiction, and unvirtuous prostitution. It may take a while, but if we work together, then anything is possible." There was low clapping from the crowd. Nothing like the cheers when the President began his speech. He had to earn the respect from the crowd over again, and by the look of his face, he was determined to do just that.

"But what is the central cause of all the violence, drugs, and prostitution? Some might say that it comes from the inner cities, individuals who were born less fortunate, or from street rats who have to commit crime in order to get by. And yes, it is true that some of the crime stems from these specific sources. But what is the real problem out there in our great cities? Who are the real criminals who run the streets, businesses, and basically the entire nation?"

Don Maretto squint his eyes and said to himself, "There's no way he's going to blame us."

"My people, the real problem stems from the Families who have built this nation on organized crime. Yes, Exodus was built from the ground up by criminal empires starting from the royal families of the Golden Age, followed by the organized crime families of the Industrial Age." The President's face looked like a burning cannon ball ready to launch an explosion of accountability. "The Seven Blessed Families are the ones to blame for the corruption! They are the criminal empires that have been committing heinous acts of violence for hundreds of years, but project themselves as decent human beings and as saviors of the nation of Exodus! But they are just criminals, that's all! Criminal empires who have overrun our homes with their lies, deception, and worst of all, mass-murder!" The crowd reacted with jeers and cheers. Jeers to defy the Seven Blessed Families, and cheers for the bravery of the President to reveal the truths against them.

Don Maretto shook his head as he watched the crowd's reaction to the President's condemnation of the Families. "He has the crowd eating from the palm of his hands now," he said to Vego. "This could end up being a dark day for our Family. Nothing good will come from the rest of this speech."

The President waited until the crowd settled before continuing on. "For hundreds of years, the Seven Blessed Families have been portrayed as the upper-echelon of our society. They have been portrayed as royalty. Kings and princes walking through our streets with their heads held high in the air because they know they have an unrelenting

346

grip around our nation, unwilling to let go so they can call it their playground. For centuries we have been toyed with. We are their playthings. Their puppets, dangling from strings as we're told how to talk and how to think. We are told where to walk and what streets to walk on. But who governs them?" He paused, as if waiting for someone in the crowd to answer him. "No one governs them. That's who…"

As the President's speech was happening at the Capital Building, Jon-Jon Rose was walking through the hallway of a south side apartment complex. The floor had multiple rooms, and the President could be heard on each and every video monitor playing.

"They walk freely among us. Men who should be locked up in chains and rot in a prison cell for the crimes they commit. And they don't commit petty crimes. They commit the worst crime of all. Murder. They are murderers, walking along the same sidewalks as our kids use to walk to school."

Jon-Jon was dressed in casual gear, a tight-fitted black jacket over a red t-shirt and black pants. His head was covered by a ball cap, and his eyes were shielded by a pair of black sunglasses to hide his identity in public. He walked in a casual manner, acting as normal as possible. But nobody would see him. Everyone was stuck in their rooms, glued to their video monitors.

When he made it to the last door at the very end of the hall, he stopped in front of it and knocked three times. He heard a bit of rustling noise, before the door was jerked open. The man standing before him was Bryant Strattburn.

"What the fuck do you want?" Strattburn asked, doped up and drunk out of his mind.

"Yes, these killers walk among us, eat at the same restaurants as us, and breathe our same air. They are in charge of the businesses we invest our good earned coin in. The sports teams that we give our undying loyalty to, and the churches where we worship and give donations from the kindness of our hearts."

For the past three hours, Alto Rose followed his uncle around town to verify his disloyalty to the Family. Palco Valone's last stop was a small, concealed building near the

Skylarks stadium, where he met a guy Alto knew all too well from the media conferences after batball games. His name was Victor Lobstein, the President of Operations for the Southside Skylarks. And not only was he involved in all the operations for the team, but he and Uncle Palco were forging his father's signatures to cover their own asses after they made the original owners of the team disappear.

The outside of the building had the appearance of a small business with one square window with closed blinds and a metal door that had been painted black. It was a nice little hideout for their shady dealings, but unless you have a place underground or in the middle of the ocean, someone's going to eventually find you out...And that's what Alto just did. He found his uncle out. The skinny pipe-smoking fuck couldn't hide this secret from his father forever. Don Maretto Rose is the king of Exodus. The Rose Family unveils every secret.

As soon as Uncle Palco entered the small building, Alto stepped out of his sports car, and walked nonchalantly across the parking lot and up to the metal door. He took a couple puffs on what was left of his cig, then tossed it to the ground and grinded it out with his shoe. Then, he loaded the clip of bullets for the Juna Typewriter he was holding with his left hand. But before he proceeded to walk through the front door, he concealed it behind his back.

The door wasn't even locked, the dumb fuck. That's how sure his uncle was of no one ever finding out about the basis of their operations. It was like walking into a candy store with nobody working behind the cash register. It was going to be easy pickings for Alto, and what might have been a good day gone to shit for his Uncle Palco.

When Alto walked inside, his Uncle Palco was leaning against the wall smoking his pipe, while Lobstein was doing paperwork behind a wooden desk. The look on his uncle's face was worth a million 'what the fuck's'.

"Alto?" Palco inquisitively said. An instant twang of fear edged out of his voice when he asked, "What brings you down here?"

"I'm looking for a couple of asshole's using my father's name to run a batball team, and I stumbled upon you, Uncle Palco," Alto replied. "Is this season looking good for the Skylarks or what? I'm a big fucking fan."

Ric Rose was as shocked as anyone by what he was hearing the President say, but he couldn't let it distract him from his mission. For a few brief moments, Miro Cicello stood as one with the crowd and listened to the amplified voice of the President as his words echoed down the block and entranced the ears of anyone listening. Ric kept his distance, but never took his eyes off the prize.

"When our people settled on this nation, we were given the freedom of land, the freedom of choice, and the freedom of raising a family. But what wasn't given to us, was the freedom of power. Power was given to only a select few. And those select few have taken advantage of that power. They don't use it for the purpose of good for our society. They use it to invoke fear into the average citizen of Exodus. The fear of pain. The fear of torture. And the fear of death.

But today I say that we fear no more of these Families. They aren't the ones who work honest jobs to support their families. They were given a precious gift and use it to benefit only them! Relics should be used for the purpose of good. Not for evil intentions!"

From high above, Zasso Cicello was using a pair of binoculars to look closely upon the gathered crowd below. As he scanned the crowd, he caught sight of his younger brother, Miro, walking around by himself. Then, he saw something that disturbed him. He was being followed. And not by just some random guy. Ric Rose was tailing close behind without Miro noticing.

"I have to go down there," Zasso told Razo and Solace.

"What are you talking about, you fool?" Solace responded. "You have a job to do."

"My brother is in danger," he said, handing the binoculars over to Razo. "He's being followed by one of the Rose brothers. The youngest one. The one my brother almost had killed. Ric Rose is up to something. I can sense it."

"This is not the time to get involved in family issues, young Cicello. Thy Master's bidding is far more important."

"It's my brother!"

"Dammit!" Solace yelled out as he pushed Zasso out of his way and stood next to Razo. "Give me those damn things!" he demanded, referring to the binoculars. Razo handed them over and Solace held them up to his eyes. "Where is this brother of yours?"

"Towards the end of the gathered crowd, two blocks south of the National Archive Building. He's wearing a shiny silver polo and sunglasses with white frames."

Solace zoomed in on the spot Zasso had described, and there he was in his silver polo and white sunglasses. "He looks like a moron." He tossed the binoculars back to Razo and said, "I'll go down and look after your brother. You stay here until it's time to do your job."

Thousands of miles away, it was a hot and muggy afternoon in the Deep South. Don Maximo Rocca and his High Consultant were cruising across the ocean surface, their speedboat bouncing off the waves. He was following the exact route from the video Salic Stone brought to him on his way to steal the Jovani Family's Relic, The Triad. Maximo had goosebumps just thinking about seeing another Family's Relic. Sure, he'd been in front of the Cicello Relic, *The Thundercloud*, but The Triad seemed more enticing. It contained powers stemmed from fire. He loved to watch shit burn.

"We're close," Maximo yelled over the boat's engine and the hard breeze whizzing through his curly hair. "I can already sense the Relic's power!"

His High Consultant just smiled and nodded as he steered the boat.

"Come on," he yelled, shoving an elbow into the Consultant's side. "Pretty soon we'll be shooting flames out of our dicks! Ha ha!" Maximo displayed his long, ivory teeth as he smiled. He was hopped up on powder as usual and loving his life right now.

They were close. The secluded island was in sight. The famous Triad Relic was nearly in Maximo's grasp. And no one had a clue he was out here in the middle of the

350

ocean, because all those morons were watching the President deliver some stupid speech. What a waste of time.

The large crowd hooted and hollered. The President waved a hand to silence them, so he could continue, but it took a few moments before they settled. "My people, we have been stepped on for far too long by the Seven Blessed Families. We have been drawn to their luxurious lifestyles, and it has made us weak at the knees." He paused and looked from one side of the crowd to the other. "We have idolized them. Envied them. And even been jealous of the way they live. I too am guilty of this sin, for I thought I had the honor in being their pet. But after being in office for the past seven years, I've had front row seats to the misery they bring our nation. Their lavish lifestyles bring nothing but pure carnage! Just ask the great Don Maretto Rose. His son was slaughtered on center stage at the historic Grand Theater."

Don Maretto winced at the thought of his son, Georgiano's death. He turned his head to the side and felt like vomiting. Nothing will change what had happened, but Maretto will never get over the death of one of his young sons. It was the only comment the President has made that Maretto agreed with.

"And who was the one responsible for this murder? It was Don Xanose Cicello's son! The son of another one of these great patriarchs of the Seven Blessed Families!" The crowd booed out of spite for the patriarchs. "But he didn't just kill one of the heirs to the Rose Family throne. No, he killed innocent men and women, including professional actors, who were putting on one of the greatest performances of their careers. Now, they may never perform again, unless it's for our great Lord up above." Light clapping emanated from the crowd, out of respect for the fallen victims.

The President paused and scratched the right side of his clean-shaven jawline, before he continued, "My people, the terror that the Seven Blessed Families bring into our homes everyday must stop. I know that it is hard to ask that the average citizen of Exodus not fear these men and women of organized crime, but it's the fear that they thrive upon. They want you to fear them. That is where they get their control over you. When they make an entire nation be afraid of their presence, then they have won! And if it continues, then they will always win!"

Don Maretto lowered his head as he heard the constant roars and jeers of the crowd, letting it be known that they were on board with the President. *Yes, we put fear into others,* he thought. *But that is the way you are supposed to rule over your people…But maybe they're not my people anymore…Maybe they never really were.*

The members of the Legislation were all nodding their heads in agreement with the President as he went on with the speech. "The Seven Blessed Families strike their fear upon you by acts of violence. Murder! If they don't get what they want, then they will take it from you! They will eradicate you from this earth to fulfill their every need, and they won't think twice about it! They have no hearts! They have no sense of purity! And they have no souls! Murder is what is in their hearts! Murder is what is inside their souls!"

Jon-Jon Rose reached over his shoulder and removed the obsidian sword that was strapped to his back. The edges of the blade glowed a bright crimson as he gripped the handle with both hands.

Bryant Stattburn's eyes grew like a pair of inflated balloons when he saw the appearance of the magical weapon. "What the…" is all he could get out of his vocal chords.

With a mighty thrust, Jon-Jon stuck the blade through Strattburn's abdomen, the glowing crimson cutting through the skin like butter. The blade penetrated all the way through his body, the tip sticking out the center of his back. When Jon-Jon retreated the blade out of his body, a gush of blood and guts spilled to the floor.

A brunette woman dressed in just a long t-shirt asked what was going on and then entered the doorway area. Strattburn turned around to face her as he held his entrails with his hands and coughed up blood out of his mouth. Jon-Jon proceeded to shove the blade of the sword through the back of Strattburn's head. The tip exited through his mouth, severing his tongue. It fell to the ground and slivered around like a worm that had just been hooked.

The woman screamed an awful shrill, and she needed to be shut the fuck up. So, Jon-Jon reached into his waistband with his left hand, pulled out a silver handgun, and unloaded three shots at the woman. Her chest and abdomen exploded with opened holes of blood and tissue. She fell to the floor in an instant, no longer causing any attention to the murder scene.

"Murder is what is in their blood," the President continued. "It has been for generations. The members of these Families were born to kill. And kill they do! Without remorse, they rid each other with a simple order from the leaders of their Families. The thugs on the street are buttons ready to be pushed with a simple nod of the head. It's that simple! Just like that," he snapped his fingers, "and you're full of bullet holes, then taken out like trash and thrown into the river."

Alto Rose revealed his submachine gun to his Uncle Palco and Victor Lobstein. While Victor sat stunned and motionless behind the desk, Palco treaded backwards and screamed like a little girl. Alto almost felt bad when he heard the horrible shriek his uncle let out, but when you fuck around with his father, you have to pay the price with your life.

Alto took aim at Lobstein first and pulled the automatic trigger. His chest opened up like a can of sardines as wood chips, documents, and checks went flying into the air, combining with a crimson mist. Lobstein fell backwards off his chair, hitting the back of his head off the wall.

The gun was then turned on Palco Valone, who shrieked and shrilled as he braced himself against the wall. Alto pulled the trigger, and Palco's white dress shirt turned into a mess of red flesh as his body was riddled with bullets. He screamed and yelled as he was being put out of his misery, then slid down the wall until he dropped to the floor, leaving long streaks of blood along the way down.

The President paused and let out a long sigh, before he continued, "The question is, my people, is will this reign of terror ever end? Will there ever be peace? Are the patriarchs of the Seven Blessed Families ever going to put down their guns and swords, call a truce on the violence, and use their magical Relics in a positive, productive manner?"

Through a tunnel of palm trees, Don Maximo Rocca walked ahead of his High Consultant as they made their way closer to the cave that inhabited the Triad Relic. Maximo could see a small pond in the close distance. It was clearer than a swimming pool. The sunlight flickered on the surface of the water.

"It's so damn beautiful down here," Maximo commented about the scenery while licking his teeth. "Maybe I'll just move my Family down here and conquer the Deep South. I'm sure there won't be any complaints about the weather." Maximo chuckled as he swatted a mosquito away from his face.

"I sure don't have any complaints, boss," the High Consultant said. He stroked his blonde ponytail, then said, "Except for the humidity. It's a real bitch on my hair."

"Fuck your hair," Maximo said with a smirk.

"I would if I could," the blonde, ponytailed douchebag said back.

Maximo shook his head in disgust. "Whatever, motherfucker." The pond was getting closer and closer. "We're almost there. Try not to fuck yourself before we get to the Relic."

Maximo's High Consultant let out a bellow of a laugh, then followed it with a shriek of pain as his throat was slit and blood spurted out of his carotid artery, making a red mess of his white t-shirt and shorts. He fell to his knees, then face-first into the sand. Standing behind him was the perpetrator, holding an obsidian dagger with a fiery orange glow around the edges in both hands. The dagger in his right hand was dripping blood unto the sand. The other dagger was caulked back and ready to go. Don Calico Jovani was ready for a battle.

After hearing the shriek from his High Consultant, Maximo lowered his head and sighed. At that moment, he knew he had been set up. There wasn't going to be any heist of the Triad Relic, he wasn't going to migrate his Family to the Deep South, and he and Xanose's alliance wasn't going to mean shit unless he left this island alive. He realized that his dream of being on top was most likely over.

"Salic fucking Stone," is what Maximo muttered to himself before he turned around to face his surprise attacker. But it wasn't a real surprise to see the man dressed in a button-down shirt with a collage of tropical flowers. The diamond stud in the middle of his forehead twinkled in the bright sun.

"You must be one hell of a smooth-talker to get to one of my guys, Don Calico. For that I respect you. But I guess we're not gonna go back to your place and have drinks while we settle our differences," Maximo said, trying to wiggle his way out of a fight to the death.

Calico stepped over the lifeless body in front of him and diligently walked towards Maximo. "You sent a spy down to my territory in order to steal my Family's Relic. Would you have a drink with someone who tried to do that to you? I don't think so, Don Maximo."

Maximo reached over his shoulder and unsheathed his obsidian sword from the strap on his back. A royal blue glow surrounded the blade. "I'm not going down without a fight."

"I would be disappointed if you didn't." Calico charged ahead, then leaped into the air, coming down hard with his wild blades.

Maximo successfully blocked the first attack, but was then hit with a barrage of unrelenting cuts and swipes. He was outmatched from the beginning. Calico was a much better fighter than he could have ever been in his youth.

Calico used unique spinning attack moves that Maximo struggled to fend off, and after only a few more swipes of his daggers, he had an open shot to Maximo's wrist. The dagger slit completely through the tissue and bone, severing off his hand. Maximo shouted to the heavens in pain, but was immediately brought to silence when Calico shoved a dagger into his eye socket.

The Rocca and Cicello alliance ended right then and there.

"The answer, my people, is no. The patriarchs of these Families are only capable of bringing harm to one another. And they will never use their Family Relics for the purpose of good. Why would they? If history has proven one thing, it's that the Seven Blessed Families have thrived because they use the Relic's powers for the purpose of violence. The blood members of these Families are trained specifically to kill. Not to use their powers productively, like cutting lumber, fighting fires, creating fire, generating electricity, or shielding others from pain." He looked over at Don Maretto specifically when he said the last part. Everyone, especially the President, knows of the Rose Family's dominant defensive powers.

The President lifted his heavy eyes away from Don Maretto and focused back on the crowd in front of him. He took a heavy breath and went on, "So, what can we do to stop this tyranny that the Seven Blessed Families have reigned upon us?" People from the crowd began to shout answers at President Payne, until it was just a jumble of yells. The President lifted a hand to silence the people. They obeyed. "My people, I have an answer for you." A small grin formed on his face, but then it quickly straightened out and became hard and serious. "I hereby make a decree! The patriarchs of the Seven Blessed Families must turn in their Relics to the Legislation and myself, so that we may begin the process of using their powers in a positive, productive manner, in order to restore the decency of our humanity! Our world will no longer suffer under the tyranny of the Seven Blessed Families! And they will comply with my decree, or be thrown inside an empty prison cell to rot for the rest of their miserable lives!" The crowd erupted in mass hysteria, agreeing with the President one hundred percent. There wasn't a quiet mouth among the citizens attending the speech. Everyone had a voice. And everyone was using it.

"What just happened?" Vego asked his boss in a cynical way.

His dark eyes staring directly at the President and his hard jaw clenched, Don Maretto answered, "He wants us to turn in our Family Relics." His voice was calm, but he was burning on the inside. "The President just made a threat against the Seven Blessed Families."

"Once again, I would like to thank the Legislation for supporting this most important decision, and I would like to thank the good, hard working citizens of Exodus for your support on this beautiful day. Have a good night and rest easy, my people." The President stepped to the side of the podium and lifted both arms as if he was celebrating a victory. The crowd reacted as if he had as well. But what victory had he won? A small victory over the Seven Blessed Families? Or just the hearts of the people of Exodus?

After the President was done waving to the crowd, he turned around and started making his way back toward the entrance of the Capital Building. His special agents were by his side, attached to him like a magnet on metal. The members of the Legislation followed closely behind him, but kept their heads down and did not acknowledge anyone, especially the media.

Don Maretto kept a close eye on the President, then made the quick decision to confront him before he had a chance to disappear with his entourage. The Rose patriarch briskly walked through the crowd and up the steps. Vego and his other bodyguards kept up with him during the pursuit, their eyes targeting every direction, looking for a perpetrator to appear out of nowhere. The Don was taking a risk being out in the open, but he had to have a word with the President before it was too late.

Maretto cut the President off just before he made it to the front doors of the Capital Building. When President Payne saw Maretto out of the corner of his eye, he turned his head toward him and smiled.

"Don Maretto Rose," the President acknowledged him. Maretto was only a couple of steps away from him. Close enough to strike him with a deadly blow of magic. "I'm sure you didn't enjoy my speech, but it is what it is. I will be expecting your full compliance."

Shaking his head, Maretto replied, "You can't expect us to just turn the Relics over because you made a decree. It doesn't work like that."

The President's smile straightened and the wrinkles in his forehead lined up in unison. "Is that so? Well, Don Maretto, maybe you and the rest of the Seven Blessed Families have been underestimating me from the very day you let me take office. I will be expecting those Relics on the front doorstep of this building, or else you will all be shipped off to prison. You have ninety days, my friend. I bid you good evening."

The President was whisked away by his special agents before Don Maretto could get another word out. In a flash, President Payne was gone. The members of the Legislation all entered the Capital Building as well, Pontius Vius being the last one. Vius stared at Don Maretto with eyes of loathing and disgust.

357

Maretto stared back, then said, "You keep looking at me like that, Pontius, and I'll rip your fucking eyeballs out of their sockets."

Vius just shook his head and replied, "It does not surprise me that you would attack me with words of violence. Typical of your kind."

Before Maretto could respond to the insult, two slick-haired ESFU agents stepped in front of him, acting as a distraction so Vius could take his leave into the Capital Building. Maretto stared at the agents as they stared at him back behind black sunglasses. Then, he gave a half smile and a nod before turning around and walking away.

When Maretto turned around, he looked out upon the dispersing crowd of people. They were drones, every single one of them. Thousands of people who were just brainwashed by the President after one elaborated speech against the Seven Blessed Families. Now they would go back to their homes and back to their simple lives, dreaming of a new world that the President promised he would give them. He served them up a silver platter of new beliefs, and their simple little minds were eating off of it with forks made of fake gold.

As Don Maretto was scanning the crowd, he spotted a balding man dressed in a white sport coat lingering around at the bottom of the white marble staircase. When the man turned around, Maretto couldn't believe his eyes. He was just the man he wanted to talk to after the fiasco of a speech in front of the Capital Building. Don Xanose Cicello had been present at the speech. He, along with Don Maretto, would have to form a new alliance in the wake of the President's decree.

Maretto darted across the black marble platform as fast as his fifty-year-old legs would take him. Vego motioned to the bodyguards and yelled for them to get the car ready, then followed his boss. Don Xanose spotted Maretto coming as soon as he reached the top of the stairs, but instead of waiting for him, he glowered and turned his back on him, before casually walking off through the now scattered crowd.

"Xanose!" Maretto yelled as he trotted down the staircase. "Xanose, wait!"

It didn't take much for Maretto to catch up to the Cicello patriarch. Xanose didn't seem in much of a hurry, even though he was basically ignoring Maretto's calling out to him.

As soon as Maretto was within ten lengths of Don Xanose, he shouted, "Xanose!" The Cicello patriarch finally turned around to face him. He had an annoyed look on his face. "Don Xanose, now is not the time to ignore one another. I believe it is time for our Families to call a truce for the time being. We can't let the President take away what has been our rightful inheritance for hundreds of years. We have to stand together and fight this atrocity of a decree. There must be peace between our Families."

Don Xanose reacted with a sigh, then looked Maretto dead in the eyes and said, "It's too late for that, Maretto Rose. There can never be any peace. He's already gone too far." With his eyes, Xanose motioned for Maretto to take a look behind him.

Slowly turning his head, Maretto looked over his shoulder, and striding through a group of lingering people, was the man who brought misery to his life. Zasso Cicello.

Zasso shoved a pair of citizens out of his way, walked a few more lengths forward, then stopped in his tracks and had a stare down with Don Maretto. He was dressed in a slick royal blue suit, with a white dress shirt underneath, unbuttoned to his chest, shiny silver necklaces dangled from his neck. His black and silver hair was flowing in the breeze, and his triangular face bore a scowl directed at the Rose patriarch. In his right hand, he was brandishing his unique obsidian sword. The transparent blue and yellow energy blended in unison as it bordered the edges of the blade.

Maretto tilted his head downward and sighed. He then looked back at Don Xanose, whose face looked downtrodden and defeated. But why? It was his son doing his bidding...Right?

When the two patriarchs were done giving each other somber looks, Don Xanose began the long walk back to his limo, which was parked along the sidewalk about thirty lengths away. His bodyguard, Rondo, stood next to the back door, waiting to open it for his boss.

For a moment, Maretto watched Xanose walk away, but then he turned around and focused his attention on the enemy at hand. Zasso pointed the tip of his blade toward Maretto and said, "Today is a day of reckoning, Don Maretto Rose. You escaped my clutches once before, but today you are coming with me." He lifted his left hand and moved his fingers into a claw-like shape. A ball of electricity formed in his palm. "Whether you like it or not."

Vego Rainze stepped in front of Maretto and drew out his pistols in a haste. Maretto grabbed the back of his shoulder and moved him to his side. "Your father has infiltrated your feeble mind, Zasso. You are going down a road in which you cannot return from. Be careful the decisions you make."

"My father?" Zasso retorted in an instant. He let out a devious laugh. "You have no idea what you are going up against, Don Maretto. I believe the feeble mind belongs to you." The ball of electricity in his palm grew until it completely surrounded his hand. "Your sons aren't here to fight for you today. And even if they were, I would butcher each one of them until you fell to your hands and knees and begged me to take you with me. But lucky for you, that's not gonna happen. So, step forward and come with me in peace."

"Your mother!" Vego shouted as he stepped in front of his boss once again.

From amidst the crowd, Razo treaded toward the action and drew out a shotgun from behind his back, aiming it at Vego. "I have a bodyguard too, Don Maretto. But I don't want to take this situation as far as using them on one another. Tell Rainze to step aside, or Razo is going to blow his fucking face off."

"He wouldn't get the shot off in time, asshole!" Vego yelled as he aimed his pistols directly at Razo. "If your little man wants to dance with a big dog, then we can dance!"

"Enough!" Maretto shouted. "This is exactly why the President wants to take away our Family Relics. We can't act out our differences in public, Zasso. Let's go talk about this somewhere private, and maybe we can bring some peace to our situation."

"Fuck the President!" Zasso yelled back. "And fuck peace! I'm getting what I want, Don Maretto Rose. It's my destiny to live out my dream."

Maretto's forehead crinkled in confusion as he said, "What are you talking about?"

Just as Don Maretto asked the question, Don Xanose was approaching the limo. He motioned for Rondo to open the door for him, and as soon as his bodyguard obeyed, there was a deafening crack, immediately followed by a tumultuous explosion. Rondo was blown apart in an instant, his body overcome by a mammoth fireball. Don Xanose was lifted off his feet and blown thirty lengths backwards until he landed on his back. His white suit had turned black and his face and arms were badly burned. He lied motionless as pieces of the limo skipped past his broken body.

The force of the explosion caused Don Maretto to fall forward on his face, while a burning tire skipped across the pavement and hit Vego in the back of the head, knocking him to the ground and knocking him out. The impact caused Zasso to fall flat on his ass, but he landed on the middle part of his back, so he wasn't hurt too bad. But Razo was caught off guard by the blast and fell backward and smacked his head off the pavement, sending him into a deep sleep.

Maretto lifted his head off the pavement and surveyed the chaotic scene. Surrounding him was a thin layer of smoke from the mighty explosion. It must have been a bomb wired to the limo. People were in mass hysterics, running as far away from the area as they could. Their screams were only a muffle, as his ears were ringing from the blast. The street was littered with charred metal and shards of broken glass. The air smelled like burnt rubber.

Turning his head to the right, he noticed that Vego was lying flat on his face, but taking regular breaths. He looked beyond his bodyguard and caught a glimpse of Don Xanose's body sprawled out on the ground. He didn't look good, but he didn't seem dead. Then, he turned his head and looked forward, and saw that Razo was knocked out cold, but Zasso was slowly rising to his feet. If he didn't do the same, then he would easily be taken prisoner. So, he mustered up all his strength, pushed himself off the pavement, and gingerly rose to his feet. He steadied himself once he was standing upright again, then with pure instinct, constructed a crimson shield in front of his body.

A few blocks away, a black sports car was parked in between two other snazzy rides next to the sidewalk. His eyes hidden under dark sunglasses, the passenger surveyed the damage. "Fuck'n hell," Salic Stone commented. "The timing was off and the blast was too big. I don't think we got Xanose enough to kill him."

The driver shook his head. "And the blast knocked Don Maretto Rose to the ground," Petro Palini observed. "That's not gonna get us in his good graces, ya know." He gritted his teeth. "Don Calio is going to be pissed."

Shaking his head and rubbing his forehead from the stress, Salic said, "We have to let him know we failed. Let's go."

Petro turned the key in the ignition, shifted the gear to drive, and then sped off down the street, leaving a mess for the Rose and Cicello Families to clean up.

Meanwhile, Zasso Cicello unleashed a bolt of lightning aimed directly toward Maretto Rose. The magical bolt of energy struck Maretto's crimson shield, but ricocheted off it. Furious by its lack of impact, Zasso charged toward Maretto with his sword in attacking position. Maretto didn't flinch, but stood still as he waited for the impending attack. Zasso took a quick swipe at his head, but he leaned back and watched the blade pass within an inch from his face. Zasso then went for a backhanded swipe, which Maretto ducked under just as the blade flung by. He tried a lunging stab to the abdomen, a forceful cross slash to his chest, and then a spinning swipe to his neck, but Don Maretto dodged every attack as if the fight was in slow motion.

With his sword stashed back at the Heritage Castle, Maretto only had his bare hands to fight back with, and as soon as he dodged a series of more attacks, he shoulder-rammed Zasso right in the chest. Crimson shadows followed his body as he slammed Zasso backward and on his back. Zasso was quick to get up, but was met by a forceful push of energy that sent him back to the ground.

Like he was twenty years old again, Maretto pounced upon Zasso, kicking him square in the gut, then grabbing him by the hair and yanking him to his feet. He gave him a forearm shot to the face, a spurt of blood launched from his nose. He kneed him in the gut, then grabbed the back of his head and gave him another forearm to the temple. He pummeled Zasso, over and over. Zasso tried to counter the elder man with a blast of lightning, but Maretto snagged him arm, twisted it, and then kicked the absolute shit out of him. Zasso fell like a bag of bricks, moaning and groaning as he slivered around the pavement, spitting up globs of blood. He tried pushing himself up, but was slow to do so.

"Don't bother getting up," Maretto told him. "You lost before you even tried to win, Zasso." He paced around the fallen young man, taunting him with his intimidating presence.

"How are you so powerful?" Zasso yelled out while huffing and puffing.

"It's knowledge as well as power, young man. I have been one with our Family Relic for years. No matter how old I get, I can still fight like a young man such as yourself. But with an even deadlier force." He went down to one knee and thunder-punched the ground right next to Zasso's head. The impact of his energized fist cracked the pavement. "Much deadlier force."

"Then kill me, you son of a bitch!"

"No," Maretto replied. "That would be too easy."

"Just do it!" Zasso yelled as a driblet of blood dripped out of his mouth. "I've already failed my mission. I'm already dead."

Maretto bent over Zasso's beaten body and said, "You die when I say you die. And I'm not ready to kill you yet."

Out of the corner of his eye, Zasso could see Razo awaking out of his abrupt slumber. Like a drunkard who had just fallen on his face, Razo stumbled to his feet and set his balance as he swayed back and forth. When he finally steadied himself, he reached down to the ground and grabbed his shotgun. With shaky hands, he pointed the barrel of the gun at the back of Don Maretto, who was standing over Zasso, clueless that he was about to get shot in the back.

Through the mist of smoke from the explosion, Vego Rainze appeared with his pistols drawn. He pulled the triggers and round after round was fired. Razo's chest exploded in a mass of blood and flesh as he was hit by every shot. The shotgun dropped to his side as he stumbled backwards, before falling flat on his back. His chest rose up and down in short, quick breathes, but in a matter of seconds, his breathing stopped and Razo was a goner.

"No!" Zasso shouted as he tried to push himself from off the ground, but Maretto prevented him from doing so with a thunderous fist to his face. He was knocked unconscious as his face was planted into the pavement. A trickle of blood ran down his cheek and into his mouth.

Vego limped his way over to his boss, who stared down at the man who murdered his son. He wiped the sweat off his forehead, then slicked back his wavy hair. "How close was he from getting me?"

"Only seconds away. His shaky hands were preventing him from pulling the trigger…Amateur hour."

Maretto shook his head. "That's too close. It would have been a major disappointment to be killed by the likes of that man."

Vego shrugged and said, "Well, he didn't, so what do we do now?"

Maretto thought to himself for a moment, then replied, "We take him with us and make him talk. If it's not his father behind all this nonsense, then maybe we can dig it out of him. Someone powerful has manipulated his mind, and we need to figure out who."

"And if he doesn't talk?"

"He'll talk…Eventually, they all do," Don Maretto said in a grave tone.

Inside Marty's Tavern, Miro Cicello was sitting at the bar while the bartender was wiping a few glasses and watching the video monitor hanging down from the ceiling above the shelves of liquors. The media was covering the historic speech the President had just delivered, but then a special breaking story developed when an explosion happened near the Capital Building. Details were few and far between at the moment, but reporters were guessing that the Seven Blessed Families were involved.

"My God," the bartender commented, "people are going to kill each other over that damn speech. Are you hearing this shit?"

Miro drained a glass of liquor down his gullet before he answered, "I don't give a fuck, Marty. How about you fill up my glass? Fill it to the top this time." He let out a yawn and stretched out his arms. His biceps were barely covered by the silver collared shirt he was wearing. His white slacks were so tight that his bulge looked like he was wearing a cup during a batball game. And his white sunglasses covered his drunk blood-shot eyes.

"As you wish, Mr. Cicello. You just sit back and relax. My man will be here soon with the shit you requested."

"Good. If I don't get high soon I'm gonna lose my fucking mind."

Ding a ling-Ding a ling... The bell above the entrance rang when a customer opened the door and entered the tavern.

Marty looked up and said, "Welcome to Marty's, my friend." The customer didn't say a word back and Miro didn't bother looking behind him to see who it was. If it wasn't the drug dealer Marty was expecting, then Miro didn't give a shit.

"You like that music box?" Marty asked the customer. "Play anything you want. I've got a pretty nice selection going."

Still, Miro ignored the customer as Marty continued wiping down glasses with a white cloth. The customer shoved a coin in the slot of the music box. It jangled until it hit the bottom of the coin box, splashing against the other coins. The customer made his selection, and the music started playing.

Miro was in the middle of taking a swig of his drink, but stopped mid-sip the instant he heard the beat of the song. His eyes lit up like a firefly as the fluid in his mouth dribbled down his chin. He was very familiar with the song. Not too long ago he played it for a few of his guests just before he put on his magic act of death...But one of the guests happened to get away.

365

"Why don't you come to the bar and have a drink, friend," Marty said to the customer, just before shots rang out and his chest burst open in four different spots. He fell back into the shelves of liquor, blood splattered all over the bottles as they fell to the floor. Marty slumped down to the floor, then a moment later took his last breath.

Miro didn't as much as flinch when Marty was shot to death just inches away from him. He didn't move a muscle. He just stared straight ahead into the vast expanse of nothingness. Typical of a soulless creature such as himself. But there was another simple reason why he didn't move. He knew exactly who was in the bar with him…And he knew that he was knee deep in shit at the moment.

"If this song didn't catch your attention, then I thought blowing your bartender friend away would. You might not be showing it, but I know it has. You're about ready to piss your pants right now, Miro," Ric Rose said as he pointed a pistol at Miro.

"Is that what you think, Ric Rose?"

"It's what I know, asshole."

Miro chuckled, then said, "Then you don't know a fucking thing about me." He spun around in his bar stool and shot an electrical charge of energy at Ric. Ric used his newly acquired skills to dodge the bolt of electricity. He was like a red shadow, moving faster than the electricity could travel, and instead of hitting him, the electric bolt struck the music box and destroyed it, cutting off the song.

Ric countered the attack with a quick shot with the pistol. The bullet struck and blew apart Miro's hand. His fingers were scattered across the bar counter and his thumb fell on his lap. He screamed and yelled in excruciating pain as blood spurted out his arm.

Miro tried shooting Ric with an electric bolt with his other hand, but Ric dodged it once again, before blowing away that hand as well. Miro was now left with only stubs for hands. He screamed to the high heavens, but no one was listening.

Ric crept toward Miro, who was flailing about with his arms, coating the bar with his blood. "I can finally see clearly now, Miro. My purpose in life right now is simple. It's to protect my Family at all costs, and avenge those who do my Family and me wrong."

Ric stood directly in front of Miro, who was leaning up against the bar, taking erratic breaths of air. "So, today I start with you." Ric shoved his pistol in his waistband, then grabbed Miro by the neck and began to squeeze as hard as he could. "Send me a postcard from hell when you get there. Let me know how hot the fire is burning down there, bitch."

With his other hand, he pulled a hunter's knife from his pocket, and shoved it deep into Miro's gut. Miro's eyes bulged out as he grunted, then Ric twisted the knife and drug it up to his sternum. Blood gushed out of the wound as Miro's eyes rolled into the back of his head. Ric let go of Miro's neck, then gave him a left hook to his head. Miro's body slumped to the floor and he bled out until his heart let out its last beat. His skin turned a pale gray and he was gone, sent to the special hell he belonged.

Ric stood over Miro's corpse, his hand soaked in blood. He thought he would feel satisfaction from the vengeful kill, but instead he felt empty. He felt like sticking a needle in his arm to let his mind drift away so he could forget about the kill. Ric wasn't a cold-blooded killer. Not like everyone else in his Family. But he wouldn't dwell on his gruesome revenge for too long. Miro Cicello was a soulless human being who deserved the death Ric gave him. He should've tortured him before he killed him, but he didn't have the time for such games. Soon enough, someone would venture into the tavern, so he needed to leave before he was caught.

Ding a ling-Ding a ling… The bell above the entrance rang. Someone had ventured into the tavern.

The stranger stepped across the floor in his slick dress shoes. He bore a black suit over a pink dress shirt and white bowtie. His fedora cast half his face in shadow, but the crisscrossing scars on his face were still visible. Ric had never seen the likes of this man before.

"My, my, what a mess you've made here," the man said as he walked through the tavern like he owned the joint. "I don't think Zasso's brother will be coming home for dinner tonight."

Ric drew his pistol and aimed it at the stranger. "Who the fuck are you?" he asked with cold malice.

"Solace Volhine," he answered, then brushed past Ric and overlooked Miro's bloodied corpse. A pool of blood had developed underneath his body, almost reaching Ric and Solace's feet. "And you can drop the pistol. It's not going to do you any good."

"Ya, I don't think so," Ric replied, still pointing the gun at Solace.

Without looking at Ric or his gun, Solace scrunched his fingers into a claw-like shape. The pistol crystalized as it began to freeze. Ric could feel the bitter cold in his hand, so he dropped the gun and watched as it shattered into thousands of pieces.

Ric's jaw dropped like an anchor. "What the fuck?"

Solace took his eyes off of Miro's corpse and geared his attention to Ric. "I know, I know. It's amazing how I can use Blessed powers and I'm not a part of any of the Families. I get it. It's old news. But I didn't come here to show off my magical powers. I came to check on Zasso's brother for him, but I can clearly see that it's too late. You have creatively disposed of him, which I am sure he is deserving of. If he's anything like his brother, then a painful death was knocking on his front door."

"Then why are you still here talking to me? If you don't care whether or not Zasso's brother is dead, then why don't you just get the fuck out of here and leave this whole situation alone?"

Solace waved a finger at Ric and said, "Now, now, young Rose, I can't just leave a situation like this the way it is. It's apparently clear that you are not just another hood on the street, cashing in his father's checks. Maybe Miro Cicello was that kind of asshole, but the young man standing in front of me seems dangerous. And anyone who's dangerous, and not on our side, is a threat to our mission."

"And what mission is that?" Ric asked in wonderment.

"Come one now, do you really think I'm going to reveal that kind of information to a member of the Rose Family? You have to be smarter than that. An offspring of the great Don Maretto Rose must be as sharp as a butcher's knife." Solace turned his head and under his breath said, "The Father of Gangster my ass. I'm the real gangster around these parts."

368

Scrunching his forehead, Ric asked, "Who the hell are you, man?

Solace scowled at Ric and answered, "I already told you who I am! Are you fucking deaf or something?"

"I heard you tell me your name, but I just want to know where the hell you came from," Ric said back.

Pondering a thought, Solace said, "As much as I would love to have a little chat over an open fire with a bottle of wine, I have precious little time on my hands. So, instead of all that, I'm just going to have to eliminate a little threat to our mission." Solace extended his arm and pointed his fingers toward Ric. "And you *are* a threat, Ric Rose." His left eyebrow raised as he cracked a devious smile.

Solace's hand turned blue as swirls of white mist revolved around his wrist. Ric could feel the cold before the magical burst of energy was unleashed upon him. He knew what was coming. An imminent death. This man was powerful. He could feel the strength from a Relic inside of him. *But what Relic does this man possess?* Ric thought. *There's no Relic with the power of ice.*

Suddenly, a loud gunshot rang out, shattering the window behind Solace. His white bowtie burst into shreds and turned a dark crimson in an instant. Blood spewed from his neck and ran down his pink shirt. His arm dropped to his side, his eyes rolled to the back of his head, and he fell forward, hitting the ground face-first with a thud. After he fell, the person who fired the shot was revealed, standing behind the shattered window with his gun still held in his hand.

Ric couldn't believe his eyes. It was like he was seeing a ghost. But it wasn't. He was real.

"Melroy," Ric said in a gasp of air with a tear falling from his eye. He stepped over Solace's body and made his way to the window. He took a hard look at his old friend, just to make sure it was actually him. His face had multiple scars, his head was shaved, his left ear was missing, and he was wearing a tight black shirt with a black leather coat, pants, and shoes; a major contrast to what his usual detective garb was. But it was definitely him. It was Melroy Statz.

Ric jumped through the broken window, grabbed the collar of Melroy's coat with both hands, and pulled him in for an embrace. He hugged him tight, patting him on the back while tears flowed down his face. Melroy shoved the gun into his waist and hugged him back.

Ric didn't want to let go. He thought he had lost his best friend a week ago, and now he was hugging him as hard as he could.

"Easy, easy," Melroy said as Ric patted him on the back again and again. "I'm not fully healed, ya know. I got pretty fucked up in that accident…Well, it wasn't really an accident."

Ric let go of the embrace, but still held onto his shoulders. "What the hell happened to you? I was told you were fucking dead. How did you survive?"

Melroy cracked a smile and replied, "I got lucky, I guess. But the left side of my body got pretty banged up. They replaced my arm and part of my chest with robotics. I'm part fucking metal now."

"Really?" He let go of Melroy's shoulders, took a step back, and looked him up and down. He noticed that he was wearing a leather glove over his hand. "That's pretty cool, I guess."

Ric had so many questions to ask his friend, but there was one that was specifically running through his brain. "So, why did you hide the fact that you were still alive?"

"My Captain made the decision. I was attacked by an unknown enemy, so he thought my life would still be in danger if I survived. But instead of hiding out in a cave for the rest of my life, I decided to stay low-key and look out for your ass." His eyes became stern and serious. "You're in a lot of danger, Ric. Your entire Family is. So, I'm gonna try to help you in any way I can."

Ric looked toward the ground and thought for a moment. Then he looked Melroy straight in the eyes and said, "Thank you."

"No problem," Melroy replied with a nod. He then lightly smacked Ric in the face a couple of times and said, "You look clean. That's good. The Family needs a clean Ric Rose."

Flowers for the Pain

The Family was together in Don Maretto's office. Jon-Jon sat in the corner behind his desk, Alto and Uncle Vetti were having drinks at the bar, Ric stood over by the window, gazing out into the starry night sky, and Don Maretto sat in his throne-like chair in the center of the room. The Rose patriarch twirled his wedding ring around his finger, contemplating the Family's next move. They were in a dangerous situation, taking the heir to the Cicello throne captive, but they couldn't just let him go, and killing him wasn't an option either. They needed information from him, but so far, they had been unsuccessful. It had been three days since he was captured and imprisoned in a cell in the depths of the Rose Family high-rise mansion, and Zasso Cicello has said nothing.

"He's not going to talk, pap," Jon-Jon said, leaning back in his chair with his hands clasped behind his head. "We've had him down there for three days without food, sleep, or a way to use the bathroom. He rather piss and shit himself than tell us what he knows and who he's working for. I'm telling you right now, he's a part of something big. Something bigger than him...Maybe something bigger than us."

Alto let out a cynical cackle and said, "Like what?"

Jon-Jon shrugged and replied, "That's the problem. We don't know."

Alto cackled again, sipped his drink and said, "Fuck that. I say we kill the son of a bitch. If he aint gonna talk, then there aint no reason to keep him alive. That fuckface killed our brother. Let's slit his fucking throat and watch him bleed to death."

"No," Vetti responded, answering for Don Maretto. He knew his older brother would respond the same. "We have to keep trying to get something out of him. He knows vital information. Your brother was killed because he tried to stop him from abducting your father. Zasso's brother tried to kill Ric and said that our whole Family was on the verge of getting wiped out. Melroy Statz was hunted and attacked by a rogue military force that we still have no idea where they came from. And then Zasso tried to capture your father again, in order to gain access to the Rose Quartet." He took a deep swig of his drink

372

and continued, "And for what? To have all the Family Relics? To stop our Family from getting stronger? Or to maybe find some hidden power deep within the Rose Quartet?" He shook his head. "Jon-Jon's right, Alto. Zasso is a part of something big. Killing him will do us no good. We *have* to make him tell us who he's working for. We all have to know. *I* have to know."

"Come on, Uncle Vetti. Let's be real about this," Alto said as he took a hit off a cig. "The Cicello Family has something in the works. That's all this is. Zasso's just following his fat tub of lard father."

"I highly doubt that, Alto," Vetti said back. "Someone attacked Xanose. He was almost killed."

"We don't even know who fucking caused that explosion!" Alto shouted at his uncle. "It could've been some fucked up junkie loser off the street! No offense, Ric."

Still staring out the window, Ric replied, "I'm clean right now, asshole."

Alto just shrugged his shoulders, put his cig out, and sipped on his drink.

"No street junkie could've caused that kind of explosion," Jon-Jon commented. "That bomb was professionally done."

"So, what?" Alto replied. "There are five other Families who all hate each other. It could've been anyone."

"And that's why we need to keep interrogating Zasso," Vetti said. "He has the answers we need."

"It's his fat-ass father, Uncle Vetti!" Alto shouted. "So, let's kill the skinny bastard!"

"Alto!" Maretto yelled out. "Enough! You will listen to the High Consultant of this Family!" The room went silent. Don Maretto's tantalizing voice could do that to a room full of grown men.

Alto didn't take getting yelled at very well. He never did. Shaking his head, he put an aggressive grip around his drink, then stormed across the room and toward the door. He stopped just before he was about to exit the room and turned to Ric. "Welcome to the Family, Ric. You're a Blessed member now, and just like me, you won't have a say in shit!" He ripped open the door, stepped out of the room, and slammed the door shut behind him.

The room remained silent for a few more moments, until Jon-Jon said, "So, we keep trying to get information out of Zasso is what we're all agreeing towards?"

"As much as I would love to do what your brother wants to do with him, it's the only way we're going to solve any of our problems," Maretto replied. "If we kill him, we lose our chance to find out who is the mastermind behind Zasso's mission. And I wouldn't be surprised if he knew the group behind Melroy's attack as well. I have a feeling that all of this is somehow related. The rogue militia that attacked Melroy is working for the same person Zasso is. I guarantee it."

Vetti and Jon-Jon nodded their heads in agreement with the Rose patriarch, then Jon-Jon said, "So, what do we do to Zasso now? Threaten to cut his balls off or something?" he asked with a grin.

"Let me talk to him," Ric broke in, as he continued to gaze out into the city.

Jon-Jon let out a slight laugh and said, "You? What makes you think *you* can get him to talk?"

Neither Maretto nor Vetti cracked a grin or said a word. Instead, they stayed silent and awaited his answer.

Ric turned toward the others and said, "I'm not saying that I'll get him to talk, but it's worth a try. Maybe I'll just happen to say the right thing to him." Jon-Jon shrugged as Maretto and Vetti stayed quiet and kept listening. "Besides, I haven't had the chance to confront that asshole since he killed Georgie. It's about time I have a few words with my brother's killer, and let him know that I took care of his own brother. That could shake him up a little."

Maretto turned his head and looked back at Vetti. Uncle Vetti just shrugged his shoulders and gave him a slight nod, as if saying, it wouldn't fucking hurt. He looked over at his youngest son and said, "Okay, Ric. You're a Blessed Family member now. It's your right to get involved. Have at it, son."

Maretto stood up and approached Ric. He grabbed his son by the shoulders and said, "It's damn good to have you back, Ricalstro." He leaned in, gave him a kiss on the forehead, and whispered, "A Blessed member of the Rose Family is bound to do great things. But only if you stay true to your blood. Your Family is your blood and that's more important than anything else in your life. And that blood is in this room, flowing through all of our veins." He patted Ric on the cheek. "Don't ever forget that, my son."

Ric nodded his head and then embraced his father in a loving hug.

The Rose Family high-rise mansion was a state-of-the-art living quarters for Don Maretto Rose and his sons, but an old-fashioned elevator located in a dark corridor near the back of the building, took its passengers down to a desolate underground passageway that led to a single room that represented a prison cell. The dirt ground felt like mush as Ric Rose traversed through the dark and murky passageway, alit by small candles attached to the cement walls. He was escorted by Vego Rainze, who limped his way ahead of Ric. Vego refused any hospital treatment after the confrontation in front of the Capital Building. He had been struck by debris from the explosion that was meant to turn Don Xanose Cicello into ash, but always the tough guy, Vego was back on the job of protecting the patriarch of the Rose Family the very next day.

Stopping in front of the cell, Vego used a rusty old key to unlock the latch on the thick and rusty iron door. Before he unhinged the latch, Vego turned to Ric and said, "I'll be right outside if you need anything, kid. Don't get too comfy with this guy." Vego drew a rare grin, then unhinged the latch and opened the door.

Ric nodded at Vego with a grin of his own, then stepped into the cell. The first noticeable detail about the old cell was its stale odor to go along with the pungent smell of humid piss. Sitting in the center of the old cell, his hands chained tight to the back of a metal chair and his feet shackled to the floor, was the bruised and beaten heir to the Cicello throne. His head was down and his silver-black hair hung over his dirt-ridden face. He had only a t-shirt draped over his upper body, but bore the royal blue suit pants he was wearing three days ago.

When Zasso heard someone enter his cell, he lifted his head and gazed through his greasy hair. A lackadaisical grin creeped upon his face once he saw and recognized the person standing before him. "Ric Rose," he said with a slight cackle. "It's so good to see you. Welcome to my new home. It's not as terrible as it seems. Other than the smell of my own piss, it's not that bad."

Ric remained silent for the time being. He stood in front of Zasso, but he looked to the side of him. He couldn't look him in the eyes just yet. If he did, then he'd rip his fucking heart out of his chest.

"I'm guessing you have become a Blessed member of your Family, or you wouldn't be down here right now, standing in front of an all-powerful man such as myself. No, they wouldn't let you come near me unless you have taken your vows. It seems as though they'll let anyone in your Family become Blessed. Even junky drug users such as yourself." Zasso waited for a response or a reaction. Anything. But Ric remained silent. "You must be proud of yourself, Ric Rose. You're an inspiration to all of those out there who can't control the amount of substances they inject into their veins. You are proof that even a junky can become a prominent individual in a Blessed Family. The Rose Family baffles me. They all act like their shit don't stink one bit, but they'll let a piece of shit like you reek up the fucking joint...Unbelievable. It really is."

Zasso got what he wanted.

"Your brother, Miro, is dead," Ric blurted out.

Zasso's eyes changed. They were more serious. More businesslike now.

"I killed him three days ago. It was probably around the same time you were trying to abduct my father."

Zasso sniffed at news. "So, this is the way you're gonna try and break me. By bringing me lies?"

"It's not a lie. I happened to spot him when I came out of the National Archive Building one day. He thought he was sly, disappearing into the middle of the city. But little did he know, I was beginning my training to be Blessed, which would take me to the same vicinity as his little hangout. He's not that smart, ya know. He frequented a tavern just a few blocks away from his apartment. Not a very good idea to become a regular somewhere when you're trying to lay low for a while." He leaned in closer to Zasso. "The stupid fuck. It made it easy for me to follow him, hunt him down, and then gut him like a fish."

Zasso's breathing became heavy. He saw Ric following his younger brother during the President's speech and agreed to let Solace Volhine look after him instead of himself. Little did Zasso know that Solace shared the same fate as his brother.

"So, you've avenged your brother's death by killing my brother. That's how this nice circle of blood usually runs, so now I'm sure we can all work on an agreement together. A truce between our Families."

Ric shook his head. "I didn't kill your brother to avenge my brother. Avenging my brother would be killing you." Ric stood up straight and walked around Zasso. "But you see, my father has informed me and my brothers that we aren't allowed to kill you. It really pissed off Alto, but Jon-Jon and I are willing to do whatever is best for our Family. So, I asked my father if I could be the one to talk to you next."

"And why's that? You think you can extract information out of me, Ric Rose? You are a baby. A junky. You don't possess the power that I have. You are nothing compared to me."

Ric came around his other side and said, "Oh, really? Then why am I freely standing in front of you, and you have your hands tied and legs shackled, while you piss your pants? Huh?"

"Because of your father. That's why I'm here."

"That's right. Because of my father. And I'm my father's son. Which means that I now have the power over you for the time being." He reached back and slapped the absolute shit out of him.

The slap may have jerked his head to the side, but Zasso winced at the minute pain. "Really? You're just going to slap me like a woman?"

Ric reached back and slapped him again, harder this time. The smack of his palm connecting with Zasso's cheek bounced off the walls of the cell.

"You little piece of…"

Slap! Ric backhanded him this time. His head jerked to the other side, his sweaty hair flailing about his face.

He spat a driblet of blood. "What the fuck is your problem?"

Slap! Ric stroked him again, catching him hard in the jaw. Zasso let out a grunt of pain as blood flew from his mouth.

Ric grabbed him by the shoulders and bent down to whisper something in his ear. "I know it was you."

"What?" Zasso replied.

Slap! He caulked him again with a backhand. Zasso's eyes bulged and his mouth hung open with blood dribbling out the side as he let out heavy breathes of pain.

"It was you there that night, watching from afar," Ric whispered in his ear.

"What?" Zasso repeated.

Slap! Ric caught him with a slap to the side of his head, rapping his ear. Zasso let out a frustrated grunt.

"You were the shadow from afar, lurking in the night as you watched her get raped," Ric whispered in the ear he just struck. "I always had a feeling it was someone from your Family, but I never found out who. But ever since I was Blessed by the Rose Quartet, I've

378

gained this strong sense that I can't even explain. And once I saw you sitting in the shadows of this cell, I knew it was you."

Squinting his eyes, Zasso said, "You're so full of shit, Ric Rose. I know nothing of what you say."

Slap! Slap! Slap! Ric ripped him three times in a row, jerking his head back and forth. Zasso's cheeks were cut up and bleeding streams of crimson. He couldn't lift his head anymore, so Ric lifted it for him with two fingers under his chin.

"The truth is, Zasso, is that I don't give a fuck whether or not you tell us the information we need," Ric said, his eyes full of contempt. "It won't bother me one bit, because when it's all said and done, and you still haven't told us who you're working for, I'll have the pleasure of watching you meet your demise. Because that is what's going to happen when my father finally gives up on you. He's going to fucking kill you. Yes, my father can be a rational man. A patient man. But I've seen him get frustrated with assholes like you as well. And it's not pretty. It's not a pretty sight. He's going to end your fucking life." Ric held out his hand, showing his reddened palm. "But until that day comes, I'm just going to constantly slap the shit out of you. Everyday. For the rest of your pathetic, pants-pissing life."

Ric reached back to catch him once again, but Zasso interrupted him and said, "He goes by the name, *Thy Master*."

Ric stopped in mid-swing of his hand. His eyes were caught like a deer in headlights. He was shocked. Ric had just got Zasso to talk. He gave him a name...*But who in the hell is Thy Master?* Ric thought as he lowered his hand. He had to delve deeper.

"Who? Thigh Master?"

Zasso shook his head. "No. *Thy* Master."

"Thy Master?" Ric asked. Zasso nodded in reply. "Who in the hell is he?"

Zasso paused for a few moments before he answered, "To be quite honest with you, Ric Rose, I have no idea who he really is or where he came from. He just contacted me

379

one night, out of nowhere, when I least expected it. It was like a dream…But it wasn't a dream. It was real. As real as you and I talking right now."

Ric didn't want to believe him, but he did. He could sense that Zasso was telling him the truth. "What does he want with my father?"

Through his greasy, sweaty hair, Zasso eyeballed Ric and answered, "He wants the Rose Quartet, of course."

"Why?" Ric asked, almost in a whisper.

"Eternal life," Zasso answered with a wide grin.

Ric scrunched his eyebrows in confusion. "What?"

"That's all he would tell me." His grin disappeared. "He wanted me to be the one who captured your father and bring him to his feet. I am the chosen one of Thy Master. He trusted no one but me." He put his head down in defeat. "But I failed him." He spat on the ground. It was a blood and saliva mix. "Now I must face the consequences of my failure by being stuck in a dirty cell, talking to the likes of you, Ric Rose."

"What do you get in return?"

The wide, sneering grin returned. "Juna," he answered. "The city of Juna would be mine. It would be my playground. I would do anything I want with it. I would be the ruler of my people…I would be king of this land."

Ric sighed, took a few steps backward, and said, "No, Zasso. You won't." He turned his back on Zasso and headed to the door.

"Wait!" Zasso cried out.

Ric stopped in stride, and then turned around to face him one more time.

"What about my father? What has happened to him?"

A moment of silence fell between them, before Ric answered, "Don't worry, your father is still alive."

"Where is he?" Zasso asked in a demanding tone.

Ric gave his own shit-eating grin and replied, "He's in the hospital recovering from his injuries. He'll be just fine, Zasso. Our Family sent him some flowers for the pain."

The heart monitor let out a steady beep as the electronic waves flashed across the screen. Connected to the monitor and lying in bed was the injured patriarch of the Cicello Family, his head, neck, and arms wrapped in gauze to temper the burn wounds. His eyes were halfway open as he watched one of his bodyguards walk into the room with a large cardboard box.

The bodyguard was a tall and husky man with slicked back hair, bearing a white suit with a black shirt. His hands were enormous, which made the box seem smaller than it actually was.

"Don Cicello," the bodyguard said, "the front desk sent this package up to your room. The delivery man told them it's a 'get well soon' gift from a very special and concerned friend. He didn't say exactly who it was from, though." He examined the sides and bottom of the box. "Nothing seems out of the ordinary, boss. Seems like a legit gift from someone."

Xanose blinked his eyelids a few times and said, "Open it." His voice was hoarse and raspy. He was barely able to verbally communicate.

"Sure thing, boss."

The bodyguard placed the box on the tray table at the end of the bed. He opened the top and looked inside. "It's a bouquet of roses. Nice ones too."

Xanose's eyes widened in panic as he tried to speak. But the words wouldn't come out.

The bodyguard grasped the vase holding the bouquet of roses and lifted them out of the box. Low and behold, inside the clear and round vase, was Miro Cicello's severed head floating in the water. The head's eyes and mouth were halfway open and the skin was sagging and bloated from being underwater.

The shock of seeing the head caused the bodyguard to flinch and drop the vase onto the floor. The glass shattered, and Miro's head rolled around until it came to a rest facing up at Xanose.

Xanose looked down at his son's severed, decomposed head and let out a raspy shrill of horror.

It was a warning to Don Xanose and the rest of the Cicello's…You don't fuck with the Rose Family.

Message received.